Marrying MR. WRONG

THE BRIDES OF HILTON HEAD ISLAND

BOOK 4

international bestselling author

SABRINA SIMS MCAFEE

Marrying Mr. Wrong
The Brides of Hilton Head Island
Book Four

Editor: GWE

Book design by Inkstain Interior Book Designing

Sabrina Sims McAfee can be contacted via her website:

www.sabrinasimsmcafee.com

TO MY DEDICATED READERS:

Wow! You have really fallen in love with The Brides of Hilton Head Island Series. Per your request, here's book four. As yes, I will keep writing this series as long as you're interested. From the bottom of my heart, I can never thank my readers enough.

XOXO,
SABRINA

For my grandmother, Katrina Lindsey, known to me as Bigma. Thanks for loving me unconditionally, supporting me, the private conversations. But most importantly, thanks for sharing your wisdom.

You're my heart.

Loving you forever, Sabrina

Chapter One

"ARE YOU SURE I WON'T be invading o n your privacy, Aunt Leslie?" Sasha Spaulding asked, drawing back the sheers inside the living room of her townhouse to peer out the window. The full moon settled in the dark night sky. A red truck was parked on the curb across the street beneath a tree.

Waiting for her boyfriend Reggie to come home so she could tell him she was breaking up with him, Sasha's whole body tensed. Nervousness knotted inside her. Oh God, how was she going to tell Reggie she was ending their relationship? Sasha thought, releasing a soft sigh. Reggie means me no good, I have to leave him. I'm sick and tired of his cheating and doggish ways. I should've left Reggie a long time ago.

Leslie Spaulding replied with, "Of course you're not invading on my privacy, Sasha. You're my niece, and you can come stay with me for as long as you'd like. I could use some company in this big old house. Who knows, you just might meet your husband here."

Sasha shook her head negatively. Getting married was the last thing on her mind. Once she got out of this absurd relationship with

Reggie, she didn't have any intentions of settling down. Once she got to Hilton Head Island, she planned on spending time with her favorite aunt, take her songwriting career to the next level, and enjoying the beach. But as far as a man was concerned, she felt like she didn't need one.

To hell with men. "I'm never getting married or having any kids, Aunt Leslie. After I get out of this horrible situation with Reggie, I'm going to take it easy and focus on my songwriting career."

Leslie replied with, "Oh, Sasha. Don't say that. Getting married to the right man can be a good thing. Don't let your relationship with Reggie change how you once felt about settling down and having children."

Reggie is a certifiable jerk. He's made a fool out of me for the last time. And I mean that. "I hear you, Auntie. Well, I'll be arriving in Hilton Head sometime tomorrow night. Again, thank you so much for the listening ear, and for always being so supportive. I don't know what I'd do without you."

"You don't have to thank me, Sasha. You're my sister's only daughter. It's my job to listen to you. And if that Reggie gives you any trouble when you tell his behind you're leaving him, just give me a call. I'll be in Nashville faster than you can blink your eyes. I can't wait to see you. It's going to be so much fun having you here in Hilton Head. Richmond, Slade, and Dirk can't wait to see you. Even stupid-behind Russell says he can't wait to see you."

"Like me, you've gone through so much with a man...Uncle Russell."

"That's how I know you're going to be okay. If I can get over what Russell did, you can get over Reggie. It ain't gon' be easy, but with time you'll be just fine. Now, get off this phone and go get some rest. You have a long drive tomorrow. I love you, Niecy."

"I love you, too." Letting the sheer drapery slip from her fingers, Sasha ended the call.

"Who the fuck were you talking to?" Reggie's demeaning voice asked from behind. Oh boy, here we go. Swallowing, Sasha slowly turned from the window to find Reggie standing in front of her. Tall, dark, and controlling, Reggie frowned. Taking a step closer to her, his lips twisted. "I know you're not telling some man you love him in my damn house."

Sasha sighed. "Reggie, I'd never disrespect you like that."

Reggie snorted. "Who were you talking to, Sasha?"

Sasha sucked her teeth. "None of your business, Reggie."

Reggie's eyes were flat, hard, passionless. "Oh, it's like that, I see." His grim tone chilled her.

Growing further irritated, Sasha rolled her eyes. If she knew for a fact that Reggie wouldn't follow her to Hilton Head after she told him she was leaving him, she'd tell him she'd been on the phone with her Aunt Leslie. However, she didn't know how he was going to react to the breakup. Or if he'd try to follow her to the Low Country.

Dreading to tell Reggie she was leaving, Sasha swallowed the big knot in her throat. "There's something I have to tell you. Let's sit down." She gestured to the sofa against the wall.

Reggie's eyes darkened. His jaw muscles flickered. He extended his hand towards her. "Give me your cell, Sasha."

Looking up at him, Sasha's nerves tensed. "I'm not giving you my cell, Reggie. Now can we please sit down and—"

Reggie swung, his fist connecting with Sasha's cheek, splitting it into. Her stomach flopped. Mouth wide open, her hand shot up to her stinging cheek. Thin blood oozed from her face onto her shaking fingers. Stunned, tears formed in Sasha's eyes.

Yes, Reggie had cheated on her too many times too count. And yes, he often stayed out till the wee hours of the morning and had recently become overly controlling. But he'd never hit her before. Her mind reeling, still cupping her cheek, she narrowed her eyes

at him. This will be the last time he ever hits me.

Reggie clutched Sasha's shoulders. "I'm so sorry, Sasha. I didn't mean to hit you."

Tears came into Sasha's eyes. "Get your hands off me, Reggie. We're through. I'm leaving you. Tonight," her voice cracked.

Reggie's eyes darted back and forth. "No, baby. Please don't leave me."

Pain rippled in Sasha's burning face as she rounded Reggie to head for the bathroom. On her heels, Reggie followed her. Standing in front of the mirror inside the bathroom, Sasha lowered her hand from her bloody face to find it swollen and bruised. Oh my God. A tear slid down over the scar.

Sasha pulled a tissue from the box. Dabbing at the ugly scar on her face, another tear streamed from her eye. Somewhat in shock, she turned to face Reggie. "I can't believe you hit me. You've stooped to an all-time low. Leave, Reggie. Just leave. Before things get ugly."

Standing slightly inside the bathroom, Reggie huffed. "I said I was sorry. If you would've just given me the damn phone like I asked you to, none of this would've happened."

Sasha tossed the bloody tissue in the trash, then took a step forward. Her eyes to his chest level, she sighed. "Whatever, Reggie. Get out of my way."

Reggie stepped to the side, letting Sasha walk past him. He's not going to take my leaving him lightly. I have to get out of here. Tonight. Right now. Not wanting things to escalate and get out of control, Sasha made the quick decision to call the police later. If Reggie thought his professional football career would be in jeopardy, there was no telling what he'd do to her.

4

Hurt beyond measure over her once beautiful relationship with Reggie, Sasha pulled open the pantry door, grabbed a plastic bag, then filled it with ice cubes. Distraught, she placed the ice bag on her cheek. Leaned her back against the kitchen sink.

Reggie stood in front of her. "What did you want to talk about earlier?" he asked in a gruff voice.

Perhaps I should leave while he's asleep. Sasha shook her head. "Nothing."

Reggie took a step forward. Tucked a piece of hair behind her ear. "How can I make this up to you, Sasha?"

She blinked, tears falling from her lashes onto her cheeks. "You can't, Reggie. You hit me." She sniffed.

Reggie's brown eyes turned black. "You're going to leave me, aren't you?" Silence filled the air, creating more tension, making Sasha ever so fearful. "I can see it in your eyes. You're planning on leaving me." Fisting his hips, Reggie turned around, took a few steps forward. As he looked at the refrigerator, he inhaled deeply, his shoulders motioning up and down. He whirled. Clenching his teeth, Reggie pointed a finger in Sasha's face. "Just to let you know, I'd rather be dead than to live without you. I'll kill you before I let you leave me!"

Reggie's death threat made Sasha's heart spin. Fear coursed through her veins. Her chest tightened. "I don't have any intentions of leaving you, Reggie," she lied, having no choice. Feeling trapped in her own home, Sasha's eyes traveled to the sharp blade lying on the counter beside the stove, then back up to Reggie's scowled face.
"I'm tired. I'm going to take a shower."

"Maybe I can join you." It'll be a cold day in hell before I take a shower with him. Reggie kissed her forehead. He jerked his chin towards the staircase. "Let's go. A little make-up sex will make you feel better."

5

Having no clue how she was going to get out of having sex with Reggie, Sasha's eyes swung to the knife lying on the counter again. With the ice pack pressed to her aching face, she began mounting the staircase in front of Reggie. *Thank God I never married him.*

Halfway up the staircase, Sasha's cell phone rang, but she ignored it. With three more steps to go before she reached the top, Reggie fisted the back of her shirt and yanked. Sasha froze in her tracks. Turned around to face him.

"Aren't you going to answer that?" he asked, taking a step upward so he'd be on the same step as her.

"No. After what just happened, I'm not in the mood to talk."

Reggie's brows dipped. "Why I do have the feeling you're cheating on me?" Insecurity lingered in his dark pupils.

"Probably because you're cheating on me."

Reggie fisted the top of Sasha's shirt, pinned her against the staircase's wall. "Give me your phone, Sasha." He snorted.

"Let go of me, Reggie."

"You're one trifling bitch, Sasha. You think I don't know about you and Travis?" *Travis? What in the world is he talking about? Travis and I only discuss music. He's considering offering me a publishing contract.* Reggie continued. "Yeah, you didn't know I knew about him, did you?" A nasty chuckle pressed from Reggie's twisted mouth. "I followed you the other day and saw you having lunch with him."

Now he's spying on me. "If you must know, Travis works for Yellow Dog Entertainment and is considering giving me a publishing contract for one of the songs I wrote. It's a big opportunity. A major artist is considering singing the song."

"You pick a fine time to tell me about your so-called friend. I saw the way Travis looked at you. You're a damn fool if you think he doesn't want to fuck you. I don't want you seeing him

6

anymore. Is that understood?" Wishing Reggie would let go of her shirt, she closed her eyes. Finally, her cell stopped ringing. Thank you, God. Just as she reopened her eyes, the darn cell started ringing again. Oh God, no.

Pinning her with his weight, Reggie dug in her front jean pocket, pulled out her cell, and eyed the Caller ID. Hard lines formed on his face. He tapped the speaker button on the cell, answering it.

Silence. Nothing. And then Sasha heard Travis say, "Hey, Sasha. I have some great news!"

Holding the cell up to his mouth, Reggie stated, "Don't call my woman anymore. If you do, you'll have to pay the price." "Hello? Who's this?" Travis asked.

"Your worst nightmare." Pressing a hard thumb to the speaker button on the screen, Reggie ended the call.

"You didn't have to do that, Reggie. Now my song will never get recorded. I hate you! You bastard!" Anger shadowed her voice. "Give me back my phone!" She snatched the cell from his grip. Stuffed it in her pocket.

Reggie gripped the sides of Sasha's head and banged it into the wall. Her eyes rolled. Head spinning, she gripped the handrail and began descending the steps. I have to get out of here now.

"Come back here, Sasha! I said get your ass back up these steps! Try leaving me! I'll kill you, woman!"

"I'm not scared of you, Reggie!" Holding onto the handrail, Sasha glanced back over her shoulder. Reggie raised his hardcovered shoe in the air and kicked her in the back. Unk. Sasha's body tumbled down the stairs. She landed hard on her face. Reggie spat, "I got something for you. Just wait and see." He jogged up the staircase and shot inside their master bedroom.

He's going to get his gun. In a desperate attempt to protect herself, Sasha crawled towards the kitchen. The knife. I have to get

the knife. Feeling as if the wind had been knocked out of her, Sasha flattened her palms on the tile floor and then staggered to her feet.

Spine aching, Sasha stumbled towards the stove, hefted the knife in her hand. When she'd told herself she'd never let him hit her again, she'd meant it. And when she'd said she wasn't scared of him, she'd meant that, too.

"Sasha! You're one dead bitch!" Reggie shouted, bustling down the staircase. He'd snapped.

Breathing raggedly, Sasha hastened to the dining room and hid behind the wall. She took her cell from her pocket, quickly dialed 911, and told them to hurry up and get there. Clutching the handle of the sharp blade, she heard Reggie's footsteps growing closer.

Then she heard him breathing harshly. Oh, God. He's standing on the other side of the wall.

"Oh, Saaasha," Reggie sang. He turned the corner and found her.

Gripping the knife behind her back, the hairs on Sasha's nape straightened.

Hatred filled Reggie's eyes. He put the barrel of the gun to her forehead. "I called the police. They're on their way. Please, Reggie. Don't do this—"

Anger simmered in his tone as he stated, "The police don't scare me. I told you I'd kill you if you tried to leave me. You should've listened." With his finger wiggling on the trigger, Reggie fired! Click. Nothing happened.

Hollering, Sasha swung the knife from around her back and plunged the sharp blade into Reggie's side. Eyes spreading wide, his mouth dropped wide open. The gun tumbled from his grip to the floor. Sucking air into his lungs, he wheezed. He gripped the handle of the sharp blade, then plummeted to the floor on his back.

Lying on his back, Reggie glared up at Sasha. Blood oozing from his wound, he chuckled nastily. "You're feisty as hell…Sasha." Gurgling, the lids of Reggie's eyes closed.

Chapter Two

PALLID SOUNDS ROLLED OFF THE   ocean and eased into Salvador Casillas' ears as he walked along the dark beach behind his cousin's estate. The full moon glowed brightly in the sky. Salvador paused in his tracks, picked up a seashell, tossed it into the water. It's time for me to get going, he thought, glancing at the back of Zeke and Taylor's mansion.   How in the world he'd let his first cousin, Zeke, talk him into coming to a couple's gathering was beyond him. Damn, he'd been mighty stupid to agree to such a thing.

Wondering what woman he was going to get in his bed tonight, Salvador peered out at the dark sea. With so many females to choose from, he pulled his cell from his back jean pocket and scrolled through his contacts. Reaching sexy   -behind Kristen's name, a smile came across Salvador's face. While Kristen was great in bed, she was too overbearing and needy at times.

Continuing to thumb through his contacts, Salvador's cell buzzed in his palm . Julie Palmer's named appeared on the screen. Thinking about the way Julie had swallowed his cock whole the last time they'd slept together, Salvador smiled, and then quickly answered his cell.

"Hello." Jeez. Julie could give some good head.

"Hi, Salvador. It's Julie. There's a great party going on tonight at Club Matrix. If you're not doing anything, I'd love for you to meet me there. Maybe we can hang out at your place afterwards. Can you come?" Julie emphasized the word "come".

Speaking of coming, it'd be his pleasure to meet Julie at the club and cum inside her mouth afterwards. "Sure. I'll meet you at the club, and we can go to my place afterwards. That is, only if you promise not to get offended if I—"

Julie interjected, "Ask me to leave after we have sex. I know we'll never be anything but friends, Salvador. And although I'd love to have more than a sexual relationship with you someday, I'm just glad you're honest about your intentions as far as I'm concerned. Thanks for not misleading me."

Salvador nodded. "Don't thank me for being honest, Julie. That's the only way I know how to be—honest." While Salvador was a lot things, he definitely wasn't a liar. Before he got a woman in his bed, he always made it a point to let them know he wasn't the settling down type. The more women, the merrier was the motto he lived by. Zeke, Richmond, and Braylon could have that marriage stuff.

Looking forward to Julie swallowing him whole later this evening, Salvador ended the call, slid his cell back into his pocket, and walked back towards the mansion. Suddenly, thunder boomed in his ears. A strike of white lightning flashed in the sky.

As he climbed the steps of the back porch, drizzles of rain sprinkled down on him. Getting wet, he pulled open the back sliding glass door and entered Zeke and Taylor's immaculate home. Loving couples packed the room. Jazz music flowed from the sound system. This is too mushy for me. I got to get the hell out of here.

In search of Zeke and Taylor, Salvador's eyes roamed over the large, spacious den. Braylon and Sandella sat in the corner talking and laughing while Richmond and Kayla stood near the bar sipping red wine from glasses. All the couples seemed so in love. Love— they could have love. Being in love was not in his nature.

Smiling his behind off, Zeke emerged in the doorway just off the kitchen. Meeting his first cousin's gaze, Salvador headed in his direction. "Enjoying yourself, cousin?" Zeke asked. Taylor walked up behind Zeke, put her chin on her husband's shoulder, then wrapped her arms around his waist.

"I'm enjoying myself thoroughly, cousin. But I'm about to head out," Salvador replied.

"Oh, why so soon?" Taylor asked.

Because I'm about to get a blow job. "I have another party to attend."

Thunder boomed, shook the house. A strip of lightning flashed, lighting up the room. Raindrops tinkered against the roof.

Taylor released Zeke's waist, then walked up to Salvador to give him a big hug. "I hate that you have to go," Taylor said, releasing him. "I was hoping you'd get a chance to meet my girlfriend, Lolita."

Looking at his wife, Zeke shook his head. "Salvador knows how to find his own woman, Taylor. Besides, Lolita is looking for a husband and—"

"I'm never getting married," Salvador interjected. So this is why Taylor kept insisting that I come…she wants to set me up with one of her girlfriends. Thanks, but no thanks. "Anyways, thanks for having me." Salvador kissed Taylor's cheek. He and Zeke slapped hands. He turned around to wave goodbye to all their guests.

"Goodnight, everyone."

"Be good, playa," Richmond said, laughing.

Cupping Sandella's hand, Braylon waved with his free hand. "Don't forget about the polo game we have coming up Saturday."

Salvador nodded. "I'll be there. I plan on destroying you."

Braylon chortled. "I'm going to make you eat your words." Patting her husband's thigh, Sandella laughed.

Damn, everybody in here is smiling and in love. Maybe being in love isn't such a bad thing after all. Maybe I should try it someday. Oh, hell no. Feeling out of place at the couple's night out event, Salvador trudged towards the front door.

Taylor opened the door for Salvador. "It's starting to rain hard. Maybe you should wait to leave until it clears up some," she suggested, a look of concern on her pretty face.

"Oh, it's just a little rain. I'll be fine. Thanks again for the invite." Salvador took off jogging in the rain towards his black BMW SUV. Soaking wet, he slid behind the steering wheel, cranked the vehicle, and began backing up out the long driveway of Zeke and Taylor's mansion.

Moments later, Salvador rounded the corner off Ocean Boulevard, passed Spaulding Drive, stopped at the traffic light. When the light flashed green, he nosed the BMW SUV into traffic, making a left.

Driving along the street, hard rain fell in sheets, pounded the windshield. Flicking on his windshield wipers, thunder roared. Lightning crackled.

Listening to an upbeat country music song by Carrie Underwood, images of his alcoholic mother came into his mind. Salvador had been blown away when he'd found out his mother was an alcoholic. Self-destructive, his mother had cheated on his father and ended up ripping their family apart. Thinking about his mother, who refused to get help for her alcohol dependency,

Salvador turned up the volume on the radio and tried to force thoughts of his mother out of his mind.

Salvador drove across the overpass, made a left at the corner, and then proceeded to drive down the long, dark road towards the other side of the ocean. Rain flooded the lightless street, making it hard to see. Anxious to get home, he increased the speed of his windshield wipers.

Boom! Thunder echoed. Too bad he didn't like cuddling, because tonight would be perfect for such a thing, he thought, picturing Julie wrapping her pink lips around his hard shaft, then licking his testicles and—

Clenching the steering wheel, Salvador peered in his rearview mirror at the car tailgating him. Bright headlights flashed repeatedly. The driver laid heavy on the horn. "Get off my tail, asshole."

In an attempt to drive around Salvador, the car behind him merged into the left lane of the two-way road. Bam! The vehicle slammed head-on into another vehicle in the opposite lane. Gripping the steering wheel, Salvador slammed on brakes. Tires screeching, his SUV skidded off the slick road and flew into a patch of grassy wetland. Right before it collided with a thick, burly tree, the SUV came to an abrupt stop.

"Holy shit!" Shocked, Salvador gave his head a hard shake. Shocked, he shoved the door open with his shoulder, flung his feet to the ground, and took off running back down the dark road. Sprinting towards the horrible head-on collision, rain pelted his scalp, drenching him.

A loud horn blasted in the air. As he jogged closer to the car accident, Salvador noticed a third car had been involved in the horrific accident. Smoke billowed from the hood of the third car that he hadn't seen until now. Dear God, please let them be okay.

When Salvador reached the third smashed car of the horrific scene, he gripped the handle of the driver's side door and yanked it open. Inside the wrecked car was an African-American woman slumped against the deployed airbag.

Salvador's heart raced inside his chest. Reaching in his pocket for his cell, he clutched the woman's shoulder and shook her. "Ma'am, are you okay?" Praying the female was okay, he dialed 911 and gave them his location.

Grunting, the woman lifted her head from the airbag and glared at him. A huge bruise stained her brown cheek, and she had fresh scratches on her forehead. Squinting, she gripped the sides of her head. "What…what happened?"

"You've been in a car accident. Help is on the way." Feeling the need to protect her, Salvador knew he had to hurry and help the people in the other cars as well. He hastened to the car in front of hers, and as soon as he reached it, gasoline fumes assaulted his nostrils. He peered inside the car to find an African-American gentleman jammed inside. The man looked hurt badly.

Salvador pulled open the door to find the older gentleman covered in blood. "Jesus Christ!" He put two fingers to the injured man's neck, checked for a pulse, but didn't feel one. No. No. No. He palmed the man's shoulder, dragged him from the car, laid him on the wet pavement, and performed CPR.

Rain steadily poured from the sky. Pinching the man's nostrils together, Salvador blew quick breaths into the old man's mouth, then began chest compressions. Breathe. Breathe. Breathe.

"Is he alive?" the soft voice asked from behind.

Salvador glanced up to find the woman he'd helped a few moments ago towering over him. Fear on her soaked, watery face, wet hair matted her scalp. Salvador put two fingers to the man's wrist. "He doesn't have a pulse."

Sirens blasted through the air. Continuing with the CPR, Salvador glanced up and spotted emergency aid vehicles racing towards him. Red and blue lights emergency lights flashed in the night.

Pumping on the man's chest, Salvador glanced up at the woman. Rain poured down over them. "I don't think he's going to make it."

Nodding, the woman turned on her heels and bustled to the man in the other car that'd caused the accident. "Oh my God! He looks dead."

The ambulance pulled up in front of Salvador. Paramedics and firemen jumped out of their vehicles and took over. Glad help had arrived, Salvador went and stood to the side of the road beside the woman.

Praying that both men would survive, he shook his head. "Sometimes you just have to be patient. On a stormy night like this, he shouldn't have tried to go around me."

"You're right. This is horrible." The woman's tone was dreary.

The harsh rain turned to light drizzles. The police approached them to take their statements. Once they were done, the officers went back over to the wreck to take photos.

Distraught as hell, Salvador glanced at the woman's car. The entire front was banged up, looking like a total loss. It looked like it'd been compacted and belonged in a junk yard. "Your car is a wreck. I'll take you to the hospital. Let's go."

The woman shook her head. "That's okay. I can call someone to come get me."

"Okay. But make sure you go to the hospital and get that knot on your head checked out. It's pretty bad."

Giving him a hurtful stare, she touched the big bump on her forehead. Fingers feeling over the bruise, she lowered her gaze to the ground as if she were ashamed, then glanced back up at his face. "I'll have my friend take me to the hospital." She reached into her pocket, pulled out her cell phone, and dialed. With the phone pressed to her ear, she nibbled her bottom lip.

Salvador's eyes beheld the woman's brown-complexioned face. From what he could tell, she was a beautiful woman. "Take care."

"Thanks."

Exhausted, he stalked towards the ambulance. The paramedics placed the elderly man he'd tried to save on the stretcher, rolled him in the rear of the ambulance, and then drove off. Curious about the other man's status that'd caused this night to go so wrong in a matter of seconds, he walked up to where he lay on the stretcher.

Salvador glowered down at the man, then looked at the paramedic. "Is he going to make it?"

The paramedic's eyes held sadness. "No. He's dead."

"That's too bad." Salvador had seen a lot of things in his life, but he'd never seen anyone die right before his eyes. Due to his own stupidity and eagerness, and his attempt to go around him, the man lying on the gurney in front of him had died.

Needing a stiff drink, Salvador headed for his SUV. His head dangling between his shoulders, water squished beneath his hard shoes. Forget meeting up with Julie tonight. Too much had happened, and now he wasn't in the mood to be around Julie. Or anyone, for that matter.

Drained, he hooked a hand under the handle of the door, clambered inside, then called Julie to cancel his date with her. After ending his call with the ever-so-understanding Julie, he inserted the key in the ignition and cranked the engine.

Still trying to calm his nerves while holding on to the steering wheel, Salvador inhaled deeply. Jesus Christ. A man had lost his life tonight, and another one was fighting for his. The woman in the car accident should really go to the hospital and get that huge bump on her forehead checked out.

Overwhelmed, he steered the SUV to the edge of the grass. He glanced to his right, and then to his left. The woman he'd helped in the car accident was walking down the street. "What in the world is she doing?" he mumbled, knowing it was unsafe for her to be out here at night alone.

Clenching the steering wheel, Salvador pulled out onto the wet road. When he reached the woman, he rolled down his window and drove slowly beside her. "What happened to your ride?"

When she turned to look at him, she looked frustrated. She shrugged. "My ride didn't answer when I called," she said, continuing to walk.

A pretty woman like her definitely shouldn't be out her all alone. "My offer to take you to the hospital still remains."

With her purse strapped across her shoulder, she shook her head. "No thanks."

"How much sense does it make to walk out here on a dark road by yourself?"

Keeping her eyes straight ahead, she replied, "Considering you're a stranger, it makes perfect sense to me."

Driving slower, Salvador's rear shifted in his seat. "The police wrote down my name, and they got my ID. I can assure you, it's safer if you get in the car with me than to walk out here by yourself. If the wild dogs don't get you—"

She swung her gaze at him. "Wild dogs?! I'll take the ride." Purse strapped across her shoulder, she hurried to the passenger's side car door, hopped in, and slammed it closed.

"I'm sorry I didn't get the car door for you, but you didn't give me time."

"Trust me, the last thing I'm worried about is you getting the car door for me, especially after what happened tonight. Can you please take me to my car so I can get my luggage?"

"Sure." Salvador pulled up beside her car and parked. Palm up, he held out his hand. "Give me your keys."

She reached into her purse to retrieve her keys and gave them to him. He climbed out of the SUV, hit a button on her key fob, and the trunk of her destroyed car popped open. Four suitcases, books, and other items were packed in the trunk of her car. With all this mess in her trunk, this woman looked like she was either leaving town or coming into town. Salvador pulled two suitcases from the trunk.

After Salvador placed the luggage in the back of his SUV, he climbed back inside the truck and extended his hand towards the seemingly timid woman. "By the way, I'm Salvador...Salvador Casillas."

Seemingly hesitant, she placed her small, dainty hand into his big palm. The touch of her soft hand made his male senses leap. Wondering where the feeling had come from, he gently shook her hand.

"I'm Sasha," she said, foregoing her last name. Still tensed, she released his hand.

Salvador proceeded to drive down the dark road, away from the accident. "Sasha, the hospital isn't far from here. Why don't you let me take you there so you can get checked out," he pushed, really concerned about her well-being and health.

Adamant about not going to the hospital, Sasha shook her head. "Ummm. I'd rather not go to the hospital."

"Why not?"

Sasha diverted her gaze from him to stare out the window. "I feel fine. Besides, I just got in town from a long ride and would like to get some sleep in a comfortable bed."

"You can always come back to my home and rest for the night. I have plenty of spare rooms."

Salvador sensed uneasiness coming from Sasha. "Thanks. But I wouldn't feel comfortable."

"Where would you like for me to take you?" he asked, understanding her not wanting to spend the night with a stranger.

She turned her gaze back to him. "You can take me to my aunt's house. I have her address stored on my cell." She reached inside her purse, retrieved her cell, and hit go on the Google navigation system.

"Make a right at the light," the woman's voice on the GPS stated.

Wondering what had brought the attractive woman sitting beside him to Hilton Head Island, Salvador made a right at the light, as the navigation system had instructed. Following the directions coming from Google, Salvador turned the volume down on the radio.

"So Sasha, tell me, what brings you to Hilton Head?"

Sasha clasped her fingers together in her lap. "I needed to get away from Tennessee and come somewhere peaceful."

"It's very peaceful here, so you've made a great decision by coming here."

The GPS in the cell announced, "You have reached your destination. Your destination is on your right."

"Leslie Spaulding is your aunt?" Salvador asked, pulling up into Leslie's driveway.

Surprise developed in Sasha's eyes. "Yes, Leslie's my aunt. You know her?"

Salvador chuckled. "Yes. I know Leslie quite well. She's one of the funniest, and prettiest, and smartest women I know. I'm good friends with her son, Richmond. In fact, Richmond and I are scheduled to play polo this coming Saturday. I just left him at a party a little while ago. He and his wife Kayla are great people."

"Wow. What a small world. Aunt Leslie loves Kayla. She brags about her and the children all the time. I can't wait to finally meet Kayla."

"You're going to love Kayla. Like your Aunt Leslie...Kayla is one of the nicest women I know." Salvador noticed the lights inside the house were off. "It doesn't look like Leslie's home."

Observing the dark house, Sasha slapped her forehead. "Oh my goodness. I totally forgot that Aunt Leslie had Bible Study tonight. She specifically told me she wouldn't be home until later. I'd hate to interrupt her while she's in church. Dang."

"Well, the invite to stay with me still stands." Seeing how apprehensive Sasha was, Salvador lifted his cell from the console, tapped the photo gallery, and extracted a polo picture of him, Richmond, Zeke, and Braylon.

Holding his cell phone up to Sasha's eyes so she could see the picture, he said, "This is a picture of me with your cousin and some mutual friends of ours. I promise, I'm harmless, Sasha. You'll be utmost safe if you decide to come stay with me for the evening." He lowered the cell to his lap.

Relief appeared in Sasha's eyes. She nodded. "For some reason, I believe you. I guess I'll take you up on your offer to stay at your place." Sasha's lips pulled into a delicate smile, causing something to stir inside Salvador.

Chapter Three

SASHA SAT IN THE PASSENGER seat beside Salvador, nervously fumbling her hands together as he drove down the road, heading towards his home. Hoping she wouldn't regret her decision to stay with him tonight, she gazed out the window but couldn't see a darn thing for the darkness. Because of everything she'd been through over the last few days, an uncomfortable feeling settled deep inside her stomach. An image of Reggie cocking a gun to her head came into her mind. She shuddered.

Reggie had abused her in the worst way possible. Had tried to kill her. If the gun hadn't jammed, he would've shot her in the head. Although she was a huge believer in non-violence, Reggie had left her no choice but to stab him in his side.

After she'd stabbed Reggie, he'd somehow managed to stand and make his way to his car. By the time the police had gotten to her home, Reggie had disappeared, and no one had heard from the evil man since. Knowing that Reggie was out there somewhere, probably wanting to seek revenge on her, made Sasha wary.

"We're here," Salvador's husky voice cut into Sasha's thoughts. He steered the SUV up into the driveway of what looked like a mansion.

Bright lights lined the edges of the grass along the driveway. Palm trees nestled in his front yard. Steep steps led up to the front porch. My gracious, the two story house looked humungous. Looked fit for a rich person. Who exactly are you, Salvador Casillas? she wondered, pushing the door open.

"Wait! Wait! I'll get the door for you." Salvador jumped out of the car and hastened to open the door for her.

"Thanks." Sasha climbed out of the SUV. "You didn't have to open the door for me."

"No woman who rides with me will ever open the door for herself. Not if I have a say in it." He lifted the latch on the back of the BMW. "Do you need all of your luggage?"

"No. Only the pink suitcase." He seems like a gentleman. Considering he's friends with my cousin Richmond, I'm sure he is one.

Rolling the pink luggage behind himself, Salvador walked along the length of the driveway. He hefted the suitcase in his arms and hiked up the steep steps to the porch.

Opening the front door, Salvador gestured for Sasha to enter first. Guarded, she crossed over the threshold into the dark foyer. Salvador shut the door behind them.

"Let me get the lights." Hands fumbling over the wall, Salvador flicked on the lights. The room brightened. "Follow me." Bringing her luggage with him, Salvador walked through the living room and entered the den.

Tired as ever, Sasha's eyes roamed over the spacious room. She'd never seen a guy's home decorated as nice as this one. A light grey color painted the walls. Rocks in various shades made up the fireplace. Dark chocolate wood covered the floors. A tan sectional centered the middle of the room. A plasma television mounted the wall above the rock fireplace.

"You have a beautiful home, Salvador."

"Thanks." He pointed to the bedroom way off the kitchen. "My room is back there. If you need anything, just let me know." Then he pointed to his right. "There's the elevator." Elevator? "The guest room is upstairs. This way." Gripping the handle of her suitcase, Salvador turned, led her up a flight of stairs, and down a hallway.

He pushed open the door to the bedroom upstairs, placed her luggage at the foot of the white sleigh bed. As Sasha stood in the center of the plush, decorated room, a serene feeling came over her. Greyish-white wood covered the floor. A cotton white bedspread with white fur pillows accentuated the queen-sized bed. Off-white paint stained the walls. Above the bed hung six glass mirrors.

"I just have to ask, did you decorate this room? It's beautiful."

"No. In hopes that Lucy would come live here with me, I bought this house and hired an interior designer to decorate it."

"Lucy? Is that your girlfriend?"

Salvador shook his head. "Oh, no. I'm not the shacking up type of guy. Lucy is my stubborn mother. Anyway, make yourself at home. I'll see you in the morning." He turned and stalked towards the door.

Just as he reached the arch in the doorway, Sasha said, "Thanks again."

His striking blue eyes seemed to bore into her flesh, making her nervous. "It's my pleasure. Sleep well." He left.

Sasha propped her suitcase up on the bed, popped it open. She grabbed her pajamas and panties and headed for the bathroom. Once inside, she fumbled through her toiletry bag. Oh crap, I don't have any soap. I guess I'll have to borrow some from Salvador.

Her hand gliding along the iron rail, Sasha dismounted the staircase, taking note of the expensive artwork clinging to the walls.

This is some house. Looks so luxurious. Way too big for a single man.

When Sasha entered the kitchen, Salvador was standing at the counter, fixing something. Perhaps a sandwich. Apparently not noticing she'd entered, he kept his back to her. Sasha's eyes roamed up and down Salvador's backside. The strong looking man had broad shoulders and bulky biceps, and he had to be at least six-one. Nice body.

Sasha cleared her throat. Salvador turned around to face her. Captivated by Salvador's gorgeous blue eyes, tanned skin, and masculine features, Sasha swallowed. Something inside her stirred.

Gazing into her eyes, Salvador hefted a sandwich to his lips. "Would you like a sandwich or something to eat?" He took a big bite.

"No, thanks. I'm not hungry. Do you have any soap I can borrow?"

"Sure. Follow me." Salvador lay his sandwich on the kitchen counter, walked down the narrow hallway towards his room. Reaching the closed door, he put the beer under his armpit, turned the doorknob. What happened next shocked Sasha.

Salvador pushed open the door to his bedroom. A sharp breath whipped from his mouth. Two naked Caucasian women were on Salvador's bed, kissing and engaging in hot foreplay. Some blondehaired woman was on top of a girl with jet black hair and tattoos. Bumping and grinding, the blonde lifted the tattooed girl's breast to her mouth and suckled her nipple into her mouth.

With her hand to her chest, Sasha blinked repeatedly. *Salvador is freaky as hell.*

Salvador further entered his master bedroom. "Julie! What are you doing here? And who's she? I cancelled our date, remember?"

The naked blonde released the tit from her mouth, then hopped out of bed. Extending her skinny arms outward, she smiled.

"Salvador, you're finally home. Good."

Salvador stated, "Answer me, Julie. What are you doing here?"

Julie swung her long blonde hair over her shoulders. "You know I don't forget a single thing you tell me. Of course I remember you cancelled our date. I just wanted to surprise you with a little fun tonight. You sounded so upset on the phone, I decided to treat you to something special." Julie extended her arms above her head into a wide V. "Surprise!"

Salvador shook his head. "Surprise? You've got to be kidding me."

The tattooed girl sitting on the bed eased up on her elbows, spread her legs wide open. "Hey, Salvador...two girls are better than one." She transferred her eyes to Sasha. "You can join us if you'd like."

Oh, hell no. Sasha chuckled mentally. "No, thanks. I'll let the three of you have at it all by yourselves." She diverted her gaze to Salvador. "Umm. Don't worry about the soap."

Just as Sasha turned around, Salvador gripped her elbow. "Wait, Sasha. I know what this must look like, but trust me, I had no idea Julie would be here with another woman in my bed."

Smiling, Julie put her hand on her hip. "He sure didn't know. Is this your girlfriend, Salvador?"

"No, Julie. I don't have a girlfriend, and you know that. She's a relative of a good friend of mine. Look, no offense, Julie, but the two of you have to leave. I have a special guest tonight."

Julie picked her jeans up off the floor. "No problem. I understand. Let's go, Kim."

Salvador walked over to the bed, picked a shirt up from the mattress, and handed it to Julie. "I hope you're not upset, Julie."

Julie replied, "Of course I'm not upset. I understand you and I are just friends, and that's all we'll ever be. Stupid me. I thought you'd like engaging in a threesome. I guessed I should've asked first." She snickered.

Salvador's brows gathered in the center of his forehead, as if he were thinking. "Yes, you should've. I still can't figure out how you got in here, though."

Covering her mouth, Julie giggled. "Oh, we climbed through the window. You left it unlocked."

Smiling, Salvador shook his head. "I need to be more careful."

Julie kissed Salvador on the cheek. "No, what you need to be is more adventurous."

Salvador chortled. "Have a good night, Julie. You too, Kim."

"Thanks," the ladies said synchronously, and then left.

After Salvador saw the ladies out, he returned to his bedroom to Sasha. "I had no clue Julie would be wild enough to get in my bed without an invitation. Sorry about that."

"Oh, you don't have to apologize to me."

"Yeah, I know. But I don't want you getting the wrong idea. Do me a favor, and keep this between us. The last thing I need is for Leslie to think I'm some kind of sex freak."

"My lips are sealed." Sasha put a finger to her mouth.

Salvador's gaze roved over Sasha's scarred face. "This has been a crazy night."

"Tell me about it," Sasha uttered. For her, not only had tonight been crazy, but the entire week had been crazy. Filled with stupidity, heartbreak, and danger.

"Oh yeah, let me get the soap for you." Salvador went to the bathroom to get the soap, and after he returned, he handed it to Sasha. Towering over her, he stared down at her face. "Wait a minute. I just noticed something. The bruise on your cheek never had any blood. You didn't get that scar from the car accident, did you? That's why you refused to go to the hospital."

Ashamed, Sasha's gaze lowered from Salvador's face to the floor. Pained over what Reggie had done to her, tears shot into her eyes. I look like a fool. Feel so stupid.

Salvador cupped the balls of Sasha's shoulders. "Sasha, look at me." Sasha tilted her head back to glance up at Salvador. I'm so ugly, she thought, wanting to hang her head between her shoulders.

"What happened to your face?" he asked.

Sasha sighed. "I don't want to talk about it."

His blue eyes showed genuine concern. "I'm sorry for prying. Just to let you know, if you ever need a listening ear, I'll be more than willing to listen to you."

"Thanks." I could use a hug, she thought, staring into those striking blue eyes of his. As if reading her mind, Salvador encircled his big, strong arms about her shoulders and embraced her tight. Inhaling the wet scent of rain on his damp shirt, she draped her arms around his waist and finally let the built up tears flow from her eyes. Salvador's hand caressed up and down her spine. "It's okay, Sasha. Just get it all out. Get it all out. If you want me to, I'll personally drive to Nashville and kick his ass for you."

Lifting her head from the sculpted muscles of Salvador's rock solid chest, Sasha released a series of light chuckles. "Why do I have the distinct feeling that you'd really go fight him for me?"

Salvador put a finger to Sasha's chin. "Because I would."

"But you don't even know me."

"You're right. I don't know you, Sasha. But I know your relatives. Leslie, Richmond, and all of the Spauldings are like family to me. You hurt one of us, you hurt us all. I sure hope that whoever did this to your face never shows up here. Because if he does, he'll regret the day his mother ever gave birth to him."

Raw emotion shown in Salvador's eyes, and Sasha knew he meant every single word he'd just said. For a reason she couldn't explain, it gave her great comfort to have Salvador on her side. To take up for her. To let her stay at his home tonight. And yes, to give her that big hug he'd just given her.

Exhausted, Sasha sighed. "Again, thanks for everything. I'm going to head upstairs to take a shower, then go to bed."

"Goodnight, Sasha."

"Goodnight, Salvador."

As Sasha left Salvador's room, she could feel his eyes burning a hole in her backside. He seems like such a nice man. Walking down the hallway, she glanced back over her shoulder, and sure enough, Salvador was standing in the doorway of his bedroom watching her. Butterflies twirled in her belly.

Long moments later, Sasha lay in the white wooden bed inside Salvador's guest bedroom, thinking of him. She thought about how kind he'd been to her, and about how handsome he was. How good it had felt to be wrapped in his muscular arms and to have leaned her head on his ripped chest.

Suddenly, her cell buzzed on the nightstand. She reached over and answered it. "Hi, Auntie Leslie. You finally got home from church, I see."

"Yes, dear. Bible Study was great. Are you almost here?"

"Actually, I got here a little earlier than anticipated. Long story short, I got in a car accident—"

Leslie's gasp came through the phone. "A car accident?! Dear God, are you okay? Are you in the hospital? Where are you?"

"I'm at Salvador Casillas' home. He says he know you."

"Yes, I know Salvador. He's a good friend of the family. Such a great guy," Leslie confirmed.

That's good to know. "Well, since I'm already in bed, I'll be staying at Salvador's tonight." Leslie snickered. "What's so funny, Auntie?"

"I hope you're in the bed inside Salvador's guest bedroom, and not the one inside his master suite. Rumor around town is…once Salvador gets you in his bed, he lives in your head and heart forever. Come to think of it, I think Salvador would be the perfect guy for you. Maybe you should get in his bed."

Sasha's mouth parted. "Auntie."

"Don't 'Auntie' me. You're a grown woman, Niecy. You deserve a good man. Give me a call in the morning, okay?"

"Yes, ma'am." Sasha ended the call. She pulled the string on the beaded lamp, and the room dimmed. Clenching the sheets to her chin, thoughts of Salvador kissing her lips slid into Sasha's mind. Oh God, why was she thinking of him like that? Knowing the last thing she needed was to get involved with a man, she forced fine-behind Salvador right out of her mind and drifted off to sleep.

Chapter Four

PAIN RIPPLED IN WAVES THROUGH Ben Haroldson's aching body as he lay in the hospital bed after the horrible car accident he'd endured. With tiny oxygen tubes inside his nostrils and IV needles pricking his arms, cold fluid trickled into Ben's veins. Tired and banged up, Ben gritted his teeth. He grunted.

Sort of wishing he'd died in the car accident, Ben looked at the vitals machine beside the bed. Terrified for his life, he tried to think of ways he could leave the hospital. I got to get the hell out of here. The hell out of Hilton Head. If he hadn't been in a head-on collision, he would've been on the expressway by now, heading to Canada. Hell, Mexico. Hell, anywhere besides the low damn country.

When Ben moved his legs, his muscles ached. Even his bones ached. Head throbbing, the top of his stomach bubbled, made him nauseous. Damn you, God. Why didn't you just let me die in the car accident? As soon as they find me, they gon' kill me anyway. It's only a matter of time before they blow my fucking head off. Kill me execution style. I would've rather died in the car accident than to let some ruthless, heartless man murder me. Make me suffer. Got damn it. I done got myself into a world of trouble with no way out.

"Why did you perform CPR on me? You should've minded your own business," Ben mumbled to himself, referring to the mystery man who'd saved his life. According to one of the nurses, some kind stranger had performed CPR on him, and if it hadn't been for the kind man's act, he'd be dead. Problem was...old man Ben Haroldson kind of wished he had died. Because he'd survived the crash, he now had to keep running. Keep living with fear.

The phone inside the hospital room rang. Ben slowly lifted the phone off the receiver and placed it to his ear. "Hello."

"You can run, but you can't hide." Hearing the familiar deep, groggy voice, Ben's heart spun. The man who wanted Ben dead continued. "You're dead meat, Ben. Deadfuckingmeat." Click. A buzzing sound rattled in Ben's ear. I got to get out of here. He's
coming. He's coming.

Ben flung the linen off his legs. Turning sideways, sharp pains coursed through his veins. He inhaled a sharp breath. Slowly, he placed his feet on the floor and stood. His life in danger, he took one step forward and fell flat on his face with a loud, resounding thud.

Why did he save me? Why? Why? Ben thought, hoping he'd suffocate while lying there with his face pressed to the floor.

Feet dragged across the tile floor. Ben slightly lifted his head to find a pair of white sneakers in front of him. In a squeaky voice, the nurse said, "Oh my goodness, Mr. Haroldson. Look at you. You've fallen, and you can't get up." The nurse stooped down, hooked her arms beneath his shoulders. "On the count of three, I need you to try to stand."

Ben groaned in pain. "I can't do it. It hurts too bad. Uuuggh."

The nurse named Tasha said, "Yes, you can do it, Mr. Haroldson. One...two...three." Nurse Tasha pulled upwards.
Palms flat on the floor, Ben staggered to his feet. Joints throbbing, he sat on the hospital bed. Tasha lifted his legs to the mattress, turned them sideways, and then recovered his legs with the linen. Waging her finger in his face, the nurse decreed, "You're in no shape to get out of the bed all by

yourself. If you need help, just press the red buzzer, and I'll come assist you."

"Thanks, Tasha."

"You're welcome, Mr. Haroldson. Is there anything else I can get you?"

Ben groaned. "Some pain medication, please. I'm hurting bad."

Tasha fisted her hips. "Now see there, Mr. Haroldson, you done went and hurt yourself even more. I'll be right back with your pain medication." She stepped outside the room. Seconds later, Tasha returned with the pain medication and administered it to him. "There, that should make you feel better. The medication is going to make you a little sleepy. Well, if there's nothing else. I'm going to go ahead and head home for the evening. Just to let you know, the shifts just changed, so when you wake up, you'll have a different nurse." Tasha left the room.

As Ben lay on his back listening to the television, his eyelids started to droop. The pain medication eased through his veins, making his pain subside. He released a long yawn. Eyes opening and closing, he thought about all the risks he'd taken just to save his wife's life, and in the end she'd died anyway.

Thinking about his deceased wife, Ben's heart squeezed. Oh, Claira. After all I done for you, you died and left me anyway. Now I'm going to spend the rest of my life on the run. Running from a got damn monster. Groggy, Ben's eyes closed, and he started dreaming.

Carrying a bag of groceries, Ben mounted the creaking steps of his old home tucked into the woods, and then opened the front door. A retired maintenance man, Ben stalked into the kitchen and found his wife, Claira, sitting at the kitchen table, holding her face in her hands. Crying her eyes out, Claira's sobs filled his ears. Broke his heart.

Deeply disturbed, Ben placed the grocery bag on the counter and hurried over to his dear, sweet wife. "Oh Claira, what's wrong, darling?"

Claira lifted her weeping head from her hands. A red color stained the white parts of her eyes. "The doctors diagnosed me with gastric volvulus today."

"Gastric what?"

"Gastric volvulus. I have an abnormal rotation of my stomach by 180 degrees. It can cause a closed loop obstruction, resulting in incarceration or strangulation. It's a rare stomach disease that requires surgery. If I don't have the surgery, I'm going to die, Ben."

Die?! Ben felt as if someone had reached into his chest and snatched his heart out. He'd been married to Claira for forty-seven years and couldn't imagine his life without her. Seeing his wife in such turmoil and hearing such horrible news, Ben's heart grappled. "We'll get a second opinion, Claira. How much does the surgery cost?"

"Twenty thousand dollars. Medicaid won't cover it all. We can't afford the surgery."

Sulking, Ben wrapped his arms about Claira's shoulders. Tears poured from his eyes as they sat crying together. "It'll be okay, Claira. I'll get the money," Ben promised.

Claira sniffled. "How, Ben? How?"

Ben kissed the side of Claira's grey hair. "You have enough to worry about. Let me worry about getting the money. Now let's go to bed."

Ben and Claira walked hand-in-hand down the narrow hallway towards their bedroom. Once inside, Ben turned back the covers. Claira climbed on the mattress and lay down on her back. Wearing a soft pink nightgown, water teetered on Claira's grey eyelashes.

Ben patted Claira's shoulder. "It'll be okay, Claira. I promise." He bent down to kiss her lips, then pulled the cover up over her chest, letting it stop at her chin. "I'll be in the den watching the news if you need anything."

After Ben tucked his wife, Claira, into bed, he walked inside his den to make an important phone call. Desperate to get money so Claira could have life-saving surgery, he lifted the phone from the receiver and put in a call to the one person he knew could help him come up with the money. It was illegal money, but still it was money.

On the third ring—

"Sleep tight, motherfucker," a thick Russian accent punched Ben's ears. Dreaming, Ben's eyes shot open. Instantly, he recognized the Russian guy standing over his hospital bed, holding a pillow over his face. Yuri! Yuri's black eyes narrowed. He slapped a hard hand to Ben's mouth. "Maybe the next time you take money from someone, you'll get the job done." Yuri chuckled nastily. "Oh, my bad. There won't be a next time."

The pillow came crashing down hard on Ben's face, smothering him. Unable to see, Ben swallowed his own screams. Hot piss shot from his shaft, soaking him. Struggling to breathe, Ben's aching body writhed. Losing consciousness, an image of his deceased wife Claira appeared inside his mind. With white wings on her back, Claira looked like an angel as she said, "Fake like you're dead, Ben." With a whiff of smoke, Claira vanished.

Hoping his angel, Claira's, plan worked, Ben flung his arms to his sides. Stilled his wild, kicking legs. Stopped writhing, and pretended to be dead.

Chapter Five

THE EARLY MORNING SUN PERCHED high in the sky above Salvador's oceanfront estate. White seagulls flew above the blue, glistening water behind the mansion. Sounds of waves crashing against the shore sailed through the open window of Salvador's room and straight into his ears.

Eyes wide open, Salvador lay in bed thinking abo   ut his houseguest—Sasha. Even with the huge knot on her forehead and the ugly scar on her face, Sasha Spaulding was one beautiful woman. If he'd met her on a night free of drama, he would've tried his hardest to get her in his bed.

Sasha is beautiful.Last night during the rain storm, Sasha's long black hair had hung in wet waves over her shoulders. Her drenched bangs had matted to her forehead. The round shape of her breasts had perched beneath the material of her wet shirt. Cinnamon   - colored sensual eyes had accentuated the brown skin on her round face. Yesterday evening, Sasha had made his insides burn. Especially when he'd held her in his arms while inside his bedroom. Now thinking about his beautiful houseguest, Salvador's balls tingled.

Reminiscing about how he couldn't take his eyes off Sasha's behind when she'd left his room last night, a smile touchedSalvador's lips.

Crossing his legs at the ankles, he clasped his fingers together behind his head. "As soon as you're feeling better Sasha, I'm going to try my hardest to get between those luscious thighs of yours." As soon as the words had left his lips, Salvador cursed. Considering Sasha was his good friend, Richmond's, first cousin, there was no way he could have sex with her and then not call her the next day, like he normally did with women. Richmond would kill him if he did such a thing, and he wouldn't blame him one bit.

Salvador cursed. Sasha Spaulding is off limits. Lo decepcionante, he thought, thinking how disappointing the realization was. "Well, it sure wouldn't hurt to make the sexy pussycat some breakfast."

Salvador clambered out of bed and walked to the bathroom. After he freshened up, he threw on a pair of jeans and ascended up the staircase to go tell Sasha good morning. Anxious to see Sasha's pretty face, he walked down the hallway and noticed the guest bedroom door was open. Good, she's up.

Rubbing his hand over his bare chest, Salvador entered the guest room to find it empty. On top of the made up bed lay a sheet of paper. Did Sasha leave? he wondered, heading into the bathroom. On the floor of the bathroom lay a pair of hot pink panties. Sasha's. He lifted the panties to his nose and sniffed the crotch. Ummm. Her pussy smells delectable. He stuffed the flimsy panties in his front jean pocket, and then went back inside the bedroom.

Noticing the paper on the bed again, he lifted the note to his eyes to read it.

Dear Salvador,

I woke up early this morning and decided to call a cab to come get me. Thanks for coming to my rescue last night and allowing me to stay here at your beautiful home. Words can never express how much I greatly appreciate your kindness.

From the bottom of my heart, I thank you.

Sasha

P.S. As promised, my lips are sealed about Julie and Kim being found in your bed. Although I have to admit, they were the highlight of my night, and I found them just as much intriguing as they were funny.

Wishing Sasha would've woken him before she left, Salvador crumbled the paper, tossed it in the trash. Sasha was the first woman that had ever left his house without telling him goodbye. Normally, he had to throw women out of his house. Or politely ask them to leave. Or come up with an excuse to get them the hell out of there. Disappointed because Sasha had left, Salvador jogged down the steps, snatched his keys off the kitchen counter, and exited his beach house through the front door.

Thirty-five minutes later, Salvador walked through the steel front doors of his business—Casillas' International Boxing Academy. Unless he had to be on television as a boxing analyst, he worked at the boxing sports complex daily. Making his way towards his office, Salvador couldn't get pretty Sasha off his mind. The nerve of her to leave without saying goodbye. Why did he care anyway? It wasn't like he could fuck her or anything.

Hating the fact that his good friend Richmond was blocking his blessings with Sasha, Salvador plopped down in the leather chair behind his desk. Right when he pressed the power button on his laptop, his cell buzzed. He spied the Caller ID. Speak of the devil.

He swiped his cell, then placed it on his ear. "Good morning."

Richmond stated, "Good morning. I just called to say thanks for taking care of my cousin Sasha last night."

Too bad I couldn't take care of Sasha like I wanted, and get between her legs. Salvador replied, "Man, you know you don't have

to thank me for seeing about your family. I'm just glad Sasha is okay."

"Yeah, thank God she's alive and only got a few nasty bruises." Apparently, Richmond had no idea that Sasha may have sustained her injuries from the hands of a man. No, make that from the hands of a chump. Real men didn't hit women. Richmond continued, "Anyway, Mom's cooking her usual big dinner Sunday and wanted me to invite you."

Salvador smiled. "Tell Leslie I graciously accept her offer."

"Okay, man. Be good. I'll get up with you on Saturday for a game of polo." Richmond sounded like his normally merry self.

"See you Saturday, man." Salvador ended the call.

With so much to do today, Salvador cupped the mouse of his computer and clicked the cursor on the Outlook Express button, opening up his email. Jeez, he'd just cleaned out his email yesterday evening before he went to Zeke and Taylor's home, and since then he'd gotten over a hundred more emails. Most of them were from people inquiring about his summer boxing camps. Too bad there were already full, he thought, his hands typing over the keyboard, replying to someone with interest.

Knuckles rapped on Salvador's office door. He lifted his head to find Zeke and Taylor's son, named Jaheem, along with a good friend of his by the name of Corey standing there.

Waving the young teenagers in, Salvador smiled. "Come on in. How are you doing this morning?" "I'm

all right," Corey stated.

Jaheem reached out and slapped hands with Salvador. "I'm good, bruh."

Salvador hovered the cursor over the red send button on his computer, then clicked. He simultaneously hit control+alt+delete, locking his computer, and then stood. He headed for the locker unit inside his office. "I hope you guys are ready to train mean and hard today." Opening the locker door, he extracted a pair of red boxing gloves and a whistle.

With a Nike duffle bag strapped over his shoulder, Jaheem stated, "I don't know if Corey is ready, but I am. I stay ready to box. I feel like tearing some ass up today."

Corey sucked his teeth. "Well, you won't be tearing this ass up. If anything, it's going to be the opposite."

Salvador chuckled. "Hey boys, what did I tell you about all that cussing?"

Jaheem's dark eyes rounded. "Excuse my expression, Coach Salvador. But after being in that group care facility for so long, it's taking me some time to get rid of the bad language. I'm working on it, though."

Salvador nodded. "Good, because how people perceive you is important in life. It can be the difference between getting a job or not. Getting a girl or not."

Jaheem stuck his chin out. "Oh, I ain't never had no problem getting a girl. Shoot. Now that the females have found out my daddy is a rich white man, those THOTS be all over me." "THOTS? What's a THOT?"

"These Hoes Out There." Jaheem cracked up laughing.

Chuckling, Salvador just shook his head. "You're too much, Jaheem. Let's go get in the ring."

Corey and Jaheem followed Salvador into the gym. Standing outside the ring, the boys put on their boxing gear. While his cousin Zeke hadn't hesitated to let Jaheem take boxing lessons, it'd taken his wife Taylor a long time to agree to it. Because of everything Jaheem and his brother Zavier had been through, their mother could be overly protective at times. And Salvador couldn't blame her one bit, he thought, climbing into the ring.

Jaheem lowered his headgear over his head, put on his sparring gloves, and gave Corey a peculiar stare. "Please know, I'm not going to take it easy on you today." He popped his mouth guard into his mouth.

Fully sheathed in his boxing attire, Corey replied, "Get ready for the whooping of your life, bruh."

Both boys climbed into the ring. Standing in front of each other, Jaheem and Corey put up their glove-covered fists and waited for Salvador to blow the whistle. "Remember what I taught you at your last lesson. Get in your fighting stance. Relax your hands until impact."

"Even during hooks, right?" Jaheem asked.

"Yes. At the sound of the whistle, begin." Salvador tucked the whistle between his lips and blew. Eeeer. Feet shuffling, the boys started punching. "Tuck your thumbs in, Jaheem."

As Salvador stood there watching the boys box, he noticed Corey's skills seemed to be off today. He blew his whistle, stopping them. He walked up to Corey. "Hey, bud. You're not putting forth any effort today. What's going on with you?"

When Corey took his headgear off, Salvador saw sadness in his eyes. "Nothing. I'm just not in the mood."

"Look, Corey, I can tell something's bothering you. Just to let you know, I'm here if you need me." Salvador patted Corey's shoulder.

Corey sighed. "It's my granddaddy. My mom and I stopped by his house this morning and found a note saying he was leaving Hilton Head Island."

Wow. That's tough. "Maybe your grandfather will come back."

Corey sucked his teeth. "He ain't even tell nobody 'bye. He just left us a stupid-behind letter." Angry, Corey threw his helmet on the ground, climbed out of the ring, and flopped down in the chair. Salvador threw his leg over the rope, and then the other, and went and stood beside the saddened teenager. "Why do you think your grandfather would just up and leave?"

Corey shrugged. "All my life, he's preached to me that the Haroldson men are strong men, and leaders, and the head of our communities. Now how in the hell you gon' teach somebody something as important as that, but don't follow your own rules?"

Corey has a good point. "Sometimes adults make mistakes, just like kids. Well, I'm going to pray that your grandfather comes back home. What's his full name, so I can pray for him?"

"Ben Haroldson," Corey said, tears welling up in his eyes.

Ben Haroldson, Salvador thought, inwardly praying Corey's grandfather would come back to his adorable grandson, who obviously loved him very much.

Chapter Six

SASHA STOOD INSIDE THE GUEST   bathroom at her Aunt Leslie's house, looking in the mirror. A big knot on her forehead, a big bruise on her cheek, her face looked hideous. This morning when her aunt had first laid eyes on her, she'd gasped. Leslie had expressed how she hated the car accident had left her face in such disarray. But these scars...these ugly scars on her face were not the result of a car accident. Nope. These scars came from the hand s of a man—Reginald "Reggie" Carter. If Leslie knew Reggie had beat her, she'd probably get in her car and go searching for him. But that wouldn't do any good. According to the police, Reggie still hadn't been found. He was still running from the police.

Tired of reliving the abuse stemmed from Reggie, Sasha left the bathroom and exited her bedroom. She walked down the hallway, descended the staircase. Scents of buttery pancakes wafted up her nose when she entered the kitchen.

"There you are, my Niecy!"   Leslie wiped her hands on her apron and gave Sasha a big hug. Squeezing her tight, Leslie confirmed, "I know I've already said this, but I'm so happy you're here. I hope you never go back to Tennessee." Leslie released her and just stared. Feeling as if Le   slie could see she'd been beaten, insecurity wavered through Sasha. She felt fragile. Leslie remarked, "I tell you, Niecy, you're such a beautiful woman. You look just like your mother, Katrina. Gosh, I wish my sister Katrina was here to see you."

Sasha wished she could stop feeling so down. "I wish my mother was here, too. I miss her so much. Thanks for the compliment, but I don't feel so beautiful, Auntie."

Leslie patted her cheek. "Oh, nonsense, Niecy. You are just as pretty as they come. Don't get any prettier than you. I hope you're hungry, because I cooked a mean brunch." Sasha's stomach growled just from thinking about food. "Hungry? I'm starving."

"Oh, good. As soon as—" The doorbell rang. A huge smile spread across Leslie's face. "Oh, goody. They're here."

"Who?"

"The crew." Leslie spun on her heels and practically ran to answer the front door. "Sasha!" Leslie yelled out a few seconds later. "Come inside the dining room."

Sasha emerged inside the dining room to find Richmond, Suade, Dirk, Kayla, and a few children standing there. Ecstatic to see her cousins, Sasha's lips hitched.

"Wow, cousin! You're sure looking good," Richmond said, giving her the biggest hug.

Sasha patted Richmond's back. "You, too, cousin."

"Hey, let somebody else get a chance to hug this pretty cousin of ours," Suade stated. After hugging Suade, and then Dirk, Richmond introduced Sasha to his beautiful wife, Kayla. He then introduced her to their three beautiful children—Carson (CJ), Richmond II (RJ), and an adorable little girl named Isabelle.

CJ pointed his finger at Sasha's forehead and asked, "Mommy, what happened to her face?"

"She was in a bad car accident, CJ," Kayla responded.

CJ shrugged. "Oh, she can't drive."

Kayla gasped. "CJ. Watch what you say. The car accident wasn't her fault." She looked at Sasha. "I'm so sorry."

Sasha giggled. "It's okay, Kayla."

Isabelle grabbed a hold of Kayla's leg. "Mommy, her face scares me. Was the monster in the car?"

Kayla's face turned brownish-red. "No, Isabelle. There's no such thing as monsters, remember we talked about that."

Isabelle blinked. "But CJ said the monster was in his room the other night."

Richmond interjected, "Isabelle and CJ...monsters are not real. Don't believe everything the other kids tell you."

Leslie requested, "Let's gather hands, please, so I can bless the food." As Leslie led the family into prayer, warmth filled Sasha's heart. It felt so good to be around people who loved her, and whom she loved. "Amen," Leslie said, ending the blessing.

"Amen," everyone said in unison, then took their respective seats at the dining table.

Sasha's eyes combed over the huge brunch spread over the dining room table. Leslie had cooked fluffy buttery pancakes. Maple sausage links. Fried chicken. Waffles sprinkled with white powdery sugar. Cheesy eggs, grits, muffins and fruit. Like Leslie had said, she'd cooked a mean brunch.

A diehard vegetarian, Sasha fixed her plate with a little bit of everything, except for the meats. She hefted the syrup bottle in her hand and drizzled her buttery waffles with the sweet molasses. "Thanks for cooking brunch, Auntie."

Leslie sliced a sausage link in half with her fork. "You're welcome. I love cooking."

Richmond said, "If you think this is something, wait until you see how she cooks on Sundays."

"She cooks enough food to feed a village," Kayla said, holding baby RJ in her lap.

Suade lowered his glass of juice to the napkin. "And it be good, too."

Sasha forked some fluffy eggs into her mouth. "Wow. Being single, I never get food like this."

Leslie patted Sasha's arm. "Well, now that you're here, you'll get this good cooking all the time. I tell you...it sure feels good to have you here, Niecy."

"Thanks. I'm glad to be here."

"How long do you plan on staying?" Dirk asked.

Right now, she felt like she could stay in Hilton Head Island forever. "I don't know, Dirk. What about you? How long will you be here for?"

Dirk scooped up some grits on his fork. "Oh, just until the weekend. I have to get back to college."

"Are you still a vegetarian?" Suade asked.

Swallowing a piece of melon, Sasha nodded. "Yes. I gave up meat three years ago and haven't touched it since."

Suade held a fried drumstick up to his mouth. "I could never give up meat." He bit into a chicken.

"So, Sasha," Richmond started, "Mom told me that you stayed with Salvador last night."

Orange juice flew out of Dirk's mouth. "Oh, hell no! Please tell me Salvador didn't try to get you in his bed." Brows dipped, Dirk dragged a napkin across his face. "Did he?"

Sasha shook her head. "No. He—"

Suade interjected, "Oh good, because I was about to pay him a damn visit. How in the hell did you end up staying at Salvador's?"

Sasha hesitated, blinked with bafflement. She had no clue staying with Salvador would be such a big deal to her guy cousins. "Salvador was at the car accident last night. His timing couldn't have been better. He provided CPR to one of the men involved in the accident. Had he not been there, both men would've probably died." Sasha wondered how the man that Salvador had saved was doing. Maybe later on today, she'll go to the hospital and pay him a visit.

Richmond cleared his throat. "Listen, you two. Salvador would never try to get with Sasha. He knows better than to cross that line." Dirk shook his head. "Yeah, right."

Sasha hefted a glass of water to her lips. "What's wrong with Salvador? He seems like a good guy." A fine one, too.

"Oh, Salvador's a great guy," Suade stated, "he's just a diehard playboy, that's all."

Leslie laughed. "My. My. My. Now look who's talking. Suade and Dirk...the two of you can't talk. You're no better than Salvador. Salvador is a great guy, Sasha. He just hasn't met the right woman to settle down with. Who knows, you just might be the girl to make him want to get married."

"Mom!" Richmond, Dirk, and Suade shouted in unison.

Sasha cracked up laughing. "Trust me, guys...the last thing on my mind is getting involved in a relationship. In fact, I never want to get married. All I want to do is concentrate on getting one of the songs I've written published."

"You're a songwriter?" Kayla asked.

"Sort of. After my mother died, I quit my corporate job at a technology company to become a full-time song writer. I've written a lot of songs, but nothing has been published yet."

"Well, someday your song will get published," Leslie said, "just keep writing and doing what you're passionate about, and it'll happen. I've already prayed over it, so it's a done deal."

"Thanks, Auntie." Hopefully, she'd get published before she depleted her savings, Sasha thought.

Brunch had been a hit. After everyone left, including Leslie, Sasha flopped down on the couch inside the den and peered out the window. As she stared at the lake running serenely behind the big house, quiet stillness filled her ears. Emptiness filled her heart.

Sitting there feeling lonely, Sasha thought perhaps she should go job hunting sometime next week. Yeah. Yeah. One day her songwriting career may take off, but until it did she needed a job to occupy her free time, keep her mind busy, and pay her a decent income. A college graduate of Spellman University, she'd earned a bachelor's degree in business and had minored in technology. With her degrees and work experience combined, she should be able to find some kind of decent work in the low country. Right?

Sasha's cell rang in her pocket. Spying the Caller ID, it read 'unrestricted'. She swiped the screen, then placed the cell to her ear. "Hello."

"Hi, Sasha." At the sound of Reggie's voice, Sasha's heart spun. Reggie! Reggie sighed harshly. "I'm so sorry for what I did to you. Can we please meet somewhere in public and talk about this?

Sasha's nostrils flared. Refusing to cry, she swallowed. "No. We. Can't. I hope the police find you and put you behind bars for what you did to me. Don't ever call me again." Click. It took no time for her cell to buzz again. 'Unrestricted' appeared on the screen, letting her know it was Reggie again. I'm not answering his call. What kind of fool does Reggie think I am? It'll be a cold day in hell before I ever get back with that abusive monster.

Sasha stood. "I'd rather be dead than to ever get back with him." Needing some fresh air, Sasha dialed the cab service to come get her.

THE YELLOW CAB ROLLED UP to the hospital and came to a complete stop. Sitting in the rear of the ride, Sasha handed the

Caucasian cab driver a twenty dollar bill. "Keep the change."

"Thanks. You have a good day, ma'am," the cab driver stated.

"You too, sir." Anxious to find out how the man who'd been in the wreck last night was doing, Sasha opened the car door and stepped out onto the pavement. The spring May air clung to her skin as she made her way inside the hospital. According to the paramedics last night, they were bringing him here.

Reaching the circulation desk, Sasha prayed that the man who's car she'd hit from behind was still alive. Had survived. Oh God, she should've never been trailing him so closely. Especially with the way it was raining. Fix it, Jesus. Fix it.

As she approached the waiting area, the Caucasian woman sitting behind the circulation desk greeted Sasha with a polite smile. "Hello. How may I help you?"

"Hi. Ummm. Last night, I was in a car accident with some man, and—" I don't even know his name. Sasha continued. "According to the paramedics, they were going to bring the man who I got in the car accident with here…to this hospital. I'm here to see him." "What's the gentleman's name?" the woman asked.

Sasha shrugged. "I don't know his name. He's an African-American man. He looked like he was in his late sixties."

Glancing up at Sasha, the woman tilted her head. "I'm sorry, ma'am, but unless you're related, I can't give out any information on him."

The corner of Sasha's mouth twisted with exasperation. "But I need to know how he's doing. I've been worried sick."

The receptionist shrugged. "Sorry."

"You mean to tell me you can't even tell me how he's doing?"

"No, ma'am. I could lose my job."

"May I have a tissue, please?" The lady pulled a tissue from the box by the computer and handed it to Sasha. She reached inside her purse. She extracted two twenty dollar bills from her wallet, wrapped the money with the tissue, and then handed it to the lady. "There's forty dollars wrapped inside the tissue."

"His name is Ben Haroldson. Fourth floor. Room 415," she quickly rumbled off.

This chick is something else. "Thanks."

"No. Thank you," she said with emphasis.

On her way to Ben's room, Sasha stopped by the gift shop.

Carrying a live green plant in her hands, Sasha walked along the fourth floor of the hospital, searching for Ben's room. Reading the number 415 to the side of the door, she stopped in her tracks. Here's Ben's room. Having no clue as to what she was going to say, she walked inside Ben's room.

Wearing a white hospital gown, Ben was sitting upright in bed, watching television. Hearing her come inside his room, he transferred his gaze from the TV to look at her.

"Hi," Sasha said, smiling.

Ben scrunched his brown, wrinkly face. A big bald spot was on the top of his head, and thin grey hairs covered the sides. "Who are you?"

"My name is Sasha. I'm the lady who crashed into your car from behind last night. May I come in, please?"

Swallowing, the round ball in Ben's throat glided up and down. A look of fear settled on his round, chubby face. "Sure. As long as you are who you say you are."

What was that supposed to mean? Who else would she be? "I'm sorry for slamming into the back of your car. I know it's not much of a peace offering, but I got you this plant."

Silence. Nothing. "Thanks. It's nice." Ben nodded to the dresser positioned beneath the television. "You can put it over there."

Sasha placed the green plant on top of the dresser, then sat in the chair beside Ben's hospital bed. "So, how are you feeling?"

"I've been better. Bones hurt. A lot. Aching all over. I see your face got messed up from the car accident." Yeah, that's what everybody thinks. Everybody except Salvador. He was smart enough to figure out that my facial scars didn't come from the car accident. I wonder what Salvador is doing. "What about you?" Ben

asked, cutting into Sasha's thoughts about Salvador.

"Huh?"

"How are you feeling?" Ben queried.

"Other than a little sore, not bad. So when do you get out of here?"

His hands in his lap, Ben twiddled his fingers. "I don't know yet. But I hope soon. The food in here is gross."

"If you like, I can go get you something to eat and bring it back," Sasha offered.

Ben's complexion lightened some. "You'd really go get me something to eat?"

"Yes. Considering I almost killed you, that's the least I can do. What kind of food do you like?"

Ben aimed the remote to the television, changed the station, and placed the remote in his lap. "Please don't feel like you need to make up for what happened to me. The accident wasn't your fault, Sasha. If the man in the other car hadn't tried to speed around the SUV in a rain storm, the accident would've never happened. But to answer your question…soul food is my favorite kind of food."

"What about desserts?"

"Anything from the bakery over there by the ocean— SugarKanes. Especially the caramel pecan pies they sell. Ooo-we— those things are delicious."

"I've heard a lot about the desserts at SugarKanes."

Worry conveyed on Ben's face. His eyes turned darker. "Look,
Sasha. I appreciate you stopping by, but really, it wasn't necessary. You really need to go—"

"I see great minds think alike," someone with a deep voice stated. Sasha's gaze swept to the door. Wearing a black-collared Polo shirt and a pair of jeans, Salvador stood in the doorway holding a big green plant. In fact, it was the same plant she'd purchased for Ben herself. "May I come in?" Oh my, Salvador's here. He's so good looking. Sasha's heartbeat kicked up a notch. "Hi, Sasha." "Hi." Her greeting came out low.

Concern shadowed Ben's face. "Who are you?" he asked.

Plant in his hands, Salvador stalked up to Ben's bedside. "I'm Salvador. Salvador Casillas."

Ben's eyes stretched wide. His crinkly lips smiled. "Salvador Casillas?! Yes! Yes! You're the boxer. I recognize you." Salvador is a boxer? That explains his lavish lifestyle. Because Sasha didn't watch sports that often, she had no clue he was a professional boxer. Ben continued. "Why, of course you can come in." He chuckled. "I've never met a professional boxer before."

Salvador's lips pulled into a handsome smile. "I'm retired from boxing. I'm now a boxing analyst, and a boxing trainer."
"My grandson—" Ben cut off his sentence.

"Your grandson what?" Salvador mocked.

Ben's smile quickly faded, and he shook his head. "Nothing. Nothing. Why are you here to see me?"

"Initially, I came here to see how you were doing."

Ben looked baffled. "I'm confused."

When Salvador sat the plant on the edge of the bed, Sasha picked it up and placed it on the dresser beside the one she'd bought. "I know you're confused, Mr. Haroldson."

"Ben. Call me Ben."

Salvador nodded. "Okay, Ben. I'm the person who pulled you from the car last night."

Ben touched his chest. "Good God Almighty. You saved my life."

"Yes, sir. I did."

Ben diverted his sad gaze from Salvador's face and stared in the opposite direction at the window. He exhaled harshly, then looked back at Salvador. "I'd be lying if I told you I was grateful that you saved my life. That being said, I can't say thank you."

Salvador folded his arms across his thick, muscular chest. "I'm not surprised to hear you say you're not grateful, Ben."

Ben's grey eyebrows lifted. "You're not? How come?"

"This is going to sound weird coming from a stranger, but you and I have something in common."

Ben shook his head. "Oh, no. We don't have anything in common. I've read all about you and have seen you fight. A rich man like you and a poor man like me don't have squat in common.
I can assure you of that."

"You're wrong, Ben. We do have something in common."

Ben shook his head. "What's that?"

"What we have in common is our love and concern for your grandson—Corey Haroldson."

Ben's head jerked backwards. "You know my grandson Corey?"

"Yes. Corey is a great kid. I train him at my boxing academy."

"I told his mother not to let him get involved with that boxing, and she done went and did it anyways, I see. Alyssa has always been so darn hardheaded."

"With me heading up his lessons, Corey's in great hands. However, he was really down this morning. He told me that you'd left a letter stating you were leaving Hilton Head. I know it's none of my business, but I'd like to make a suggestion that you pay Corey a visit before you just up and leave town. Corey loves you like a father. And being that his father is absent from his life and walked out on him, please...I'm begging you to not do the same. If you do, it may damage him forever."

Ben's eyes grew watery. "You're right, Salvador. My problems are none of your business. Thanks for the plant. Please see yourself out." Ben looked at Sasha. "And you, too. Both of you, just go. Get out of here."

Alrighty then. Feeling sorry for Ben and this Corey kid, Sasha stood. "I'm sorry if I inconvenienced you. I hope you feel better."

Both Salvador and Sasha began making their way out of Ben's room. Right when they reached the doorway, Ben said, "Hey, Salvador. Please don't tell Corey you saw me. It won't do nothing but upset him. I have no intentions of seeing him before I leave. So the less he knows, the better."

Salvador's face scrunched. The corners of his blue eyes slanted. "You're a very selfish man, Ben. Let's go Sasha."

Walking in complete silence, Salvador pushed through the double doors of the fourth floor and descended the staircase. Dismounting the steps behind him, Sasha hated seeing Salvador so upset. Apparently, this Corey kid meant a lot to him.

Salvador flung open the door on the first floor and stepped outside. Clenching his teeth, he balled his fists. "I tell you...that Ben Haroldson is one old selfish bastard. The mere fact that he plans to leave Corey without giving him a reason why pisses me off."

Sasha's hand instinctively began caressing Salvador's arm. "Maybe Ben has a good reason for not saying goodbye to his grandson."

"I'm sorry. But there's never a good reason to leave a child without giving them a proper explanation of why you're doing so. I'd never just up and leave my family. Only punks leave their family like Ben is doing. Corey is upset. Ben's daughter, Alyssa, is upset." "And you're upset." The way Salvador cared so much for this Corey kid spoke volumes, as far as Sasha was concerned. "While there's nothing you can do to get Ben to change his mind, there is something you can do for Corey."

"Like what?"

"Pray. I'll pray with you." Sasha grabbed Salvador's hands. "Close your eyes."

"I don't know about this, Sasha. I'm not good at praying when I'm angry."

"It's okay. I'll do the praying. All you have to do is close your eyes, and I'll do the rest." Salvador released a deep breath, then closed his eyes. Sasha closed her eyes, too. "Heavenly Father. We come to You and ask that You somehow get Ben to change his mind about seeing his grandson before he leaves. Lord, we ask that You help guide Ben to do what is right for both him and his grandson. Thank You for listening, God. Amen." She opened her eyes.

Salvador's right eye popped open, and then his left one. "Amen." When she tried to ease her hands from his, he briefly held them tight. "That was a beautiful prayer, Sasha. I must admit, I feel calmer."

"Prayer works."

Finally, he released her hands. "Yeah. You may be right. How did you get here?"

"I caught a cab."

"Well, if you don't have anything planned, I'd love to take you to lunch."

"Leslie cooked a huge brunch today. If I hadn't ate so much, I'd take you up on your offer. Not only that, I need to go pick up a rental car so I'll have something to drive while I'm here. If you can take me to get a rental, I'd greatly appreciate it."

"Sure, no problem. I'll take you." Salvador and Sasha walked side by side in the hospital's parking lot. Using his key fob, he popped the locks on his BMW SUV, opened the door for her, and she climbed inside.

He rounded the rear of the BMW, hopped in, stuck his key in the ignition. His hand gripping the steering wheel, Salvador looked at Sasha. All that male dominance and handsomeness made her female senses stir. Somebody as good looking as Salvador had to be special.

Salvador's eyes seemed to hold a sheen of purpose. Pride. Dignity. "Don't worry about picking up a rental car. You can borrow one of my mine."

Is he for real? "Are you sure? I have insurance, and I hate imposing on people."

"I wouldn't have offered if I wasn't sure. Like I said before, you're a Spaulding. Family to one of my closet friends." Salvador's blue eyes gleamed. When his tanned lips drew into a sexy smile, Sasha's heart swirled. Dear Lord. He's gorgeous.

Sasha hated depending on men. Even more, she hated that the man sitting beside her had just made her feel something sensual. "You know what…thanks for offering me your car…but I'll just get a rental car."

His blue eyes looked like glassy hand-blown art. "Okay, that's fine. If you don't mind, I'd like to stop and pick myself something up to eat real quick, and then I'll take you to get the rental car."

"Of course I don't mind. I'm riding with you, so I'm on your schedule."

"You are indeed on my schedule." The way he'd responded made her feel as if he were up to something.

Salvador made a left at the traffic light, drove down a road called Ocean Boulevard. Enjoying the view of the glistening ocean to her right, a feeling of peace washed over Sasha. She had the distinct feeling Hilton Head Island was the perfect place for her to be right now in her life.

The sound of tires rolling over gravel caused Sasha to look slightly to her left. Salvador pulled up into the lot of the famous bakery—SugarKanes. Aunt Leslie and Ben love this bakery.

Salvador put the gear in park. "I'm going to run in and out. It won't take long."

"Please don't feel like you have to hurry because of me. If you want to sit and eat, I can have a cup of coffee or something while you enjoy your lunch."

"Okay. I'll eat inside. Let me get the car door for you." Sasha waited for Salvador to round the SUV and pull the door open for her. His eyes gleaming like a blue sea, holding the door open, he stepped to the side.

"Thanks." When Sasha went to lower her feet to the SUV'S running board, she missed it and slipped. On her way downward, Salvador caught her in his strong boxer arms. What in the hell? Surprised she didn't hit the ground, and embarrassed as hell, she glanced up at Salvador as she lay in his arms.

Their gazes hooked, he helped her into a straightened stance, kept his arms wrapped about her shoulders. Tilting her head back, her sheathed breasts pressed to his thick chest, her pointed nipples tingled. Desire flooded her, crept to her center. Her moist labia lips fluttered like butterfly wings.

"Be careful, these rocks are slippery." His minty breath fanned her face.

Can't be any more slippery than my vagina. How dare
Salvador get her so wet!

Chapter Seven

MENTALLY ORDERING HIS SHAFT TO stay soft, Salvador pushed
through the door of SugarKanes. A sweet , sugary flavor crept up
his nose, making him hungrier. People packed the inside of the
popular bakery. Noise from patrons spread throughout. Waitresses
and other staff walked about.

With Sasha by his side, Salvador stalked towards the host
stand. Normally, he didn't take girls out in public in the daytime.
On occasion , he'd take a woman out a t night, but that was only
when he knew he'd get a blow job or some pussy after wards. To
his surprise, he didn't mind being seen out in public with Sasha. He
didn't care if people thought they were a couple or more than
friends. The reason he felt this way made no sense to him. Maybe
he felt like this because Sasha was Richmond's cou sin, and he
couldn't get her in his bed even if he wanted to. Damn.

When he'd put his hands on her a few moments ago and had
captured her so she wouldn't fall, he'd been tempted to thrust his
tongue into her mouth, wrap his tongue around hers, and kiss he r
erotically. He'd also been tempted to take her back to his place and
try his damn hardest to get into her panties. He could already see
it, keeping his hands off the sexy pussycat named Sasha was going

to be one helluva challenge.

Standing behind the glass display, Sandella spotted him, smiled, and made her way over to the hostess stand. Sandella spread her arms and hugged him. "Salvador. It's so good to see you," she said, releasing him.

"It's good to see you, too, Sandella. Please meet my friend, Sasha." *The woman I want to take to bed, but can't.*

Sandella smiled prettily. "Welcome to Hilton Head Island, Sasha. Kayla called me earlier and told me all about the big brunch Leslie cooked for you. She also told me how pretty you were. And that indeed you are."

Sasha's cheeks turned a brownish-red. "Thanks, Sandella. You're very pretty, too."

"Thanks. Are you staying here, or are you picking up something to go?"

"We're staying here," Salvador confirmed.

"Follow me." Sandella gathered two menus in her hands and showed them to a table by the window. Seating them at a table with an ocean view, Sandella spoke, "Sasha, maybe after you get settled, we can get together with some of my other girlfriends and have lunch or something."

"I'd like that. Thanks, Sandella."

"You're welcome." Sandella walked off.

Sasha's sexy lips curled upward, exposing a dashing white smile. "She seems so nice."

You seem nice, too. "Sandella is very nice. She's a good person to know and hang out with. You should try the caramel pecan pie she makes. It's delicious."

"Everyone rants about her caramel pecan pies. I'm going to try the pie, and get a cup of coffee to go with it."

After the waitress took their orders, Salvador and Sasha sat at the table, thoroughly enjoying each other's company. While making small talk, thoughts of Corey and Ben crossed Salvador's mind and threatened to make him angry. Not wanting to let negative thoughts of Ben ruin his date with Sasha, he forced them aside. Wait. He wasn't on a date with Sasha. He was just having a friendly lunch with her—the pussycat who'd made his loins hurt.

Sasha's cell buzzed. She extracted it from her purse. "Excuse me. But I really need to take this call." She scooted the chair back and walked outside.

The waitress lowered a glass of sweet, lemony tea in front of him. "Thanks." Gazing out the window at Sasha as she talked on her cell, he admired her breathtaking beauty from her side view. The sun glistened on her brown skin. Strands of silky black hair paraded over her shoulders and down her back. Her breasts perched high beneath the red cotton shirt she wore. And those damn jeans she wore rode her plump bubble ass like a cowgirl riding a wild bull.

Balls tingling from looking at Sasha, Salvador lifted the drink to his mouth. Imagining his tongue rolling over the bud of her dark clitoris, he sipped. Sweet, sugary tea glided down his throat. I wonder if Sasha's sex tastes as good as this tea. Betting her sex would feel like silk on his probing tongue, he lowered the beverage to the table.

Standing on the other side of the window, Sasha tapped a button on her cell, then glanced sideways. Their gazes linked. Locked. Salvador's shaft knotted. Heat rushed him. He fought to tear his gaze away from hers, but he managed to. If he would've kept looking into her sensual eyes one second longer, the tip of his shaft would've leaked. He hadn't even touched her yet, and he could imagine the musky scent of her sex.

"Sorry about that," Sasha said, retreating back to her seat at the table across from him.

"No problem." He yearned for her in the worst way possible.

The waitress lowered a roast beef sandwich piled with mushrooms and overflowing with melted Swiss cheese in front of him. She then lowered a thick slice of caramel pecan pie in front of Sasha.

After blessing her food, Sasha forked a piece of pie into her mouth. "Oh. My. God. This is delicious," she said, chewing her food. Damn, he even liked the way her mouth moved whenever she chewed.

Hating he cared about what Richmond would think if he slept with his cousin, Salvador bit into his roast beef sandwich. Juices squirted from the meat, wetting his mouth. He sure wished a different kind of brown, tender flesh was squirting on his lips— Sasha's vagina. Aroused, his rod slightly hardened. Grew an inch inside his underwear.

"Want some pie?" Sasha forked a piece of pie onto her fork and extended it across the table towards him.

Hell yeah, I want some of your pie. "Do. I. Ever. Want some pie." Salvador leaned his head across the table, wrapped his long, pink tongue around the fork, and sucked the pie off. Just like he'd do to her pussy cat if he was eating it.

Sasha dropped the fork, and it clinked against her plate. An astounded look shot to her pretty face. Yeah, baby, I want to eat you. Glad you know it. Looking at the scared look on Sasha's face, Salvador cracked up laughing on the inside.

He purposely pinned her with a heated gaze. Her bottom lip quivered. As horny as you have me, you better be scared. "I'm so clumsy." She picked up the fork with her trembling hand, sliced into her pie, and continued eating the dessert.

Salvador held his roast beef sandwich up to his mouth and took a huge bite. Juices spilled onto his mouth. What man wouldn't want any of your pie, Sasha? Using the tip of his tongue, he trailed a circle around the outlines of his mouth. Sasha shuddered. Deciding to do Sasha a favor whether she liked it or not, Salvador finished his lunch. He dragged a napkin across his mouth, paid the bill, and the two of them left.

Steering the SUV down Ocean Boulevard, Salvador laid a gentle hand on the middle part of Sasha's thigh. "Mind if I roll the windows down?"

"No. I'd like that."

Salvador tapped a button, rolling down all four windows. He then left the roof back. Wind blew into the inside of the truck, brushing strands of hair across Sasha's brown lips and face. Having had a wonderful afternoon with Sasha, he wished like hell it could end in an even better night. A night in his bed. Stroking. Poking. Licking. And kissing.

On his way home, Salvador stopped by his boxing academy to get some paperwork. After giving Sasha a tour of his sports facility, they left. Ten miles later, he drove his SUV into the driveway of his oceanfront home and parked.

White seagulls flew over the shimmering sea behind his home. The orange sun lowered to the horizon. From where he sat inside the truck, he could see the beige, sandy beach.

Sasha averted her gaze from Salvador's two story beach house and looked at him. "Whose house is this?"

"Mine."

"I thought you were taking me to get a rental car?"

You thought wrong. Salvador smiled. "I changed my mind."

Her cinnamon-colored eyes were serenely compelling. Drew him to her like a magnet. "What? How am I going to get around? I need something to drive."

Salvador pressed a button near the rearview mirror. The garage door lifted. Inside the overly expansive garage sat five luxurious cars——his big boy toys. "You can drive any one you want to. The choice is yours."

Sasha's mouth parted. "Wow. Why do you have so many cars?"

Salvador shrugged. "I love collecting cars. I have ten more at my home out in California.

"I had no clue you were a famous boxer until Ben had mentioned it earlier today."

"Yeah. I'm a retired boxer."

"Retired? How old are you?"

"Thirty. And you?"

"I'm twenty-six." A spark of some indefinable emotion portrayed in her eyes.

"In the world of boxing, I wasn't really that famous. In fact, I'm more famous as a boxing analyst than I ever was as a professional boxer. People don't group me in the same category as Floyd Mayweather or Manny Pacquiao, or Evander Holyfield. I'm ranked a little bit beneath them. Rightfully so." He exited the car.

As Salvador and Sasha headed for the garage, a cool afternoon breeze rolled off the ocean from behind his home and sailed down over their heads. "It feels so good out here."

"Yes. It's nice and windy. Perfect spring weather. With the summer quickly approaching, it won't last long, though." Speaking of long, Salvador sure wished he could long stroke the woman standing to his right. Sasha continued. "With it being so dark out last night, I really couldn't see the outside of your home. It's beautiful. Absolutely gorgeous. So big. Why does a single man like you need such big things?" she asked, her eyes staring at his white Panamera Porsche.

Salvador laughed. "I just like big things. I think big. I dream big." "Did your mother teach you to dream big?" Sasha inquired.

Salvador's lips fell into a straight line. Lucy hadn't taught him anything. In fact, he'd practically had to raise his mother, instead of the other way around. "No. She didn't. So which car are you going to borrow?"

Sasha's eyes roamed over the Porsche, then transferred to the Mercedes, and then went to the BMW. Lastly, she looked at the Corvette and his Bentley.

She patted the hood of the Panamera. "I like this one."

"The Porsche it is, then. Let's go inside so I can give you the keys." They entered the kitchen through the back garage door. Salvador pulled open the drawer by the refrigerator, tossed her the keys, and she caught them.

"I hope I don't wreck your car," she said in a worrisome tone.

"If you do, it's all good. I can always buy another one."

"Let me ask you something, why are you being so nice to me?"

Salvador took a step forward. "I told you...the Spauldings are like family to me." He took another step forward. "But there's another reason I'm being so nice to you, Sasha. I'm sure you have a clue as to why." As he closed the distance between them, Sasha began walking backwards. Oh yeah, now he had her backed into the kitchen door. Right where he wanted her. Towering over her, Salvador put a flat hand to the door above her head. Using his free hand, he touched a finger to her dimpled chin. He dropped his face close to hers. "You're a very beautiful woman, Sasha. Although I've only known you for one day, you make me burn. Ever since you arrived at the hospital earlier today, I've been dying to do this..."

Salvador slanted his mouth over Sasha's and kissed her feverishly. Twining his tongue with hers, he groaned huskily. While kissing her, an image of Richmond holding up a fist appeared inside his head. Ready to take Sasha to his bed and make wild, burning love to her, Salvador decided he wouldn't try to seduce her. Sasha was delicate and special, and had to be treated as such.

Sasha broke their heated kiss. Breathing raggedy, she blurted, "I'm not having sex with you. The nerve of you to think just because you let me borrow your car, I'd have sex with you!"

"That's was not my intention—" Frowning, Sasha flung open the kitchen door and stormed into the garage. "Where are you going?" he asked, standing in the doorway.

She gripped the handle of the white Porsche, swung the door open, and slid between the seat and steering wheel. "I'm going home! Goodbye!" She slammed the door, cranked the engine, and sped off.

Watching the Porsche speed out of the driveway, Salvador burst into laughter. Feisty Sasha had turned him on. Had set his balls on fire. "You got away today, Sasha. But it'll never happen again. I'm getting in her panties. Soon. Real soon." Rod hard enough to split a brick, Salvador closed the door and headed to his bedroom.

Salvador walked inside his master bedroom. Standing at the foot of his bed, he reached into the front of his jean pocket and pulled out Sasha's pink panties that he'd found on the guest bathroom floor this morning. He turned the hot pink panties inside out, sniffed the crotch area, and then licked it. Mmmm. Remnants
of Sasha's pussy taste great.

Aroused, Salvador pulled open the drawer beside his bed, retrieved a tube of lubricant. He sat on the edge of the bed, lowered the zipper of his jeans. He reached into his underwear and pulled out his tanned cock. Blood filled his throbbing mushroom head. He squeezed the cool lubricant on his erection, wrapped Sasha's panties around his shaft, and fisted himself.

Thinking of Sasha flawless complexion, her round bubble butt, and that pretty smile of hers, Salvador mashed his steely erection up and down in his tight grip. He groaned. Wishing Sasha was bouncing her sex up and down on his rod, cum boiled inside his balls. Needing to release himself, he grunted. Started jerking himself harder. Wilder.

Semen flew from Salvador's slit into the crouch of Sasha's panties. It's only a matter of time before I take you to bed, Sasha.

Only a matter of time.

Smiling because Sasha had worked up his loin's area into a high fever, Salvador cleaned off in the bathroom, and then headed for the den. The beautiful ocean behind his home was a pretty shade of baby blue. The sand, a nice beige. He opened the sliding glass door. The soft sounds of water brushing up against the sand caressed his ears as his feet pivoted.

Hefting the remote in his hand, he clicked on the television, flopped on the sofa. Threw his feet up on the table. Watching the local evening news, he couldn't stop thinking about Sasha.

Whew. Sasha was one hot cookie. A cookie he couldn't wait to devour with his mouth. Taste every inch of her delectable body.

Yep, she'd slapped him because he'd kissed her today, but the next time...oh, the next time hopefully he'd be slapping her instead. Slapping her curvy rear with the palm of his hand. Hopefully, she was the kind of woman that could appreciate a good spanking.

A sudden thought caused his mood to sour. Considering some clown had struck Sasha and had beat the living crap out of her, maybe she wouldn't like a spanking after all. Boy, did he wish he could get his hands on the bastard who'd hit her. He'd choke the shit out of him with his own hands. Throttle the jerk. Then step on his neck with his hard boot.

Speaking of jerks, he knew another jerk. Ben Haroldson. In Salvador's book, Ben wasn't worth a dime. A freaking nickel. Ben was a worthless piece of crap.

Poor Corey. He had a loser for a grandfather. What kind of person left their daughter and grandson without saying goodbye? Sasha felt Ben maybe had a good reason to do what he was doing. If he did, what on Earth could it be?

"Are you in some type of trouble, Ben?" Salvador mumbled, dying to figure this difficult puzzle out.

Chapter Eight

BEN'S HAND SHOOK UNCONTROLLABLY AS   he lifted the
spoon covered with apple sauce to his lips. Swallowing the food, he
eyed the two green plants on the dresser inside his hospital room
and felt horrible for how   he'd treated his guests earlier. He'd
thrown Salvador and Sasha out. Had acted like he couldn't care less
about his grandson, when it was just the opposite. I love Corey.

Heart broken, Ben's bottom lip folded under. Ben loved Corey
and his daughter, Alyssa, with all his heart. With every fiber in his
body, he loved them. That's why he had to leave. He couldn't put
their lives at risk.

The man he owed the money towas named Laurente. Laurente
wouldn't hesitate to kill his daughter Alyssa and his grandson   ,
Corey. Laurente was of Russian decent, and ruthless.

Several years ago, before Ben had retired as the maintenance
man at an elementary school, he'd met Laurente while at work.
Laurente had come to the elementary school to pick up his son at
the time. When Laurente had spotted Ben inside the office fixing
the hinges on the door, he'd told him he wanted him to do some
maintenance work for him at the gift shops he owned. Ben had
agreed to help the heartless man out. Now, the same man who had

once treated him kind wanted him dead.

Ben's chest ached. Rubbing a heavy hand on his tight chest, he lowered his spoon to his tray. "I regret the day I ever met you, Laurente." His mind switched to his beautiful wife, Claira, before she died. "But it was all for you, Claira. Now you're in heaven. You left me here by myself," Ben uttered, sulking.

Several months ago, when Claira had gotten sick and had needed to have an emergency surgery that'd cost a ton of money, Ben had called up Laurente and asked the heartless man if he could borrow some money. As broke as Ben was, he didn't have a choice but to go to Laurente for the money. Laurente had agreed to give Ben the money, but it came with a condition—Laurente wanted Ben to burn down the structure of a multimillion dollar business. So in exchange for the money, Ben had agreed to commit arson. Dumb him, he'd tried to set the building on fire, but things went wrong. Now Laurente wanted Ben to pay for the huge mistake with his life. Regretting the day he'd ever met Laurente, Ben cursed. Closing his eyes, his mind burned with the memory of the night he'd tried to set the building on fire.

At three in the morning, Ben drove his car down the long, dark road and parked on the curb. Scared out of his mind, he eyed the huge warehouse-looking building across the street and felt like puking. Damn, he'd never done anything criminal in his whole entire life. He hadn't even gotten as much as a parking ticket and was now about to burn down somebody's business. But if he didn't do it, then Laurente wouldn't give him the money. And his wife, Claira, well, she wouldn't be able to get the surgery and would end up dead.

Feeling as if there was only one resolution to his problem, Ben got out of the car, opened his trunk, and hefted the red container filled with gasoline. Shaking like a leaf, Ben walked briskly towards the huge building.

Wishing he could get the money some other type of way, Ben walked past a huge oak tree. Bats shot out of the tree, terrifying Ben.

He jumped. Almost had a heart attack. His legs turning to gelatin, he heard crickets chirping and birds squawking. The different sounds coming from the night animals creeped him the hell out.

Ready to get home to his beloved Claira, Ben doused gasoline on the back of the building, struck a match, and tossed it. Orange flames ignited, and the building caught on fire.

Inhaling smoke, Ben scuttled as fast as he could away from the fire. He jumped in his car, cranked the engine, and got the hell out of there. On his way home, he stopped by Laurente's and collected the second half of the money the ruthless man owed him.

A short while later, just as the sun began to rise, Ben arrived home. Smelling like gasoline and burnt wood, he walked inside the bedroom where Claira lay in their bed asleep. Standing over their bed, Ben studied Claira's natural beauty. The sun slipping through the blinds radiated on her rosy cheeks. Her soft, shiny hair looked like grey silk. Her wrinkly lips were naturally mauve. Because of him, Claira could now get the surgery and live longer, Ben thought, feeling somewhat relieved.

Anxious to tell Claira he'd gotten the money, Ben cupped her shoulder and shook her. "Claira. Wake up, I have something to tell you." When Claira didn't move, Ben shook her again. "Claira, honey. Wake up." When she didn't respond the second time, fear coursed through Ben's veins.

Ben put two fingers to Claira's wrist to check her pulse. Nothing. He put two fingers to her jugular vein and couldn't get a pulse there either. He dropped his head to her chest and didn't hear or feel a thing. Claira Haroldson had died in her sleep that night.

"Oh no, Claira! Oh no!" Ben scooped his beloved Claira into his arms and held her until the rescue squad got there.

As Ben stood outside watching the paramedics roll Claira's cold corpse into the back of the emergency aid vehicle, his cell rang. "Hello."

"Ben. Ben. Ben," Laurente said, in his thick Russian accent. "You took my money and did a half-ass job."

Watching the ambulance pull off with Claira's corpse, Ben's heart shredded. "Huh? What are you talking about?" he asked Laurente, tears flowing from his eyes.

"I drove by the building you were supposed to burn down, and it's still standing, Ben. Other than burnt shrubbery, ain't shit burned. I paid you to torch the building! Not the fucking trees!"

Pain shot to Ben's temples. Oh God. Oh God. His wife had just died, and now this. "I'm sorry, Laurente. I thought I'd did as you requested. Please forgive me. My wife died, so I won't be needing the money. I'll bring it back to you today."

Laurente laughed wickedly. "I'm afraid not, Ben. A deal is a deal." Shaking his head, Ben realized his life was spiraling out of control. "But I don't need the money anymore. Claira died. She's dead."

"Too fucking bad! A deal is a deal. You have two choices now. One—you go back and burn the building down as you promised. Or two—I burn your ass. You choose, Ben."

"How's my favorite patient doing?" Hearing the familiar voice, Ben's eyes shot open to find Nurse Tasha standing at his bedside. Patting his shoulder, Tasha smiled. "Glad to see you finally ate something."

Ben nodded. "When is the doctor going to come check my leg out?" Ben asked, having injured it worse when he'd taken a hard fall the other night. "It's starting to swell."

"The doctor should be here shortly. Let me take a look at your leg." Tasha rolled Ben's hospital gown up to his hips. Ben's hurt leg had reddened and was swollen around the knee. "Oh wow, Mr. Haroldson. I think you may have fractured your leg. If my assumption is correct, you're not going to be getting out of here anytime soon."

Terrified that Laurente may send one of his boys back to the hospital to murder him tonight, Ben shuddered.

Chapter Nine

"KEEP YOUR LIPS TO YOURSELF, Salvador!" Sasha warned as she and Salvador stood inside his den.

Smiling his tail off, Salvador clutched Sasha's shoulders. "You know you want me, Sasha. Just admit it."

Sasha rolled her eyes. "You're so conceited, Salvador. Listen, and listen good. I do not want you. I came to Hilton Head Island so I could get away from a man, so why on Earth would I want to get involved with one as soon as I get here?"

A cocky smile appeared on Salvador's handsome face. "Because the man you were with before was a pompous jackass. And me, well, I'm nothing like the jerk. I know how to treat a woman." Desire flickered in Salvador's blue eyes. He pressed his hard shaft into Sasha's belly, and then his lips came coaxing down on hers.

Unable to resist his advances, Sasha returned Salvador's kiss. Latching onto his tongue, her nipples tingled. Her sex clenched. Her clitoris hardened.

Salvador broke their sensual kiss and smiled. "I knew you wanted me."

Sasha said breathlessly, "Make love to me, Salvador."

He made his thick rod glide against her belly. "Oh, so now

you're begging for it?" He jerked her off her feet.

While Salvador toted her in his arms, Sasha heard her cell buzz. "Oh, wait. Put me down. My cell is ringing."

"Ignore the call. What we're about to do is more important."

"No, seriously, put me down, Salvador," Sasha said, kicking her feet.

Salvador frowned. "Gladly." He tossed her. Hands flailing, legs kicking, Sasha hit the floor.

Buzz. Buzz. Buzz. The cell on the nightstand buzzed. Sleeping in her comfortable bed, Sasha's eyes fluttered open. Thank God, she'd been dreaming. Buzz. Buzz. Buzz.

"What time is it?" She rolled over to her side and read the red numbers on the alarm clock sitting on the nightstand. 7:57 am. Buzz. Buzz. Buzz.

Just as she picked up her cell, the call went to voicemail. Who was calling her so early in the morning? she wondered, hoping it was Salvador. Remembering how he'd kissed her yesterday, she smiled. A warm feeling spread throughout her.

Could she have been wrong for slapping Salvador when he'd kissed her? Knowing she liked it, why exactly had she slapped him? Well, she definitely didn't come to Hilton Head to get involved with a man. That was for sure. Men could be doggish at times. And according to her cousins, Salvador was a diehard player, and definitely not the settling down type. Only a foolish woman would get involved with Salvador after her cousins had warned her. Besides, she'd just gotten out of an emotionally abusive relationship.

"I'm not going to be your fool, Salvador. Been there, done that." Sasha eased up on her elbows. Yawning, she stretched her arms above her head. Stretched her legs on the soft linen. Leslie's house was so cozy, she felt like she could live here—forever.

Bing. She got a text message. She lifted her cell from her lap and brought it to her eyes.

Salvador: Good morning. I just tried to call you, but I guess you're still asleep. Hope I didn't wake you up. What do you have planned for today? I'd like to take you to lunch.

Somewhat flattered, Sasha smiled. Her insides beamed. "No, thank you. I'm not wasting my time with a playboy."

Sasha: Good morning. I have a lot I have to get done today. But thanks for the offer.

Salvador: What about dinner?

Sasha: Sorry, I'm busy.

Salvador: I hope you're not avoiding me because of the kiss we shared. I would apologize for kissing you, but I thoroughly enjoyed it too much to do so.

"The nerve of you," Sasha said, thinking of what to text next.

Sasha: Just make sure it doesn't happen again.

Salvador: Why not? Did you not enjoy the kiss as much as I did? It sure looked like you did. Your mouth was all over mine. The little slap you gave me didn't fool me. In fact it was quite a turn on.

Fingers on her cell, Sasha's mouth dropped. "Oh, no he didn't!

You're so full of yourself, Salvador."

Sasha: Whatever.

Salvador: Anytime you want to kiss me again, just let me know.

Have a good day.

Sasha: I see you're very conceited. You have a good day, too.

Salvador: I'm not conceited. Just confident. By the way, if you suddenly become available and would like to go out with me, give me a call. I'm free all day and night. And in case you're wondering, if we hook up, I do indeed plan on kissing those sweet lips of yours again.

Half-frowning and half-smiling, Sasha touched her lips. Fire shot through her body. Mmph. Salvador had turned her on via text messaging, and she hated that he had the ability to make her hot like that.

She slid back down on the mattress, pulled the cover up over her breasts. Still hotter than melting lava, she licked her lips. Salvador was a good kisser. Well, a great kisser.

Visions of how Salvador had captured her mouth yesterday sailed inside Sasha's head. He'd wrapped his long tongue around hers and had suckled it into his mouth. Wetness formed between her legs just from envisioning the way he'd kissed her. Nibbling her bottom lip, she spread her legs on the mattress, slid her hands into her panties, and rubbed circles on her clitoris. Oh, Salvador.

Circling her hips, she felt her entrance grow slick with need. Aroused, she rolled her finger over the hard bead. Secretly wishing Salvador was there so he could flick his tongue over her swollen clit, Sasha released a low moan.

Playing with herself, she imagined Salvador kissing her breasts. Kissing her mouth. Kissing between her thighs. And yes, kissing her throbbing nubbin.

"Oh, Salvador," she cooed, her clitoris exploding.

As Sasha finished off her orgasm, her cell rang. Smiling, she placed the phone to her ear. "Yes. I'll go out with you."

"Thank God you finally came to your senses." Reggie's deep voice stabbed her ear, knocking the smile right off her face.

Creeped out, Sasha hung up. "Darn you, Reggie. You messed up my morning." Knowing she could never go back to sleep now that Reggie had called her, she crawled out of bed and headed for the bathroom. I hope the police find Reggie and lock his behind up.

I've never had a man hit me before. Never.

After freshening up, Sasha headed downstairs. When she walked into the kitchen, Leslie was standing at the stove, stirring a spoon inside of a pot. Humming to the upbeat tune streaming from the kitchen's intercom, Leslie bobbed her head to the music. "Good morning, Aunt Leslie." Lying the spoon on the stove, Leslie turned around. Sasha gave her aunt a morning hug.

"Good morning, Sasha. Don't you look pretty this morning. Got some grits and eggs, and fresh blueberry muffins if you're hungry."

"Thanks. I'll have a little bit before I leave." Sasha fixed her plate.

Leslie had such a huge smile on her face. "You have big plans today, don't you?" she asked, scooping grits into a bowl and then dumping some scrambled eggs on top.

Taking her seat at the round kitchen table, Sasha shook her head. "No. I don't have any big plans. What makes you think I have big plans today?"

Leslie took a seat across from Sasha. "Because you brought home a mighty big car yesterday—Salvador's car. All the women in town is going to be jealous once they see you riding around town in his Porsche. He sure has the hots for you, I see."

Sasha laughed. "Well, if he has the hots for me, then too bad, because I'm not crossing that line with him." She forked some cheesy eggs into her mouth.

"Why not? You're single. He's single. Both of you have a lot of great qualities. Me personally, I think he'd be a good guy for you to get to know." Leslie scooped some grits onto her utensil and blew onto the food, cooling it off.

"Although my relationship with Reggie has been over for a long time, we officially just ended things this week. I'm not mentally ready to get involved with another man. To be honest, I don't think I'll ever be ready. Being single and unattached just seems so much easier."

Leslie cleared her throat. "Sasha, dear. If it's okay, you're Auntie wants to give you some advice." Sasha nodded. Leslie continued. "Don't judge all men based on one bad relationship. When Russell and I first got married, for a long time he was a great husband. But after time passed, Russell started cheating with younger women and became a horrible husband. I'm so glad I divorced him. However, he gave me something I'll forever be grateful for."

"What's that?"

"His sperm." Sasha giggled. Leslie continued. "Because of Russell, I have three beautiful sons. Although I experienced a lot of pain, I'd go through all of it again. The hurt made me stronger, and wiser, and brought me closer to God. Now that I'm older, I will admit I get lonely sometimes, and I wish I had someone special in my life. I'd hate for you to end up older and lonely like me someday. Especially when you could've had a man like Salvador."

Sasha tilted her head. "Oh Auntie, you're a beautiful woman. You'll find somebody to share the rest of your life with one day."

With a twirl of her wrist, Leslie shook her head. "Psssh. I don't know about that. Only God knows. It's much harder to find a man once you get my age. But you, on the other hand, you're still a spring chicken. And the pickings aren't slim for a pretty girl like you. Do you in the least bit think Salvador is attractive?"

He's freaking gorgeous. Had me playing with myself this morning.

"Yes. He's attractive."

"Is he your type?"

Heck yes. Sasha nodded. "Yes, he's my type. But—"

"But don't miss out on a good opportunity when Salvador makes his move."

"So you really think he's going to make a move on me?" Well, he'd already made a move, but not a serious one.

Leslie raised her eyebrows. "Trust me, if he let you drive his car—it's only a matter of time before he makes a hot, lusty move on you." Leslie laughed. "Wait till I tell Willa and Kayla's mother, Veronica, about this. Oh yeah, and another thing..."

"What?"

"Don't let Richmond, Suade, or Dirk talk you out of getting with the most eligible and most desirable bachelor in Hilton Head—Salvador. Your cousins are being overprotective. Salvador is a good man. He hasn't put down his player's card because he hasn't met the right woman." She cupped Sasha's hand. "I strongly believe you're the woman that's going to make Salvador Casillas settle down."

Putting her elbow on the table, Sasha fisted her chin. "I don't know about that, Auntie."

Leslie fanned the air with her hand. "Chile, please. Older people can sense things others can't. You're the right woman for Salvador. I can feel it in my bones."

While Sasha appreciated the way Leslie thought so highly of her, she still had reservations about taking things further with Salvador. When Sasha remembered the way Salvador had slurped the caramel pecan pie off the fork yesterday, tingles ran wild through her body. If he ate the pie between her legs the way he'd ate the other pie, there'd be no turning back for her. None whatsoever.

Sasha thanked Leslie for the delicious breakfast, and for the advice. She stood, walked outside, slid into the Porsche behind the steering wheel, and then left.

Cool air blew into the open windows of the white Porsche, whipping Sasha's hair into a tangled mess as she drove down the road lined with beautiful oaks on either side. Mounting up the overpass, she took in the view of the glistening river beneath. Bopping her head to Beyonce's song Dangerously In Love, she marveled at the serene scenery of Hilton Head.

If she spent time with Salvador, just like Beyonce sang, she could see herself falling Dangerously In Love with the fine stallion. Maybe Leslie was getting ahead of herself. For all she knew, Salvador only wanted one thing from her—sex. And she wasn't going to have sex with him unless he asked her to marry him.

Sasha cringed from her own thought regarding marriage. Where in the hell had the thought of marriage come from? She never wanted to get married anyway. Not to Salvador, or anyone for that matter. Her ex, Reggie, had showed her how doggish men could be.

Needing to get some items out of her wrecked Honda, she steered the Porsche into the tow yard and parked. A few seconds later, she entered the building and walked up to the receptionist desk. The brown-haired girl sitting behind the desk was smacking the crap out of a piece of gum. Lifting her head, she blew a bubble.

It popped on her face.

"How may I help you?" she asked, smacking.

Sasha answered, "My car was towed here, and I need to get somethings out of it before it's sent to salvage."

The girl's fingers tapped over the keys of the computer. "What's the make and model of your car?"

"A silver Toyota Camry."

"Follow me, please." The woman led Sasha to the back of the tow yard's building. "Your car is over there." She pointed at Sasha's Honda, then headed back inside.

Wrecked cars crowded the area out back. Sasha's sandals clacked against the pavement as she walked towards her car. She pulled open the car door, slid into the driver's seat, and spotted a brown shoebox in the passenger seat. Momentarily confused, she glanced back over her shoulder. Old clothing, black garbage bags, and an old stereo system junked the back seat.

Holding on to the steering wheel, Sasha said, "What is all this stuff doing in my car?" She lifted the lid off the shoebox to find a bunch of letters and pictures inside. Baffled, she lifted one of the wrinkly envelopes to her eyes and read the sending address: Ben Haroldson. "This letter is addressed to Ben," she mumbled. The man I hit. She noticed the return addresses said Claira Haroldson. Why is his stuff in my car?

Wait a second, this wasn't her car. Yes, it was the same color and the same make, but this car was different on the inside. Did she and Ben have the same car? She yanked open the glove compartment, pulled out the registration information from the black binder. Sure enough, this was Ben's car. Returning the registration info, she shut the glove compartment door. She'd been so shocked the night of the accident, she'd never noticed they'd had the same car.

Sasha flipped the envelope over to find the seal broken. Letting curiosity get the best of her, she slid the letter out and began reading it.

My Dearest Ben,

The night before you left to go off to Vietnam, as you laid in bed beside me, I stayed up all night and watched you sleep. Although you were about to go off to war, you slept like a brave solider. That's because you are a soldier, Ben. My soldier. My brave hero.

At one point while you'd slept on your side, I'd bent down and kissed your lips. I'd traced your ear and eyebrows with the tip of my index finger, and you didn't even stir. It gave me great comfort to know you could sleep soundly and your departure was just a sunrise away. Ben, you're the bravest man I know, and I'm so happy to be your wife.

You've always said that we were poor, and had so little. I disagree. Now that you're gone, I can clearly see we're not poor at all. We're rich, Ben. Rich in all the things that matter. Like family. Honesty. And loyalty. We're rich in the love we share for one another. I can't wait for you to come home so we can continue growing and nurturing our rich marriage.

As I sit here writing this letter, my heart is pounding so hard because I can hardly stand the fact that you're gone, and you're not here to hold me. Or kiss me. Or make love to me.

Oh Ben, I miss everything about you. I miss you leaving the toilet seat up. I even miss you snoring loudly in my ears at night and awakening me. I miss every little quirk about you. God, I'd give anything to have you here with me, burping and whatnot. I had no clue how good I had it until you left me to go off to war.

My precious heart, please come back home to me. Please, Ben. Please. Your

wife,

Claira.

Holding the heart-wrenching letter in her hands, Sasha sniffled. Refolding the letter, a tear slid down her face. The letter from Claira to Ben was one of the sweetest letters she'd ever read. Claira's love for Ben was so obvious in the letter. Wondering why

Ben felt the need to leave Hilton Head, Sasha reached to the back of the box and pulled out a black and white photo of the most beautiful woman she'd ever seen.

Dark, curly hair, high cheekbones, and full lips, the woman in the photo had to be Ben's wife, Claira. This must be Claira.

She reached into the box again and pulled out another photo. A little girl, along with Ben and Claira, was in the photo, and they all were smiling. "This must be your daughter, Ben. Why would you pack up and leave here without saying goodbye to your own daughter?"

Sasha slid the letter and the photos back inside the box where she'd found them and covered it with the lid. I have to find out why Ben is so desperate to leave Hilton Head. Wondering what part Claira played in Ben's leaving, if any, Sasha picked up the box and exited the car.

Spotting her own Honda that looked exactly like Ben's, she crossed the pavement, retrieved her items. Ben...I don't care how mad you got with me yesterday, I'm paying you a visit today. Box in her hands, Sasha got back in Salvador's white Porsche and headed to the hospital.

TWENTY-FIVE MINUTES LATER, SASHA ENTERED Ben's hospital room carrying a teal box from SugarKanes in one hand and a brown box with Ben's pictures in the other. Ben was sitting on the bed, aiming the remote at the television, clicking through the station. When he heard Sasha come in, his gaze transferred from the TV to her, and then back at the television. Apparently, he still didn't want to see her. Well, that was okay. She'd drop off the pie and pictures and leave.

Girding herself with resolve, Sasha braced herself for a possible rejection. "Good morning, Ben. I brought you something. A caramel pecan pie and your pictures."

Ben's round eyes looked at the box. "My pictures? That's my box. How'd you get my box?"

Sasha lowered the box containing the photos to Ben's lap. "I went to the tow yard today to get some things out of my car. Come to find out, we have the same identical car. They showed me to your car instead of mine."

Ben laughed. "Talk about a coincidence."

"I don't think it's a coincidence. I think it's fate."

Ben's right brow hiked. "Fate? What makes you say fate?"

"Everything in life happens for a reason. I think we were supposed to meet," Sasha declared.

Ben shrugged. "If you say so."

Sasha pulled back the lid on the teal SugarKanes box. A whiff of sweet caramel entered her nose. "I brought you a caramel pecan pie from SugarKanes."

Ben's brown, wrinkled lips pulled into a handsome smile. "That was mighty sweet of you, gal. Mmm. The pie looks and smells delicious." "Would you like for me to cut you a piece?" she offered, feeling his mood was lightening.

"Sure. That'd be nice."

Sasha lowered the cake box to the dresser, retrieved the plates and forks from her oversized purse strapped to her shoulder, and cut two big pieces of caramel pecan pie. She handed a plate and fork to Ben, kept one for herself, and then sat on the foot of the bed.

Ben cut the pie with his fork and ate it. "Mmmph. Mmmph. This is so good."

Sasha forked the pie into her mouth. She savored the rich caramel flavor. "Ooo, this is so delicious. I see why everyone rants and raves about Sandella's special pie recipe."

"Everything Sandella cooks at SugarKanes tastes good. I done had almost everything off the menu. Everything! The entrees and desserts."

Sasha laughed. "So you're one of SugarKanes' regular customers, huh?"

"Oh, yeah. I eat there all the time. Sandella and Braylon are a beautiful couple. Reminds me of how my Claira and I used to be." Done with his pie, he placed the empty plate on the nightstand beside his bed. Ben lifted the lid off the brown box in his lap and pulled out an envelope. "Claira used to write me letters all the time. Even after we got married, she'd write me letters from time to time." He slid the folded letter from the envelope, and then unfolded it. "I can't even see how to read this without my glasses."

"I'll read it to you."

"Will you really?" Ben asked. Sasha nodded. "You're such a sweet gal." Ben extended the letter towards Sasha.

Sasha lowered her empty pie plate to the bed, took the letter from Ben's hand, and began reading the letter to a man she hoped would someday become her dear friend. "My Dearest Ben," Sasha said.

My Dearest Ben.

It's Friday night in Hilton Head Island. As I'm sitting in bed writing you this letter, my heart is filled with love and longing for you. I long for you to hold me. I long for you to kiss me, and to make love to me. Wishing you were home with me instead of Vietnam, I just pray that you're okay.

Although today was a good day, last night was weird. It was weird because of the dream I had about you. You're never going to believe how the dream I had ended up being a reality. Oh Ben, I hate having to tell you about the reality in a letter. But here goes...

Early this morning as I slept in bed, I had a dream about you. I dreamed you were in Vietnam, just like you really are. Fighting a horrible war.

Dressed in camouflage, you and the other Marines were cantering through the forest with guns clenched in your hands. A bullet had whizzed by your head, and then a big bomb had exploded. All the events happening in my dream had seemed so real. Like it was really happening. I pray to God that those things didn't really happen to you.

Anyway, in my dream the detonated bomb had shaken the Earth and had forced you to your knees. Covered in grimy dirt, you started moaning my name. Then the dream switched up. You kept moaning, but except now you weren't in the forest anymore. You were moaning while making love to me, Ben. Isn't that hilarious?

Right after we finished making love, while you were on top of me, your mouth pulled into a handsome smile. You told me this, "Claira, why, I think I got you pregnant." Then kapoosh, you vanished. The dream ended there. When my eyes opened, my heart felt like it was about to jump out of my chest.

As I sat at work hemming and sewing all day, I couldn't get the dream off my mind. Especially the part about you getting me pregnant. Feeling nauseous, I asked my boss if I could leave work early so I could go to the doctor. And guess what? You're never going to believe it.

I'm pregnant, Ben! You're going to be a father. So now when you get home, there'll be two people glad to see you, instead of one. Me and the baby.

86

I love you, my heart. Please come home to me and the baby, Ben. Please. Yours truly, Claira.

Refolding the letter, tears slid down Sasha's cheeks. "That's a beautiful letter."

Water filled Ben's eyes. "Claira was in my dream the other night. She——" Trying not to cry, Ben's face drew a blank.

I wonder whatever happened to Claira? Sasha wondered, caressing Ben's kneecap.

Chapter Ten

RUTHLESS LAURENTE LAGOUNOV SAT ON the couch inside his den attempting to read the news paper, but he was distracted. He was irritated. Pissed. And furious because Ben Haroldson hadn't been murdered like he'd ordered the other night.

Anger coursed through Laurente's damn veins. Uncrossing his legs at the ankles, he grunted. Laurente's henchm an, stupid ass Yuri, had been ordered to murder Ben, and he had failed. Now he had to not only kill Ben, but Yuri, too.

Turning to the next page of the newspaper, Laurente huffed. "I don't need any pussies in my organization." They'll hold me back, and I won't be able to fly. Yuri is a pussy. Just like Ben, Yuri had to die. Thinking about how Ben thought he was safe in the hospital, Laurente chuckled.

Had old man Ben burned down Salvador Casillas' building like he'd been instructed to, he wouldn't have to be hiding. Hiding like a wimp. So what , Ben was old? He should've thought about that before he took his damn money in exchange   for burning down Salvador's building.

Laurente folded the newspaper, lowered it to his lap, then glanced out the window at the river behind his home. Boats cruised along the blue, glistening water. Men stood on the dock fishing.

You think you've outsmarted me, Salvador, but I will have the last laugh. Just thinking about Salvador made Laurente cringe. Salvador wasn't about shit. Wasn't worth the dirt on the bottom of his shoes.

The land should've been mine. Salvador had put in a bid for a piece of land that Laurente had wanted to buy for his precious wife, Zena, behind Laurente's back. When Zena had found out that Salvador had gotten the land instead of her husband, Zena had wept like a baby in Laurente's arms.

Staring at the river behind his mansion, Laurente grumbled. How dare Salvador steal the land he wanted to purchase for his wife right from under his damn nose? The fucker thought he could treat him any kind of way just because he was once a professional boxer. And wealthy.

Apparently, Salvador had no clue as to who he was. And for now, Laurente wanted it to stay that way. However, right after he took care of Ben and Yuri, he was going to burn down Salvador's building, like it should've been done the first time. If someone tried to get in his way, he'd burn them down, too. In the mood for burning shit, Laurente's gut twisted with irritation. Hearing his wife Zena's feet dragging across the marble tile, Laurente inhaled deeply and tried to push his anger aside. Zena came to stand in front of him, looking ever so beautiful. His eyes raking up and down his wife's sexy figure, Laurente's lips pulled into a smile.

Zena's white, creamy skin glowed. Her deep blue eyes gleamed. Wearing a white hat with a big bright ribbon, blonde hair paraded down over her big tits. The fake tits he'd paid thousands for. Flat stomach, little waist, and petite, Zena had on a peachcolored, tight dress.

Zena's peach painted lips pulled into a soft smile. "Good morning." She bent over and pecked his lips.

MARRYING MR. WRONG

Madly in love with his wife, Laurente's cock stirred. "You look beautiful today, Zena. So beautiful, you make me want to eat your pussy for breakfast." Wanting to bury himself inside Zena's womb, he clenched her hips and pulled her down in his lap. Putting his nose to her neck, he mashed his erection to her lower spine. "You feel that?" he asked, holding his precious jewel.

Zena giggled. "Yes, I feel that." Caressing the back of his hand, she said, "I have a brunch date today with the girls. We're going to have lunch on the ocean at the Balfour Hotel."

"Sounds like fun. Speaking of the Balfour Hotel, every time I think about how Zeke Balfour killed his own brother, I want to send him a trophy in the mail. I didn't think the little pussy had the balls to do something like that."

Zena turned sideways to look at him. "Well, other than attending some of the same functions, you really don't know Zeke well enough to say what he is or isn't capable of, do you?"

"Uuh. I know birds of a feather flock together. And since he hangs with pussies, he must be one. Wouldn't you think?" Laurente chuckled.

Zena smiled. "You're cruel, Laurente."

The head of Laurente's shaft throbbed. "Speaking of pussy, how about you let me fuck you before you leave?"

"But Laurente...then I'd have to take a shower and would end up late."

Laurente lifted his right brow. "A quick dick sucking would do."

Zena put her nose to the tip of his. "I'd love to suck my husband's dick for breakfast like a big, juicy sausage."

With a big smile on her face, Zena got on her knees in front of Laurente, zippered down his dress pants. She reached into his drawers, pulled out his erection, and fisted him tight. She placed her peach-colored lips on his swollen tip, opened her mouth wide, then swallowed him whole.

Glaring out the window at the river behind his home, Laurente palmed the back of Zena's head and thrust his tool deep into her throat. Ah, her hot mouth felt wonderful on him.

Rocking her head back and forth on his stem, Laurente watched Zena suck hard on his throbbing stem. Angling his erection downward, Zena brought her lips to the tip of his stem, flicked her tongue over his hard knob. She scraped her red nails against his testicles.

Feeling cum build at the base and work its way to the top, Laurente groaned. Zena jerked him wildly in her tight fist. "I love fucking your mouth, Zena. Oh, fuck. Shit. Suck this cock. Suck it."

Laurente fisted Zena's blonde, silky hair, rocked his hips, then froze. Sperm charged from his pulsating stem into Zena's mouth, and she gladly swallowed his spunk.

Heart beating against his ribs, Laurente released a harsh breath. Now this is why I have to kill Salvador. He stole my precious Zena's land from her. And no one makes my wife cry. No one. Except for me.

Chapter Eleven

CLOTHED IN A BLACK TANK and sweats, Salvador stood inside the boxing ring at his gym, training Jaheem and another boy named Ivan. Throwing punches, the boys' feet shuffled. Jaheem punched the other kid named Ivan in the face. Sweat flew off Ivan's face, and the poor kid fell on his rear.

Shaking his head, Ivan looked distraught. Like he was clueless as to where he was. Determined to keep fighting, Ivan blinked repeatedly. Mashing his boxing gloves into the floor, he stumbled to his feet.

Sweating profusely, Ivan put his fists up in front of his face. He bared his teeth, exposing his mouth band. He swung, then stumbled.

Salvador jumped between the two boys, stopping the fight. He placed a hand on Ivan's shoulder. "Are you okay, Ivan?"

Ivan nodded. "I'm a little dizzy."

"Have a seat in the chair."

Ivan sat in the chair. Salvador stooped in front of him, checking for signs of injury. "You look okay. Let me know if you start feeling ill." Salvador stood. His gaze traveled to the front door of the boxing facility.

The door flung open. In walked Ivan's father Laurente Lagounov.

With jet black hair, Laurente had a glass blue eye, and the other one was brown. A short scar ran was on the side of his face. Approximately sixfour, he had on a black business suit.

The business owner of a stream of gift shops, Laurente stalked towards the boxing ring. Seemingly disgruntled, he frowned. Eyes squinting at Ivan, he stopped beside the ring.

Salvador climbed out of the ring and stood in front of Laurente. "My man, Laurente. How's your day going?"

Laurente glared at his son Ivan. Still sitting in the chair tucked in the corner of the ring, Ivan lifted his headgear from his head. A sad look was on Ivan's face.

"It'd be better if my son wasn't getting his ass kicked. I pay you a lot of money to train my Ivan, but it doesn't look like it," he grumbled in a thick Russian accent. "I saw the way the other boy punched him. He almost knocked his ass out."

Salvador shook his head. "He's just having a bad day."

Folding his arms across his chest, Laurente nodded. "Get up Ivan, and fight."

Salvador slid his hands inside his sweats. "Ivan's had enough for today. Let the boy rest."

Pushing past Salvador, Laurente walked to the corner of the ring to stand beside where Ivan sat. He glared up at his son. The muscles in Laurente's cheeks flickered. "Lagounov men don't fight like weaklings. We fight like strong warriors. Ivan! I said get your ass up and fight!"

Ivan jumped to his feet, hastened to the center of the ring, and threw up his fists.

Salvador clenched his molars, then walked up to Ivan's father. "Laurente. This is not a good idea. He was just dizzy a few minutes ago. Ivan, come out of the ring."

Ivan looked at his father, then back at Salvador.

Laurente spat, "He's my son. If I say he fights, then he fights.

Hit him, Ivan." Ivan didn't move. "I said hit him!"

"You don't give the orders here, I—"

Ivan swung and punched Jaheem in the face. Jaheem took a step back. "Coach Salvador, I don't want to fight him. He don't look right. He don't have on his headgear."

Irritated, Salvador felt his face hardening. "Unlike his father here, I understand, Jaheem. Get out of the ring and go get your things, Jaheem. Your father will be here any minute to pick you up."

"Yes, sir." Jaheem clambered out of the ring and headed to the locker room.

His face beet red, Ivan put a hand to his lower stomach, walked over to his father, and climbed down out of the ring. Laurente gently slapped the back of Ivan's head. "What's wrong with you, son? How you let some wimp beat you like that?"

Salvador shot daggers at Laurente. He felt like punching the egotistical man in the face. "Watch your mouth, Laurente. No one comes up in here and talks badly about the kids I train. None of my students are wimps. You will not stand here in my face and disrespect my place of business. If you have a problem with the way I operate things, feel free to leave and not come back."

Laurente's eyes turned dark. Or was that just his imagination? Salvador wondered, a bad feeling washing over him.

Laurente burst into laughter. "Chill, man. I'm just trying to have a little fun, that's all." Smiling, he clapped Salvador's back. "Lighten up."

He's got to be bipolar. "No, you lighten up. Take it easy on Ivan. He's a great kid, with a lot of talent. As I said earlier, he was just having a bad day. Isn't that right, Ivan?"

A look of despair shone on Ivan's reddening face as he nodded. "Yes, sir. I don't feel well."

"Go get your things, and let's go," Laurente ordered Ivan.

Getting a bad vibe from Laurente, Salvador watched him and Ivan as they exited the gym. Hoping the construction on his new gym was going well, Salvador pulled his cell out of his pocket and called the general contract manager.

"Good morning, Salvador," Lee answered.

"Good morning, Lee. How's the construction for the new gym going?"

"Considering a fire took place, it's going quite good," Lee responded.

"Does it still smell like smoked wood?"

Lee stated, "Yes. According to the restoration people, it's going to take a few weeks for the odor to completely dissipate."

"Gotcha."

"Do the police have any idea who set your building on fire?" "No. Not yet. And that's probably a good thing."

"Why's that good?" Lee asked.

Frustration threatened to build inside Salvador. Because if I knew who burned my gym, they'd have hell to pay. "Let's just say I plan on making it very hard for the person who deliberately set my building on fire. Keep me posted on the progress." Salvador ended the call.

On his way to his office, images of how he'd kissed Sasha yesterday came into his mind. Dying to kiss those sweet lips of hers again, a smile tugged at the corners of his mouth. "Sasha," he mumbled her pretty name. The way he'd intimately said her name frightened him. He'd said her name like it had meaning. Like she'd gotten permanently inside his head. To hell with falling for a

woman. That's not in my nature.

Salvador plopped down in his seat. Hit a button on his laptop. The screen brightened. Not appreciating the way Laurente had come up in his business trying to run things, Salvador snorted. He

better not ever try me like that again. If he does, I will no longer do business with him.

Although he simply adored Ivan, he refused to allow anyone to disrespect his place of business. A business he'd built from the ground up. When he'd first started out boxing, when no one knew his name, Salvador had dreamed of someday having a large sport complex so he could train kids to do what he loved doing—boxing. Because of his love for boxing and the constant growth of his business, he'd wanted to build a newer and bigger facility. Kids, teenagers, and young adults from all around the world flocked to his training sessions, especially during the summers. Salvador snarled. Right when he'd went and built a newer and bigger sports complex, some idiot tried to burn it to the ground.

"Pisses me off," he grumbled, clicking the cursor in the web browser. "Pisses me off, just like Ben pisses me off." He typed Ben Haroldson's name in the Google search bar, then hit enter. No information came up regarding Ben. Something about this whole Ben thing didn't sit right with Salvador. Tired and frustrated, he depowered his computer, locked his office door, and headed out.

"OH, YEAH! NOW THAT WAS a fun day!" Ben's throaty chuckle floated out into the hallway of the hospital. Walking towards Ben's room, Salvador scowled. Unless he'd called his daughter and grandson and told them he was still alive, how could he laugh at a time like this?

Salvador emerged into the doorway of Ben's hospital room. Shocked, his heart jostled. Sasha was sitting at the foot of Ben's bed, laughing right along with him, holding pictures in her hands.

Wondering what the hell was so funny, Salvador cleared his throat.

Sasha's head snapped in his direction. Seeing his face, her smiling lips formed into a straight line. Her facial expression serious, she brought her fingers to her lips and touched them.

Sasha's reaction amused Salvador, causing him to gloat inwardly. *She's still thinking about the kiss, I see. Well, if she thought the kiss on those lips was something to remember, wait till I feast on the lips between her legs.*

Ben rolled his eyes at Salvador. The older gentleman cleared his throat. "Oh, Lordy. I thought I kicked you out yesterday?"

Salvador stalked up to Ben's bed. "Hello, Sasha." He nodded. "Hello, Ben."

Sasha softly said, "Hi, Salvador."

Ben looked at Salvador, then at Sasha, then back at Salvador. "Man, is this your lady?"

She would be if I wanted one. "No. We're just good friends."

Ben shook his head. "What brings you by?"

"Look, Ben. I'm going to get straight to the point. I came by to see if there's any way I can get you to change your mind about going to see your daughter and Corey before you leave town," Salvador stated in a firm tone.

Ben's brows scrunched. "I know you're Corey's coach, but this has nothing to do with you."

Salvador's annoyance increased. "I disagree, sir. As Corey's trainer, it's my business to make sure he's happy and makes good grades. And grow up to be a respectable citizen. He's not happy because he thinks you left him. When actually you're sitting up here in the hospital, still planning on leaving him and your daughter without saying goodbye."

Ben folded his arms over his big belly. "I guess that means you haven't told Corey we met, huh?"

Salvador shook his head. "No, sir. I haven't. The last thing Corey needs is to get his hopes up and think you'll come say goodbye, and then you don't."

Sasha extended a photo to Ben. "Here's another picture of you with your wife, and your daughter and Corey. The four of you look so happy."

Ben folded his arms across his chest and stared out the window. "I don't want to see any more photos. Thanks for bringing me my box. But you can leave now."

Sasha said, "But Ben, what about Claira? Are you leaving because of her?"

Ben's eyes grew watery as he stared at Sasha's face. When he shook his head, a tear slipped from his eye. "No. Claira's dead. Look, I know the two of you are only trying to help, and I appreciate it. But no one can help me. It's in everyone's best interest that I leave Hilton Head."

Disconcerted, Salvador wanted answers. "What kind of help do you need?"

Ben's eyes met Salvador's despairingly. "The less you know, the better."

Salvador probed further. "Are you sick? In danger? What are you running from, Ben?"

When Ben shifted in bed, he groaned. "Damn, that hurts. Discussion over. Thanks for coming by." Ben slid down on the bed to his back, pulled the cover up to his chest, then closed his eyes. "Goodbye," he said, keeping his eyes closed.

Salvador pulled his business card from his wallet and laid it on Ben's chest. "I'm going to leave my business card with you, Ben. If you ever need anything, please don't hesitate to call me. And remember, no one can help you if they don't know what you need help with."

Sasha placed the brown box on the dresser, then walked over to Ben's bedside. "I have the feeling you could use this." She bent over and kissed Ben's cheek. Ben's wrinkled lips trembled. "I left your pictures on the dresser. Take care of yourself, Ben."

Salvador walked towards the door, with fine-behind Sasha following him. Although he didn't know Ben, Salvador felt bad for leaving him. He loved elderly people and hated that Ben was old and alone. And from what he could observe...Ben was scared. Salvador paused in the doorway and turned to look at Ben. Ben laid still in the bed, with his eyes closed. "Call me if you need me, Ben.
Please call me."

Salvador pushed through the door of the staircase. Sasha looks hot as hell in those damn jeans. I can't wait to sample her lips again. Descending the steps, he came to a sudden stop when he reached the second floor. Sasha bumped into the back of him, her tits brushing his back. Needing to get something off his chest, Salvador turned to face her. They stood so close to one another that even a sheet of paper would have a hard time getting between them. "You look beautiful, Sasha."

"Thanks." Sasha swallowed. Breathing intensely, her breasts heaved up and down. Like she was getting hot or something. Maybe she was thinking about the kiss he'd branded her with.

Desiring to slam his mouth on hers, Salvador asked, "I love the fact that we keep running into each other like this."

Her gaze as soft as a caress, Sasha swallowed. "You do? Why?"

"Because." He cupped her biceps. He dropped his face close to hers. "It gives me the opportunity to try something," he breathed on her lips.

Sasha's tongue protruded from her mouth, licked her lips. "What do you want to try?" she asked in a low voice.

Salvador's balls tingled and grew warm. "This." He slanted his mouth over hers and kissed her smoothly. Because they were in the hospital's staircase, he ended their kiss sooner than he'd wanted to. Letting her biceps go, he turned his face sideways. "You can slap me if you want," he teased, chortling.

Sasha put her soft hand on his jaw and motioned his face to look at her. "I don't want to slap you, Salvador."

Salvador smiled. "I didn't think so. Would you like to join me for dinner tonight?"

The question sent her lips smiling. "Sure. What time?"

"I'll pick you up at eight." Salvador descended the rest of the steps, pushed through the door of the hospital, and as he walked towards his car, he thought about how he planned on getting in Sasha's panties tonight.

Chapter Twelve

DRESSED IN A CHARCOAL HUGO Boss business suit and wearing a pair of Gucci men sunglasses, Laurente stood in the center of an abandoned warehouse, surrounded by five of his most important goons. Tapping his shoe on the pavement, Laurente brought his diamond Rolex up to his face to read the time. Anger boiled his veins. "I can't stand an incompetent asshole," he spat in a gruff tone.

Tired of waiting for his henchman , Yuri, Laurente snorted. Yuri was tardy as hell. Was supposed to be there by now. It was a damn shame things had to come to this. It really was. But if he wanted respect from the men in his organization, then he had to set an example and send a message. One that was loud and clear. And who better to make an example out of than Yuri? He wasn't worth a damn anyway.

"What's this meeting about, Boss?" Rob, his third in charge goon, asked.

"You'll see in due time , Rob." I'm about to make an example out of someone.

His second man in charge, named Troy, stated, "Yuri's ass been slacking lately. Seem like he's losing respect for what we stand for. And for what we trying to accomplish."

Laurente snapped, "Work on your grammar, Troy. It's what we're trying to accomplish. Impressions are important."

Troy nodded. "You're right, Boss."

The door at the side of the warehouse cracked open. In walked Yuri, wearing a black tank top and his damn sweatpants sagging around his ass. Didn't he tell him about sagging like a damn thug? The men in his organization all wore business suits. Had good jobs. Had people thinking they were smart, hardworking, and would never do anything illegal. Seeing how inappropriately Yuri was dressed only heightened Laurente's temper.

"What it be, Boss?" Yuri extended his hand towards Laurente, but the mobster just left it hanging.

Pulse ticking in his chest like a fucking rocket, Laurente cleared his throat. "I'm not too happy with you, Yuri," he scoffed.

Concern came onto Yuri's face. "What's wrong, Boss?"

Tempted to kick Yuri's ass in the stomach, Laurente slid his hands into his pockets. Shifted his weight. "The mere fact that you have to ask me what's wrong pisses me off even more. Are you that dumb? Or is it that you just don't give a fuck?"

Yuri shook his head. "Nah, Boss. I care. Oh, are you mad because I didn't kill Ben like you told me to?"

Laurente clapped his hands, his mouth turned upwards. "You figured it out. You figured it out." He chortled but didn't find a damn thing funny. Yuri joined in on his laughter. And so did Troy and Rob, and the other guys. A sudden frown shot to Laurente's face. "Shut up. All of you. There's nothing funny. You see, that's what's wrong with this here organization. You want to play follow the leader, but are not good leaders. Especially you, Yuri."

Yuri thumbed himself in the chest. "Who, me?"

Laurente gritted his teeth. "Yes, you, you dummy. You come in here dressed like a fucking thug. Just look at you. Your pants are hanging around your waist, and you have on a wrinkled tank top.

Your hair looks like black shit sitting on top of your skull. I've told you time and time again not to dress like that, but still you disrespect my wishes. So now, Laurente is mad. Not only is Laurente mad because of how stupid you look today, but Laurente is also mad because you didn't kill Ben like I told you to." Laurente tilted his head. "Tell me, Yuri, how did you let an old man like Ben Haroldson trick you like he was dead?" Silence filled the warehouse. As Laurente waited for Yuri to answer, a death stench filled the air. He could smell Yuri dead and stinking already.

Regret shot into Yuri's eyes. "I'm sorry, Boss. I tell you what, I'll get the job done tonight. I'll go back to the hospital and take care of Ben Haroldson once and for all."

Laurente waved his finger. "It's too late to make up for a mishap. That's not how this organization works." Laurente snatched off his sunglasses. "Since you disappointed Laurente... Laurente must now disappoint you."

Yuri's eyes stretched wide. He looked at Rob, and then at Troy, and then back at Laurente. Sheer fright jumped on Yuri's face. He took off running towards the side door entrance.

Laurente pulled back the lapel of his blazer, whipped his gun from his holster, and fired. Pow! The powerful blast emanating from the gun popped in his ears. The bullet shot into Yuri's back.

Yuri's feet halted. His knees buckled. His sagging sweatpants slouched down to his feet, exposing his underwear. Laurente fired another bullet into Yuri's back. Yuri plummeted hard to the ground on his face.

Strong scents of gunpowder crept up Laurente's nose. He walked over to Yuri's body and kneeled. Putting two fingers to Yuri's neck, he checked for a pulse. Knowing he'd sent a loud and clear message to his other henchmen, Laurente stood. Slid his sunglasses back on his face.

Maintaining a cool authority, Laurente pushed his shoulders back.

"I hope everyone here has learned a valuable lesson today. Do as Laurente says, or you will have hell on your hands. Troy and Rob, get rid of Yuri's corpse." God, he smells.

"Yes, Boss," Troy and Rob answered synchronously.

Moments later, Laurente drove his burgundy 750 Li BMW down the long road, heading back towards his house on the river. Thinking about how that jerk Yuri had tried his patience, and how that conceited bastard Salvador had tried to tell him what to do with his own son, Laurente fought hard to cool his temper. The last thing he wanted was for Zena or Ivan to see him like this.

Yuri deserved to die. Inhaling a deep breath, Laurente pulled into his driveway beside an unfamiliar car. Wondering who was visiting his home, Laurente's temper threatened to come back. Zena knew he didn't allow her to have company unless he knew about it first and approved it. She'd better have a good explanation for this mess.

I mean…a good explanation, he thought, entering his home through the front door. Scents of spicy broiled steak lingered throughout the house as Laurente stalked towards the kitchen. On his way there, he heard giggling, so he turned and walked into the den. Two other women, along with his wife, sat on the sofa chatting.

When Zena spotted him, she rose from the sofa. "Laurente. Good, you're home. I want you to meet my friends."

Laurente removed his sunglasses. Hoping Yuri's body was in the river by now, Laurente greeted the women. "Good evening, ladies."

"Good evening," the ladies said in unison.

Zena said, "Laurente, this is Sandella." Zena then looked at the other pretty lady. "And this is Taylor. Taylor and I discovered today that our sons know each other. Ivan and Jaheem both take boxing lessons from Salvador."

His day getting worse by the minute, Laurente's chest tightened. He didn't want that kid Jaheem anywhere near his son after what'd happened today in the gym. Ready to toss Zena's unwelcomed guests out of his house, laughter filled Laurente's ears. He turned his gaze towards the staircase. Ivan, Jaheem, and another little boy came running down the stairs.

Laurente cursed inside his head. Now this really pisses Laurente off.

"All right, boys, it's time to go," the woman named Taylor exclaimed.

"Do we have to go, Mom?" the kid with the curly hair asked.

Taylor ruffled the kid's hair. "Yes, Zavier. It's getting late."

Zavier shrugged. "But it's not like we have real school. We're home schooled and can get up whenever we feel like it."

Taylor's head tilted. "Zavier, home school is real school. You should know by now that just because you're home schooled, doesn't mean you get to stay out late and get up when you want to. You're on a busy schedule, just like the kids who go to public school."

"Okaaay. I called the front seat first!" Zavier said and shot towards the front door.

Jaheem smiled at Laurente. "Nice seeing you again today. See you tomorrow, Ivan."

Looking like he felt better, Ivan smiled. "Bye."

Sandella hugged Zena, then released her. "We'll have to do this again real soon."

Taylor stated, "Getting together with the kids was so much fun. Thanks for joining us for lunch."

Smiling her butt off, Zena replied, "Thanks for inviting me. You ladies know how to have fun."

"Nice meeting you ladies," Laurente stated, wishing they'd stop with all that mushy stuff and get to stepping. He'd never been a fan of Zena hanging out with a bunch of females.

"Nice meeting you, too," Sandella and Taylor said in unison.

Zena showed Sandella and Taylor out. As she stood to the side holding open the front door, a big smile plastered Zena's white face. He'd die if Zena ever left him, Laurente thought, knowing it was about to go down inside his home.

Zena shut the door. "What a wonderful day." "When will dinner be ready, Mother?" Ivan asked.

"In fifteen minutes. All I have to do is cook the sides." Zena caressed Laurente's back.

"Yes! Intercom me when it's done." Ivan jogged up the staircase.

Laurente snapped, "Ivan! Get back down here now!"

Ivan came running back down the stairs and hastened up to Laurente. "Yes, Father?"

Something told Laurente that Ivan had been faking ill earlier while at the gym taking boxing lessons. "How are you feeling, son?" "I feel good."

Laurente clenched his molars. "So the little tummy ache you had earlier is gone?"

Ivan nodded. "Yes, Father."

Zena put the back of her hand on Ivan's forehead, checking for a temperature. "Ah, he was sick earlier? What was wrong, Ivan?"

Ivan shrugged. "I just got dizzy."

Tired of Ivan's lies, Laurente thwacked Ivan's face with his back hand. Ivan's mouth dropped. "Ouch, Father!" He cupped his reddened jaw.

Zena gasped. She jumped in front of Ivan. Tears welled in Zena's eyes. "What's gotten into you, Laurente? Why did you hit my son like that?!"

Teeth clenching, Laurente pinched the bridge of his nose. "Because our son here embarrassed me today. He stood in the ring like a big pussy and let that Jaheem boy whip his ass," he stated grotesquely.

Eyes blazing like fire, Ivan pushed his shoulders back. "It was only practice, Father."

"It's never just practice, Ivan! Our family comes from a history of strong men. Lagounov men lead their families and their organizations. You can't be a leader if you give up as soon as a challenge comes your way. I don't care if you had to shit or puke, you should've kept fighting till you passed the hell out. My gut instinct tells me that you weren't sick today. You pretended to be sick because you're scared of Jaheem, aren't you?"

Ivan's eyes lowered to the floor, then back up to Laurente's face. "Yes, Father. I must admit, I got a little scared. Jaheem is such a great fighter."

Laurente patted Ivan on the back. "Thank you for being honest, son. Starting tomorrow, you will be working for me. It's high time you come and meet the men in my organization."

Zena shook her head. "No. Laurente. He's too young. He's only sixteen. He's smart and has a bright future. I don't want him getting involved with your business. I want a better life for Ivan."

Laurente despised the comment Zena made. A better life for Ivan? Did this woman not see how he provided the finer things in life for her and Ivan? A big house. A big, fancy car. Fancy clothes and shoes. Not to mention all the big diamonds he'd bought for her over the years.

Laurente snorted. "Life don't get any better than this, Zena. Do me a favor...stay out of this, sweetheart. Ivan is sixteen. He's almost an adult. If something happens to me, Ivan needs to be in a position to run the organization. He needs to learn the gift shop business and what comes with it." Laurente turned his attention to Ivan. "Ivan, my son, your mother will call you when dinner is ready.

Until then, go upstairs."

Ivan nodded. "Yes, Father."

Laurente watched Ivan walk up the stairs. Shoulders sagging, Ivan's head was bowed. If he'd said he was sorry for slapping some sense into Ivan, he'd be lying. Ivan was his only child, born from the only woman he'd ever loved—Zena. He wasn't going to raise his only son as a punk. Ivan came from a strong line of Russian men. Therefore, he had to be trained as one. Act like one. Become one— fierce and strong, and powerful. Knowing this, it was high time Ivan watched his father murder someone— maybe that person would be Ben. By this time tomorrow…just like Yuri…Ben Haroldson will be sleeping in his grave.

Zena's watery eyes were stony with anger as she said, "Getting Ivan involved in drugs is wrong, Laurente. And I don't like it one bit."

"When it comes to how I run my business, I don't care what you like, Zena. I'll do anything to make you happy, as long as it doesn't involve how I operate my organization and make my money. Another thing, I forbid you to hang out with Taylor and Sandella," he stated grimly.

Zena's cheeks turned bright red. "Why, Laurente? Taylor and Sandella are such nice women. I just met them, and like hanging out with them."

"Perhaps they are nice. But haven't you read the paper lately? Taylor and Sandella have a way of drawing the cops to them. And the last thing we need is for the cops to start sniffing around my gift shops, trying to find out how I really make my money."

Zena sniffled. "But I like them, and—"

"Cut them off, Zena," he snapped tersely.

"I'm sick of you choosing my friends for me, Laurente." Tears streaming down her cheeks, Zena jogged up the staircase. She hastened inside their master bedroom and slammed the door.

Laurente's gut twisted. The last thing he'd wanted was to make Zena or Ivan cry. But he knew what was good for them. At some point, they were going to have to stop questioning him. They'd never done it before, and they weren't going to start questioning

him now. I'm the king of this castle, and what I say goes.

Laurente slid his hands in his pockets, walked into the den up to the window, and gazed out at the boat dock behind his home. If he wanted to make a man of Ivan, he had to make his son watch Ben get murdered. Yeah, that's what I'm going to do. I'll let Ivan watch

me kill Ben. Ready or not, you're about to become a ruthless sonofabitch just like your father, Ivan.

Chapter Thirteen

INSIDE THE BATHROOM, LOOKING IN   the mirror, Sasha applied light foundation to her face, trying to cover up her scars. While the knot on her forehead had started to fade, the scar on her cheek had developed a scab. Wishing her face would heal faster, she grabbed a tube of red lipstick and traced her lips. Loving the way the red lipstick made her lips pop, she pursed them together   , smoothing out the vibrant color.

Salvador never mentioned where he was taking her for dinner tonight. So she decided to wear a pair of navy   blue jeans with a simple red shirt and a black short sleeve blazer, along with a pair of red high heels. She'd made sure to cover up her breasts and dress a tad bit on the conservative side. The last thing she needed was for him to think she was ready to have sex with him   , because she wasn't. In fact , the only reason she was going out with him was because she'd just moved to Hilton Head and could use a good friend. Yeah, that's all she and Salvador would ever be—friends.

Noticing it was almost eight o'clock, Sasha picked her red clutch up from the bathroom counter, tucked it under her armpit, and headed downstairs. R eaching the first level, she turned and walked into the den. Leslie sat on the couch, watching the hit show

Empire.

"Aunt Leslie," Sasha said, standing behind the couch.

Leslie looked over her shoulder and gazed up at Sasha. "My, my, my. Don't you look pretty? I like the red lipstick on you."

"Thanks. I'm about to head out. Salvador and I are going to dinner."

Leslie's mouth fell open. "I knew it! I knew he had the hots for you!"

Sasha laughed. "We're just friends, Auntie."

Leslie wagged a finger at her. "I bet you're not going to be friends for too long. Salvador knows a good thing when he sees it. And if he can't see you're a good thing, then he needs to have his eyes examined."

The doorbell rang.

Nervousness crept up inside Sasha. "That must be him now."

"I sure wish I had a man to go out with instead of sitting here watching Empire. Don't get me wrong, I love me some Terrance Howard and Taraji P. Henson, but there's nothing like having a man to spend your life with, chile. Enjoy your date."

"Thanks. You'll find somebody one day, Auntie. And this is not a date."

Leslie's head jerked back. "If it's not a date, what is it then?"

"It's just two friends hanging out, trying to get to know one another." The doorbell rang again. "I'll talk with you tomorrow." Clutch in her hand, Sasha strutted in her high heels towards the dining room.

Leslie shouted, "Oh, no Cookie didn't!"

Her hand gripping the door knob, Sasha drew in a deep breath, and then opened the door. Sasha's heart swirled.

Salvador stood on the porch holding a bouquet of colorful flowers in his hand. The porch light beamed down on his tall, muscular frame. Wearing a white collared shirt and a pair of black jeans, he looked so freaking gorgeous. Fine. Like a stallion.

Salvador's striking blue eyes flickered as they raked up and down Sasha's body. "Wow. You look beautiful."

Sasha blushed. "Thanks. You look handsome."

"Thanks." He extended the colorful flowers towards her. "These are for you."

Sasha grabbed the flowers. How thoughtful. "Thanks. They're beautiful." As they walked towards his SUV, her heels clicked against the pavement. Climbing into the truck, flowery scents streamed from the bouquet and sailed up her nose. He shut the door, rounded the truck, and climbed in on the driver's side.

"Where are we going?" Sasha asked, a delicious tomato aroma creeping into her nose. What's that smell?

Glancing sideways at her, Salvador steered the SUV down the road. "It's a surprise."

Sasha smiled. "I love surprises."

Salvador focused on the road ahead. "Which one do you love the most?"

"What do you mean?" Sasha asked.

Giving her a serious look, his lips pulled into a handsome white smile. "Do you love surprises the most, or kissing me the most?"

Crossing her legs at the knee, Sasha snickered. "I refuse to answer the question."

"I was hoping you'd say you loved kissing me more." A country song by Carrie Underwood came on.

"Carrie can sing."

"You like country music?" Salvador queried.

"Yes. I love country music. I've written several country songs. I'm hoping to get one of them published one day."

An amused look came on his face. "I didn't know you write music."

"Yes, I'm a songwriter. I haven't had anything published yet. I came real close, but things didn't quite work out," she said, thinking how Reggie had screwed things up for her with...

"What happened?" Salvador asked, bopping his head to the music.

"Right when I was close to getting a publishing deal, my ex screwed things up for me."

"How so?"

Hesitant to talk about her ex-boyfriend while on her first date with Salvador, she contemplated what to say. "The night before I got ready to move here, the publisher called me, and my ex answered the phone. He told the publisher not to call me anymore. Not only that...he threatened him, too. I haven't heard from the publisher since. I've tried calling him to apologize, but he hasn't returned my phone calls."

"I'm sorry to hear that. Whatever is meant for you, will be. Just keep writing your songs. I can't wait to hear something you've written." He pulled off the main road onto a dirt road. Deep, dense forestry and darkness engulfed the SUV as he drove deeper into the woods.

"I have a few of the songs I've written downloaded on my cell, if you'd like to hear one now."

The BMW SUV rocked and shimmied over the dirt road. "Sure, I'd love to hear it," Salvador stated, bringing the SUV to a stop in front of a small wooden house. Beyond the brown, isolated home ran a wide lake. On the deck attached to the side of the home sat a picnic table with gleaming post lights.

In the rear beyond the lake nestled a forest. Bright stars twinkled around the full moon in the dark sky. Where are we?

"I have my song I've Changed on my cell."

113

"Let me hear it."

"Okay." Curious as to what he'd think about her song entitled I've Changed, Sasha pulled her cell out of her purse, downloaded her song, and pressed play. Her voice, along with the slow music, eased through the speakers.

When I was with you, you were all I could see
When I was with you, so much negativity
When I was with you, didn't think I could live without you,
The thought alone brought me to my knees
When things ended, my life collapsed
When things ended, my heart shattered
When things ended, it nearly destroyed me
I cried and cried, asked God to help me
Now I've changed
I'm not the person I used to be
I've changed
I let you go cuz you wanted to be free
I've changed
Now you wanna come back
But I don't love you anymore
I've changed
Love for you no longer lives in my heart
I've changed
Please leave me alone, get lost
I've changed
Goodbye, be gone
It feels so good not to want you anymore The
slow music, along with Sasha's voice, faded.

"Wow. I love your song. I felt every word in the song, and I'm not an emotional man. Did you write the song by yourself?"

Sasha nodded. "Yes. It's not finished yet, though."

"The woman who's singing it can sing her tail off. Her voice is sultry, and soulful."

"That's me."

Salvador's eyes stretched wide. "That's you singing? Wow, woman. You're just as talented as you are beautiful. I tell you, Sasha, your song is a hit. Don't ever give up on your dreams. If I can be of any help to get you published, just let me know."

Smiling, Salvador's gracious offer probed her soul. "Thanks. I'll keep that in mind."

"We'd better hurry up and eat dinner before it gets cold."

"Dinner? There aren't any restaurants out here, is it?" Her eyes traveled over the wooden house, and then the forestry.

"Nope, we're having a picnic." Salvador clambered out of the SUV.

After opening the door for her, he pulled two bags from the back seat and led her towards the lake house. Walking beside him, her heels dug into the thick grass. Reaching the picnic table, he placed the bags on the table. "We're having dinner out here. Let me show you the inside of my home first." He inserted a key into the rear door lock. "It's not much too it. Real small," he said, pushing open the door to his lake house.

Sasha entered the home through the back door and walked into a small den. A blue rug covered the brown, polished wooden floor. A light blue couch sat close to the wall. Above the log fireplace, a deer head was mounted to the wall. "It's very nice and cozy in here."

"Thanks. It's two bedrooms. Whenever I have large family gatherings, my family stays here if there's not enough room at the beach house."

"Let's eat." Salvador led Sasha back outside to the deck area. Standing beneath a post light, he pulled a white tablecloth from the bag, spread it on the wooden table. He then set a candle in the center of the table, lit it with a lighter.

He reached into the other bag. "Our dinner is in here." He sat two aluminum containers on the table. When he removed the lid from the first one, the tomato aroma she'd smelled when she'd first entered the car wafted up her nose. "I hope you like Spanish food. This is paella. Because I wasn't sure if you like seafood or not, I put it on the side."

"I'm a vegetarian. I'm glad you put it on the side."

"A vegetarian? Oh no. What are we going to do with all of this, then?" He pulled a box of fried chicken from the bag.

Sasha burst out laughing. "Why do people think that all Black people love fried chicken?"

Laughing, he placed the box on the table. "I didn't buy the fried chicken because you're Black, Sasha. I bought it because I like eating it, and I hoped you did, too. I hope you're not offended, because it wasn't my intention."

"No. I'm not offended. I'm sorry for even thinking like that. However, I used to love fried chicken. Back in college, that's all I ate."

He pulled a bottle of red wine from the bag. "I have some tossed salad, and grilled vegetables and chilled wine, too." Salvador fixed Sasha a vegetarian plate filled with rice, salad, and grilled vegetables before fixing his own. He stuck the cork remover in the cork, then pulled. Pop. The sound of the cork's removal from the bottle resounded throughout the air. Bottle in hand, he filled her glass first. The wine bubbled at the surface. After filling his glass, he took a seat across from her.

She eyed her plate. This looks so good.

Sasha spread her napkin in her lap. "Did you cook all of this?"

"Nope. I picked it up from one of the finest restaurants in Hilton Head." He eased his arms across the table and cupped her hands. "I'll say the blessing."

"Amen," they said in unison as he ended the blessing.

He placed his cell on the table, tapped the Pandora app, and slow renditions came from the tiny speaker. He'd thought of everything, hadn't he?

Sasha scooped a forkful of seasoned yellow rice into her mouth. The flavors piped on her tongue. "This is so delicious." As Sasha sat enjoying her tasty meal, crickets chirped in her ears. A light breeze rolled off the lake, sailed through her hair. The cool breeze caused her to shiver. The ambiance is romantic. "The grilled squash is delicious."

"Their food is always good." Inside the candle jar, the tip of the wick danced with fire. Gnats encircled the light post in the distance. Ducks treading the water quacked.

It's so peaceful out here. "Thanks for doing this for me. I'm having a wonderful time."

"I'm glad you're enjoying yourself. I thought about taking you to a fancy restaurant. But I wanted to spend some quality time with you without any distractions. I love the way the moon illuminates your lovely face. Love the way the wind is turning up the ends of your hair. Love the way your mouth moves when you chew."

His sweet words made her nipples tingle. "Are you always this charming with all the women you take out?" He's just saying all this sweet talk to me so he can get in my panties. Well, he's not getting in them tonight. Maybe next time. Oh, Lordy. She mentally slapped her forehead. She shouldn't be thinking about sleeping with Salvador. If she slept with Salvador, she'd probably end up falling in love with him, and then what? And then nothing...because men like him didn't settle down.

"Nope. I don't tell women what I just told you. Believe it or not, I've never said those things to anyone but you. You're one of a kind, Sasha."

Yeah, right. "Salvador, what makes you think I'm one of a kind? You hardly know me."

Glints of light radiated in his eyes. "I don't have to know you to see how special you are. Normally, my perceptions about people are right on point. Hopefully, you'll keep going out with me so I can see that I'm right about you."

"Please don't take this the wrong way, but I just got out of a serious relationship, and I'm not ready to get into another one."

Salvador held his wine glass to his lips. "Well, if it'd make you feel any better, I don't believe in serious relationships." Tilting the glass to his lips, he sipped at the red wine.

Sasha suddenly became slightly irritated. If Salvador didn't believe in serious relationships, then why in the hell had he asked her out? To waste her time? To get her in his bed? Men. Considering she'd just said she didn't want to be in a serious relationship, why in the hell did she even care if he wanted to be in one or not? Lord help her, she was too confused.

"Sasha." At the sound of Salvador's husky voice, Sasha snapped out of her trance and looked at him. "You'd drifted off." She nodded. "Let's take a walk on the boat dock."

"Okay."

As Salvador and Sasha walked along the boat dock, the floor boards of the wooden dock creaked beneath their shoes. A cool breeze descended down on her. He draped an arm about her shoulder, caressing the round ball of her arm.

Now at the end of the dock, she leaned against the railing, peered out into the darkness at the forest in the near distance. Salvador's woodsy cologne enticed her. The soft sound of water treading soothed her. And so did Salvador's arm, lingering about her shoulders. This evening was definitely a night to remember. No, he hadn't taken her out to a fancy restaurant. And no, he hadn't spent a fortune on her. But he'd done something much more special…he'd put a lot of thought into the date. She didn't care about money anyway.

"Your fragrance turns me on, Sasha." The underlying sensuality of Salvador's words captivated Sasha.

Now how in the hell was she supposed to respond to that? "You smell good, too." Did that sound cheesy, or what?

His arm still draped about her shoulder, Sasha gazed up at Salvador's face, their eyes linked. Her heart swirled. Oh, my. My. My.

Moments passed with them standing there, not uttering a single word. Salvador's head slowly moved downward until his forehead touched Sasha's. "I muero por probar tu boca." His thick Spanish accent punctuated her ears. Set her soul aflame. Sent her female senses to whirling.

Clueless as to what'd he'd uttered, Sasha asked, "What did you say?"

His minty breath fanned her face. "I said I'm dying to taste your mouth."

Heart thundering inside her chest, Sasha anticipated one hot kiss coming her way. Kiss me. Kiss me.

"But since you're not looking for a serious relationship and only want a friendship, there's no use in me kissing you. No use in us taking this further. Is it?" She pondered over how to respond. "The last thing I need is for your cousins to think I'm trying to use you, Sasha."

Salvador had her so hot and bothered right now, she couldn't care less about what Richmond or Suade or Dirk would think. All she cared about right now was kissing on those manly lips of his.

Oh God, his lips were so close to hers. Dying to kiss him, water streamed from the pores inside her mouth and filled it. Gazing into his flickering blue eyes, she swallowed. Why doesn't he just go

ahead and kiss me?

She swallowed the built up saliva inside her mouth. "I'm a grown woman, Salvador. What I do with my life is no one's business except for my own. My cousins can't control my decisions."

He removed his arm from around her shoulder. "I know. But as a friend of the family, it's my job to make sure you're protected. The last thing I'd ever want to do is to pretend I'm something I'm not. And I'm definitely not the type of man to settle down. Your cousins know this, and they'd have a fit if things between us went further and didn't work out. Knowing this, we must remain friends." He slid his hands in his pockets and began walking back towards the picnic table.

Walking beside him, she desired for him to cup her hand. Perhaps she shouldn't have opened her big mouth about not wanting to be in a serious relationship. Darn, I was looking forward

to him kissing me. "Thanks for being honest."

"I may be a lot of things, but a liar isn't one of them. I'm very upfront."

"I guess that's why Julie wasn't mad when you told her to leave your house. She clearly understood the two of you were just friends." Cleaning up their mess on the picnic table, Salvador laughed.

"Exactly. That was one crazy night. Thing after thing kept happening."

"Yes. I could've never predicted the guy that'd end up helping me would turn out to be best friends with my cousin. I think God arranged our meeting."

Salvador shrugged. "Perhaps He did. What do you like to do for fun?"

"Other than writing, I like to swim, read, and travel. What about you?"

"I have a lot of hobbies. Of course, boxing. But my other favorites are surfing, polo, and stargazing."

Salvador's domineering presence didn't seem to balance with his desire for stargazing, Sasha thought. "Watching stars? I never would've guessed that about you."

After cleaning up their mess, walking side by side, they headed back for the SUV. "I come out here all the time just to relax and stargaze. I find it to be the most relaxing and interesting thing to engage in. Would you like to watch the stars with me tonight?"

"Sure."

At the rear of his SUV, Salvador hooked his hand under the latch and lifted the door. He grabbed the stand for the telescope, positioned the legs in the grass, and mounted the telescope on top. Peering through the eyepiece, he adjusted the lens, pointing it towards the starlit sky. "Tonight is perfect for stargazing. If it was a clear, moonless night, there'd be thousands of more stars. Here, take a look." He stepped behind her.

With Salvador standing closely behind her, Sasha positioned her eye over the eyepiece and witnessed the sky like she'd never seen it before. Stars twinkled bright in the black sky. They seemed so much closer than they really were. The star to the east glittered brightly, then started falling.

Sasha jumped up and down. "I see a falling star! It's falling! It's falling!"

"Make a wish. Hurry." Sasha closed her eyes. Please let Salvador kiss me before tonight is over. Salvador stated, "And don't wish for me to kiss you, because it's not happening." Her eyes shot open. Turning to face him, she frowned. "You know what, Salvador...you are so conceited."

His lips pulled into a sexy smile. "You were wishing that I'd kiss you, weren't you?"

Rolling her eyes, she folded her arms over her breasts. "No, I wasn't."

Salvador chuckled. "If you want me to kiss you, Sasha, just say it." Sasha sucked her teeth. "You're too conceited for you own—"

Salvador clutched Sasha's shoulders, dropped his mouth down on hers, and thrashed his tongue inside her mouth. Curling his tongue with hers, his firm lips glided over her mouth. Oh yes, this was exactly what she'd wanted. Why had she tried to fight this kiss? Ooo, he could kiss.

Sasha twirled her tongue around Salvador's thick flesh, swallowed his saliva. His shaft turned to hard stone against her belly. Feeling his rigid erection pressing into her navel, electricity shot through her body. Moisture seeped from her entrance into her panties. Her clitoris throbbed. Lord help her. Why couldn't she resist this man? Did she even really want to?

Not knowing what the hell she wanted, Sasha broke their sizzling kiss. "I thought you said you didn't think we should take things further because of who my family is and your relationship with them?" she said, trying to catch her breath.

His eyes smoldered with fire. "Truth is, Sasha...while I respect your family, I want you. You make me burn, woman. It's a challenge for me to set boundaries and keep my damn hands off you. I can't promise you anything, because I just don't know what'll happen if we cross the line. All I can promise you is this...I won't do anything you don't want me to do. And I promise to always be honest with you about how I'm feeling. Quiero hacerte el amor, Sasha," he stated in Spanish before saying, "I want to make love to you."

Oh my, how she'd love nothing more than for Salvador to make tender love to her body. But a warning inside her head told her she shouldn't sleep with him. At least not yet. He'd already admitted he didn't desire to be in a serious relationship. So if they had sex, that's all it'd be—just sex, and nothing more. It'd be quite dumb of her to sleep with a man like him and get her heart all involved.

A dull ache formed in Sasha's moist center. "As much as I want to make love to you, I can't."

"I respect your decision, Sasha. I was a fool for thinking you'd let me eat your pussy tonight." Her sex clenched. Ohmygoodness. He pecked her lips. "Come, I'll take you home. Oh yeah, if you have any photos of yourself, text them to me."

Chapter Fourteen

ON HIS WAY TO THE club after dropping off Sasha, Salvador drove down the long, dark street and couldn't stop thinking about the fine woman. Everything about Sasha impressed him. From her sweet and often feisty personality, to her lustrous, curvy body, to her talented songwriting skills, he was smitten with the sexy pussycat.

Reliving the erotic kiss he'd shared with Sasha inside his brain, Salvador's shaft hardened inside his underwear. Balls tingling, his heavy rod pushed against his zipper, and the tip threatened to leak fluid. Damn, he needed some pussy. Maybe I can meet a woman at the club and fuck her tonight. Needing to release himself inside of a woman, he steered the SUV up into the lot of the club and parked.

Pushing through the door of the club, loud music blasted the air. Shook the building. Semi-erect, Salvador slid on the stool at the bar. A waitress came up to him, placed a napkin down in front of him. "How you doing tonight, Salvador?"

If he'd gotten in Sasha's panties like he'd originally planned, he would be doing better and wouldn't be feeling like he had the blue balls. "I'm good, Abbie. How are you?"

Abbie smiled. "I'm good. Are you having your usual?"

Salvador nodded. "And you know it."

"I have one Dirty Martini with two olives on the rocks, coming up." Abbie headed to get his drink.

Sitting on the bar stool, his eyes roamed over the club in search of someone he could take home and bang. A pretty blonde standing in the corner by the DJ's booth with her tits spilling from her top winked at him. My, she's pretty. Looks easy. Maybe I'll take her

home tonight.

"Here's your Dirty Martini," Abbie said.

Taking his eyes off the sexy blonde, Salvador turned around. "Thanks, Abbie."

"You're welcome, Salvador." Abbie put her hands on her hips. "You always come in here by yourself. Do you have a girlfriend? If not, I know the perfect girl to introduce to you. I mean, she's perfect for you."

"No, Abbie. I don't have a girlfriend."

"Aren't you going to ask who I want to introduce you to?" Abbie shrugged.

"Who?"

Abbie leaned into the bar, placed her mouth to his ear, and whispered. "Why, of course I'm the perfect girl for you. I'd do whatever you want me to." Abbie stood erect and gave him a cute smile. As pretty as Abbie was, she wasn't his type.

Salvador chuckled. "You're a nice, cute girl, Abbie, and can do better than me."

"Oh, it don't get any better than you. Thanks for putting me down easy. I better go check on my other customers. Good seeing you, Salvador."

"Likewise, Abbie."

The jamming tune playing faded, and Where Do Broken Hearts

Go, by One Direction, came on. "Where do broken hearts go," Salvador sang, his mind drifting to how beautiful Sasha had sounded when she'd sung to him earlier. Sasha can blow. Can sing her butt off.

Salvador hefted his dirty martini to his mouth, sipped, and swallowed. The blonde he'd been checking out earlier slid her rear onto the barstool beside him. Obviously vying for his attention, she tossed her long hair behind her shoulder.

Lowering his drink to the napkin, Salvador turned and met her gaze. Desire for him lit up her pretty green eyes. "Can I buy you a drink?" Salvador asked.

Her eyes raking up and down his body, she nodded. "Yes. I'll have a Long Island Iced Tea." Her squeaky voice had a hint of twang to it.

Salvador waved Abbie over and ordered up a Long Island Iced Tea. "What's your name?"

"Chelsea," she said, staring with longing at him.

"Nice meeting you, Chelsea." He stuck out his hand. "I'm Salvador."

Chelsea placed her soft hand in his, shook it. "Nice meeting you, Salvador." When he went to release Chelsea's hand, she clenched it tighter, like she didn't want to let it go. "I've read so much about you in the papers. I must say, it's a pleasure to meet you in person."

"Thanks, Chelsea," he said, practically having to snatch his hand away. Jeez.

"So what's a handsome man like you doing in here all by yourself?" she asked in a seductive voice.

Wasn't he supposed to ask her what was a pretty young woman doing in here by herself? "I just stopped by to have a drink." The bartender named Abbie lowered the Long Island Iced Tea in front of Chelsea. Her eyes hooked with his, Chelsea lifted the drink to her hot pink painted lips and sipped. "What about you? What are you doing in here by yourself?" he asked, just for the hell of it.

"I'm a cowgirl in here, searching for a cowboy. And why, I think I've found myself one." Chelsea traced her lips with her tongue, licking off the alcoholic beverage.

Salvador laughed. "Is that right?"

"Yep, that's right. You look like a cowboy to me." Chelsea turned sideways on the stool. When she crossed her long legs at the knees, her short skirt rose to her hips, exposing her creamy thighs. Chelsea's green eyes twinkled. "Just to let you know, this here cowgirl loves to ride rough and hard. And it won't cost you a thing. Why don't we get out of here and go somewhere nice and quiet?"

"Give me a second to finish my drink." Salvador chugged down his dirty martini, and then paid the bill. He jerked his head towards the door. "Let's go."

With a big smile on her face, Chelsea hopped off the stool and followed Salvador outside. As Salvador crossed the parking lot with Chelsea by his side, his cell buzzed. He pulled his cell from his back jean pocket. Noticing he had a text message, he tapped the yellow button on his cell. A beautiful picture of Sasha smiling and wearing a sexy red dress appeared on his screen, halting his stride. The text beneath Sasha's lovely photo read: Thanks for the wonderful date.

Enjoyed it. Especially watching the stars. And the kiss, too. ☺

Warmth spread through Salvador's whole damn body. Glad she'd sent the picture like he'd requested, his fingers pecked the keyboard on his cell.

Salvador: Thanks for letting me take you out tonight. Why don't you come to my house tomorrow? Perhaps we can go horseback riding on the beach.

Sasha: Sure. I'd love to.

Salvador: Bring your bathing suit and a backpack. See you tomorrow.

Sasha: Okay. Goodnight.

Salvador: Goodnight. By the way. I still want to eat you.

Salvador waited for Sasha to respond, and when she didn't, he guessed his last comment was just too much for her to handle. Good, hopefully he'd given the little pussycat something to think about. Nothing would please him more than for Sasha to go to bed deliriously aroused and thinking about what he'd said about eating her. Maybe she'd dream about his tongue delving in and out of her hot puckered channel.

Feeling like he could text Sasha all night, Salvador slid his cell in his back pocket. There was only one woman that could soothe his insatiable sex craving tonight, and it definitely wasn't this Chelsea chick standing beside him, looking like she could swallow his cock whole.

Chelsea licked her lips. "So where are we going, cowboy?"

Nodamnwhere. "Chelsea. Please forgive me, but something came up and I have to change my plans. I'm sorry."

Fisting her hips, Chelsea sucked her teeth. "Ah, shucks. But I was looking forward to you and I having a little wild sex tonight." Smacking on a piece of gum, she blew a bubble. The bubble popped on her face. She looked down at his crotch. "You're hung like a horse. Look like you could blow a girl's back out with that big weapon between your legs."

Salvador shook his head. "Nice meeting you, Chelsea." He pulled open the door of his BMW.

"Call me if you change your mind. 843-523-1578! Call me sometime...my boxing cowboy!"

Ignoring Chelsea as she rambled off her digits, Salvador cranked the engine, and then pulled out onto the road. Thinking

Out Loud, by Ed Sheeran, came on. If he and Sasha had a love song, this song on the radio would be it, he thought, wondering where in the hell had that stupid thought come from. Looking forward to spending tomorrow with Sasha, Salvador sang, "Baby we found love right where we are. Baby now. Take me into your loving arms. Kiss me under the light of a thousand stars. Oooo. I'm thinking out loud."

Sasha's name kept slipping through his thoughts as he sang the love song.

Driving down the dark two lane road deep into the low country, he spotted a man walking down the street with a trash bag strewn across his shoulder and something in his hands. The poor man must be homeless. Never the one to pass by a homeless person without giving them any money, Salvador pulled a fifty dollar bill from the wallet lying in his console.

Slowing the car, he rolled down the passenger side window. Fifty dollar bill in his hand, he extended his arm towards the window. "Here, sir. Take this. It's a fifty dollar bill." The gentleman stopped walking, dropped his trash bag to the ground, and turned his head to look at him. Shock ran through Salvador. Ben! "Ben. It's that you?"

Grief filled Ben's eyes. His chubby face contorted. "Get lost! Don't be following me." Ben picked up the big trash bag, hefted it over his shoulders, and kept on walking.

Salvador drove at a snail's pace alongside Ben as he traipsed down the road with his head dangling between his sagging shoulders. Salvador stated, "For your information, I'm not following you. I just happened to be riding down the road and stumbled upon you."

Ben lifted his head to look at Salvador. "Beat it! I don't want a ride."

Salvador frowned. "Oh, don't worry, you're not getting one. The last thing I'm going to do is help you leave Corey and your daughter without saying goodbye to them. So long!" Salvador hit the button on his door, rolling up his window. Frustrated, he continued on his route.

Damn Ben. He was too stubborn for his own good. Clenching the steering wheel, Salvador glanced in his rearview mirror. Ben dropped the black garbage bag and the brown box in his hands. Grabbing his chest, Ben fell to the ground on his knees.

Oh, shit. Is he having a heart attack?

Salvador slammed on brakes. Panic stricken, he threw the gear in reverse and sped backwards. Reaching Ben, he jumped out of the car and scurried towards him. "Ben!" Salvador got on his knees in front of Ben and clutched the elderly man's shoulders.

Releasing his chest, Ben shook his head. "Damn. You came back. I'm okay. I got strangled on my own spit. Has that ever happened to you?"

A good lashing pushed at Salvador's lips. He clenched his mouth tight to keep from cursing. "Are you serious? You got strangled on your own spit?"

Nodding, Ben shrugged. "Well, don't look so surprised. That can happen, you know?"

"You scared me half to death." Salvador stood, extended his hand to Ben. When Ben gripped his hand, Salvador helped pull him into a standing position.

"Thanks for helping me up. This right leg of mine gives me such a hard time, especially since I fell in the hospital. Thank God I didn't break any bones. Now if you'll excuse, I need to get going. I don't want to miss my ride at the bus station."

"Look, Ben. Why don't you just let me give you a ride to the bus station?"

Ben looked over his shoulder like he was looking for someone. "Well, I guess it wouldn't hurt if I took you up on your offer." Salvador placed Ben's bag into the rear of his SUV, shut the latch. He pulled open the passenger side door for Ben. When Ben lifted his right leg to climb upward, his knees buckled and he fell backwards. Salvador caught him with his arms. "Thanks for catching me. The last thing I need is to break my spine."

"Don't mention it. Hold on to my shoulder and climb in."

Doing as Salvador requested, Ben held the brown box in one hand, gripped Salvador's shoulder with the other. Putting all his weight on him, Ben clambered inside the SUV.

Salvador jogged around the front of the SUV, hopped in, and proceeded to drive down the road. He locked the SUV. "I am not as dumb as you think I am."

"What's that supposed to mean?" Ben asked, holding the brown box in his lap.

"Ben, I know you didn't choke on your own spit. You fell because your leg is injured. I'm taking you back to the hospital," he stated frankly.

Fear developed in Ben's eyes. "Please don't take me back to the hospital. If you do, he'll kill me."

Salvador frowned. "Kill you? Who's trying to kill you?"

Ben gave his head a hard shake. "Nobody. Forget I said that."

Salvador's mind was spinning. "How in the hell can I forget what you just said? Who wants you dead? Who wants to kill you? And why?"

Ben's mercurial eyes darkened. "The less you know, the better. I've already said too much. I don't know why I'm even running at this point. He's going to find me."

"I'm taking you to the police."

Ben hit the dashboard repeatedly as he barked, "No! No! No! If I go to the police, they'll kill my daughter Alyssa, and my Corey. Please, Salvador. No police."

Silence loomed inside the truck. Salvador thought long and hard about what he should do. It sure was hard to make a decision when he didn't know what in the hell was going on. Right now, he could only think of one thing to do. "I tell you what, Ben. Why don't you come to my house and stay for a while? I'm sure that whoever wants you dead wouldn't think to look for you at my place. I have a guest house attached to the main house, so you'll have plenty of privacy. I'll have my private physician care for you until your leg gets better, and after it heals, if you still want to leave, you can."

Shaking his head, fear remained in Ben's eyes. "I don't have any money to pay for rent or doctors. To be honest, I don't even have any money for food. I'm broke." Ben sighed. "Broke," he choked out.

"I don't want any money from you, Ben."

"Well, how can I earn my way? I ain't in no shape to cut the yard." Who would want to kill an old man like Ben? Only a bully. "The only thing I want from you is to get better, and to take care of yourself."

"Okay. I can take care of myself."

Salvador stuck out his hand. "You promise?"

Ben smiled. He gripped his hand and shook it. "I promise."

"You should do that more often."

"What?"

"Smile."

Ten miles later, Salvador steered the SUV into his driveway.

"Thanks for helping an old man like me out."

Salvador pulled the key out of the ignition. "The pleasure's all mine." Ben gripped the door handle. Salvador said, "Hold up, I'll get the door for you." Salvador hurried to the passenger side door and helped Ben out of the SUV. He placed Ben's arm around the back of his neck and helped him up the length of the driveway.

Now at the guest house positioned to the right of the main house, Salvador inserted his key in the front door, pushed it open, and entered. Old white sheets covered the furniture inside the den. A stale scent permeated the air. The guest house needed to air out.

Ben's arms slipped from around Salvador's neck. Dragging his leg behind him, Ben hopped to the couch. "Nice place you have here. Your guest house is bigger than my whole house."

Salvador pointed towards the small-sized bedroom. "There's some washcloths and towels inside the closet inside the bathroom. There should be some soap in there, too. Do you need your bag out of the trunk?"

A look of mild relief shone on Ben's face. "Not tonight. There's nothing but the clothes I wore to the hospital in there. They're dirty. Need washing. I feel horrible for possibly putting your life in danger. I hope he don't show up here."

Salvador's head jerked back. "I don't know who he is. Or who we're talking about. But I wish he would step foot on my grounds with the intent to hurt me, or you, or anyone I care about. If he does, I can promise you, he'll have a big surprise waiting for him."

"What you gon' do? Beat him bad like you used to do your boxing opponents?"

Salvador shook his head. "No, sir. It'll be way worse than that. Way, way, worse." I'll kill the bastard. "If you need anything, just dial 333, and it'll ring up to the main house. Goodnight. And thanks."

Holding onto the counter, Ben shifted his weight. "Thanks for what? I ain't helped you. You helped me."

Salvador pat Ben's shoulder. "Thanks for letting me help you.

Everyone needs help at some point in their life."

Ben's brows hiked. "Even you?"

Yes me, especially when it comes to dealing with my mother Lucy. "Yes, even me. Goodnight."

"Goodnight. Thanks again." Ben's gratitude was evident.

Salvador pulled open the door, and then shut it behind him. Crossing the grass towards the main house, he sought his brain for ways he could help Ben without involving the police.

First thing tomorrow morning, he was going to get Ben a new cell phone and put a GPS tracker on it. Afterwards, he was going to call a private investigator, Don McQuade. Don had helped Richmond and Zeke, and he had done a marvelous job. Don will help me figure out who's trying to kill Ben, and how to best help him.

Wracking his brains out about what kind of trouble a man Ben's age could possibly be in, Salvador entered his house through the side kitchen door. Walking over to the fridge, his cell buzzed. Pulling the cell from his pocket, he hoped it was Sasha calling.

Spying the Caller ID, he frowned. What does she want? Disgruntled, he placed the cell to his ear. "Yes, Mother?"

"Why you got to say my name like that?"

Because I'm sure the only reason you're calling is because you need something. "What do you need, Mother?"

Salvador heard when his mother Lucy sucked her teeth. "What makes you think I need something?"

He pulled a beer from the top shelf of the refrigerator, shut the door. "Because you only call when you need something," he said, twisting the cap off his beverage.

Lucy's sigh came through the speaker of the cell. "Don't say that, Salvador. That's not true. I call you quite often, but sometimes you don't answer because you're busy."

"I don't mean to be rude, but I just walked in the house, and I'm very tired. Just tell me what you need. Okay?"

Lucy got quiet before saying, "I hate asking you this, but I need some money to pay my rent."

I knew she was calling for money. "What did you do with all the money I sent you the last time? Did you spend it on alcohol? Drugs? What?"

"I gave it to some needy children." Lucy sounded like she was lying.

"Bullshit, Lucy! Bullshit. I gave you fifteen thousand dollars. That's a lot of money to blow in four months. I'm not going to enable you any longer. If you want help, I'm willing to help you. But I will not enable you. Do you hear me? I will not enable you, Mother!"

"All that money you have…what kind of son are you? If it wasn't for me, you would've never became a boxer. Thanks for nothing!" Bam! Lucy slammed down the phone in his face.

Steaming, Salvador tilted the beer bottle to his lips and chugged down the whole darn thing.

Chapter Fifteen

SPRING BID FAREWELL TO THE low country, ending the cool, breezy nights. Right around the corner, the summer month of June arrived. Along with it came hot summer days and sultry , warm nights. On this particular June afternoon , white wispy clouds floated near the yellow s un. Black birds flapped their wings over the tall trees heading towards the ocean.

Sun gleaming through the windshield, Sasha squinted. She steered Salvador's white Porsche into the driveway of his oceanfront mansion and parked. Sheathed in a pair of jean shorts, a red tank top, and a pair of white sneakers, she exited the car. Backpack strapped across her shoulder, she mounted the steps to the porch and rang the doorbell.

Waiting on Salvador to answer the door, Sasha turned to look out at his immaculate front yard. Palm trees nestled throughout. Slender emerald grass looked like thick plush carpet covering the ground. It's so pretty out here. So relaxing. She heard the door crack open and turned to find Ben standing there.

Sasha's heart jostled. "Ben! Wh at are you doing here?" She stepped over the threshold and gave him a big , tight hug. Thank God you came to your senses she thought, releasing him.

Ben's dark lips eased into a heartfelt smile. "I ran into Salvador last night, and he invited me to stay here. He has such a big heart."

"Yes, he does."

"Right when you rang the doorbell, he got a phone call and asked me to get the door. My leg is bad, so I'm going to go back into the den to sit down." As Ben made his way back towards the den, he periodically held on to the furniture or walls for support.

Who was Salvador on the phone with? Sasha wondered. A tinge of jealousy threatened to creep up inside her. She hoped he wasn't on the phone with some woman that was trying to get with him.

She entered the spacious den area.

Ben flopped down on the sofa, making himself right at home.

Sasha walked over to the wide bay window overlooking the blue, glistening ocean. Two white horses stood outside on the sand. The horses' reigns were tied to a black trailer that read: Spaulding Equestrian Center. He'd gotten the horses from Richmond's business.

Just as Sasha turned to face Ben, Salvador emerged inside the den. Stubbles of hair peppered his tanned face. His solid chest muscles looked cut beneath the tank top he wore. Biceps bulged like hard, ripe peaches in his arms. Tall and manly, he was all muscles.

I bet his rod is one big muscle, too. Desire tugged at Sasha's heart like a harpist's fingers plucking at strings. Pulse beating at the base of her throat, the flesh on her arms pimpled.

Salvador walked up to her, pecked her forehead. Her heart melted. "Good afternoon."

Nipples growing thick beneath her bra, Sasha smiled. "Good afternoon."

"Are you ready to go riding?"

"Yes."

"As soon as the doctor gets here—" The doorbell rang. "That must be Dr. Vest now. Excuse me." Salvador went and answered the door, and then returned with a Caucasian man. He made the introductions. Salvador met Ben's gaze. "Ben, you're in good hands with Dr. Vest. He's going to give you a thorough examination, make sure your leg looks okay. In the meantime, Sasha and I are going to head out. If you need me, my cell number is written down on a sheet of paper on the table inside the kitchen, and I plugged it in the cell phone I bought you this morning."

Ben's eyes watered. "I can't tell you how much I appreciate your kindness. I'm going to spend the rest of my life repaying you. Thanks, Salvador."

Salvador patted Ben's shoulder. "Don't mention it." He looked at Dr. Vest. "Thanks for coming by at the last minute."

Dr. Vest responded, "Sure. Nice meeting you, Sasha."

"Nice meeting you, too, Dr. Vest." She strapped her backpack on her back.

Salvador pulled open the sliding glass door, stepped out onto the back deck, and descended the steps to the beach. He strode over to the white horse on the far end. "How about you ride this one? Her name is Pearl."

Pearl's eyes looked like black, shiny marbles. Sasha glided her hand over Pearl's white, thick fur. "You're so beautiful, Pearl."

As Salvador clenched Sasha's hips, he put his nose to the crook of her neck. "You look fine as hell in these shorts." His hoarse, seductive tone made her insides bubble with joy. "Here, let me help you up."

With one hand on the reign and the other flattened to Pearl's side, Sasha stuck her foot in the stirrup. Mounting the horse, she eased her rear on the saddle.

Salvador loosened the reigns from the trailer, and then hopped on the other black horse like he'd been riding all his life. Perhaps he had. "Follow me." He steered his horse towards the ocean.

Sasha steered Pearl beside the horse Salvador rode. "What's your horse's name?"

"His name is Blanco."

"Nice name for a horse."

"I figure we can ride down the beach to the boardwalk. You ready?"

Sasha nodded. She teased, "If you have trouble keeping up with me, I'll meet you at the boardwalk."

Salvador chuckled. "Get serious. I can assure you...you're not a better rider than me."

"It depends on what's being rode." Smiling, Sasha yanked on Pearl's reign, and the animal began galloping.

Salvador's firm ass bounced up and down on the saddle as he rode the horse.

"I'd love for you to ride me!"

"I bet you would!" Riding the white horse named Pearl, Sasha's breasts jiggled inside her bra.

Horse's hooves cantered on the ground, kicking up the beige sand. Waves splashed against the hot earth. Joyfully riding the horses along the beach, the beige sand sparkled like colorful glitter. Million-dollar estates perched in the grassy area beyond the mounds covered with tall willows.

The wind slapped at Sasha's face. "It's a beautiful day."

Admiration for her sparked inside Salvador's blue pupils. "Anytime I'm with you, it's a beautiful day." Huskiness lingered in his tone.

"I feel the same way."

"I'm glad you're finally starting to admit how much you like me, and how much you want me." There was an air of efficiency about him that fascinated her. Like he was close to perfect.

"I never said anything about wanting you."

His lips drew into a handsome smile, disturbing her in every way. "Maybe your mouth didn't, but your pretty brown eyes did."

Well, considering she was falling head over heels for him, there was no use in responding to his comment. One look at her, and she was sure anyone could see how fond she was of Salvador. What woman wouldn't be fond of Salvador? Salvador can have any

woman he wants, and he definitely doesn't want you, her consciousness whispered. Girl, please, Reggie didn't even want you, and he ain't even half the man Salvador is.

Restaurants, shops, and activity rental booths positioned on the boardwalk appeared before them. They brought Blanco and Pearl to a stop in front of a patch of brown, long willows. Dismounting Pearl, Sasha inhaled the salty air.

Salvador tacked Blanco's reign to the railing first, and then he did the same thing with Pearl's. Standing in front of Sasha, he cupped the ball of her shoulder. Oh, how she loved when he touched her. After he gets in your panties, he's not going to want

anything to do with you, fool! her conscious screamed inside her head again. Go away. Can't you see I'm having a wonderful day?

"We can take a walk along the boardwalk. Rent a jet ski. Grab a bite to eat. Or if you want, we can do all three."

"I say let's do all three."

"Would you like to start with the jet skis?"

"Yes." Salvador waved over the beach attendant. Sasha took off her shoes, placed them in her backpack. "Would you like to put your shoes in my bag?"

"Yeah." Salvador removed his sneakers from his feet. Mercy. Mercy. Even his toes were handsome. She longed for the feel of his arms squeezing her in a tight embrace.

"How may I help you?" the young blond-haired teenager asked.

Salvador told the young boy, "I'd like to rent a jet ski. How much is it?"

"Fifty dollars for half an hour." After Salvador handed the teenager two one hundred dollars bills, he asked, "Which jet ski would you like?"

"Get the black and gold one," Sasha said, making a suggestion. Excited about exploring the ocean, her insides beamed.

Salvador stated, "The lady wants the black and gold one."

"I'll be right back." The teenager took off running. He grabbed two life jackets and looped them around the gears of the jet ski. He then pushed the ride towards the edge of the ocean.

"Do you have a beach towel in your backpack?" Salvador asked, his eyes squinting against the sun.

"Yes."

"Great."

Tugging her hand, they walked to the edge of the beach. Wet, warm sand pressed into the heels of her feet. Salty ocean water brushed against her legs.

Salvador pushed the jet ski into the ocean, climbed on. She clambered on behind him, wrapped her arms around his six pack.

"Hold on tight," he decreed over his shoulder. Clenching the black handles of the jet ski, Salvador rotated the gears and the ride cruised into the ocean.

Joyfully riding across the sea, the bright sun warmed Sasha's skin. Water kicked up from the ocean, splashing Sasha's face. Her hair tousled in the wind.

The sea was crowded with various water sports. Sailboats cruised about. Colorful canopies from parasails floated in the air. Her arms wrapped around his six pack, Sasha's breasts pressed against Salvador's spine. Loving the feel of her boobs touching his hard body, her lips curled into a smile. He sure knew how to have fun.

Thoughts of how they'd shared in stargazing last night entered her mind. The kissed they'd shared entered her brain, too, making her hot between the legs. Maybe she should just go with the flow, and whatever happened between them just happened, she tried convincing herself.

Sasha glanced back over her shoulder to find that they were far away from the mainland. Oh hell, they were halfway across the sea, out in the middle of nowhere. Okaaayy. It's time to turn around.

"Hey. Don't you think we should turn around? We're out pretty far."

"I know a little private island I want to take you to."

"Hilton Head has private islands?"

"They're more like private pieces of land. But I like to call them islands."

"Well, are we almost there?" I don't like being out here without any lifeguards. This is scary.

"Yes. We'll be there in a second."

Sasha put her chin to his right shoulder. "You sure are adventurous."

"Yes, I am. That's the only way I know how to live. If you stick around, maybe you'll adapt to my adventurous habits."

Desiring to suck on his earlobe, she licked her lips. "Do you want me to stick around?"

"I've been with you every day since I've met you. I don't know what it is about you, but I can't get enough of you," he said with meaning and severity.

A circular piece of land crowded with trees came into view. Salvador drove the jet ski up to the land and parked it. Cutting the engine, he got off.

"Do you come out here often?" she asked, stepping down.

"No. Not at all. In fact, it's only my second time out here. I came out here once. Before a boxing championship to clear my mind and run in the sand. I haven't been out here since."

"Did you win the championship?"

"Yeah. After I won, I retired. "

"Do you think you'll ever fight again?"

"No. I'm done with fighting. My career ended with a win, and I want to keep it that way. I just want to concentrate on training the younger generation. I was hoping my new sports training facility would be built by now, and up and running. It would've been if someone hadn't tried to burn it down."

"Do you have any idea who tried to burn it down?"

"No. But when I find out who did it, their ass is grass." Uh oh. Salvador pointed near the bed of grey sea rocks beside the palms. "Let's sit over there."

The bright sun kissed Salvador's handsome face as he plopped down on the sand. Sasha pulled her big beach towel from her backpack, spread it on the ground, and sat beside him. Shimmering blue water surrounded the circular piece of land covered with tall trees. Reminded Sasha of the movie The Blue Lagoon. "This does look like a private island."

"Maybe it can be our special place." His husky voice held a touch of sincerity.

Beholding his tender gaze, she drew her legs up to her chest, wrapped her arms around her knees. "Our special place. Does that mean I get another date with you after today?"

Tenderly, his eyes melted into hers. "The way I feel right now, yes."

The idea that this private island may be their special place excited her. "Do your feelings normally change quickly when it comes to women?"

Salvador tipped his head towards the blistering sun. "Nope. Normally, I have very little interest in women from the beginning. But I don't feel that way about you. There's something special about you. You intrigue me. You captivate me." His face started leaning into hers. "You turn me on, and I haven't been able to stop thinking about you since the first time I laid eyes on you." Sweat wet his forehead. He cupped her ear. "God, you're so beautiful. Let's go for a swim."

Salvador stood. He pulled his shirt over his head, tossed it on the ground. Sasha gawked at the grooves and contours making up his muscular torso. Her body ached for his touch. Imagining her tongue licking his hard nipples, her tongue involuntarily protruded from her lips.

His eyes locking with hers, Salvador yanked down his jeans. His shaft looked like a huge, ripe banana beneath his swim trunks. Mercy. Mercy.

"Did you remember to bring your swimwear?" he asked, towering over her like a fierce soldier.

"Yes." Sasha pushed herself into a standing position. She rolled her shirt over her head. Pulled her shorts down her legs. A red two-piece bikini clung to her skin.

Salvador took a step back. His eyes raked up and down her figure. "Sasha. Sasha. Sasha. You look amazing."

"Thanks. You, too." And so does your manhood. He linked his fingers with hers. They jogged straight into the ocean. The cold water immersed Sasha. "Ooo. It's cold."

"Climb on my back." He stooped in the water.

Sasha held on to his broad shoulders, wrapped her legs around his waist. Salvador plunged into the cool water and began swimming. Feet kicking, arms flailing, he swam like a big fish in the sea.

Weee, this is so much fun. Get it, Salvador. Swim, she mentally cheered him on.

Coming to a stop, a big wave crashed into them. Sasha slipped off Salvador's back, plunged into the ocean. Gravity sucked her towards the bottom. Her feet kicking, salt water shot into her nose and mouth and burned her eyes. Swallowed up by the rough currents of the sea, she felt rough hands clutch her shoulders and jerk her from the water.

Coughing, she blinked sporadically. Water burst from her mouth.

Drenched hair matted to her scalp. The salty water caused her eyes to momentarily burn.

Clutching her shoulders, Salvador held Sasha tight to his chest. He chuckled. "Oh, my pussy cat, sabes nadar?" "Huh?"

He called me his pussycat. I like it.

"Can you swim?"

She coughed. "Yes. I can swim."

"It sure doesn't look like it."

"Stop laughing at me or—"

Salvador tossed back his head, letting loose a hearty chuckle. "Or you're going to what?"

"Or I'm going to knee you in your balls." Really? Was that the best she could think of? "Or I'm going to do this—" She reached beneath the water and pinched his nipple. "Now."

145

Salvador chortled. "I hope I'm not supposed to be affected because you pinched my nipple, because it turned me on." He laughed. "See." He pushed his erection into her stomach. Sasha scrunched her face. Salvador continued. "I don't take lightly to people trying to mistreat me for no good reason. How would you feel if I—" Using his fingers, he twisted her nipple back. "Pinched your nipple."

That felt so good. "Forget you, Salvador," she said, trying to pretend like she didn't like it, when in fact he'd made her insides jangle.

Salvador pecked Sasha's lips. "You can't forget me even if you wanted to. I know I sure can't forget you."

With his massive erection still pressed to her stomach, water saturated his gorgeous, tanned face. His blue eyes sparkled. Gripping her hips, he slid his tongue into her mouth and tongued her down. Groaning, he cupped her behind. He lifted her until his penis connected with her center. Her fingers curled around his shoulders, she wrapped her legs around his waist.

Their sexes touching, he rocked his rigid rod into her opening. Knocked his hard tool against her clitoris. Slurping on his thick tongue, Sasha groaned huskily. Nipples tightening, her center grew slick.

The constant friction of their sexes pounding against one another pushed her towards a clitoral orgasm. One hand on her spine, he slid his free hand over her right breast, thumbed her nipple. Sensual desire shot through her. OhmyGod. I'm about to cum. Yes. Unable to stop the madness, her hands left his shoulders and palmed the back of his head.

Feasting greedily on his tongue, she circled her hips. Her breathing escalating, she moaned deep inside her chest. Oh, I'm so close. So close. On the verge of exploding, she lolled her head back, letting the sun kiss her arched neck.

"Oh, Salvador." Bucking on his elongated shaft, Sasha's clitoris throbbed. Biting her bottom lip, her body tensed, her clit burst into a powerful orgasm. Oooo. Oooh. "Ahhhh."

As her orgasm tapered off, Salvador held her to his muscular chest. "I'm glad I was able to bring you pleasure, Sasha. And though I'd like nothing more than to make passionate love to you out here, I'm not."

What? Huh? "Why not?" Sasha asked, ready to spread her legs wide open for him.

The light in Salvador's eyes grew dark, almost cold. "Because. Just because." Salvador tucked a piece of wet hair behind Sasha's ear. "I guess we should get going before it gets dark."

She felt the nauseating sinking of despair. Now, here she was considering having sex with him, and he'd turned her down. But why? Was there someone else in his life? Did he all of a sudden not find her attractive? Did he have deep issues she wasn't aware of? Or could it be that he had so much respect for her family that he didn't want to risk her falling in love with him, only to turn around and dump her? If that was the case, then it was best that they didn't take things further.

Sasha wrapped herself up in a cocoon of anguish. She climbed behind Salvador on the jet ski, wrapped her arms around his waist, and held on tight as the ride jetted across the ocean.

A short while later, Salvador and Sasha rode on the horses, heading back towards the estate. Still trying to figure out why Salvador didn't try to make love to her, Sasha's butt bounced up and down on the saddle.

Ever since they'd left the private beach, Salvador had been quiet and distant. Like he'd been in deep thought. His mood had switched quick on her. Perhaps they shouldn't have been kissing like that. Oh goodness, what if he'd decided he wasn't going to have anything to do with her after today?

Clenching the horse's reign, Sasha steered Pearl up to the trailer beside Blanco, parked her, and then dismounted. One by one, Salvador placed the horses into the back of the trailer, tied them up, and then shut the door.

Seemingly upset, he gave Sasha a weird look, and then headed up the back steps with her by his side. Sasha paused. "What's wrong, Salvador?"

Standing on the step above her, Salvador peered down at Sasha. "Nothing's wrong."

Sasha released a deep breath. "Are you sure? You haven't said two words to me since we left the private beach."

He placed a hand on her shoulder. "Please forgive me if I seem a little distant." Not offering an explanation, he turned to continue his hike up the steps. Coming to a stop in front of the sliding glass door, he glanced over his shoulder back at her. "You can go home if you want."

What in the hell? "Fine. I'll go home," she snapped, disliking the fact his happy mood had suddenly turned sour.

When Salvador pulled the sliding glass door open to his mansion, a sharp gasp whipped from his mouth. Fists balling, he flinched. "What in the heck are you doing here?" The outlines of his face hardened.

Maybe she's the problem, Sasha thought, waiting for him to introduce her to the woman standing inside his den.

Chapter Sixteen

"MOTHER. WHAT ARE YOU DOINGhere?" Pinching the bridge of his nose, Salvador drew in a sharp breath. Hating his mother had shown up without apprising him first, Salvador felt his face grow hot. He surveyed his mother. You look terrible,Mother. Awful.

Lucy looked frail and thin. Scraggly bangs on her forehead, a troubled expression rested on her pale white face.   When she inhaled, Lucy's bony shoulders motioned up and down.   "It's that any way to greet your mother? Whatever happened to a hug? Or 'Hi, Mom, it's great to see you'?" Her raspy speech was slurred.

Jesus Christ, she better not be drunkSalvador took three steps forward. An alcohol stench drenched his mother's clothing. His nose twitched. "My God! You wreak of alcohol,   Mother. Please don't tell me you came here drunk."

Guilt appeared on   Lucy's pale face. Her bottom lip folded under. "I'm not drunk, Sal. I only had a few drinks. Just a few. I promise."

"A few drinks, my ass," he barked, feeling a headache coming on.

Lucy pouted. "Watch how you talk to me, Sal. I'm still your mother." She looked at Sasha. "Well, aren't you going to introduce me to her?"

Salvador transferred his gaze to Sasha. "This is my mother... Lucy."

Sasha's soft lips pulled into a smile. "It's nice meeting you, Lucy," she said, shaking his mother's hand.

"Nice meeting you, too. You're pretty." Lucy's throat sounded clogged.

Sasha blushed. "Thanks."

"Is this your girlfriend, Sal?"

"You need to mind your own business, Mother."

Lucy stared at him with pitiful eyes. "I'm sorry, Sal. Please don't be mad at me."

Salvador felt sorry for his mother and hated her dependency on alcohol. Grave disappointment for his mother entered his soul. I have to help her. She needs me. "Did Ben let you in?"

Lucy looked around at her surroundings. "Ben? No. I let myself in. It's not safe to leave your doors unlocked. Who's Ben?"

Sasha interjected, "Excuse me. I'm going to see myself out." She looked at Lucy. "Have a good evening." She headed for the door.

Lucy nodded. "You, too."

Salvador told his mother, "You stay right here. I'll be right back." Lucy had some nerve to show up at his house unannounced. Disgruntled, he pulled open the door for Sasha and walked her to the car.

Sasha stood by the driver's side door of his Porsche. Longing radiated in her brown, cinnamon-colored irises. "I had a great time with you today. Thanks."

"I had a great time, too." Tempted to kiss her soft lips, he pulled open the car door instead. Disappointment shone in Sasha's eyes. She slid behind the steering wheel, and then left.

Walking up the steps, Salvador grumbled. More than anything, he'd wanted to kiss Sasha. Earlier today while in the ocean at the private beach, he'd wanted to make love to her, but his feelings for her had scared him. More like terrified him. That's why he'd decided to pass up the opportunity to make love to her. Deep down inside, he felt like she deserved a man much better than him. One that could love her for all eternity. The last thing a woman like Sasha deserved was for a man like him to get her in his bed and then lose interest.

Maybe I won't lose interest, Salvador thought, entering his home. Who was he kidding? He always lost interest in women after he had sex with them. Sasha definitely didn't deserve an egotistical man like him. She deserved much better than him. Way better.

When he reentered the den, Lucy was sitting on the couch. She stood. "If you want me to leave, Sal, I can."

Observing his mother's rough appearance, a combination of joy and sorrow intermixed inside Salvador. "You don't have to leave. Please excuse my frankness earlier, I'm just surprised to see you."

Lucy gazed at him speculatively. "How long can I stay?"

Salvador gestured to the sofa. "Have a seat, Mother." Lucy and Salvador sat beside one another. God, she smells horrible. She needs a bath, bad. Salvador stated, "What's going on? Are you in some kind of trouble?"

Lucy sniffed. She folded her arms across her chest. "Well, you're going to find out anyway, so I might as well tell you. I lost the house."

Struggling to hide the severity of his disappointment, Salvador sighed. "Considering all the money I give you, there's no excuse for you to have lost your home."

Lucy sighed heavily. "I know, Sal. You're right. But please don't lecture me. Not right now. It's been a long day. Just please let me stay here for a few days until I get myself together, and then I'll leave. I promise. Just a few days is all I need."

You need more than a few days to get yourself together. "As long as you promise not to drink, you can stay here as long as you like. I'll get rid of all the alcohol inside the house so you won't be tempted. What about your AA meetings? Are you still going?"

Lucy nodded. "Yep. Yep."

Salvador had the distinct feeling Lucy was lying about attending her AA meetings. "Come, let me show you to your room."

"Oh. I already found it. My suitcase is in there and everything." Salvador chuckled. "You're a funny woman."

Lucy pinched Salvador's cheek. "It's so good to see you smile when you look at me, Sal." Her eyes watered. "Normally all I do is make you frown. I just break your heart. All the time." The tear sitting on the rim of her eye rolled down her cheek. She swiped at it.

Salvador wrapped his arms about Lucy's shoulders and embraced her. A sour stench socked him in the nose. He'd been waiting for a long time for Lucy to come live with him, and though she came drunk, he was still happy that she came. With her living under his roof, maybe now he could save her from destroying herself. Love for his mother filled Salvador's heart. "I'm going to do everything in my power to help you, Mother."

Lucy caressed his back. "Thanks, Sal. I need all the help I can get."

Just as Salvador let go of Lucy, Ben emerged inside the den. Ben stated, "Oh, I'm sorry. Didn't know you had company."

"It's okay, Ben. This is my mother, Lucy."

Sniffling, Lucy touched her hair. Her eyes wandered over Ben's entire body.

"Lucy," Ben extended his hand to her, "nice meeting you." Something mysterious passed between Ben and Lucy as they looked at each other and shook hands, but Salvador couldn't quite put his finger on it.

"Are you the butler?" she asked.

Ben laughed. "Although I'm a great cook, I'm not the butler. I'm a guest."

"Oh."

Salvador exclaimed, "Ben is a new friend of mine. He's living here temporarily."

Ben smiled. "You raised a mighty fine man here, Lucy."

Sadness dulled Lucy's eyes. "I can't take credit for how my Sal turned out. He practically raised himself. Didn't you, Sal?" Lucy's stomach growled.

Salvador watched the play of emotions on Lucy's tired face. "You helped some, Mother. Are you hungry?"

Lucy rubbed circles on her stomach. "A little."

"What would you—"

Ben interrupted, "I can cook for the two of you, if you like. Just tell me what you like, and I'm sure I can whip it up for you." He smiled.

"There's some fresh salmon in the refrigerator. If you think you can do something with the fish, have at it," Salvador stated.

Smiling his behind off, Ben nodded. "I can cook a mean salmon dish. I can make it take like you're in a five-star restaurant." "Really?" Salvador couldn't wait to taste Ben's cooking.

"Yes, really. How would you like it prepared?" Ben queried.

"It doesn't matter. Surprise me. Now if you'll excuse me, I have a few phone calls to make." Leaving Ben and Lucy in the den by themselves, Salvador headed for his bedroom.

Now instead of having one guest living with him, he had two. Turning into his master suite, he headed straight for the window and lifted it. Sounds of the ocean rolled through the window.

Sitting on the edge of the bed, Salvador pulled his cell from his pocket, checking to see if Sasha had texted or called him. She hadn't. After the way he'd gone all silent on her, he couldn't blame her, not one bit. Damn.

Confused about what kind of relationship he wanted from Sasha, he cursed. It'd only been a week since he'd known her, and she'd somehow gotten under his damn skin. Inside his heart. Oh, crap no. She ain't inside my heart, is she? He didn't know what the hell he felt for Sasha because he'd never felt like this before.

Salvador released a deep breath. Maybe I should call Sasha. Or better yet, maybe not. Maybe it's best if I don't see her again. No need to ruin a perfectly good friendship just because I want to make tender love to her delicious looking body. Because I want to nibble on her delectable clitoris. Or because I want to insert my cock inside her snug pussy.

Cell in his hand, Salvador thumbed through his contacts, and then dialed. Three rings later, a familiar voice came on. "Salvador, I was just about to call you," Don, the private investigator, exclaimed.

"You have any news regarding Ben for me?"

"Nothing real concrete. Just a few basics. I must say, Ben's resume is quite impressive. He retired as a Marine. Fought in Vietnam. Ben was married to a woman by the name of Claira. They had one child together, a daughter named Alyssa. Alyssa lives here in Hilton Head Island and has a son named Corey."

Yeah, yeah. He already knew all of that. "What about his record?"

"Ben's record is squeaky clean. I wasn't able to get a hold of his cell records today. But I have the gut feeling once I get them, I'll be able to put a few more pieces of the puzzle together."

"Thanks, Don."

"You're welcome."

After ending the call, Salvador headed into the bathroom to shower. Standing inside the shower, hot water sprayed his back. Circling the bar of soap on his chest, he thought of Sasha. Thought of how it had felt to have her sex gyrating on his cock earlier today while in the ocean. Thought of how it had felt to kiss her brown, soft lips. How he'd clenched her hips. And how he had cupped her round bubble ass in his hands. More different than alike, he admired everything about the beautiful African-American queen.

Scrubbing his aching balls with the soap, Salvador's rod stiffened. It seemed like forever since he'd been inside of a woman. Twice, he'd passed up the opportunity to get laid because of Sasha—once with Julie and Kim, and the other with Chelsea. An expletive left his mouth. Sasha had a hold on him, and he didn't like it one bit. None whatsoever.

Balls aching and rod stretched to the max, he pushed the shower door back. Water dripping down his legs, he stepped onto the mat. "Damn woman got my cock hurting, and she isn't even here." Toweling off his back, he contemplated whether or not to masturbate. Forget it, I'll just order up some pussy from somebody I don't love— He said an expletive.

It was impossible for any man to fall in love with a woman after only knowing her for a few days. Wasn't it? Love? What was love? How did it feel to be in love? he wondered, putting on some clean lounge wear.

Damn Sasha. She had him confused as hell. Perhaps he shouldn't call or go out with her until he figured out what it was he was feeling. Fully dressed, Salvador left his bedroom, entered the hallway. A flavorful aroma lingered in the air. Mmm. Smells heavenly.

Salvador entered the kitchen to find that Ben had cooked a delicious looking meal. On the stove inside a rectangular baking dish were four salmon steaks drizzled in a buttery looking creamy sauce. To go along with it, Ben had cooked some cheesy scalloped potatoes topped with bread crumbs, and crunchy green bean with sliced almonds.

Salvador patted his stomach. "This looks great, Ben."

Ben's eyes rolled over the food on the stove. "I bet you gon' think it tastes as good as it looks, too. I found the potatoes in the pantry. There's nothing like homemade scalloped potatoes. I can't stand that box stuff."

"Me either," Lucy said, entering the room looking fresh. Taken aback by Lucy's attempt to clean up, Salvador stared at her. Lucy's freshly shampooed hair hung in wet curls over her shoulders. Sheathed in a pair of dark blue jeans, her breasts perched from the red shirt she wore. "This food looks delicious. Quien te enseno a cocinar, Ben?" Lucy asked in Spanish.

Apparently understanding Spanish, Ben stated, "My deceased wife, Claira, taught me how to cook when she was alive."

Surprise covered Lucy's face. "You speak Spanish?" Ben seemed to have impressed her.

Ben nodded. "Some. I know a little French, too. Learned it many years ago when I was in the Marines."

Lucy put her hands on her hips and smiled. "Impressive."

Everyone took their seats. Lucy picked up her fork and dug in, eating fast like she'd hadn't eaten in days.

"If you don't mind, I'd like to bless the food," Salvador said.

Lucy stopped chewing. "Oh." She dropped her fork on her plate and swallowed. "My bad. Go ahead."

Salvador extended his one hand to Lucy, and the other to Ben. "Let's please gather hands." Ben and Lucy grabbed his hands, and then they held each other's. Bowing his head, Salvador closed his eyes. "Heavenly Father, thank You for the food on the table. Bless the hands and the person that prepared it. May the food on the table be nourishment to our bodies." "Amen," Lucy blurted.

Salvador's right eye popped open. "I wasn't finished, Mother."

"Ooops. Sorry."

Salvador continued. "As I was saying...Father, thank You for this union between me, Ben, and my mother. Amen."

"Amen." Lucy cut the end of her salmon with the fork, then stuffed it in her mouth. "Oh my God, Ben," she said, chewing around the food, "this is sooo good."

Ben smiled. "Thanks, Lucy."

"Slow down, Mother." Salvador forked a piece of salmon into his mouth. A buttery lemon pepper piped on his tongue. Mmmm. He swallowed. "Ben, this is delicious."

Ben smiled. "Thanks."

Lucy smacked on the green beans. Crunch. Crunch. Crunch. "Wait till you taste these green beans."

"They smell heavenly." Salvador tasted the green beans, and then the scalloped potatoes. Ben was right. His food was just as good as a five-star restaurant. Salvador took a drink of his water. Lowered the glass to the table. "Thanks for cooking. Everything is delicious."

Ben replied, "It's the least I can do, considering all you've done for me. If it's okay with you, I'd like to cook for you in exchange for the rent."

Salvador swiped the napkin down his mouth. "You don't have to cook for me, Ben. As far as I'm concerned, you don't owe me a thing." Salvador patted his chest. "My kindness towards you comes from here...my heart."

"I know, Salvador. But it'd make me feel better if I could do something nice in return for you. Let me cook for you. Just buy the groceries, and I'll make whatever you want."

"We gladly accept your offer, Ben," Lucy remarked, blinking those long eyelashes of hers.

Eating the cheesy scalloped potatoes, a sudden thought occurred to Salvador. Please don't tell me she's flirting with Ben. Continuing to eat his tasty meal, Salvador prayed Lucy's sudden presence in his home wouldn't be a disaster.

Chapter Seventeen

A WEEK LATER, KNUCKLES RAPPED on the door of the guest suite where Ben stayed. Excited about his day with Salvador, Ben hurried to the door and flung it open. Surprised by his unexpected visitor, Ben felt his eyes squint. What is she doing here?

Lucy stood on the porch wearing a pink, skimpy sundress. Her thin lips smiled. "Hi , Ben." With her hair pulled back into a high ponytail, she strutted past him to the inside.

"Good afternoon, Lucy. I thought you were Salvador." Wondering what in the heck Lucy wanted, Ben shut the door. Lucy looked Ben up and down and started laughing. "What's so funny?"

Snickering, Lucy pointed at Ben's kneelength socks. "I just find it weird looking when grown men wear long socks with flip flops."

Ben looked down at his long white socks and flip flops. "I think it looks rather nice."

"I'm not saying it looks bad. It's just an odd combination." Lucy's eyes traveled over the spacious guest suite. "My Sal has done quite well for himself. Don't you think?" She flopped down on the sofa, crossed her legs at the knees.

Ben nodded. "Your son has done better than okay. He's done great. He's such a good, good, kind man. I owe my life to him."

Inwardly thanking God for Salvador, he sat on the sofa next to Lucy.

"That's what I gather."

Glancing out the window at the ocean, Ben clasped his ashy, rough hands together. "Salvador has done so much for me. I just wish there was some kind of way I can repay him."

Lucy turned sideways. Staring into his eyes, her head tilted. "I know how you can repay Sal."

Ben's brows lifted. "You do? How?"

"You can pay my Sal back by paying his momma some attention." Lucy jumped on top of Ben, knocking him backwards to the curb of the sofa. Stunned, Ben smelled alcohol all over Lucy. Her breasts pressed to his chest, she fisted the top of his shirt. Puckered her sour-smelling lips. "Kiss me, Ben." Lucy lightly brushed her lips against Ben's.

Ben pushed Lucy off him and jumped to his feet. "Got darn you woman!" He dragged his backhand over his mouth. Wagging his finger at her, Ben firmly stated, "If you think something's going to happen between us, you're sadly mistaken. I'm too old for relationships."

Still sitting on the couch, Lucy's gazed traveled from Ben's face to his manhood. "Does it still work?"

"Hell yeah, it still works! But only for the right the woman. I don't even know you."

Lucy shrugged. "And?"

"And besides, you're drunk! You better hope Salvador don't—

" A hard fist banged on the front door. "That's Salvador now."

Lucy's eyes stretched wide. Jumping to her feet, she whispered, "Oh no. Please don't tell Sal I've been in here. He'll get the wrong idea. Think I'm trying to do something I'm not with you." Nah, Lucy. Sal knows his mother very well. Lucy continued. "He'll get so angry with me. I'm going to go hide in the closet." Lucy hastened to the master suite, hid inside the closet.

Seems like Lucy's life is just as big of a mess as mine. I'm a loser. A big fat zero. Ben cracked the door open.

Salvador stood on the porch holding a pail and two fishing rods in his hand. "You ready?" He handed one of the fishing rods to Ben.

"Yes, I'm ready." And so is your momma. She's ready to jump my bones. Especially the one inside my pants. Ben closed the door behind himself and headed for the beach.

Crossing the sand behind Salvador's mansion, Ben pulled his sun visor down on his head. He inhaled the fresh air and salt water. Boy, was this mighty kind of Salvador to invite him to go fishing with him. Other than his daughter and grandson, no one ever paid him any attention or spent any time with him. Well, that wasn't exactly true. Sasha had spent some quality time with him. Had even spent her own money and bought him a caramel pecan pie. She'd been kind and read him some of the letters Claira had written to him, too.

Ben walked up the wooden steps of the pier behind Salvador. Reaching the end, Salvador dropped the empty pail on the floor. "Hopefully, the fish are biting today."

Yeah, well I know who is biting today. Your momma. She tried to bite my lip off. The sun gleamed bright in the sky. Ben put his bait at the tip of the line. "It's a great day for fishing." Ben placed the rod over his shoulder, then tossed the line into the sea. Salvador did the same. "I know I keep saying it...but I really appreciate everything you're doing for me."

"Please stop thanking me. What good is life if you don't give back to people when they need help? Makes me feel good to help someone. Now that I know someone has made a threat on your life, I agree with you, it's best that you don't contact your daughter or Corey. Ben, if you tell me why this man wants you dead, or what the problem is, I may be able to help you."

Ben shook his head profusely. "I messed up, Salvador. Big time. There's nothing you can do to help me."

"Do you owe somebody money? If so, maybe I can pay your debt off."

"My situation is complex. The less you know, the better." Ben had already tried giving Laurente the money back, but Laurente had refused the money. The evil man wanted him to keep his commitment and burn the building down. Why did Laurente want the building burned down so badly? Ben wondered, feeling his line tug.

"So you're not going to let me help you?" Salvador asked in a harsh, raw voice.

"Nope." The fishing line jerked. Gripping the fishing rod, Ben reeled the line inward. A big grouper popped from the sea, wiggling at the end of his pole. "Now ain't that a beauty. Gon' make a tasty dinner for us tonight." He placed the fish in the bucket.

"I love grouper."

"How do you want me to prepare the grouper?" Ben tossed his line back into the sea. "I can blacken it or grill it. Or make an encrusted grouper. I can even fry that sucker."

"Surprise me—" Salvador yanked hard on his line. A monk fish popped up from the ocean, flapping from side to side. "Do you have any clue what kind of fish this is?" he asked, reeling the fish upward.

"That's a monk fish. I'll cook that baby so tender, you'll think you're eating lobster."

Placing the monk fish in the bucket, Salvador smiled with his eyes. "I love lobster." He threw his line back into the water.

"Me, too. A poor man like me don't get to eat it that much, though. It's too expensive." Silent moments passed as they stood alone on the pier fishing. "You've asked me about my personal life, so I feel comfortable asking you about yours. Can you see?"

Salvador looked at Ben. "Can I see? Yes, I can see. What kind of question is that?"

Ben held up two fingers. "How many fingers do I have up?"

Salvador gave him a profound look. "Two. Where are you going with this?"

"Yep, you can see all right. See what you want. Being that your vision is good, it's too bad you can't see how wonderful a woman Sasha is."

Salvador returned his gaze to the ocean. "What makes you think Sasha is a wonderful woman when you barely know her?"

"At this old age, I can sense things many young people can't. I strongly sense the chemistry you and Sasha share. When the two of you are in my presence, I can feel electricity shocking the air." Ben laughed. "Me and my Claira used to have that same kind of energy for each other. God, how I miss my Claira. Anyway, if I were you, I wouldn't let a woman like Sasha get away from me. Especially when you have apparent chemistry like you obviously have."

Salvador kept his eyes on the ocean. "I agree. Sasha is a special woman. But considering I don't ever want to get married, I'm not going to pursue her."

Now that's just stupid. "Why you don't want to get married?"

"There's too many women out there to settle down with just one."

Ben rolled his eyes. "That's a bunch of fried bologna. Yeah, it may be a lot of women out there, but they all won't bring you the same kind of chemistry you have with that gal Sasha. Let me tell you something, young man, getting married to the right woman is the best thing a man can do with his life. If you have the right woman, it's the sweetest feeling in the world. God intended for men to find a wife and have children. Don't go and be a fool and pass up a great opportunity. It's no fun growing old by your lonesome."

"I hear you, Ben. I hear you."

"Don't just hear me. Act upon it."

Ben and Salvador spent a solid hour fishing and conversing. After their fishing excursion ended, Ben picked up his pail and headed back towards the guest house so he could clean the fish and prep them for dinner. When they reached the back of the estate, Ben and Salvador parted ways. Salvador mounted the back steps to the deck, and Ben headed for the guest house.

Tired and beat from the brutal rays of the blistering sun, Ben grasped the doorknob and entered the guest house. Smelling like the beach, he dropped the fish off in the kitchen and headed to his bedroom. When Ben stepped inside the bedroom, his mouth shot open. "Dear God."

Lucy lay asleep on the bed, clenching a beer bottle to her boobs. Her pink dress was rolled up to her hips, and her legs were spread wide open, revealing her white panties. What should I do? Should I call Salvador? Should I toss her out? If Salvador thought he was fooling around with his mother, his feelings for him would change. And he'd be out on the streets. Perhaps that would be a good thing. For all of them. Little did Salvador know, but as soon as his leg got to be one hundred percent healthy, he was going to leave anyway. The longer I stay here, the more I put Salvador, Lucy, and Sasha's life in danger. I can't risk them getting hurt.

Ben stalked up to the bed where Lucy lay asleep. When he withdrew the beer bottle from Lucy's grip, she stirred. He tossed the empty bottle in the trash beside his bed. Hoping Salvador didn't find out she'd been drinking, Ben placed a hand on Lucy's shoulder and shook her. "Lucy. Wake up."

Lucy's eyes slowly peeled open. Yawning, she eased up on her elbows. "I've been waiting on you, Ben. What took you so long to get back?"

She's drunk as a skunk. "Lucy, you can't be coming in here doing stuff like this."

"Stuff like what?"

"Like getting in my bed and waiting for me."

Another yawn eased from Lucy's mouth. "Like Goldilocks, I just fell asleep in Poppa Bear's bed." Ben couldn't help but shake his darn head. Lucy looked to the right of the mattress, and then to the left. "Where's my beer? I know you better not had drank it." She gave Ben an accusing stare.

Ben sighed. "I didn't drink your beer, Lucy. I don't even drink, lady. The bottle was empty, so I threw it in the trash. I don't mean to be rude, but I think it's time for you to go. I'm about to clean some fish for dinner. Why don't you go up to the main house, get cleaned up, and join Salvador and me for some good eating later?"

Lucy turned her legs sideways and got out of the bed. Her hands came down hard on Ben's shoulders. A sensual glow in her eyes, she pressed her boobs to his chest. "If you want something good to eat, how about eating me?!" Ben's jaws dropped. Goodgodalmighty! Lucy threw her arm around his shoulder, whipped out her cell, and held it up in front of them. "Say cheese, Ben." Holding the camera above their heads, she snapped a photo of the two of them.

Chapter Eighteen

I HAVE SOME SERIOUS WRITER'S block. Sitting on the bed with her legs folded on Sunday afternoon, Sasha put the tip of the ink pen in her mouth and sought some words to finish crafting her R&B breakup song. Of course   , the song's idea had originally stemmed from her breakup with Reggie. Humming a slow melody, Sasha began writing the song she hoped someday would get published.

Verse Two
    When I was with you…you wanted to hang out with your boys
    When I was with you…you treated me like a windup toy
    When I was with you…you treated me so bad
    You used me, abused me took my kindness for granted
    When things ended, I felt broken
    When things ended, I felt alone
    When things ended, it nearly destroyed me
    I cried and cried, and asked God to hold me

    Rereading what she'd just written, Sasha had to admit, she felt it was good writing material. At least she hoped so. Desperately wanting to finish the breakup song she'd entitled   I've Changed today, she glanced at the clock on her nightstand. Just as the red digits flashed to three, the intercom inside her room clicked on.

"Sasha. Everyone has arrived," Leslie said, her voice streaming through the intercom. "Dinner is ready and will be served shortly."

Anxious to see her cousins, Sasha placed the pen on top of the pad and exited her room. Her hand gliding down the handrail as she descended the steps, she smelled yummy cornbread dressing. Loud laughter filled the house.

Smiling, Sasha entered the living room to find it super packed. Everyone and their adorable children were present. Richmond and Kayla, Zeke and Taylor, Sandella and Braylon. Dirk and Suade. An older gentleman she wasn't familiar with was there also. And even Salvador was present. Salvador stood off in a corner, talking with Richmond.

Meeting Salvador's gaze, Sasha's smile faded. Darn, why had Leslie invited him? After all that kissing and grinding in the ocean over a week ago, he hadn't bothered to call her. Or text her. Well, if he didn't want anything to do with her, then so be it. She didn't want jack crap to do with him either.

In fact, as soon as she purchased her brand new car tomorrow, she was going to return his Porsche to him and never go out with him again. Well, not that he was asking her out anyway, but still.

She mentally sucked her teeth. Just be happy you didn't sleep with him, dummy. Her subconscious laughed her butt off at her inside her head.

She'd been a fool to entertain the thought of the two of them having a relationship. Deciding not to let Salvador's presence stir her emotions into a frenzy, Sasha smiled. "Hello, everyone."

Smiling and waving, everyone spoke to her in return. Ignoring Salvador's penetrating gaze, Sasha walked towards the living room and began making small talk with Kayla, Taylor, and Sandella.

"So how are you adjusting to Hilton Head?" Sandella asked.

"I'm adjusting quite well."

"Staying here with Leslie, I'm sure you are," Kayla stated.

"Leslie spoils me like I'm a child. She's been a blessing to me," Sasha acknowledged. "As soon as I get on my feet, I plan to get my own apartment."

Taylor touched Sasha's arm. "Let me know if you'd like someone to accompany you when you go look for a place to stay." Sasha nodded. "Zeke told me how you and Salvador have been spending a lot of time together."

Sandella's mouth stretched wide. "Are the two of you——"

"Dating?" Kayla interjected. "Give us the scoop, girl."

"Salvador and I are just friends," Sasha commented. He stopped calling me out of the blue.

Taylor smiled. "Mmm hmmm. Let Zeke tell it, Salvador let you borrow his Porsche. Trust and believe...Salvador is not the type of man to let any woman drive his car unless he's feeling her."

Sasha slid her hands in her jean pockets. "He's just being nice, that's all."

"So have the two of you went on any dates?" Sandella pried.

"A few." Gosh, I wish they'd changed the subject. The man doesn't have any interest in me.

Taylor stated, "Girl, Salvador has the hots for you. He's a wild one to tame, but if anybody can tame him, I think it's you, Sasha."

Sandella nudged Taylor. Clenching her teeth, Sandella muttered,

"Don't turn around, Sasha. Salvador is heading this way."

Salvador approached Sasha from behind. "Hello, Sasha." When Sasha turned around to face Salvador, her heart melted. She could feel the sexual magnetism that drew her to him. God, she missed him. How did she let herself fall for him so fast? In the blink of an eye, at that.

"Hi, Salvador," her voice came out like a weak whisper.

"It's been a while since I've spoken to you. How are things going?" His voice was calm, his gaze steady.

Sasha glanced over at Kayla, Taylor, and Sandella. The three of them stood there with huge smiles on their faces. Like something magical between her and Salvador was about to happen. For crying out loud, Salvador could care less about her.

She returned her gaze to Salvador. "Things have been well on this end. How have you been?" And why haven't you called me? She didn't dare ask. You made me have an orgasm in the ocean at the private beach, and just stopped calling. Like nothing had ever happened.

"I've been busy. Trying to get my mother acquainted. She—" The unfamiliar man she'd spotted earlier walked up to them. "Isn't anyone going to introduce me to this beautiful woman?"

Zeke stated, "Uncle Colton, this is Sasha Spaulding...Leslie's niece."

Colton extended his hand to Sasha. When she placed her hand in his, he brought it up to his white lips and kissed her backhand. "I see pretty women run in this family. You're just as pretty as your beautiful Aunt Leslie," Colton said, letting go of her hand.

Sasha blushed. "Thanks, Colton." If Colton's single, he'd be a good match for Aunt Leslie.

Something sparkled in Salvador's eyes. "I agree, Uncle. Sasha is a very beautiful woman."

Whatever. "Thanks." A part of Sasha was kind of glad Salvador had come now.

Leslie lowered a pan of macaroni and cheese to the table with the rest of the food. "Can everyone please gather around the table?"

All the guests encircled the dining room table. How in the world did she end up next to Salvador? Sasha thought, standing beside him. Leslie continued. "Will everyone please join hands so I can bless the food?" Salvador cupped Sasha's hand. A sensual feeling swirled in her stomach. She closed her eyes and listened to Leslie as she said a beautiful prayer. As the prayer came to a close, Leslie pronounced, "Amen."

"Amen," everyone said in unison.

Salvador leaned over and whispered in Sasha's ear, "It felt good to hold your hand."

Screw you. Before Sasha knew it, she'd rolled her eyes. If Salvador thought she was going to respond to his comment, he could forget it. For all she cared, he could go jump in the lake behind Leslie's house. Why are you so mad at Salvador if all you wanted was to be his friend? You're such a liar! her subconscious screamed at her.

Leslie stated, "I'd like to thank everyone for coming here today. But I'd like to especially thank Zeke's father, Colton, for coming. When Zeke called and asked if his father could join us for our usual Sunday dinner, I gladly said yes. Colton has been through a lot lately. Because I know the power of being around people who love and care for you, I thought it'd be great for him to join us. We care, Colton. Thanks for coming."

A mist covered Colton's eyes. "Thanks for the kind words, Leslie. And thank each and every one of you for praying for me. I still have a rough road ahead of me, so please…continue to pray. Now enough about me, let's eat some of this good cooking this pretty lady has cooked for us."

Leslie's cheeks flushed a brownish-red as she took her seat at the head of the table. "Cut it out, Colton. There's nothing pretty about me."

Colton sat at the other end of the table. "I beg to differ. You're a very beautiful woman, Leslie. And from what I hear, you're just as beautiful on the inside as you are on the outside."

Smiling, Leslie blushed. Something magical seemed to have transpired between Colton and Leslie, Sasha thought, taking her seat beside Salvador—Mr. Can't Call Nobody. Hey, that just may make a good title for a song.

Ding dong. The doorbell rang.

"I wonder who that could be?" Leslie said. Right when she scooted her chair back, in walked her ex-husband, Russell.

Russell entered the room and went to stand beside Leslie. Wearing a plaid shirt, cowboy hat, and hard shoes, his eyes roamed around the room. "Good afternoon, folks," Russell greeted, removing his hat from his head, then placing it to his chest.

A dark cloud seemed to have fallen over the silent room.

Sasha slowly stood. "Hi, Uncle Russell."

"Oh, Sasha." Russell smiled. "When I heard you were in town, I couldn't resist stopping by here today to see my niece."

Sasha gave Russell a big hug. "It's so good to see you, Uncle Russell." Happy he stopped by, she released him, and then took her seat.

"She's not your niece," Richmond spat.

Russell stared at Richmond and nodded. "You're right, son. I have no right to claim Sasha as my niece. Especially after what I did to you."

Richmond responded, "I didn't make the comment because of what you did to me. Salina put you in a bad situation. With the help of Kayla and mom, I've finally accepted that. I made the comment because of how you lied, and what you did to Mama."

Holding a ceramic bowl in her hand, Leslie scooped a heaping of dressing onto her plate. "Don't be mad because of how your father mistreated me. I got over Russell a long time ago. Forgave him and everything. Maybe you should trying forgiving him, too." Lowering the bowl to the table, she glanced up at Russell. "Have a seat, Russell, and help yourself to some of this good food."

Russell's brows hiked. "Really?"

Leslie looked Russell up and down. "Yes, really. Look how skinny you done got. You look like you could use a good meal. Sit down and help yourself."

Russell's eyes went to the opposite end of the table where Colton sat. "Good to see you, Colton."

Colton stabbed the roast beef on his plate with a fork, then sliced it with a knife. "Likewise, Russell."

Great conversation partook inside the dining room as everyone sat enjoying their meals. Being around her family like this made Sasha's heart beam. Overflow with joy. She'd lost so much while living in Tennessee, but she had gained so much more by coming here—her family and a new group of friends.

"This is some good food, isn't it?" Salvador asked Sasha.

"Yes, it is. It's so tasty."

When Salvador took out his cell and began texting at the table, Sasha became irritated. It's so freaking rude to text at the table.

He's probably texting some freak. Or Julie.

While chewing on some seasoned meatless cabbage, Sasha's cell buzzed in her pocket. She retrieved her cell. Spying the text message from Salvador, she frowned.

Salvador: Speaking of tasty, your lips look tasty with every bite you take.

As if Salvador wasn't sitting right next to her, Sasha's fingers tapped the keyboard on her cell.

Sasha: Forget you. Don't talk about my lips.

Salvador: What's with the attitude, beautiful?

Sasha: I don't have an attitude.

Salvador: Oh, I know why you're mad.

Sasha: I'm not mad!

Salvador: Are you mad because I haven't called you after you tried to suck my face off in the ocean?

Sasha: Nope.

Salvador: Liar. You know you miss me. Admit it...you want me. Sasha thought, He thinks a lot of himself. The nerve of him to

suggest I want him. He's fine, but he's not that fine. Well, okay. He's super fine. But that doesn't mean I'm going to fall at his feet.

Sasha: I couldn't care less if you call me, with your arrogant self. Sasha saw Salvador smiling from her peripheral view.

Salvador: Flipping someone off is rather rude, lovely. An emoji such as this one would have been more pleasant. At least the emoji looks like I feel. Dying to lick all over your sexy body with my long, pink tongue.

A spark of excitement surged through Sasha. Her entire body warmed. Heat rushed to her cheeks. Shot to her center.

Richmond cleared his throat. "The two of you are texting away. Must be important."

Sasha's gaze snapped up and captured Richmond's face. "I'm sorry. One of the music publishers in Tennessee contacted me about writing a song for them," she kind of lied. Yellow Dog Entertainment had reached out to her, but that was a long time ago. Before Reggie had run them off.

Not offering an explanation, Salvador slid his phone in the clip attached to his belt.

Salvador has made me so hot. Finding it difficult to sit beside Salvador without her nipples and sex tingling, Sasha excused herself from the table. Flustered with sated desire, she went to the bathroom and closed the door. Standing in front of the mirror, she retrieved her cell. Refusing to let Salvador have the last word, she texted him.

Sasha: You will NEVER lick this body.

Glad she'd had the last word, she placed her cell on the counter and began combing her hair with her fingers. Bing. Her cell chirped. Picking up her cell, she brought it to her face to read the text message.

Salvador: That's a lie. I will lick your body. Just wait and see.

Fuming, Sasha leaned her back against the counter and folded her arms. "I can't believe that egotistical jerk. He goes a whole week without calling me, and when he finally sees me, he does all this flirting." *Darn Salvador.* He'd gotten her mad and hot at the same time. Trying to tamp down her mixed emotions, Sasha closed her eyes. Images of how Salvador's big shaft had rocked against her clitoris and made her cum entered her mind. She'd cum so hard while grinding him in the sea. Remembering how the hard knob of his shaft had pressed into her center, she groaned. "Mmm." Her eyes remaining closed, she placed her hand to the base of her throat. Licked her lips.

At the sound of the knock on the door, Sasha's eyes fluttered open. *I won't let Salvador get to me.* Body temperature heated from thinking about Salvador, she opened the door. Her heart spiraled.

Salvador's lips drew into a delicious smile. "There you are. I've been looking all over for you." Blocking her way, he stepped inside the bathroom, locked the door. His large frame towered over her like a tall warrior.

Her head tilted back, Sasha frowned. "Get out of my way." When she tried to go around him, he stepped in front of her. "Move."

Light smoldered in his blue-flecked eyes. "I've missed you, Sasha."

She folded her arms across her chest. "I can't tell. Move."

"Do you want me to move like this?" He pressed his chest into hers.

Sasha rolled her eyes. "No. I want you to move so I can leave. You like playing games, don't you?"

"If all I wanted to do was play games with you, I could have. But as I said before, I'm a very upfront man," he admitted throatily.

"You're not too upfront. Are you? You went completely silent on me last Saturday and refused to tell me what was wrong with you."

"Please forgive me for acting like an ass, Sasha. Last weekend was one of the best times of my life, and it, well...being with you scared me," he stated indulgently.

"Scared you? Why?"

Salvador's eyes brimmed with tenderness and passion. "Because I feel something for you that I've never felt for any other woman. I think about you all day. I lay in bed thinking about you all night." His stem hardened on her stomach. Curling his thick fingers around her wrist, he lifted her hand, placed it over his beating heart. "Feel what you do to me."

Strong beats from Salvador's heart pounded against Sasha's flat hand. "I'm falling for you, pussycat. Fast."

Complacent buoyancy filled her heart. "I'm falling for you, too, Salvador."

"I know you are." He slanted his mouth over hers. Kissed her rough and hard.

Groaning, their lips glided. Twining her tongue with his, Sasha's moist sex clenched. Their breathing heightened.

Kissing her with a sense of urgency, Salvador fisted the back of Sasha's hair. Using his free hand, he unbuttoned her jeans, lowered her zipper. Feasting on her mouth, he slid his hand inside her panties and broke their kiss.

When his hand touched her soaked entrance, her labia fluttered. "This is payback for texting me an emoji that had its middle finger up." He slowly slid his middle finger up in her sex and twirled. Sasha's body jerked. "Ahhh. Your pussy is soaked. Su clítoris se hincha." His husky Spanish accent heightened her arousal.

Bucking on his finger, Sasha cooed. "What did you say?"

Salvador stroked her wet channel deliciously. "I said your clitoris is swollen. I want to suck it."

Ohmygod. With one hand on his bulging bicep, Sasha's head gracefully fell to his muscular chest. Softly rocking her hips, she rode his thrusting finger. He caressed her back. When he groaned deep in his chest, she felt the vibration on her ear.

Pleasuring her, Salvador inserted a second finger inside her heat. As his fingers slid in and out of her core, she rocked her clitoris into the palm of his hand. Letting him finger fuck you in Leslie's bathroom
with a house full of people...you're so nasty! her conscience yelped.

Juices streaming from her core, Sasha's body tensed. Salvador scraped her G-spot with the tip of his finger, pulling her orgasm from her. He's pulling it from me. Pulling it. Yes. Yes.

Sasha groaned huskily. Her body shuddered. Her sex erupted into a powerful orgasm. Just as she parted her mouth to scream, Salvador slapped his free hand to her mouth.

Her sex beating hard, she bit the inside of his hand and kept cumming.

Knock. Knock. Knock. "Sasha, are you in there?" Richmond asked. "I need to speak with you about something very important."

Sasha gasped. Salvador withdrew his fingers from her drenched panties. Terrified, she didn't know what to do. She got on her tiptoes and whispered in Salvador's ear, "Hide in the shower."

Salvador shook his head no, and then whispered back in her ear, "Real men don't hide from their problems. Only pussies."

She whispered, "Well, I'll hide." Sasha quietly stepped inside the shower, pulled back the thick curtain. Feeling like a little kid who'd engaged in a bad act, her nerves jangled.

Salvador stated, "She's not in here, man."

"Oh. I need to speak with you, too. So I'll wait," Richmond stated.

Sasha became frightened. Oh my goodness, I hope Richmond didn't figure us out. She heard the bathroom door open. Salvador stated, "I just took a dump. Do you have any air freshener?"

"There should be some underneath the counter."

"I checked; there isn't any."

Richmond laughed. "I guess it's going to have to stay stank, then. The guys are about to go play a game of polo. Would you like to join us?"

"Sure," Salvador said, pulling the door closed behind him.

Her heart thudding in her chest, Sasha climbed out of the shower. Whew. That was close. As she looked in the mirror, she noticed the button on her jeans was still loose and her zipper was still lowered. Fixing her jeans, she felt good on the inside. Good because Salvador had said he cared for her.

Buzz. Her cell vibrated. She read it.

Salvador: The coast is clear. You can come out now.

Sasha: Thanks for letting me know.

Salvador: Meet me at the Balfour Hotel at seven this evening for dessert.

Sasha: I thought you were going to play polo?

Salvador: I'd much rather play with you instead, my beautiful Sasha.

Sasha: I'll be there at seven. Friend.

Salvador: Don't call me your friend anymore.

Sasha: Well, what would you like for me to call you?

Salvador: Your man.

He wants me to call him my man. Wow. Sasha felt gleeful. "I have no problem calling you my man, Salvador," Sasha said softly. Smiling, she flushed the toilet like she'd used it and went to rejoin her family.

Chapter Nineteen

SALVADOR PULLED OPEN THE SLIDING glass door at the
Balfour Hotel, stepped out onto the balcony on the eleventh floor,
and took in the scenery. Lavender hues colored the evening sky.
The reddish sun had lowered to the horizon. Salty ocean waves
brushed up against the beige sand.

Gripping the handrail, a warm breeze blew over Salvador. With
his mind on Sasha, he drew in a deep breath. He couldn't deny the
fact that Sasha had gotten under his skin. In the worse way possible
she'd crawled her way into his heart. In a matter of weeks, she'd
managed to do it quick, too. Which surprised the hell out of him.

Over and over, Salvador had heard his married friends state that
when the right woman for him came along, he'd know it. Well,
now he understood what they'd meant. Undoubtedly, Sasha is the
woman for me. A nonbeliever of love, the fact that he'd fallen for
her so fast just blew his mind. Literally.

Salty scents of the beach spiraled from the land into his nose.
Imagining his tongue suckling Sasha's dark nipple into his mouth,
he shuddered. Warmth infused his heart. Sasha Spaulding just may
be the woman to make him settle down and put a ring on her finger.
Still in disbelief that he could actually like a woman as much as he

did, Salvador stalked back inside the grand hotel suite. Standing inside the luxurious bedroom, he glanced at his watch. Sasha should be there any minute.

If his mother and Ben hadn't moved in with him, he would've taken Sasha back to his home. But considering he needed privacy in an upscale romantic setting, what better place for him to invite Sasha than the Balfour Hotel & Resort?

Knowing he'd made the right decision to be in a committed relationship with Sasha, Salvador's lips drew into a smile. He lifted the lighter and hurried to light the candles inside the bedroom, the bathroom, and the entrance area. Yep, he was going to make love to Sasha in every single room throughout this damn hotel suite. Pretty sure he wanted to date just one woman now, he flicked off the lights in the bedroom and closed the door behind him.

Hearing knocking on the door, Salvador crossed the room. When he pulled open the door, his breath caught in his throat. Whoa! Dressed in a fitted red dress with a low dip in the front, a clear gloss painted Sasha's succulent lips. Ringlet-like curls hung over her shoulders and down her back.

His eyes lingering over Sasha's curvy body, Salvador's gut did some wild trick he'd never felt before. "Wow. You look stunning. I like your hair curled like that."

Sasha's eyelashes shadowed her cheeks when she blinked. "Thanks. You, too," she said, entering.

When Sasha strutted past him, Salvador got a whiff of her sweetscented perfume. His shaft tickled. I'm getting in her panties. Tonight.
"Thanks."

Standing in the center of the room with a clutch purse in her hand, her eyes roamed over the large, spacious area. "This suite is huge. It must be the presidential suite."

"Yes, it is. The biggest one they have. Nothing but the best for you, beautiful."

Her eyes traveled to the candles on the end table, and then to the ones on the kitchen counter. "The candles are pretty. There's a lot of them."

"Considering I don't know a thing about how to be romantic, I hope what I have planned for you this evening turns out okay."

Her glossy lips hitched. "And what exactly do you have planned for me this evening?"

Salvador clenched the end of her clutch, slid it from her hands, placed it on the sofa. Gazing into her eyes, he cupped her hands. "I invited you here for dessert, remember?"

Strong chemistry sparked the air. Salvador's balls tingled. Within arm's reach of the woman he'd grown to care about, he swallowed. His shaft threatened to ache.

A sensual glow radiated in Sasha's eyes. "Dessert, huh? It's that all my man invited me here for?"

Salvador put a finger to the side of Sasha's face, trailed it down over her cheek. "Call me your man again."

She twined her arms around the back of his neck. "Are you sure you want to be my man?"

"I'm positive. I took an entire week to think about what I wanted from you, and what I was willing to give you." He paused.

Her eyes gleamed. "I need to hear in detail what it is that you want from me, and what you're willing to give."

"I'm not good with words when it comes to expressing my feelings, Sasha. The only way I know how to put it is like this…I want to be in a monogamous relationship with you. I want us to spend a lot of time together and see what could come from doing so."

"I want the same thing."

"Did you save room for dessert?"

"Yes."

"I had them deliver dessert earlier. It's out here," he said, walking onto the balcony. Two chairs and a table sat on the balcony.

On top of the table was a silver dessert plate. He lifted the lid off the plate, exposing the delicious looking treats. "I hope you like what I selected. There's chocolate-covered strawberries, chocolate cake drizzled in raspberry, and vanilla cheesecake."

Sasha eyed the desserts. "Everything looks so good. I don't know what to choose." He pulled the chair from beneath the table, and Sasha took a seat.

Sitting across from her, he pointed to the dessert in the center.

"Do you like chocolate?"

"I like anything chocolate."

Using his fork, he cut a small piece of chocolate cake and held it up to her mouth. Sasha giggled. "Are you thinking what I'm thinking?"

She nodded. "Probably so. Remember how you—" "Ate the caramel pecan pie off the fork at—" "SugarKanes," they said in unison, laughing.

Salvador chuckled. "I made you so nervous that day."

Nodding in agreement, Sasha wrapped her lips around the fork and ate the cake. "You really did."

Salvador popped the cork from the bottle of wine chilling in the bucket beside him and filled their glasses. She's perfect, he thought, holding up his wine glass. "I'd like to make a toast." Sasha lifted her glass in the air. "I'd like to toast to the beginning of our promising relationship. May it be everything we both hope for."

Their glasses clinked. "Cheers."

Sasha tilted the glass to her mouth and sipped.

"Oh, yeah...before I forget...I have something for you." He slid his hand into his pocket, pulled out a tiny purple box, and handed it to her.

Her eyes shone bright in the light of the evening sun. "Salvador.
What's this?"

"Open it up and see."

Sasha popped back the lid on the box. Her mouth slightly parting, her eyes lit up. Inside the box lay a pair of sparkling diamond earrings. Seemingly amazed, she glanced up at him. "Salvador, they're beautiful. This is so thoughtful of you. What did I do to deserve a beautiful present such as this?"

Salvador's eyes fell from her face to her neck. Then to her budding cleavage. I'm going to suckle on her breasts like a newborn
baby. He lifted his eyes to her pretty face again. "It's not what you did; it's what you're going to do."

Sasha's head titled. "What am I going to do for you?"

"You're going to marry me." Huskiness lingered in his tone.

"Marry you?!" Sasha laughed. She fanned a hand in the air. "Ah, stop teasing me."

You're the one for me, Sasha. You're going to be my wife. He slid his hand across the table to cup hers. "I'm not playing, Sasha. I'm serious." Dead-ass serious.

Sasha's smiling lips set into a straight line. "The beautiful scenery, the romantic mood, you're just caught up in the moment. You couldn't possibly know whether or not you want to marry me so soon."

"I think I know what I want, my pussycat. Only time will tell."

"I like when you call me pussycat." I can't wait to lick all over the pussycat between your thighs, he thought, stifling the low groan dying to spurt from his throat. Sasha removed her silver loops and replaced them with the diamonds. The jewelry glittered on her lobes. "How do they look on me?"

"They're beautiful."

She scooted her chair back. "I'm going to go take a look." She hurried to the bathroom.

Salvador stood and leaned against the railing on the balcony, gazing out at the ocean. Wait till the fellas found out he'd turned in his player's card. Quick as hell, at that. Before he even got in Sasha's panties. "A man knows when he's found the right woman," Richmond's comment came sailing into Salvador's mind. Yeah, but how was Richmond going to feel once he found out that woman was Sasha? His cousin? he wondered.

Sasha came and stood beside him. Leaning up against the rail, she clasped her hands. Turned to look up at him. "I love the way the earrings look on me. You have great taste."

Beholding Sasha's sensuous gaze, Salvador's heartbeat kicked up a notch. Turning his back to the railing, her cupped her arms and gestured for her to stand in front of him. His chest to her breasts, he draped one arm around her waist and retrieved a square piece of chocolate cake from the saucer on the table.

He placed the molten chocolate piece of cake to her luscious lips. Slowly parting her mouth, she took a tiny bite. Popping the remainder into his mouth, he noticed frosting smeared on her lips. "You have chocolate frosting on your mouth." He cupped the back of her head. "Let me get it off." He trailed the tip of his tongue around the outlines of her sweet-tasting lips.

Sasha's tongue protruded from her lips, licking his. Her lips forming a circle, a ragged breath expelled from her mouth. As he pressed his lips to hers, Sasha's long lashes lowered, shadowing her round cheeks.

Pressing his mouth into hers, Salvador closed his eyes. He sucked Sasha's tender lips into his mouth. Tongues curling, their kiss deepened. From the roof of Sasha's mouth to her teeth, his tongue explored it all.

As Sasha's saliva filled Salvador's mouth, heat coursed through his veins. His balls grew heavy. His shaft stretched long. The head throbbed. Need clawed at his gut. Keeping one hand to the back of her head, he opened his eyes. He stopped kissing her. "I want to make love to you, Sasha."

Nodding, her cinnamon pupils glowed. "I want that, too."

Cupping her hand, he led her back inside into the sitting area. He grasped the door knob to the bedroom and pushed open the door. Red rose petals were sprinkled on the bed. Glowing candles illuminated the room.

Her eyes traveling over the dim room, Sasha brought her fingers to her mouth. "It's beautiful in here."

Desperate to get deep inside her sex, his balls ached. "I wanted our first time to be special. Just like you."

Standing near the foot of the bed, Salvador reached behind Sasha's back, lowered the zipper on her dress, and removed it. He took a step back to get a good look at her. His eyes raked up and down her luscious body.

Her brown breasts perched from the black lace bra she wore. Pointed nipples pressed into the fabric. His gaze lingered further down her body, stopping at her curvy hips and the black sexy panties covering her sex. His eyes then traveled over her luscious thighs to her red painted toenails. Ready to devour her body like a starving wild animal, his gaze slowly traveled back up the length of her body to the glowing skin of her brown face. "You're beautiful, Sasha." And mine.

Swallowing, Salvador removed his shirt. Unbuttoning the buckle of his belt, he held her gaze. Sensed her nervousness. He took off his pants, kicked them to the side, and then removed his underwear. His erect column pointed straight out like thick pipe.

Sasha's gaze fell to his hard shaft, then shot back up to his face. Don't be scared, my precious little pussycat.

Salvador took a step forward. When the hard, bulging tip of his erection pressed into Sasha's navel, she gasped. He nudged the tip of his rod deeper into her navel, and she shuddered. Her chest heaved with every breath she took. He pushed her bra straps to the side, unhooked the back, let the material fall to the floor.

Seeing Sasha's dark areolas with erect nipples caused Salvador's shaft to jerk. Desire charged through him. His head falling, he scooped her left round mound up into his hand and squeezed. Brought the tender flesh up to his mouth. Using the tip of his tongue, he flicked at her hard, dark nipple. Heat smoldered in her eyes. A soft moan eased from her lips.

His mouth found its way to her right breast. His tongue flicked at that nipple, too. Sucking her areola, he fisted the length of his shaft. Motioning himself up and down, he put his mushroom head to the crotch of her panties, pushed at her entrance.

Sasha's hands softly held on to Salvador's shoulders. Cooing, she rocked her hips back and forth. As he rolled her panties down her legs, her breast fell from his mouth.

Now crouched down in front of her on his knees, Salvador touched Sasha's hot sex. She flinched. Using his finger, he spread her vaginal lips apart, and then drove his tongue up in her center. Palming the sides of his head, a husky groan spewed from Sasha's mouth.

Twirling his tongue inside her channel, he felt the head of his shaft leak with fluid. While sucking on her swollen clitoris, he inserted a finger inside her heat and pumped. Squishing sounds emanated in his ears. Turned him on. Drove him mad. Made him feel like his cock was about to shoot sperm.

Sasha wildly humped her drenched sex on his thrusting tongue. "Mmm...mmmm," she hummed. Juices streamed from her core onto his mouth. Her creamy essence coated his tongue. Tasted like a mixture of salty and sweet.

CIRCLING HER HIPS, SASHA LOLLED her head back. This feels. So. Oh. Good. Salvador gently tugged at her blood-filled clitoris with his sharp teeth. What happened next caught Sasha off guard.

Simply blew her mind.

Aroused out of her mind, Sasha's sex pounded ferociously. While gnawing ever so tenderly on her throbbing clitoris, Salvador thrust two fingers up inside her channel. His thrumming fingers and mouth worked her pulsating sex up into a wild frenzy. Yes. Yes. Yes. It was like a hot fire had brewed up in her core and was spreading rapidly, getting out of control.

Holding on to his head, an orgasm sat at her entrance, made it feel heavy. Like it was dying to burst and break free. Needing to climax, Sasha's knees buckled. Here. It. Comes.

Gazing down at Salvador, Sasha's legs shook violently. Her clit and G-spot erupted into powerful orgasms. "Ohmylivinggod!" As Salvador's mouth probed at her sex, their gazes linked. Juices squirted from her core, soaking his face.

The intense orgasm weakened Sasha's strength. Her limbs seemed to turn to gelatin. As her body dwindled in a downwards slope, Salvador caught her. His arms secured around her waist, he scooped her into his arms and placed her on the edge of the bed.

Out of breath, Sasha gazed down at the wild, erect beast between Salvador's legs. The circumference of his swollen head glistened with precum. She circled her fingers around his still tool, fisting him. Using her thumb, she smeared the precum down under the deep groves of his shaft. His hoarse grunt echoed inside the room.

Gripping him tight, Sasha pulled the skin up over Salvador's bulging head, and then mashed her hand down his length to his base. Rotating her wrist, she worked Salvador's thick rod in her grip. Pumping her hand, he groaned rough inside his throat.

Wanting to feel him inside her, Sasha lay back in the center of the bed and spread her legs wide. As he rounded the foot of the bed, his tanned shaft swung like his name was Tarzan. He quickly pulled a condom from his wallet on the nightstand, rolled it down his thick erection. Like white on rice, Salvador climbed on top of Sasha. "You nearly drowned my face with your sweet little cunt, pussycat." She could smell scents of her musky sex on his breath.

I squirted on his face. This is so embarrassing. Unable to compre- hend why she'd cum in such a huge amount, Sasha felt shamefaced.

"I've never had that happen before. This is so embarrassing."

Salvador reached between them, fisted his steely stem. "Don't be embarrassed." He put the hard knob to her soaked opening. "I enjoyed it so much and can't wait to make you squirt again."

When he inched a little bit of his shaft inside her, it stung. Sasha's body tensed. With his hands flat on the mattress at her sides, he slowly drew his manhood back out of her, then slowly slid back inside.

Salvador's big lance felt like hot wood between her walls as it stretched her to the max. Hissing, Sasha eased up on her elbows. "Hold up. Wait. Stop."

"What's wrong?"

Clenching her teeth, she squealed. "You're big. It hurts."

"Do you want me to stop?"

Sasha shook her head. "No. Just go slow. Very. Slow."

"You're tight like a virgin," Salvador recognized. It'd been many months since she'd had sex, Sasha thought as Salvador inched his slithering snake to the bottom of her deep sea. Feeling the pain subside, Sasha lay down on her back. "Oh, baby, night after night I've dreamed about this moment." He twirled his stem inside her, bestowing pleasure her way. "Making love to you is everything I've dreamed of, and more." Rocking his hips, he captured her mouth and kissed her erotically.

Their loud moans bounced off the walls.

Driving into her at a slow pace, Salvador's round spheres brushed Sasha's buttocks, heightening her arousal. His mouth left her lips to kiss her cheeks. Her nose. Her eyes, and then her neck.

Heat engulfed Sasha. Bucking on his tool, perspiration formed on her forehead. He rolled the tip of his tongue over her right nipple, and then her left nipple. Cupping the sides of her breasts, he mashed them together. Lapped at her nipples one at a time like they were dots of ice cream.

Sasha's coos filled her own ears. Salvador wasn't just making love to her body, he was making magic inside the bedroom. He was capturing her heart. Her soul. Her mind.

Tilting his head back, he released her breasts. Moaning, his face scrunched. His speed quickened. The mattress squeaked. The headboard banged into the wall.

Pounding her insides hard, his long shaft felt as if it were buried past her navel. Her breast jiggled. Her sex squished.

Thrusting in and out of her, he reached between them, put a heavy thumb to her clitoris, and pressed. Sasha squeaked out in pleasure. "Cum, Sasha. Cum."

Salvador withdrew his manhood. Fisting his length, he circled the head of his erection on her clitoris. Over and over and over again. Oh God. Oh God. Putting his head to her entrance, he slammed back into her. Sasha coughed. Corkscrewing her sex, he reached between them again and squeezed her clitoris.

"Oh. Oh. Oh!" Sasha cried out.

Pinching her clitoris, his stem jerked wildly inside her drenched channel. "Exijo vienes ahora!"

"Huh? Ooo. Ah. Huh?" An intense orgasm pooled at her entrance.

Salvador thrust harder. "I demand you cum! Como!" At the sound of Salvador's husky demand, Sasha's sex shattered with an orgasm.

"Ahhh! Salvador!" Squirting clear juices, she saw colorful fireworks right before her eyes. Thought she'd heard them pop loud, too.

SASHA'S SEX THROBBED VIOLENTLY ON Salvador's shaft. Her sex walls squirted his cock from the head to the base. She'd even wet his roasting balls. If the pretty woman didn't look so whipped, he'd ask her to suck his cock. But since she was obviously worn out, he'd save that for another time. Oh yeah, there would be more times after tonight, he thought, slanging his shaft up inside her core.

"Are you tired, my little pussycat?"

Sasha nodded. "Yes."

"Just relax, then. I'll take it from here." Salvador withdrew his stem from Sasha's center, flipped her to her stomach, then drove back inside her.

Making love to her from behind, Sasha's curly ringlets paraded down her back. Sweat glistened on her spine. Her round bubble butt perched, enticed him.

As his pelvis slapped against her perched rear, he loved the beautiful contrast of their skin tones. Loved the way his tanned cock looked as it glided between the glistening lips of her dark sex. Sliding in and out of her slick walls, he pressed the pads of his fingertips into her rear, kept his gaze on his throbbing erection.

Seeing his member mating with Sasha's womanhood pushed him over the edge. Drove him mad. Out of his got damn mind.

Clenching his teeth, he gripped her hips. This pussy is mine forever. "Este cono es mio para siempre." He said exactly what he'd been thinking out loud.

Sasha looked back at him over her shoulder. Eyes glowing, her lips pulled into a soft smile. "Tell me what you said?"

Circling his hips, he stroked her hard. Her breasts clapped, making slapping sounds in his ears. "I said...this pussy is mine forever."

"Yes, it is." Her eyes still clinging to his, she eased up on her elbows and knees, pushed her sex backwards on his length. Squeezing her eyes shut, she refaced forward. The inner muscles of her hot sex clenched his rod. Sucked him hard. Deeper.

Salvador jeered. Hot cum boiled inside his balls, traveled up his length, bubbled inside his round head.

Peering down at her sex twisting around his manhood, Salvador roared. "Ah, fuck!" Heavy loads of semen shot from his slit into the condom, filling it. He'd cum so hard, he felt a headache coming on. Salvador withdrew from her entrance to find his shaft bare. "Shit!"

"What's wrong?" Sasha asked, dropping to her side, then rolling to her back.

"The condom. I don't see the condom," he stated in a calm tone, but his heart was beating fiercely.

Sasha looked at his bare member and gasped. "Where is it?" she asked, her eyes combing over the bedspread.

"It must be inside you. Open your legs." Sasha spread her legs wide. Salvador inserted a finger up in her sex and pulled the cumfilled rubber from her entrance. When he squeezed the top open part of the latex together, cum leaked from the bottom tip. He cursed.

"What?"

He held the condom up to his face. "The condom broke."

Fear shot to Sasha's face as her eyes rounded. Her mouth flew open. "Oh, no." She slapped her forehead. "Please don't tell me this really happened."

Salvador scooted to the edge of the bed, tossed the condom in the trash can beside the nightstand, and then rested his back on the headboard. "Are you on birth control?"

"No. I haven't been on them for months now. Since I wasn't engaged in sex, I stopped taking them. Dear God. What if you got me pregnant?"

Salvador grabbed her in his arms, cradled her to his chest. "Sasha, if I got you pregnant, I honestly don't think it'd be that big of a deal," he said, his hand moving up and down her perspired back.

She lifted her head from his chest to look into his eyes. A wary look settled on her beautiful face. "How can you say that? Getting pregnant unexpectedly is a big deal. A very...big... deal."

"Yes, it is, but it doesn't have to be. If I got you pregnant, I'll stand by your side. I'll take care of you and the baby for the rest of my life. You have my word. So don't worry." Meaning every single word, Salvador pecked Sasha's forehead and felt like he could spend the rest of his life with her.

As Salvador lay in bed holding Sasha to his chest, she kissed his chin. Threw her leg over his thigh. Soft sounds of the ocean streamed through the open sliding glass door, bringing with it a gentle breeze. Romanticizing the mood.

Their limbs intertwined, Salvador stroked the back of Sasha's hair with his fingers. His eyes traveled beyond the open sliding glass door to the white moon perched in the sky. Relentless satisfaction filled Salvador. Sasha had made him feel things he'd never felt before. Things he couldn't explain. Things he never wanted to let go of. If you're pregnant with my child, I'm going to marry you right away, Sasha. No child of mine will be born a bastard.

Chapter Twenty

PATRONS PACKED THE INSIDE OF Smokehouse Bar, which was situated at t he end of a dead end road and surrounded by woods. Loud pop music blasted inside the bar. Strong scents of tobacco filled the air.

Sitting on a bar stool, Laurente focused his gaze on the stripper dancing on the stage. A big breasted stripper named   Champagne with blonde hair slid down the pole on the stage. Landing in a split, Champagne licked her red painted lips. Breasts spilling from her bikini top, Champagne pulled her knees into her big bosoms, threw her legs up in the air, and spread them into a wide V. She made her plump vaginal lips pulse against the crotch of her red thongs.

The men in the crowd roared!

One gentleman threw a twenty dollar bill on the stage. "Pop that pussy, Champagne!"

"Make it shake!" another gentleman yelled, tossing money at the talented stripper.

Enjoying the show while sitting at the bar, Laurente picked up his cigar from the ashtray and smoked it. Expelling a deep breath, thin white smoke spiraled from his lips. As much as he loved Zena, he wouldn't mind fucking that fine-ass stripper named Champagne.

Champagne's hips swayed as she made her way back into a standing position. Circling her hips, she unsnapped the front of her bikini top, let it fall to the floor. She cupped her nude breasts, mashed them together. Smiling, her gaze traveled towards the bar and landed on Laurente. Gyrating the air and still cupping her breasts, she winked at him, then licked her nipple.

The men bellowed.

Laurente's rod jerked inside his underwear. Got slightly hard. Sorry, Zena, but I'm sleeping with Champagne. Tonight. Inhaling the cigar, he drew in a deep breath, then blew the smoke from his lungs.

The side door of the bar swung open. In walked a thin woman with scraggly bangs. Wearing a black tight dress and a purse strapped over her shoulder, her eyes wandered around the club. Spotting the bar, her lips smiled.

Walking in and out of the tight crevices of the tables, she made her way towards the bar. Almost there, the woman tripped and fell flat on her face. Laurente jumped off the bar stool and hurried over to the fragile-looking woman.

"Are you okay?" he asked, grabbing her shoulders.

Pressing the flat palms of her hands into the floor, she stood and peered into Laurente's eyes. "Yes, I'm fine. Can't you tell?" Seemingly drunk, a horrible stench wafted from her mouth. Shoulders sagging, she stumbled to the bar and took a seat.

Laurente slid back on the stool beside the drunk woman. Dang. She arrived wasted.

The bartender walked up to the woman, placed a napkin on the bar. "Hey, Lucy. This is your third time in here this week. I thought you'd be tired of the place by now?"

Lucy stated, "Nah, I ain't tired of coming here. This place is a lot of fun. Probably the only fun spot here in Hilton Head. Give me my usual."

"One cucumber gin and tonic with blueberries, coming up," the waitress said, walking away.

Lucy turned around on the bar stool to look out at the stage. She then looked at Laurente. "Thanks for helping me when I busted my ass."

Lucy is filthy drunk. "You're welcome," Laurente remarked.

Lucy's eyes roamed over Laurente's clothing, and then his face.

"You the manager?"

Laurente shook his head. "No."

Lucy sucked her teeth. "Oh, that's too bad, because I was going to ask you for a job." Lady, the only thing you look like you know

how to do is drink. Lucy's eyes glanced over Laurente. "Wearing that fancy suit and sharp white dress shirt, you sure look important.

Like you own the place."

"I'm a business owner, but I don't own this place."

"Oh, yeah? What kind of business do you own?"

"I own several gift shops throughout South Carolina."

Lucy smiled. "I knew you were important. You married?"

"Yes. Happily married."

"If you're so happily married, what are you doing in a place like this? You and the wifey had a fight or something?" Very perceptive

woman. Cigar at the tips of his lips, Laurente's jaws flexed inward as he inhaled. Yep. He and Zena had had a fight. A horrible fight. She was still mad because of the way he'd struck Ivan a while back. Not only that, she was angry with him because he was hell

196

bent on teaching Ivan how to run his organization. On how to become one of the best entrepreneurial drug lords in the world. But even if they hadn't had a fight, he'd still be at the Smokehouse Bar tonight. He frequented his favorite locale at least once a week. The Smokehouse was a place he could come to if he wanted to relax. Or have fun. Or get some pussy without any strings attached. "If she's that heavy on your mind, maybe you should just go home." Lucy's voice cut into Laurente's thoughts about Zena.

"I will." Right after Champagne gives me a blow job.

"Here's your drink, Lucy." When the waitress lowered Lucy's drink on the napkin, she turned around, thanked her. Lucy lifted the glass to her lips and took a big gulp. "Ahh. This is nice and strong. Like I like it."

With his back to the bar, Laurente spotted Champagne coming his way. The closer the lovely Champagne got to him, the harder his balls got. When Champagne reached him, she slid in his lap, wrapped her arm around his neck, put her red lips to his ear, and whispered, "I seen the way you've been looking at me all night. You can't keep your eyes off me. Would you like a lap dance?"

Laurente's shaft jerked inside his pants. He shook his head. "No, thanks. What else do you offer?"

Champagne smiled. "Depending on how much you're willing to pay, I offer a lot. What is it that you want?"

Laurente hefted his drink to his lips, gulped it down, then lowered the empty glass back to the table. He slid off the bar. "Follow me."

Laurente pushed open the side door of the bar and walked outside. Humidity inundated the dark night air. Anxious to get the sucking of a lifetime, he stalked towards the woods where he'd parked his car.

"Where are we going?" Champagne asked, her heels clicking against the pavement.

"To my car."

"You parked in the woods?"

"Yeah." Reaching his car, Laurente pulled his keys from his pocket, unlocked his vehicle. He opened the rear door behind the driver's seat, gestured for Champagne to go inside first. Climbing in behind her, he shut the door.

Champagne's round eyes lowered to his zipper, then back up to his face. "So, you never answered my question."

"What was your question?"

"What do you want me to do to you?"

Looking into her eyes, Laurente zipped down his slacks, pulled out his heavy erection. "Suck my dick."

Champagne held out her hand. "I'm not cheap. I charge one hundred dollars to do something like that."

Laurente reached into his pocket, pulled out some cash, and slapped a crisp one hundred dollar bill into Champagne's open hand. She stuck the money into her bra, grabbed his tool at the base, and then dropped her hot mouth down on him. Fuck yeah. Flicking her tongue over the top of his tip, Champagne hummed over his shaft like it was the best thing she'd ever tasted.

Laurente groaned. Thrusting in and out of Champagne's mouth, he palmed the back of her head with both of his hands, mashed her face downward. Saliva coated his rod. Her chin grazed his balls.

"Suck this cock. Suck it, damnit. Suck the cum out of me." Champagne clenched him with both of her hands, jerked him wildly. Sucked him ferociously. Thick white cum shot from his cock into her sucking mouth, and she drank it like a tall glass of white, creamy milk. "Whew. That was good."

Champagne licked her sticky lips. "Is there anything else you need?"

"Nope. Thanks, baby." He patted her back.

"You're welcome. Well, I got to get back to work. Goodnight." Champagne hurried out of the car and left.

Laurente pushed open the rear door of the car and climbed into the front seat behind the steering wheel. His balls feeling as light as a feather now, he cranked the engine and pulled the car from out of the woods onto the pavement behind a yellow cab.

The woman named Lucy, whom he'd met a little while ago, burst from the club door looking like a wild woman. "She's really tore up now." With strands of her hair going every which way, Lucy staggered towards the cab. Right when her hand touched the door, she slipped and fell, landing on her back.

Not again. Laurente threw the gear in park, hopped out of the car, and hastened to Lucy. Looking up at him with bloodshot eyes, she looked confused. Laurente lifted Lucy into his arms.

Lucy half-smiled. "Oh. Hey, you." She patted the top of his head. "You rescued me again." She laughed. Her breath smelled sour.

Laurente opened the back cab door and placed her inside. "Get home safe, lady." He slammed the car door.

As the cab began leaving the parking lot, the ringing of a cell phone captured Laurente's attention. His gaze fell to the ground to find a phone lying on the gravel. Oh, it must be Lucy's. He reached down, picked up the phone, and brought it to his eyes.

Spying the Caller ID and holding the buzzing cell in his hand, shock stormed through Laurente. A picture of Lucy hugging Ben Haroldson appeared on Lucy's screen. Ben? Lucy knows Ben?

Laurente flung open his car door, hopped inside, and followed the cab. The cab exited the wooded area, made a right, and then drove along an overpass. After making a left, fifteen minutes later the cab rolled up to a house on the ocean and parked alongside the road.

Keeping a safe distance behind the cab, Laurente cut the car lights and then brought the car to a complete stop further down the road. Hoping Lucy had led him to Ben, adrenaline coursed through Laurente's veins.

Lucy exited the rear of the cab and began stumbling up the long driveway. The cab driver pulled off. Suddenly, the door to the guest house cracked open and out walked Ben Haroldson. Look at this here. The pissy drunk woman led me to Ben.

Laurente's anger for Ben became a scalding fury. "I finally found you, Ben." Laurente reached into his glove compartment, pulled out his gun, and rolled down the passenger side window.

Her legs wobbling as she walked up the driveway, Lucy waved at Ben and fell face forward. Ben's mouth dropped. Leaving the guest door open, he scurried up to Lucy and helped pull her to her feet. Lucy draped her arm around Ben's shoulders as he encircled his arm around Lucy's waist and escorted her up the driveway.

Remembering how Ben had failed to burn down Salvador's building after he'd already paid him to destroy it, anger coursed through Laurente's veins. He seethed with mounting rage. Keeping his headlights off, he cranked the engine, drove towards the house.

"A deal is a deal," Laurente mumbled. Slowing his car when he reached the driveway, Laurente put his finger on the gun's trigger, pointed his loaded weapon at Ben's back, and fired. Pow!

Ben dropped to his knees.

Lucy plummeted to the ground, landing flat on her face.

Laurente flooded the gas. The tires on his car screeched. Speeding down the street, he made a sharp left at the corner. His heart thudding, a wicked smile came to his face. Ben Haroldson is finally dead, Laurente thought, thinking the night couldn't have ended better.

Chapter Twenty-One

QUIET STILLNESS LOOMED INSIDE THE luxurious hotel suite where Salvador and Sasha lay sound asleep on the king -sized bed. Glows of the moon slipped through the open sliding glass door, forming a bright circle over their naked bodies. With her spine cocooned to his chest, Sasha felt something hard grow against her buttocks. Stirring, her eyes slowly opened.

Staring at the full moon, her mind revisited what'd happened earlier this evening . The condom had burst. What if she was pregnant? Placing a hand on the lower part of her belly, she felt Salvador's shaft elongate against her butt cheeks, like a hard cucumber. Becoming aroused, a dull ached formed in her center. Her nipples got pointy. She curled into the curve of his body.

Salvador's muscular chest shifted against her back. Using his finger, he traced a line down her spine, over the crack of her butt. His fingers floundered at her labia, making it flutter. Her eyes still on the moon, her heartbeat quickened. Her breathing intensified.

Spreading her labia lips apart, he slipped the head of his erection inside her channel and stroked. "Are you awake?"

Sasha enjoyed the feel of the sleek caress of his strokes. Intense pleasure throbbed at her entrance. Oh God, that feels so good. "Yes," she hissed. "You need to put on a condom."

Groaning, the hard tip of his circular head caressed her silky entrance. He pushed the hair from her nape, kissed her neck. "Why do I need a condom? You're already pregnant," he said, continuing to stroke her.

Just because the condom broke, doesn't mean I'm pregnant. "We don't know that for sure."

Keeping just the head inside her, twirling it, Salvador squeezed Sasha's right breast. Her mouth fell open. "You may not know for sure. But I know for sure that you're pregnant."

Unable to stop their risky lovemaking session, Sasha's clitoris throbbed. She bit her bottom lip. "What makes you think you know for sure that I'm pregnant?"

He flicked his finger over her nipple. "Because when I ejaculated, I saw fireworks. And I ain't never saw no damn fireworks while making love before. Something other than sex occurred between us. I think we created life."

"We can't risk me," Sasha squeezed his shaft with her sex, "getting pregnant," she roughly rocked her hips forward. Salvador's erection slipped out of her channel.

Salvador groaned. He cursed. "It felt good as hell to have my bare cock inside your wet pussy."

Sasha rolled to her side to face him. She cupped his jaw. Fire flickered his blue irises. "I'd love to make love to you without using a condom, but it's too risky. Maybe I'll think about it after I get on birth control pills."

"This is torture, Sasha." He reached between them, fisted his stem, slapped it between her perspired thighs. Rocking his hips, his tool slid back and forth against the outside of her sex, between her inner thighs. Liquid heat flooded her veins. "Let me stick just the head in for a few seconds."

Struggling to resist him, Sasha lifted her top thigh, beckoned him to slide back inside her opening. Salvador put the tip of his erection at her core. Trailing the tip of his tongue over the edges of her lips, he slowly pushed further into her. Mmmm.

Buzz. Buzz. Buzz. His cell phone vibrated on the nightstand. After a few seconds passed, it stopped ringing, only to start up again. Buzz. Buzz. Buzz.

"Aren't you going to answer your cell?" Sasha asked, enjoying the feel of his head nudging against her G-spot.

"No." He groaned huskily. "I want to stick my whole entire dick inside you, pussycat." His voice was so throaty.

Circling her sex on his throbbing head, Sasha gazed into his eyes. Mmm. Slick fluid filled her channel. "I think you should answer your phone. What if it's an emergency? Or your mother calling you?"

The cell stopped ringing.

"I'm glad the phone stopped ringing, so I can concentrate on this," he uttered, stroking her.

On the verge of exploding, warning thoughts entered Sasha's mind. Stop having sex with him. Make him put on a condom. He's
going to cum inside you, fool. Gently bucking her sex on the tip of his rod, Sasha's toes curled. Her sex pulsed. Her chest heaved up and down.

Salvador exclaimed, "Jesus Christ, I don't want to stop making sweet love to you." His husky moans filled her ears. But I better, before I cum." When Salvador attempted to withdraw his tool from her channel, Sasha's drenched walls clenched his erection, held him hostage.

"Oh, Salvador." Her G-spot exploded around the circumference of his penetrating head.

"Fuck, Sasha!" Salvador clenched his length, snatched it out of her. His eyes stretched wide. Sasha gazed downward at his thick erection. Cum flew from his slit and shot onto her stomach. Disbelief was on his face. "Do you realize what you almost did?"

Shrugging, Sasha giggled. "Who cares? According to you, I'm already pregnant, remember?"

Salvador chuckled. "Touché."

I've lost my damn mind, Sasha thought, feeling the hard beats of her sex subsiding.

Buzz. Buzz. Buzz. "Who keeps calling me this time of morning?" Salvador rolled to his side and hefted his phone from the nightstand. "It's Ben." He placed the phone to his ear. "Yes, Ben." Silence. A frown. "Calm down, Ben. My mother? She what?" Salvador's face contorted. "She's been shot?!" Water sprung into Salvador's eyes. Sasha's heart flopped. "What hospital is she in? I'm on my way!" Salvador flung his feet to the floor and leapt out of bed. "We gotta go." He threw on his shirt.

Terrified, Sasha bolted from the bed. "What's wrong?"

He yanked his jeans up over his hips. "My mother's been shot."

"Shot?! Oh my God. What happened?"

"I don't know." He buttoned his jeans. "Just hurry up and get dressed."

Sasha hurried to put on her clothing. Grabbing her clutch off the sofa, she ran out the door behind Salvador.

SALVADOR SPED HIS SUV UP to the hospital lot, parked in a vacant space, and then hopped out. Jogging towards the emergency entrance, his heart pounded harsh in his chest. Breathing raggedly, he hastened up to the circulation desk and let the nurse sitting behind the desk know what he was there for.

The nurse pointed at the elevator. Moments later, Salvador and Sasha stepped off the elevator, walked down the hallway, and hurried inside the intensive care unit, where Lucy lay unconscious.

Salvador took one look at his mother lying in the hospital bed and his heart grappled. Standing beside her hospital bed, his eyes roamed over her body. Tubes and crap ran from her nose and arms.

"Oh no, Madre," he choked on his words. "Que paso?"

Sniffing, Sasha caressed Salvador's back. "She'll be fine, Salvador."

Despair flooded throughout him. "Her skin is so white. She looks dead."

"But she's not. Lucy is going to come out of this like a champion.
We have to pray to God and believe that He will help save her life."

Because of Lucy's dependency on alcohol, Salvador had often envisioned something bad happening to his mother. But he'd never imagined her getting shot. A horrible car accident...yes...but not shot. Salvador wanted answers, and he wanted them now. And the one person who could give them to him wasn't anywhere to be found. Where are you, Ben?

The doctor stalked into the room and walked up to Salvador. "Are you her son?"

Heartbroken, Salvador nodded. "Yes."

"Hi. I'm Dr. Joseph Vacanti." They shook hands. "Can we step outside the room and talk, please?"

Swallowing, Salvador nodded. "I want you to come with me, Sasha." Salvador and Sasha followed Dr. Vacanti out into the hallway. The expression on Dr. Vacanti's face worried Salvador.

"Your mother is in critical condition. She was shot in the side of her back. The bullet exited through her front side. She lost a lot of blood. She had a lot of alcohol in her system."

Jesus, help me. "Is she going to live?"

Dr. Vacanti continued. "Only God knows whether or not she will pull through this. Right now her condition is touch and go, and it can go either way. She's very weak. If you believe in prayer, now will be a good time do so. Do you have any questions for me?"

"Yes. Did my mother come here with someone?"

The doctor confirmed, "She was brought here by ambulance, and she was alone."

"Thanks, Doctor."

"You're welcome. If you need me, just have one of the nurses page me." Dr. Vacanti walked away.

Salvador had never cried a day in his life since he'd become a teenager, and now he felt like he was about to. He sniffed. He'd bet any amount of money that the bullet his mother had received had been meant for Ben.

Standing to the side of his mother's room, he pulled out his cell phone and dialed Ben. Ben answered on the first ring. "How's Lucy?"

Salvador ached with inner pain. "Not good. What happened to my mother, Ben?"

Ben's sigh came through the phone. "Earlier this evening, she said she was going out to have some fun. She didn't say where to, though. She got all dressed up and just left. Some hours later, she returned home in a cab. Noticing her staggering up the driveway, I figured, well, I thought she may be drunk, so I went to help her. Halfway up the driveway, a car drove by and opened fire. That bullet wasn't meant for your mother, Salvador. It was meant for me. I should be lying in the hospital fighting for my life, not

Lucy." A raw and primitive grief overwhelmed Salvador as he said, "Ben, I need for you to tell me who's trying to kill you. Especially now that they've shot my mother."

"Trust me, the kind of man I'm dealing with will not hurt your mother or you. Lucy got shot by accident. I'm the person he wants. And he won't stop until he kills me."

Salvador spoke through clenched teeth, "Damn you, Ben. Tell me who's after you. You owe me."

"I do owe you. But I can't tell you. If he finds out you know about him, he'll finish the job on your mother. And then he'll come after you and Sasha, and your whole entire family could end up in a bloody war. I'm not going to be responsible for any more mishaps than I already am. If your mother dies, it'll kill me, Salvador. I wouldn't be able to handle it. Kiss your mother for me, and please tell her I'm sorry. Thanks for the hospitality. Even more, thanks for the friendship. I'm gon' be on my way now." Click. The line went dead.

"Ben...? Ben...?" Disappointment sliced Salvador's heart in half.

Sasha placed her hand on Salvador's shoulder. "What did Ben say?"

"Nothing," Salvador lied, not wanting Sasha to know any more than necessary. "Come, I'm going to take you home."

Disappointment came into her eyes. "But I don't want to go home. I want to stay with you."

"Please don't take this the wrong way, but I need to be alone for a while."

Sasha nodded. "I understand."

"Thanks for being so understanding." Leaving Sasha standing outside the door, Salvador reentered his mother's hospital room and stalked up to her bed. Observing Lucy's pale white face, sorrow weighed him down. "I'm going to find out who did this to you, Mother, and when I do, they'll pay with their life for hurting you." He leaned over, kissed Lucy's cheek, and went and got Sasha so he could take her home.

Thirty minutes later, Salvador pulled up alongside his home and parked on the side of the road. Cop cars and grey sedans were parked alongside the road. Police officers combed the lawn area. Others examined the bloody driveway.

Salvador exited the SUV and stalked up the driveway towards the police officers. Blood saturated the concrete. Seeing his mother's blood soaking up the concrete, his heart shattered. The nerve of some sonofabitch to come to my home and open fire. Nobody shoots my mother and gets away with it. No damn body.

An African-American man wearing a pair of black pants and a blue collared shirt walked up to him. "Salvador Casillas, right?"

"Yes, sir."

"I'm Detective Derrick Johnson. Although I wish the circumstances were different, it's nice meeting you."

Salvador put his hands on his hips and glanced around his home. Someone had invaded his damn privacy. Had treated his home like he was some chump. "Do you have any idea who did this?"

Detective Derrick Johnson shook his head. "No, sir. Do you?"

"Not a clue."

"Does your mother have any enemies that you know of?"

"No." My mother was an innocent bystander. After the police finished questioning Salvador and left, he went inside and grabbed his gun from the top drawer of his nightstand. Making sure his Glock was loaded with ammunition, he went to go find the one person who could give him answers—Ben.

Thank God he'd been wise enough to install the GPS tracker on Ben's cell phone, Salvador thought, sitting inside his SUV behind the steering wheel. Angry, he tapped the GPS app on his cell, and it gave him Ben's exact location. Marshland Road? There wasn't anything but old buildings and abandoned warehouses in that area.

Ben, you're going to tell me who wants you dead, and why. If you don't, I'm going to kick your old ass my damn self. Temper flaring, Salvador cranked the engine and headed for Marshland Road to go confront Ben.

Chapter Twenty-Two

BATS FLEW OVER THE TALL   oaks. Owls hooted. Beaten and broken, Ben walked down Marshland Road with his head dangling between his shoulders. He'd screwed up royally. Guilt ate at his conscience like flesh-eating bacteria.

Tired of running for his life, Ben paused in his tracks and stood beneath the tall tree. Heartbeat palpitating wildly, he glared at the abandoned warehouse where Laurente and his crew held their meetings and partook in criminal activities. A pulsing knot balled in his gut. My time has come to die

Anxiety spurted through Ben. He'd fought the war in Vietnam and had survived it. But the mess he was fighting now with a vicious drug lord, Laurente, scared him more. Dying for his country was one thing, but dying because he'd cost Lucy her life and didn't have the courage to finish a felony was another.

The bullet that had struck Lucy was meant for me,   Ben thought, his chest tightening. Sick to his damn stomach, he imagined how blood had poured from Lucy's back while she lay on the ground, struggling to breathe. Lucy had lost so much blood. There was no way she'd make it. If it hadn't been for him, Lucy wouldn't be in the hospital fighting for her life. And now that Laurente knew he'd been living with Salvador, what if he tried to harm his only friend? What if once Laurente found out he'd shot the wrong person, he went and hurt his daughter, or his grandson? Poor Salvador, his mother may be dead because of him.

Salvador had done so much for him. Had given him a home. Had provided him with food. But more than anything, Salvador had offered him a friendship he'd never forget. That being said, it was his duty to give his life up to ensure no more harm would come to Salvador, or his daughter Alyssa, or his grandson Corey.

Feeling discouraged and nowhere ready to die, Ben walked across the dry ground. Sticks crunched beneath his shoes. He rounded the rear of the warehouse to find cars he recognized parked in the back. When he yanked on the door of the BMW, the alarm resounded in the air, just as he'd wanted.

The back door of the warehouse flung open. Laurente and his men came running out with their weapons drawn.

Ben's hands flung up in the air. Bile scratched the back of his throat. His stomach churned.

"Hold your fire," Laurente ordered. The men lowered their guns to their sides. Confusion shone in Laurente's eyes. He frowned. "I was for sure I killed you."

Ben swallowed in fear. "You shot the wrong person."

Laurente rolled his eyes. An expletive tore from his mouth. "Don't tell me I shot that drunk-ass bimbo, Lucy?"

How did Laurente know Lucy? Had she been the one to lure Laurente to Salvador's house? "Yes. You shot my friend. You killed her."

Laurente shrugged. "And? The drunken slut didn't look like she was worth much anyway. I gotta give you credit, you're pretty brave to have come here. Go get the gasoline," he ordered one of his henchmen.

212

MARRYING MR. WRONG
SABRINA SIMS MCAFEE

"You gave your word that if I came to you at my own free will, you wouldn't hurt my family," Ben reminded Laurente.

With a scar running down his face, evil dulled Laurente's eye, including the blue glass one. "You have my word. Does that include Salvador…the little pussy who you've been staying with?" Ben felt like his chest was about to burst wide open with fear. "Yes. Salvador is my family." My only friend.

"As long as the little pussy Salvador minds his business, I won't bother him." The henchman returned with the gasoline. "Ivan!" Laurente shouted.

A young teenager appeared in the doorway of the warehouse. "Yes, Father?"

"Come here, my son." Sliding his hands in his pockets, Ivan walked outside. Laurente jutted his chin at Ben. "Dump the gasoline on this worthless piece of shit standing here."

Ivan's eyes grew wide. "But he's just an old man, Father."

Laurente snapped, "I don't give a shit, my son. He didn't do what he promised, so he must die." Tears filled Ivan's eyes. "Stop the fucking crying." He slapped the back of Ivan's head. "Hop to it. This will make a man out of you. Prepare you to run my business someday."

One of Laurente's henchman handed Ivan the red gasoline container. Crying, Ivan began tossing the gasoline on Ben. "Please don't make me watch him burn, Father. Please." Ivan dropped the gasoline container to the ground. "He's an old man."

Laurente clutched his son's shoulders and glared into his eyes. "I promise you, once you see somebody die in this nature, it won't be as hard the next time. It'll get easier and easier."

Gasoline saturated Ben's clothing. The strong, potent fluid burned his nostrils. Terrified, Ben shook violently. Oh, Claira. I'm about to join you. "Heavenly Father, forgive me for all my sins." Laurente struck a match, held it up in the air. An evil smile appeared on his face. Trembling uncontrollably, bile rushed to the top of Ben's throat. "Our Father. Which art in heaven. Hollowed be thy name—"

Laurente's nasty chuckles spurted from his twisted lips. "There's no use in praying to God, Ben. He's not real." Laurente tossed the match.

Poof! Flames ignited! Ben's body caught on fire. Engulfed in orange, hot flames. Screaming, Ben's arms flailed, his feet stomped. Running, he dropped to the ground and rolled.

Chapter Twenty-Three

SALVADOR LISTENED TO THE GPS tracker direct him to Ben's location. Clenching the steering wheel, he made a sharp left and turned onto Marshland Drive. Grey moss spiraled from huge oaks on either side of the dark road. An abandoned warehouse came into view.

"You have reached your destination," the GPS tracker announced. Slowing his car a few feet away from the warehouse, Salvador lifted his cell from the console and spied the GPS tracker. According to the red circle on the tracker, Ben was at this location. At least the cell phone he'd given him was.

Loud sounds of gunning engines startled Salvador. His eyes shot to rear of the warehouse. Three cars shot from behind the building, sped across the grass, and then zoomed away in the opposite direction.

An eerie feeling crept up inside Salvador. He grabbed his gun from the passenger seat, tucked it between his spine and waistband. Just as his hand grasped the door handle, a human figure engulfed in orange flames came running and screaming from behind the warehouse. The man dropped to the ground and rolled.

Panic shot through Salvador. "Ben!" He hopped out of his SUV, bolted to the rear, and grabbed an oversized blanket. His heart thumping madly, he scurried towards Ben.

Rolling on the grass, Ben hollered. His burning arms flailed. His firelit legs kicked. "Ahhh! Ahhh!"

Salvador threw the blanket over Ben's burning body and smothered the flames. Huddling over Ben, he wrapped his hot body up in the blanket. Smoke shot into Salvador's open mouth. Burned his lungs. His heart beating ninety miles per hour, Salvador hefted Ben in his arms. Running for his SUV, burnt flesh attacked his nostrils. "Oh God, Ben! Oh God, Ben!" Salvador placed Ben's body in the rear of the SUV, slammed the latch, and went and hopped in behind the driver's seat. Adrenaline pumping, he mashed on the gas and rushed for the hospital.

BEN'S SMOKED BODY ROCKED INSIDE the blanket in the rear of the SUV. His head peeping from the top of the blanket, pain immersed him. His charred skin burned. His lungs contracted and expanded.

Struggling to breathe, an image of his dead wife Claira burst into thin air. With wings attached to her back, silky strands of gray hair hung over Claira's shoulders. "Claira," Ben mumbled, wondering if he was seeing things, or dying.

"I'm here for you, Ben," Claira said, extending her hand towards him.

Seeing the only woman he'd ever loved, Ben's lips trembled. "Oh, Claira. I miss you so much." She came to get me. She really came.

A white glow encircled Claira's figure. Claira said softly, "Your work on Earth is complete, Ben. It's time for you to come home. Heaven's waiting on you. Come home, Ben. Come home." Still holding out her hand, Claira's lips drew into the prettiest smile ever, accentuating her pink, rosy cheeks.

Ben clenched the top of the blanket, spread it open. Lifting his arm in the air, he smiled. When his hand connected with Claira's,

all his pain dissipated.

Claira said, "Get ready, Ben…you're about to fly." Smiling, she tugged Ben's hand. Ben's spirit lifted from his charred flesh and ascended into heaven with his loving wife, Claira.

Flying above the twinkling stars, Ben threw his arms about Claira's shoulders. "Oh, Claira. We're finally together again."

"Oh, Ben, you're going to love heaven," Claira said, releasing Ben.

Ben grabbed Claira's hand, and they began walking along the sky towards heaven. "How long will it take before I get to heaven?"

Claira's eyes twinkled. "Not long."

"Oh, wait." Ben stopped in his tracks. Standing amidst the stars, his gaze fell downward to the Earth. He could see Salvador speeding up to the hospital in his SUV. Salvador jumped out of his SUV, hefted his corpse into his arms. "Goodbye, Salvador." Ben kissed the palm of his hand and blew. Rough winds spiraled from Ben's lips and began descending downward towards Earth.

STANDING AT THE REAR OF his SUV, holding Ben in his arms, Salvador heard Ben say, "Goodbye, Salvador." Out of nowhere, a strong force of wind descended down on Salvador and shook him. His knees buckled. Whoa!

Cradling Ben's body to his chest, Salvador cantered through the hospital's emergency entrance. "Help! Help!" Doctors and nurses bustled up to Salvador. "Somebody set him on fire!"

"We'll take it from here." Two men wearing white medical coats took Ben from Salvador's arms, placed him on a gurney, and then wheeled him through a set of double doors.

Feeling as if he were about to vomit, he plopped down in the chair. His fingers stung. He turned his hands over to find them red with blisters and burned lightly. Gut wrenching, Salvador dropped his face in his aching hands. Who had done this to Ben? Who, dammit, who? He'd bet it was the same person who'd shot his mama. Wait till he found out who did this shit. Just wait.

"Excuse me, sir," a male's voice said.

Salvador lifted his head to find a doctor towering over him. Deep regret filled the doctor's eyes. Swallowing, Salvador stood. Staring at the doctor's hurtful glare, he shook his head. "Please, Doctor. No. No."

"I'm sorry, sir. The man you brought in died."

"Okay. Okay." Tears sprang into Salvador's eyes. Standing in the center of the emergency room, Salvador felt like he was about to lose his damn mind. Spotting the restroom, he hurried inside. Standing at the sink, he turned on the faucet. Trying to calm his nerves, he repeatedly doused his face with water. A sudden outburst tore from his mouth, and he quickly swallowed it. When I find the person who did this, I'm going to step on his throat, crush his Adam's apple, and then break his damn neck in half.

Determined to hold back his feelings, Salvador flung open the door and stalked outside into the dark, dreary night.

Chapter Twenty-Four

FIVE DAYS LATER, WHITE SHEETS   of rain poured from the afternoon sky, drenching the grounds at the Low Country Memorial Cemetery. Heartbroken over Ben's death, Salvador stood beneath the green tent beside B   en's grandson, Corey, and listened intently to Sasha as she sang "Amazing Grace". Standing beside the casket and wearing a black dress, the sweet melody flowed from Sasha's lungs.

Sasha sang, "Amazing grace. How sweet the sound. That saved a wretch like m e. I once was lost, but now I'm found. Was blind, but now I see…"

I once was blind, but now I see, too. See how important Sasha is to me. See how much I love her. Watching Sasha's lips move so delicately, deep love for her filled Salvador's heart. I'm in love.

Although he hadn't shared his feelings with Sasha yet, Salvador did indeed love her. He'd come to the realization the day after Ben had died. And as soon as the time was right, he was going to let Sasha know how he felt. Hopefully, she'd feel the s ame way about him, too.

After Sasha finished singing, she came to stand beside him. As the pastor led them into prayer, he grasped her hand, squeezed it tight. Bowing his head, Corey's heartfelt weeps entered Salvador's ears. Poor fella. How could someone kill an old man? Ben had a family that loved him. People that cared deeply for him. People like

me. People like my mother.

Speaking of his mother, she was getting released from the hospital today. Thank God, she'd gotten better. And had a full recovery. Now that she was better, Lucy had promised him she wouldn't drink anymore and that she'd go live at an alcohol rehabilitation treatment facility, where she could get around the clock help. Too bad it took Ben's death to make her see how bad off she was.

"Amen," the pastor stated.

"Amen." Salvador lifted his head. He turned to Corey, patted his shoulder. "Corey, I know this is hard. Although no one can replace your grandfather, I'd like to at least try to pick up where he left off. Maybe sometime I can take you fishing. Or to play football at the park. Or just do whatever you like."

Corey sniffed. "Thanks, Coach Salvador."

Ben's daughter, Alyssa, gave Salvador a bland smile. "Thanks, Salvador. Thanks for taking my father into your home and providing care for him. I appreciate everything you did for him."

"The pleasure was all mine, Alyssa. Ben helped me to gain a new perspective on life. And I'm eternally grateful for him and what he brought into my life," he said, remembering how he'd clearly heard Ben tell him goodbye right before he'd died. Then a strong force of wind had hit him like a tornado. Had almost knocked him over while holding Ben in his arms in front of the hospital's emergency entrance. Never a believer in angels before, he bet Ben was now an angel. He and Claira were probably in heaven, having a good time together. Salvador managed to smile internally.

Sasha said, "Ben brought a lot to my life, too. I loved reading

him the letters from your mother."

A single tear streamed down Alyssa's face. "Thanks for reading him the letters, Sasha. Maybe after time passes, I'll someday read them for myself."

"You're welcome. Call me if you ever need anything. Even it's a listening ear, I'm here for you and Corey." Sasha gave Alyssa a hug, then released her.

"Take care, Alyssa." Salvador nodded, turned to walk away.

Stepping from beneath the green tent, Salvador let his umbrella up over Sasha's head, and then handed it to her. "Thanks. You're getting soaked, Salvador. Why don't you get up under the umbrella with me?"

"I'm good." Rain pelted Salvador's scalp, drenched his black suit. Crossing the grass, water squished beneath his shoes. In deep thought, grief and joy intermixed inside him. He was grieving because of what'd happened to Ben, but he was joyful because of how bright his future with Sasha looked.

Reaching his white Porsche, he pulled open the driver's side door for Sasha. Sasha stated, "Oh, by the way…I'm getting a new car at the end of the week, so I'll finally be giving you your car back."

"Why get a new car when you can just have this one? I'll pay it off. Put the title in your name and everything."

Standing behind the door, Sasha shook her head. "Thanks, but I could never accept a gift such as a car like this from you. That's asking way too much." She smiled. "Besides, knowing you, if you gave me this car, you'll probably think you own me."

"I already do own you, Sasha. You're mine. All. Mine." He pecked her lips. "I'll call you later." Salvador turned and walked away. The rain steadily pouring down over him, he slid behind the steering wheel of his SUV, cranked the engine, then pulled out of the cemetery.

One hand on the steering wheel, he picked up his cell from the console and dialed.

"Hello?" Richmond answered.

"Hey, man. Are you busy?" Salvador asked, anxious to speak with Richmond.

"Nope," Richmond responded.

"Good. I need to speak with you. Can I drop by your home for a few minutes?"

"Sure."

"I'm on my way."

Driving down the street, Salvador made up in his mind that he would live life to the fullest from this day forth. And he wouldn't take things for granted. Life was too short not to live every day like it could be your last.

He flicked on the radio. Sugar, by Maroon 5, came on. Bopping his head to the music, Salvador thought of how Sasha was sweet like sugar. And how he needed some permanent sweetness in his life.

Short minutes later, Salvador stood on Richmond's porch at his oceanfront home, ringing his doorbell. Sliding his hands in his pockets, he waited. Contemplated what he was going to say to Richmond. Either way, I'm doing it.

The door cracked open. Richmond smiled. "Hey, man," Richmond said, slapping hands with Salvador. "You're wet as hell. Come on in."

"Yeah, I'm soaked." Salvador stepped over the threshold. "Where are Kayla and the kids?" Salvador asked, following Richmond into his den.

"Man...the kids and she went shopping with my mom. I think they're going out to eat afterwards. How did the funeral go?"

Salvador already missed his friend Ben. "Ben had a nice homegoing."

"So what's up? Why you wanted to see me?"

SABRINA SIMS MCAFEE

Salvador took a deep breath. "You may want to sit for this." "Okay. You're making me nervous." Richmond sat on the sofa. Thinking about how he was going to break the news to Richmond, Salvador sat on the couch across from his pal. Clasping his hands together, he drew in a deep breath. "There's something I want to talk to you about."

"This sounds serious as hell."

"It is. Well, um, you know how you and Zeke and Braylon have always said that when I find the right woman, I was going to change my mind about getting married? I—"

Richmond burst into laughter. "Holy shit! You done went and fell in love." Laughing, he clapped his hands. "Ahh. This is funny as hell. Who is she? What's her name?"

He may not find it so damn funny when he finds out I've been boning his cousin. "Sasha."

Richmond's smile flew off his face. He frowned. "What did you just say her name was?"

"Sasha," Salvador repeated. "Your cousin, Sasha."

Richmond leapt from the couch. "Oh, hell no! Man, I know you ain't been fooling around with my cousin. Sasha deserves better than you. I know you. You're a player!"

Salvador stood. "Look, man. I gave up my player's card. Those days are over for me."

Richmond fisted his hips. He rolled his eyes. "Yeah, right. Damn, man. You know how you are. You should've never gotten involved with Sasha. End your relationship with her before it gets too serious." Frustration laced his voice. The room fell silent.

Richmond's brows dipped. "Oh, no. Please don't tell me you've slept with my damn cousin." "Yes. I have."

Richmond threw his hands up in the air. "Fucking Christ! You're going to break Sasha's heart."

Salvador reached into his pocket and pulled out a box. He popped back the lid on the box and held it up to Richmond's face. The big diamond ring inside the box sparkled. "I'm not going to break her heart, bro. I love Sasha. I want to ask her to marry me, but I don't want to do it without your approval. I love Sasha. I love her, man."

Richmond slapped a hand to his chest. "Whoa. That's a big ass diamond ring." Richmond nodded. "So you really love her, huh?"

"Yes."

"And you promise not to hurt her?"

"Yes. You have my word."

"I know you. You wouldn't have bought her a ring if you didn't feel that you really loved her." Richmond smiled. "You have my approval. I wish you and Sasha the best of luck."

I was going to marry her regardless of what you said, Salvador thought, smiling. "Thanks for your blessing, man."

"But it's so soon."

"When you meet a woman like Sasha, it's not soon enough." Glad he'd gotten Richmond's blessing to marry the only woman he'd ever loved, warmth infused Salvador's heart.

Chapter Twenty-Five

THE FOLLOWING DAY, SASHA ENTERED   her bedroom, closed the door, then tossed her purse on the bed. Nerves onedge, she sighed. Pacing back and forth, she nibbled her fingernails. I'm just stupid. Stupid. Stupid. Stupid.

Inhaling a deep breath, Sasha stopped walking, stood at the foot of the bed, "Okay, I need to calm down. I'm probably freaking out for no reason." My period is late. Not ready to face the inevitable, she pulled back the flaps on her purse and retrieved the early pregnancy test she'd just purchased from Walgreens.

Nauseous, she entered the bathroom and ripped open the package. Standing over the toilet, she lowered her bottoms, spread her legs, and urinated on the stick. She laid the stick on the floor, closed the toilet seat, and sat on top of it. Waiting for the pregnancy test's confirmation on whether or not she was pregnant, her mind traveled ba ck to the night the condom had burst while she and Salvador had made love.

If his shaft wasn't so big, then none of this would've happened. If she would've gotten her behind on some birth control as soon as she knew she had the hots for Salvador, then shewouldn't be sitting here on the toilet seat inside the bathroom like a scared teenager. Darn. When Salvador had said that he'd take care of her and the baby if it turned out that she was pregnant, had he meant it?

The test should be ready by now. Sasha leaned over, lifted the test in her hand, and brought it up to her eyes to read it. Two lines! She slapped a hard hand over her mouth. Dear Lord, I'm pregnant. How am I going to tell Salvador I'm pregnant with his child? How, God, how?

Sasha tossed the test in the trash, rinsed her hands, then walked back out into the bedroom. Overwhelmed, she eased onto the bed, crossed her legs. Her whole life was now changed. She'd changed.

Bing. Her cell phone chirped on the nightstand. She picked it up to see who'd texted her.

Salvador: Let's go for a ride tonight.

Sasha: Okay. Where to?

Salvador: To the lake house where we shared our first date.

Sasha: What time should I be ready?

Salvador: At eight. I can't wait to see you.

Sasha: I'm looking forward to seeing you, too.

Sighing heavily, Sasha put her cell on the pillow. Wondering how she was going to tell Salvador she was pregnant, she slid down the mattress, folded her arms over her breasts. Lord help her, she was having a baby from a man that had never told her he loved her. Well, he did say he wanted to marry her a few weeks ago. But he hadn't mentioned it since then. For all she knew, he may have said he wanted to marry her just so he could get her in his bed.

He likes me, but he doesn't love me. He may never love me. God, but I sure do love me some him. Some fine-behind Salvador.

226

Placing her hand on her belly, Sasha managed to smile. "I'm pregnant with Salvador's baby." As she lay in bed thinking about how much she loved Salvador and trying to adjust to being pregnant, her cell phone buzzed. Not bothering to look at the

Caller ID, she answered it. "Hello?"

"Hi, Sasha." Hearing Reggie's voice, Sasha bolted upright in bed. Pinching her lips together, her chest heaved up and down. "I know you're there, I can hear you breathing. Sasha, I miss you, babe. I want us to be together. Please give us once more chance. I promise I'll act right. I want us to get married. I've changed."

"I've changed, too, Reggie. Love don't live here anymore. I don't want you. I hope the police find you and put you in jail for what you did to me." Click! She hung up in his face.

Agitated, she picked up the notepad and pen lying on the mattress in front of her and started working on her song, I've Changed. Tip of the pen on the tablet, Sasha began writing.

Verse 3
When I was with you, you didn't have time for me
When I was with you, you hung out with her instead of me
When I was with you, you stopped taking me out
Trying to act like you were single, and like you had clout
When things ended, I felt ashamed
When things ended, thought I was to blame
When things ended, thought I'd die
I cried and cried, asked God to lead me

Chorus
Now I've changed
I'm not the person I used to be
I've changed
I let you go cuz you wanted to be free
I've changed
Now you wanna come back
But I don't love you anymore

I've changed
Love for you no longer lives in my heart
I've changed
Please leave me alone, get lost
I've changed
Goodbye, be gone
It feels so good not to want you anymore

Thanking God because she was completely over Reggie and had finally completed her break up song, Sasha wrote the copyright date at the top, and then signed her signature at the bottom—Sasha Spaulding. Clenching the notepad in her hands, she brought the paper up to her face and kissed it. A perfect print of her red stained lips was on the line next to her signature.

"I feel this song has the potential to be a hit if it ever got to the right publisher." Anxious to sing her finished song, Sasha took out her cell, hit record, and began belting out the words.

Three minutes later when she finished recording her song, Sasha thought about how Salvador had said she could have his Porsche. He'd even stated he'd sign over the title to her and pay it off. The kind gesture blew her mind.

For him to offer her a car such as a Porsche, or a car at all, spoke volumes as to how much he cared for her. She'd never dated a man as generous as Salvador. But then again, she'd never dated one with as much money as him either. Even if Salvador was poor, she'd still like his fine behind.

The way he'd made passionate love to her, and had taken his time, and had made sure she'd cum first, had her now hooked. Hooked on his lovemaking. Hooked on his long, pink tongue. Hooked on the way he kissed her lips. So tender. Sasha's center ached from thinking about how Salvador had touched her there.

For more reasons than one, Sasha couldn't wait to see Salvador tonight. Lord, have mercy. How was Salvador going to react when he found out he was going to be a father? Goodness gracious.

Noticing the time on the clock, Sasha lowered her feet to the floor, walked over to the closet, and searched for something to wear. Grabbing hold of a hanger, she opted to wear a casual grey dress that stopped to her knees and a pair of cute sandals.

Rolling the dress down over her head, someone knocked on her door. "Just a minute," she said, sliding her feet into the black sparkling sandals. Fully dressed, she walked over to the door and opened it. Leslie stood at the door wearing a black maxi dress, looking absolutely fabulous. A pink tint on her cheeks, her hair was curled loosely. "Wow. Don't you look nice, Aunt Leslie."

Leslie's sweet perfume flowed from her body up into Sasha's nose. She smiled. "Thanks. You look nice yourself. I'm about to head out for the night."

Auntie is so pretty. "Where are you going, dressed up like that?"

"Oh, nowhere special. Just over to Colton's," Leslie said nonchalantly.

Taken aback, Sasha smiled. "Over to Colton's? You mean Zeke's father? That Colton?"

Leslie nodded. "Yes, that Colton. He hasn't been feeling well lately, so I'm taking him some of my natural roots and herbs to see if they'll help him feel better."

"One look at you, Auntie…and trust me…Colton is going to feel a whole lot better. I'm sure if anyone can nurse Colton back to good health, it's you." Winking her eye at Leslie, Sasha giggled.

Leslie laughed. "Chile, hush your mouth. Colton ain't no more interested in me than that fine-behind Terrence Howard on Empire. Terrence is too fine for his own good."

"Yes, he is. Have fun on your date, Auntie."

Leslie's head tilted. "It's not a date, Sasha."

"Okay, if you say so."

"He's dying, Sasha. I'm just trying to help, that's all." Leslie turned and walked away.

Sasha headed to the bathroom to do her hair. Yes, Colton may be dying, Auntie. But he ain't dead yet. The light I saw in Colton's eyes when he looked at Auntie said he was very much alive. Alive and waiting to make her his. I can feel it.

Sasha grabbed her tiny purse off the bed, strapped it over her shoulder, and descended the steps. Right when her foot left the last step, the doorbell rang. She pulled open the front door to find Salvador standing there, looking handsome as ever. Looking a lot better than the last time she'd seen him at the cemetery, which was quite understandable.

"Hi." Stepping out onto the porch, she closed the door behind her. Dear Lord. How am I going to tell this man I'm pregnant with his child? Fix it, Jesus. Fix it.

Dressed in a casual navy shirt and a pair of blue jeans, Salvador's blue eyes gleamed as he looked at her. "You look pretty, as always." When he lowered his face to kiss her cheek, the woodsy scent of his cologne sailed into her nose.

"And you look handsome, as always." After Sasha slid into the passenger side of the SUV, Salvador rounded the vehicle and got in on the driver's side. "How have you been feeling?" she asked, waves of apprehension sweeping through her. Oh God, I'm pregnant.

Salvador backed the SUV out of the driveway. "I've had better days, that's for sure. I still can't get over the way Ben died." Driving down the street, Salvador glanced at Sasha. Something sensual passed between them, and she felt connected to him like never before.

"Me, either." Sasha patted his leg. "I'm so sorry you had to see Ben die the way he did."

There was a disturbing calmness in his eyes. "Me, too. Although it's been hard to get out of my mind, I've learned a valuable lesson. And that's to never take life for granted. You can be here one day, and gone the next."

Maybe when he learns about the baby, he'll feel better. "Let me know if there's anything I can do to make you feel better."

Gripping the steering wheel, he glanced sideways at her and smiled. "Since you mentioned it, there is something you can do to make me feel better."

His blue pupils glowed with desire, and Sasha had a feeling she knew exactly what he needed to make him feel better. "Oh, yeah? What's that?"

The smile he gave her contained a sensuous flame. "I'm not going to tell you right now. You'll see later."

Cupping her stomach, Sasha sought the right words to tell Salvador she was pregnant. "Salvador, I'm...ummm."

"What?"

"Nothing. I'll tell you later."

"Are you copying me, my little pussycat?"

"Copying you? How am I copying you?"

"I say I have something to tell you, but will tell you later. Then you say you have something to tell me, but will tell me later. That's copying." Salvador's smile widened.

Sasha smiled in return. "I'm not copying you."

"Yes, you are, but it's okay. Copy me doing this." He slid his hand up her thigh, eased a finger into her heat, and twirled. Sasha squirmed in pleasure. "Copy me, and play with your pussy so I can watch."

"Oh, Salvador," Sasha cooed, softly bucking on his stroking finger.

Chapter Twenty-Six

WITH ONE HAND ON THE   steering wheel and the other fondling between Sasha's hot thighs, Salvador steered the SUV off the main road and into the thick forestry. As he swirled his finger in Sasha's wet heat, the SUV rocked and shimmied over the dirt road, making Sasha's breasts bounce inside her bra.

Rocking her clitoris against Salvador's finger, soft moans eased from Sasha's succulent lips. Her slick sex clenched his finger, drenched it.

"You like my finger in you, pussycat? This pussy is wet. I can't wait to eat it."

Licking her lips, Sasha closed her eyes. She clenched his wrist, forcing his finger further up into her. Slowly gyrating her hips, her mouth slightly parted. "Mmm. Ahhh." Body tensing, her sex began exploding on his finger.

Salvador's cock knotted. "I love the way your pussy is cumming on my finger. Can't wait to feel it explode on my tongue." When Sasha opened her eyes, Salvador withdrew his soaked finger from her channel, slid it in his mouth, and then sucked her creamy juices off. "Mmm, your pussy tastes delectable."

The brown, wooden lake house surrounded by trees came into view. In the sky, the half-moon glowed. Salvador put the gear in park and exited. Before he had the chance to get the door for her, she'd already gotten out and had met him in the front of the SUV.

Nervous about proposing to Sasha, Salvador's gut jittered. As they crossed the lawn to the lake house, he prayed Sasha didn't think the way he proposed to her was cheesy. Yes. He'd thought about taking her to a fancy restaurant to pop the question. He'd also thought about renting a private jet and proposing to her while flying high in the sky, but he'd decided the lake house would be best because it held a very special memory for him. He'd fallen in love with Sasha here. Yep. It'd taken him a long time to admit it, but it was true. He'd loved Sasha ever since they'd looked at the stars together.

Salvador stuck his key into the rear door of the lake house, pushed it open, and they entered. Standing beyond the door, Sasha placed her hand on her left breast. Her appraising eyes roamed over the den area.

Candles inside glass jars burned on the end tables. Inside the log fireplace, the orange roasting fire crackled. Slow music streamed from the speaker of the tiny radio sitting on top of the mantel.

"I see you've already been here today?"

Standing behind Sasha, Salvador wrapped his arms about her shoulders. Kissed the side of her face. "Yes. Wanting to do something romantic for you, I stopped by here before I picked you up." Although it was summer, he still lit the fireplace. If what he had planned turned out the way he wanted, it was about to get even hotter inside the lake house.

Sasha glanced back over her shoulder up at him. Worry showed on her face. "Thank you."

"Is everything okay? You look worried. Seem pensive."

Her eyes became misty. "You know me well. Remember when

I said I had something to tell you in the car?"

"Yeah. Are you ready to tell me?"

She nodded. "Yes."

"Let's sit down." Salvador and Sasha sat on the couch beside one another inside the dim room. He cupped her face. "I think I know what's causing that look of anxiety on your beautiful face." He caressed her bottom lip with his thumb.

Sasha's gaze lowered to her lap, then back up to Salvador's face.

"I'm so nervous to tell you."

"Don't be afraid. You can tell me anything."

"I'm…" She swallowed.

Salvador cupped Sasha's face. "Please tell me you're pregnant with my child."

Sniffing, she lowered her thick black lashes, then stared at him.

As Sasha's head nodded in his hands, her eyes looked glassy. "Yes. I'm pregnant. You're going to be a father, Salvador."

"Oh, baby. You've just made me the happiest man on Earth." He pulled her into his arms and embraced her tight. "I love you, Sasha."

Sasha pried herself out of his arms. "What did you just say?"

He clenched her chin with his index finger and thumb. Longing filled her medium brown pupils. "I said I love you, Sasha Spaulding. I've loved you ever since our very first date here at the lake house. I love you."

Tears sprang into Sasha's eyes. "I love you, too, Salvador," her voice cracked.

Salvador's heart beat harsh inside his chest. "Do you love me enough to be my wife?"

Swallowing, she looked at him with dreamy eyes. "Yes."

Salvador reached into his pocket, pulled out a velvet box, popped the lid back. The expensive round diamond sparkled. Sasha gasped. "Do you love me enough to be my wife and marry me next week?"

Tilting her head, her watery eyes widened. "Next week?"

"Yes, Sasha. By the end of next week, I want you to be my wife—Mrs. Sasha Casillas. And now that you're pregnant, I don't see any need for us to wait to get married. I don't want my child to be born a bastard. Not only that, I don't want to spend any more days than I have to in my house without you. Before I go to sleep at night, I want your face to be the last thing I see. When I wake up in the morning, I want your face to be the first thing I see. I want to spend the rest of my life loving you, woman."

SASHA'S HEART SWELLED WITH JOY as she sat listening to Salvador proclaim his undying love for her. Thumps pounded hard at the base of her throat. The tear in her right eye threatened to fall.

Salvador sat patiently awaiting her answer. He lifted the box to her eyes. "If you're thinking it's too soon for us to get married, it's not. You can't put a time limit on true love. Marry me, Sasha." The huge rock of a diamond sparkled inside the box's slit, right before her eyes.

"Yes. Yes. I'll marry you." The tear sitting at the rim of her eye fell. Salvador leaned into her and kissed her tear-stained cheek.

"We're going to be so good together." He plucked the ring out of the slit, grabbed her hand, and slid the ring up her wedding finger. He brought her hand up to his mouth, kissed it. "The ring is beautiful. I love it."

Love flashed in Salvador's blue eyes. "A beautiful ring for a beautiful woman. Thanks for agreeing to be my wife. I'm going to spend every waking hour making you happy."

"I'm going to do the same. I'm so happy right now. I don't ever want this feeling inside me to end."

"It won't. I'm going to make sure of it, my soon-to-be-wife."

A smile touched Sasha's lips. She twined her arms around his neck. Never in a million years did she think she'd get married to a man so fast. But then again, Salvador wasn't just any man. He was a great man. A powerful man. A strong man with a kind heart who loved her. "It blows my mind that a man like you could love a girl like me."

"I don't know why. You're a beautiful woman. Inside and out." Salvador covered her mouth with his, then slid his tongue between her lips. His kiss was tender. Smooth. Enticing.

He broke their kiss. Pulled her grey dress over her head, threw it behind the sofa. Removing her bra, desire flickered his eyes.

Thinking Out Loud, by Ed Sheeran, came on, serenading the room. "I dedicate this song to you."

"I love this song. It's beautiful."

"Just think," Salvador said, flicking his finger over her taut nipple, "after we get married, I'll get to suck your breasts every night." Lowering his head, he curled his hot mouth around her nipple, sucked it into his mouth. "Get to suck them in the morning, too." Flicking the tip of his tongue against the hard substance, he groaned.

Tingles wavered throughout Sasha's body. When she attempted to roll his shirt up over his head, her breast fell from his sucking lips. Their eyes linked, and her hands touched his muscular chest.

Aroused, she swallowed. Smoothed her hands over the hard muscles of his chest. Down his six pack, to the inside of his pants.

Love whirled in the air.

Sasha caressed the head of Salvador's shaft with the pad of her thumb, found it slick with pre-cum. She wrapped her fingers around the length of his erect shaft. It felt like hot steel in her grip. As she motioned him up and down, he expelled a sharp breath.

Peered intently at her.

"Sasha," Salvador groaned out her name. Beholding her gaze, he unbuttoned his jeans. When he yanked his zipper down, the sound ripped in the air. His fly free, Sasha pulled his steely tool over the band of his underwear, mashed him up and down. "I muero por follarte."

Sasha's gaze fell from his handsome face to the hard knob of his erection. Fluid seeped from the slit of his round, glorious head, then trickled beneath the deep, circular groove. Veins pressed at the sides of his tanned rod, forming bulging lines.

"Okay." About to submit to his request, Sasha got on her knees in front of the couch. The tip of his shaft at her eye level, she put her mouth on his mushroom head. She parted her mouth wide, then slid her mouth to the base of his manhood. Salvador's salty pre-cum tasted yummy, she thought, bobbing her head up and down on his erection. Performing fellatio, spit slid from the cracks of her mouth.

Salvador groaned huskily. "I said I was dying to fuck you. Not suck my cock."

"Do you want me to stop?" she asked, her mouth full of him.

"No. Hell no." Gently cupping the sides of her head, he thrust his tool inside her mouth. "Oh, yeah. Suck it, my little pussycat." Mmm. Salvador tasted so good. She could suck him all night long. Angling his pulsating stem downward in her tight fist, she brought her mouth up to the tip, flicked her tongue around his salty tasting head, then pressed her mouth back down to his base. He groaned throatily. "You have no idea how bad I want to cum in your mouth." "Go ahead," Sasha offered.

"Not until you cum first." Salvador grabbed his stem, snatched it out of her mouth. "Whew. I almost came in your mouth. That was close." He stood.

As Salvador removed his jeans, Sasha rolled her hot pink thongs down her legs, kicked them to the side. Towering over her, Salvador cupped Sasha's butt cheeks. His hips rocking, his member glided back and forth on her navel. Feeling as if she were melting like sizzling butter, moisture pooled in Sasha's center.

He walked and stood behind her. Putting his hands to her hips, he lowered to his knees. Twirling his nose on the crack of her buttocks, he sniffed. Trailed the tip of his tongue down over her butt crack. Sucked on her labia. Then slipped his probing tongue inside her tingling entrance.

Chill bumps pimpled Sasha's flesh. She gently fell forward to the sofa. Her hands pressed flat on the cushion, her buttocks perched high in the air. Glancing down at the huge diamond on her finger, she felt blissfully alive. Had never been happier.

Salvador's fingertips pressed into Sasha's buttocks as he continued circling his tongue on the inside of her throbbing sex. Rocking her hips backwards, she mashed her sex on his tongue, forcing his flesh to dig deeper.

Eager to release herself, she reached between her legs, pinched her clitoris, and held it. Electricity ignited in her core. Her knees buckled. "Oooo." Breathing harsh, Sasha's sex exploded on Salvador's probing tongue. Her clitoris shattered with pleasure on her finger.

Salvador rose to his feet. He lifted her right leg, placed it on the sofa cushion, and then did the same thing with her left leg. With her knees pressed into the cushion, Sasha held on to the curb of the sofa.

He got on the sofa behind her. "Hold on." He gripped his shaft with one hand, spread her labia with the other, and then inserted her. As he thrust his rod up in her, she turned her head sideways, her gaze went to the fireplace. Bright orange flames roasted the wood inside the fireplace. Sweet, slow music serenaded the room.

Madly in love with her fiancé, Sasha's heart stirred. Embedding the precious moment inside her head, tears wet her eyes.

Clenching her hips, Salvador banged her hard, made her breasts clap. Clap. Clap. Clap. Salvador's shaft felt like it was in her stomach. Grunting, he lowered his chest to her perspired back.

"Who fucks you good, Sasha?"

Ooo. His dick is in my freaking stomach. "You do."

"Say my name."

"Salvador," she said in a moan.

"Say my name louder!" Bam! He slammed into her.

Ouch! Sasha's gaze snapped from the fireplace to the wall in front of the sofa. "Salvador!"

He slammed into her again. "Say it again!"

"Salvador! Your name is Salvador!" And you can… "You can fuck. Yes. Yes! Yes!"

"Work that pussy on my dick. Fuck me. Fuck this cock." His shaft jerking wildly inside her, Salvador roared.

Loud moans and groans echoed inside the room, bounced off the walls. Salvador's spunk shot into Sasha's womb, forcing her to climax with him. The hard thumps of his tool tapered off as his

240

orgasm ended. Slipping out of her entrance, he kissed her arched spine.

He laid down on the sofa, putting his back to the curb of the arm rest. He extended his arms towards her. "Let me hold you."

Sasha crawled between Salvador's thighs, rested her back on his chest, and stared at the blazing orange fire inside the log fireplace. As he tenderly held her, she gazed down at the sparkling ring on her finger. "I still can't believe I'm getting married next week. It's all happening so fast."

Holding her, he squeezed her tighter. "Not fast enough for me. I'd be fine if we went to the courthouse on Monday and got married. But I feel you deserve a wedding. Not to mention, Richmond would have a fit if we eloped. He's looking forward to walking you down the aisle."

Sasha shifted in Salvador's lap and glanced back over her shoulder at him. "Richmond knows about us?"

"Yes. After the funeral, I paid Richmond a visit and asked him for his approval to marry you. Thank God he said yes. Because even if he'd said no, I was going to ask you to marry me anyway."

"You would've jeopardized your friendship with Richmond just so you could be with me?"

"Yes, Sasha. I love you. I can't imagine my life without you. I want to spend the rest of my life with you." He kissed her lips.

"I want to spend the rest of my life with you, too."

"I hope you're pregnant with twins. They run in our family. I—" Salvador's cell phone buzzed on the coffee table. He reached over and answered the phone. "Hello?" A dark glare appeared in Salvador's eyes. "Hold on for a second." Covering the speaker on the cell, Salvador got up from the sofa, put on his jeans, and then walked outside to take the phone call.

Wondering why Salvador needed to take the phone call in private, Sasha had a distinct feeling it was something bad.

Something real bad. Who are you on the phone with, Salvador? she wondered, entering the master bedroom so she could take a hot shower.

Chapter Twenty-Seven

WITH THE CELL PRESSED TO his ear, Salvador stood on the porch of the lake house beneath a dim light, glancing out at the woods behind his quaint home. Sounds from crickets and bullfrogs crept into his ears. "I'm back. Go ahead, Don."

"As I was saying, I think I have a lead on who may have shot your mother. It's not hing concrete, but it sure looks like it. You may want to sit down to listen to this one."

Bracing himself, Salvador sat in the white wooden chair on the porch. "I'm sitting."

Don continued. "Good. As you already know, your mother went to the Smokehouse Ba r on the night she got shot. I went to the Smokehouse Bar today and pulled their surveillance cameras, and what I found out is about to blow your mind." Salvador swallowed. Don cleared his throat and continued. "The surveillance camera showed Lucy stumblin g out of the bar. Right when she reached the cab, she tripped and fell and dropped her cell. A man helped Lucy into the cab. After the cab drove off, the man picked up Lucy's cell and looked at the screen. He then got back in his car and followed the cab out of the parking lot."

"Do you know who the man is?"

"Do I ever. Are you still sitting?"

"Yeah."

"The man that helped Lucy into the cab and kept her cell is none other than Laurente Lagounov."

Salvador's heart flopped over. Holy crap. Laurente? "I know Laurente. I train his son—"

"Ivan. Yes, I'm aware of that. After digging further, I found out Laurente owns several gift shops here in Hilton Head. However, his gift shops aren't selling crap. Laurente uses the gift shops to conduct the affairs of an enterprise through a pattern of racketeering involving money laundering, bank fraud, and drug trafficking."

Trying to process everything, Salvador shook his head. "Holy crap, Don."

"Laurente is a vicious Russian mobster. His criminal activity is traced all the way back to Russia. To say he's dangerous is an understatement, Salvador."

Confused, he shifted in his seat. "My gut feeling tells me the bullet that ended up in my mother was meant for Ben. I still don't understand. Why would Laurente want to shoot Ben? Why would he set him on fire and kill him? Do you think Ben was involved with money laundering? Or drugs?"

Don stated, "I was getting to that. A large sum of money was deposited into Ben's checking account on March fifteenth of this year."

Salvador's brows dipped. "March fifteenth." He frowned. "That was the same day the building for my new sports facility was burned."

"According to one of Ben's close friends, Ben was trying to scrape money up so his wife, Claira, could have an emergency surgery. The friend confirmed Ben somehow had gotten the money on March fifteenth, but didn't know how."

Anger rushed through Salvador. He stood. Pressing his lips in a hard line, he walked out to stand in the middle of the grass. Putting two and two together inside his head, he swatted at a gnat. Salvador told Don, "Back in October of last year, Laurente had wanted to purchase the land the facility is on, but I outbid him. He'd come to see me about it. He'd offered to pay me more than it was worth so he could have it, but I wasn't interested. Shit. That fucker hired Ben to set my building on fire."

Don exclaimed, "And when the building didn't burn to the ground, Laurente decided Ben would have to pay for not completing the job with his life. Men like Laurente kill people when they do a half-ass job. It's no negotiating with them. I know you're not going to like what I have to say next...but if I were you, I'd leave well enough alone. I'd forget about Laurente and go on with my life."

Annoyed, Salvador gritted his teeth. Still standing in the middle of the back yard, he glared out at the black lake running behind his wooden home. "You're right, I don't like what you had to say. Laurente killed my friend, Ben. He shot my mother in her damn back. No one murders my friend and shoots my mother and gets away with it. No one. I'll take care of Laurente, that's for damn sure." I'm going to kill the sonofabitch.

"Don't go do anything crazy, Salvador. Don't——"

"Thanks for your help, Don. Be good, man." Click. Salvador hung up. Furious, he shuddered. Stared out at the dense forest.

Salvador turned to face the house. He noticed Sasha's shadowy figure standing at the window, covered with a sheer white drape. Her figure looking curvy, she drew back the sheer drapery, exposing her naked body. Salvador's heart swirled.

Long hair hanging over her shoulders, the skin on Sasha's flawless face glowed. Nipples puckered on her brown, perched breasts. Curvy hips, her thighs looked toned. Smiling, she crooked her finger at him, beckoning him to come back inside.

God, I love her. She's carrying my baby. If Laurente hurts Sasha, he'd never forgive himself. Knowing a bloody war was about to take place in Hilton Head, he had to protect Sasha. That being said, he was going to marry her next week. Afterwards, he was going to transfer his life insurance, and his bank accounts, and his estate, and everything he owned to Sasha's name. Once all of his finances were in Sasha's name, he was going to do what he had to do and disappear. He was going to make Sasha think he didn't love her. That their marriage was a huge mistake. For their honeymoon, he'd take her somewhere nice, out of the country, and leave her there. And then he'd return to Hilton Head and murder Laurente with his own bare hands. I'm going to snap that fucker's neck in half.

With death on his mind, Salvador smiled at Sasha and began walking towards the house. "You've met your fucking match, Laurente," he uttered.

DAYS LATER, A SWEET AROMA lingered in the air inside Sugar- Kanes. White, peach, and orange balloons sat tucked in the corners of the eatery. A three-layered cake with the same hues sat near the window at the front. Laughter and chatter from women of various ages intermixed as Sasha sat at the head of the table opening her bridal shower presents.

"Open my present next!" Leslie shouted, anxious for Sasha to see what she'd gotten her for her bridal shower.

Sasha's eyes roamed over the presents sitting on the table. "Which one is yours, Auntie?"

"The yellow box," Leslie confirmed.

Standing beside the table with the presents, Sandella handed Sasha the rectangular yellow box. Sasha's fingers stripped the yellow paper from the box. Lifting the top, her mouth dropped. Inside the box lay a beautiful glass picture frame, with Salvador and Sasha engraved at the bottom. "Oh, Auntie. This is beautiful." Proud of her present, Leslie's cheeks turned a rosy color. "You're welcome, Sasha."

Kayla handed Sasha her present. "Now open mine."

Sasha reached into the teal bag, pulled out a red, sexy lingerie, and held it up in the air. "Now I like this!"

Taylor's mother, Veronica, grabbed her chest. "Good God. You're going to give poor Salvador a heart attack if you put that on."

Taylor laughed. "Trust me, Mama…Salvador can handle that, and much more."

Leslie exclaimed. "I agree. Salvador is a manly man. Ain't nothing soft about him. Heck, if I had a body like Sasha's and had a man, I'd wear it myself."

All the women's mouths fell open, and then they burst into laughter.

"Would you really wear something like this, Auntie?" Sasha asked.

Leslie folded her arms across her budding bosoms. "I sure would. But considering I don't have a man, I don't have to worry about that."

Laughing, Veronica shook her head. "You don't have a man? Yeah, right."

Leslie gave Veronica a strange look. "What's that supposed to mean?"

Veronica waved her hand in the air. "Nothing. Forget I said anything."

"Don't you 'nothing' me. I want to know what you're thinking. Tell me, Veronica. Tell me. Don't leave me hanging," Leslie urged Veronica to spill the beans.

"Okay. Well, since you asked. When I was driving down the street the other day, I saw you coming out of," Veronica snickered, "ooo, Lordy...I saw you coming out of Colton's house with a huge smile on your face."

"Psssh. Chile, please." Leslie laughed.

"You're dating Colton?!" Kayla shouted.

Sandella said, "Oh my goodness. Colton is fine!"

"I knew my father-in-law had eyes for you," Taylor exclaimed, laughing. "Ever since you cooked dinner for him, you're all he talks about, Leslie."

Smiling her butt off, Leslie shook her head. "There's nothing going on between Colton and me. I was just visiting the man. I took him some natural roots and herbs to make him feel better."

"Natural roots and herbs?" Sandella asked. "Kayla's grandfather used to use natural methods to heal people."

Leslie smiled. "Yes. And I'm hoping to heal Colton the same way he did."

"You're going to heal him, all right. But it ain't gon' be with no natural herbs. It's going to be with natural loving!" Veronica belted.

All the ladies burst into laughter. Sasha laughed so hard, water came into her eyes. After Sasha opened up all her presents, she glanced at the women who'd come to support her, who'd put together a beautiful bridal shower at the last minute. Thankful and grateful for what they'd done, she wanted so badly to tell them she was pregnant, but she decided to wait until after the wedding.

"If I can have everyone's attention, please," Sasha said, interrupting the many conversations taking place throughout the eatery. The room fell silent. "I'd like to thank everyone here for putting a shower together for me. Even after I said I didn't have to have a bridal shower because it was so last minute, you ladies still got together and planned this for me." Trying not to cry, Sasha sniffed. "Thank you so much for everything. The food. The cake. The presents. But most of all, thank you for welcoming me into your lives. I know many of you may have reservations about Salvador and I getting married so soon, but——"

Leslie interjected, "Not me. If I had a man as fine as Salvador wanting to marry me, I'd marry him right away, too."

Veronica laughed. "You do have a fine man...Colton. But anyhow," Veronica said, giggling. "Back to you, Sasha...no one here is judging you for getting married so quickly. It's your life. And from the looks of it, you're very happy. Salvador is a great guy, and I wish you two the best of luck."

"Let's make a toast." Leslie lifted her drink in the air, and the other women followed her lead. "To Sasha. May Salvador and she have a long, beautiful life together. Cheers."

"Cheers," the women said in unison, clinking their glasses together.

The front door of the bakery opened, and in walked a delivery guy, carrying a gigantic silver box in his hands. "This is for Sasha Spaulding," the gentleman said.

"I'm Sasha." Sasha reached up, grabbed the big box, and lowered it to the table in front of her.

The gentleman smiled. "You beautiful ladies have a great day."

"You, too," Veronica said with emphasis, apparently thinking the guy was handsome, and fine.

"That's a mighty big present," Leslie said. "Who's it from?"

Sasha searched the card and box for a name, but she didn't see one. "I don't know." She lifted the card from the box, flipped it over. Maybe it's from Salvador, she thought, her insides warming. Anxious to see what Salvador had surprised her with,

she slid her fingernail under the seal of the envelope, slitting it, and then pulled out the card. The card read: Inside the box represents how I feel
about you.

Her heart giddy, Sasha lifted the lid from the box to find a piece of cardstock with a bold number zero written on it. Below it read: You're a big fat ZERO! You're absolutely NOTHING!

Sasha's heart dunked. Ohmygod. Who would send a present with an insulting note inside? The name Reggie shot to Sasha's mind.

Leslie rubbed her hands together. "Don't just sit there. Tell us what's inside the box."

Sasha forced a fake smile to her face. "It's personal, Auntie. That Salvador is something else." Refusing to let Reggie ruin the mood of her bridal shower, Sasha lowered the lid to the box and began crossing the room towards the front door so she could go put the box in the car.

Leslie shouted, "Oh my. Did Salvador get you some whips and chains?!"

"Salvador gon' tie Sasha up!" Veronica laughed.

The women sitting around the table looked at one another, and then burst out into wild bouts of hysterical laughter.

Chapter Twenty-Eight

WHITE SEAGULLS FLEW OVER THE   blue, glistening ocean behind the Balfour Hotel & Resort. Ivory flowe rs decorated the wedding arch. Sitting slightly behind the arch, the harpist's fingers plucked at the strings on the instrument, playing a lovely tune.

White chairs draped in peach fabric for the guests situated about the beige sand. Burning torches made a path down the aisle leading up to the wedding arch. The orange evening sun lowered to the horizon. Attendees sat in the chairs talking, smiling, and eagerly waiting for the wedding to start. Carrying his bible, the Pastor went and stood by the flowery wedding arch.

Dressed in a white tuxedo, Salvador exited the back door of the hotel, passed the pool, and then walked through a sandy path with brown, tall willows on either side. Making his way towards the wedding arch, warm beige sand pressed into his bar e feet. A cool breeze ruffled his face. Glad to be marrying the woman of his dreams, he went and stood beside the pastor, smiled at his guests.

Clasping his hands together, Salvador gazed at the beautiful beach scenery and the elegant decorations Sasha had come up with. Simple, but romantic. Joy and grief built vigorously inside

Salvador. Joy because he was marrying the woman he loved more than anything on Earth. And grief because right after he married her, he had to disappear. Disappear until he killed Laurente for shooting his damn mother, and for killing his good friend—Ben. Hating things had to be that way, Salvador's heart thudded against his ribs.

When the music switched up, Colton began escorting Leslie down the aisle. His Uncle Colton was stepping in as his father today, while Leslie was serving as Sasha's mother. With her arm looped through Colton's, Leslie's satin peach gown flowed around her feet. Wearing a white tuxedo, Colton looked a lot healthier today than he had in a long time. Maybe those roots and herbs Leslie was giving him really worked. Once they reached their seats, Russell walked Lucy down the aisle, and Lucy looked as if she couldn't have been happier to be hanging on Russell's shoulder. Well, if she had any ideas about the two of them hooking up, she could forget it. Because right after the wedding, he was going to ship Lucy off to a great rehabilitation center far away from Hilton Head.

A few seconds later, the remainder of the bridal party appeared in front of the brown, tall willows, and began making their way towards Salvador. The bridesmaids wore orange gowns, while the guys wore white tuxedos with orange cummerbunds and bowties. Zeke and Taylor were paired. Sandella and Braylon walked together. Serving as her maid of honor, Kayla walked by herself and wore a peach gown.

Now with everyone standing at the front beside the wedding arch, tunes of the bridal march serenaded the air. It's time for my bride to come, Salvador thought, his gaze going beyond the rustling willows. Filled with immeasurable joy, his heart sang inside his chest.

Finally, Richmond and Sasha appeared on the sandy path, with rustling willows on either side. Seeing his dashing bride making her way towards him, he swallowed. Inhaled a deep breath.

When Richmond and Sasha stepped from the sandy path out into plain view, Salvador's heart flopped. "Oooo"s and "aaah"s resounded from the guests. Staring into her eyes, his gut swirled. Love made his domineering emotions stir. She looks beautiful. God, I love Sasha. She's carrying my baby. I'm going to be a great father.

Beholding his gaze, Sasha's red, painted lips pulled into a smile. With her hand looped between Richmond's, Sasha held an orange and peach bouquet in her hand. The trail of Sasha's elegant gown flowed behind her as she made her way down the aisle, with torches blazing fire on either side.

That's some wedding dress. The white chiffon dress Sasha wore had sexy sheathed shoulder straps made of beaded crystals that plunged into a deep V, exposing her suggestive cleavage. The slit in the front of the dress stopped at the middle of her thigh. With a white veil covering the top part of her face, she wore her hair in a low bun, with dangling curls on the sides.

When Sasha finally reached Salvador, his heart took a perilous leap. Mira mi encantadora novia, he thought, thinking how beautiful his dashing bride looked.

SALVADOR'S BLUE EYES BLAZED WITH love as he stared at Sasha. His lips drew into a smile, exposing his snow white teeth. The white tuxedo he wore made him look like a king. He was a king…her king.

Reaching Salvador, the man whom she loved with all her heart, Sasha's lips curled upward into a wider smile. Love filled her heart, stretched it to the max. The baby growing inside her stomach had to be happy, too—happy that his or her parents were getting married. After all the hardships she'd had, her life had finally come together.

Richmond released Sasha's arm. Salvador held out his hand towards her. When she placed her palm into his rough, callous hand, he mouthed, "You look beautiful."

She mouthed back, "Thanks. You, too."

During the entire ceremony, all Sasha could think about was how much she loved Salvador. And how she was going to try her hardest to be a great wife, and a great mother. After they exchanged their vows, the pastor told Salvador, "Sasha has a surprise for you." "A surprise?" Salvador asked.

A nervous giggle escaped her. "I wrote a song for you that I'm going to sing." She looked at the saxophonist, and then nodded. Swallowing, she noticed the look of anticipation on her guests' faces. She parted her lips and let the sweet melody flow from her lips. "Because of you…"

Because of you I'm
so happy
Because of you
I feel light and free
You came into my life
Filled it with joy
You love me for me
Promised me eternity
Today we're getting married
Before God
Exchanging beautiful vows
Promising to love
Today and tomorrow

Forever and always
I just want to thank you
For choosing me
I just want to thank you For
loving me
I just want to thank you For
marrying me
I just want to thank you
Because you love me for me

A glassy sheen appeared in Salvador's eyes as Sasha brought the song to an end. He looked like he was struggling to hold back tears. Sasha quickly glanced out at the audience and saw many of her guests were teary-eyed. She then transferred her gaze back to Salvador.

Looking proud, Salvador cleared his throat. "That was the most beautiful song I've ever heard. Thanks for the dedication," he said, lifting her veil. "Hurry up, Pastor, and tell me I can kiss my beautiful bride."

The crowd laughed.

The Pastor announced, "Sasha and Salvador, through their words today, have joined together in holy wedlock. Because they have exchanged their vows before God and these witnesses, have pledged their commitment each to the other, and have declared the same by joining hands and by exchanging rings, I now pronounce that they are husband and wife. Those whom God hath joined together, let no one put asunder. You may now kiss the bride!" "I love you, Mrs. Casillas," Salvador stated huskily. Sasha's heart melted. "I love you, too, my husband." The wedding attendants applauded.

A gentleman standing behind the arch released two dozen white doves into the air.

Salvador's mouth gently descended down on Sasha's, and he gave her the most amazing tongue kiss ever. I'm Mrs. Sasha Casillas now, she thought, breaking their kiss. With one hand draped around her waist, he put his hand to the lower part of her belly and quickly removed it. Ah, how sweet. He was thinking about their baby.

Smiling, Sasha glanced out at her guests and noticed three unfamiliar men walk up. They went and stood to the far left of the brown willows. Oh my, they're late, she thought, noticing the tallest gentleman of the three was dressed in a black tuxedo. He pulled back the lapels of his coat, took out a cigar, and lit it. Who's
that? Sasha wondered.

Salvador's eyes seemed to harden. Continuing to smile, though, Salvador tugged Sasha's hand, led her down the aisle. When they reached the end, Salvador told Sasha, "Stay right here. Let me go say hello."

Sasha looked at the three men to her far left, then back at Salvador. "Who are they?"

"Some people I know." He sounded evasive, like he had something to hide.

ANGER PRICKED LIKE NEEDLES IN Salvador's chest. The nerve of Laurente to show up uninvited to his got damn wedding. Desperate to strangle Laurente's ass, Salvador kept a cool demeanor. Laurente brought his damn goons with him, too.

Salvador stalked up to Laurente. His temper seething, Salvador glared him down. "Laurente. I didn't know you were invited to my wedding."

Laurente squinted his evil glass eye. "I don't need an invitation. The last time I checked, the beach was free." The

Russian mobster put the cigar to his lips, smoked it, and then blew smoke in Salvador's face.

Inhaling the potent toxins, Salvador's nose wrinkled. This *sonofabitch is trying me.* Not wanting to make a spectacle of his special wedding day, Salvador decided he'd get Laurente back when he least expected it. "You need to leave."

Laurente's eyes bore into Salvador's. "I will leave, but not before I say what I came here to say. Rumor has it that you've been going around town asking about me. Well, not you, but the little private investigator you hired." Laurente snapped his fingers. "What's his name? Oh yeah, Don." Tempted to throw a punch, Salvador clenched his molars. Laurente continued. "It's a shame you don't trust me, Salvador. I've paid you a lot of money to train my Ivan. My boy will no longer be receiving boxing lessons from you. In the future, if there's anything you want to know about me, just ask Laurente himself."

Salvador's temper flared. Forcing his emotions to remain cool and not to explode, he glanced back over his shoulders at Sasha...his beautiful bride. Entertaining their guests, his bride was smiling and waving for him to come. He looked back at Laurente. "No one comes to my wedding and disrupts it. Now get out of here. You piece of shit."

"Be careful how you talk to Laurente." Laurente put the tip of the cigar to his lips and smoked it. Smoke spiraling from his lips, he winked. "Let's go," he told his goons.

"I thought so." Salvador's temples bulged.

Laurente frowned. "Keep in mind...no one knows Laurente like Laurente knows Laurente. Oh, except for maybe Ben and your mama." Anger shot through Salvador. Before he knew it, he'd lunged forward, closed the distance between him and Laurente. Glaring into Laurente's eyes, Salvador shuddered.

Laurente barked, "Don't be a fool and ruin your wife's wedding day. I'd hate for anything to happen to her."

Fists balding, Salvador's chest rocked. Tempted to knock his ass out, he sharpened his gaze on Laurente's face.

Richmond stalked up behind Salvador and asked, "Everything okay?"

In control of his seething anger, Salvador responded, "Everything is fine. My friends here were just leaving."

Laurente smiled. "As I was saying…it was good seeing you. Again, congratulations, my man. Enjoy the rest of your wedding." Laurente turned, and he and his goons walked away.

Braylon and Zeke walked up to where he and Richmond were standing.

Braylon asked, "Who was that?"

"One of my clients," Salvador stated, leaving it at that.

As Salvador made his way back to his adorable wife, Sasha, anger flooded his veins. Laurente all but admitted that he'd killed Ben and had shot his mother. Most people feared Laurente, but not Salvador.

Surrounded by his happy guests, Salvador placed his hand in the small of Sasha's back and kissed her rosy, blushing cheek. "Sorry about that." Laurente will pay for interrupting my wedding, and for threatening my wife. Sooner than he realizes.

Chapter Twenty-Nine

LAURENTE STALKED DOWN THE HALLWAY of the second level at his home. When he reached his son's bedroom, he peeped through the crack in th e door. Zena was sitting beside Ivan on his sleigh bed, caressing his back.

Ivan's bottom lip turned under. "But Mother, why can't we just leave?"

Zena's head tilted. "Because, Ivan...we don't have anywhere to go."

Ivan sighed. "Why can't we just go stay w ith Grandma? She'll let us."

Zena replied, "Ivan, I don't want to leave Hilton Head. This is my home, and I like it here. I know your father can be tough on you sometimes, but he's a good man. He loves you, and me. We're his life."

Ivan folded his arms acr   oss his chest. "Father doesn't love anyone except for himself. If he loved me, he wouldn't have made me do what I did."

"What did he make you do?" Zena asked.

On the verge of being a damn snitch, Ivan swallowed. "He made me pour gas—"

Laurente burst into the room before Ivan could finish his sentence. "There's my two favorite people in the whole wide world. Towering over Zena, he bent down and gave his precious wife a kiss. "How was your day, Zena?"

Zena seemed uncomfortable. "It was wonderful."

Laurente felt like knocking the hell out of that wussy Ivan. "You're not in here bothering your mother with foolishness, are you?"

Ivan shook his head. "No, Father."

This boy is a scary little pussy. Pisses me off. Perhaps I need to give him a bigger challenge the next time one of my adversaries gives me a hard time. A sudden thought stormed inside Laurente's head. "Good. Because your mother already has enough on her plate to worry about. Zena, please leave Ivan and I alone. I need to speak with our son in private."

"Yes, darling." Zena slid off the bed and walked out of the bedroom.

Laurente shut the door to Ivan's bedroom and stalked back over to him. Enraged, he was tempted to strike Ivan, but decided to speak with him instead. "Look, son, I overheard you trying to convince your mother to leave me, and I don't like it one bit. I do a lot for you and your mother. I take great care of the two of you, and you would be nothing without me. If I ever hear or learn that you've been speaking badly about me behind my back...there will be consequences for your actions." He patted Ivan's back. "Do I make myself clear?"

"Yes, Father. May I ask you something without you getting mad?"

"I can't promise I won't get mad, but I will try to control my temper. Go ahead. What is it that you want to ask me, son?"

Ivan sighed heavily. "Why do I have to kill people and work with people that sell drugs? I really hate doing it, Father. It's not in me. I don't think like you."

SABRINA SIMS MCAFEE

260

This boy is the biggest punk ever. "Because, Ivan. Being a mobster runs in our family. It's a part of our history. It's how my family has always made their money. Don't question the family business, my son. There's nothing you can say to change my mind."

Ivan's eyes watered. "I've been having nightmares ever since you set that old man on fire. I can't stop thinking about him. I don't want to kill anybody else."

"Too bad, because you will." Folding his arms across his chest, Ivan's head bowed. Tears dripped from his eyes onto his shirt. Laurente patted his shoulder. "Since the mood is already gloomy, I might as well tell you…you're not going to be taking boxing lessons anymore."

Ivan's head shot up. "Why, Father? Why? I love taking boxing lessons!"

"Well, you're not taking them."

"But why not? Why?!"

"Because…let's just say that Salvador and I had a disagreement. He's a no-good bastard."

Ivan huffed. "Salvador is a good man, and you know it. Boxing is all I have, and you're taking that away, too."

Salvador stole land from me and had me investigated. "Taking that away, too? What do you mean, too?"

Pain ladened Ivan's eyes. Trying to get him to become a man was going to be a lot of work. Not as easy as he'd originally thought. "You've already stripped me of my dignity and pride. I hate myself for what I did to Ben. Just hate myself. Salvador treats me like a son. He's good to me. He taught me how to be a real man."

Laurente thumped Ivan upside his head with his fingers. "No. I've taught you how to be a real man. Not that idiotic asshole." He waved his finger in Ivan's face. "You better not ever insult me like that again. I know you're just saying that because you're upset about Ben. But like I told you before, the more you kill, the better you'll become at it."

Ivan climbed out of bed. Stood face to face Laurente. "I'm not killing anybody again. I don't care what you say. I won't be a killer," he barked.

Laurente fisted Ivan's shirt, drew back his fist.

The door flung open. "Don't, Laurente!" Zena ran up to Laurente and grabbed his fist. "Don't you hit him! I mean it!"

Fuming, Laurente lowered his fist. "You two make me sick to my fucking stomach!"

"Oh, yeah? Well, you make me sick back!" Ivan shouted.

Laurente grabbed Zena's shoulders, threw her out of the way, tossing her against the wall behind him. He drew back his fist and punched Ivan in the nose. Ivan's nose went lopsided. Blood squirted from his nostrils onto his face and shirt.

Cupping his broken nose, Ivan hollered, "You broke my nose!" Zena stood with her back to the wall, crying and shaking.

Dismayed, Laurente despised his family at this moment. Glaring down at Zena, he was tempted to spit on her. She's starting to get beside herself. "No one inside or outside this house questions me!" His knuckles hurting, Laurente marched out of the room, slammed the door behind himself.

Enraged, he began descending the staircase. All of this was because of how Ivan felt about Salvador. Talking about Salvador taught him how to be a man. Salvador hadn't taught his son shit but how to be a wimp. Let's just see how he felt about Salvador after he killed the chump ass boxer and put him in the ground, six feet under.

Fueling with anger, Laurente slung open his front door and headed for his car. I'm going to put an end to this Salvador shit tonight. Send him a message that's loud and clear.

Chapter Thirty

THE BRIGHT MOON CAST A   glow down on the hot, humid
earth. Salvador and Sasha's wedding night had ended beautifully.
From the beach wedding itself to the reception, everything had
turned out perfect, Sasha thought, sitting in the r   ear of the
limousine, tongue kissing her gorgeous husband.

I's married now. Cupping Salvador's jaws, Sasha curled her
tongue with his and couldn't wait for him to make tender love to
her. Wondering where they were going for their honeymoon, Sasha
regretfully ended their hot, searing kiss.

"I love you so much, Salvador."

"I love you, too, Sasha." He cupped her neck. "Please don't
ever forget how much I love you. Even if I die someday, don't ever
forget how much I love you, and our unborn child. True love lives
forever. Promise me you'll never forget that." There was an edge
to his voice.

"I promise. I'll never forget how much you love me, and our
child."

"There's one more thing I want you to promise me," he said,
rubbing his thumb across her lips.

"What?"

He grinned. "Promise me that you'll sing the song you wrote for me while sucking my dick."

Sasha giggled. "I promise, my husband."

"Yes. You're my kind of wife."

The limousine rounded the corner of the airport, drove to the rear. The Balfour private charter jet owned by Colton sat on the runway, preparing to take off. "Let's go, Mrs. Casillas." Salvador opened the rear door of the limousine before the driver had a chance to.

Loving her new last name...Casillas...Sasha's heart jostled. "Oh, how I love the sound of my last name." Still wearing her wedding dress, Sasha placed her hand in Salvador's and stepped out onto the pavement. Crossing the pavement towards the private aircraft, her pearl white Christian Louboutins with red bottoms clicked against the concrete. The humid air clung to her flesh. She couldn't wait for Salvador to tell her where they were going for their honeymoon. Maybe he was taking her to Paris or to Italy. Or to South Africa or to Barcelona. Oh my.

When they reached the steps of the private aircraft, Salvador jerked Sasha off her feet. He carried her up the flight of stairs, entered the aircraft, and took her straight to the bedroom in the rear. Holding her in his arms, he kicked the door closed with his hard shoe, dropped her in the center of the bed.

Eyes blazing with lust, Salvador's fingers worked swiftly to unbutton his tuxedo shirt. "I've been waiting to get inside you all day," he stated, shrugging his arms from the sleeves. Rip! He yanked down the zipper, removed his pants and underwear. His tanned shaft pointed straight out. He fisted the base of his rod, massaged it up and down. Bulging veins pressed against the gliding skin of his massive erection. That thing looked like it could split bricks. Break glass. Splinter wood.

Aroused, moisture puddled at Sasha's hurting entrance. Her

nipples hardened beneath her wedding dress. Sensual feelings spread through her system, making her whole body hot. Yearning to make love to her husband, Sasha watched her husband selfpleasure himself. Licking her lips greedily, her clitoris tingled.

"You look so beautiful in the wedding dress. I want to fuck you in it."

"Let me keep my promise first." Sasha scooted to the edge of the bed, fisted his tool above his fist, and sucked the head of his erection into her mouth. She sucked on his hard knob like it was delicious lollipop. As she'd promised in the limousine, Sasha started singing the song she'd wrote for him around his shaft. Humming the sweet melodies she'd written with especially him in mind, fluid trickled from her clenching sex into her panties.

Thrusting in and out of her mouth, Salvador gripped her shoulders. Groaning, he slid his manhood to the outer part of her lips, let it rest. Palming the back of her head, he slowly slid his pulsing stem back inside her mouth. Her mouth motioning back and forth on his stem, saliva slid from the cracks of her lips, down her chin.

Sucking him deliciously, she groaned hoarsely. She glanced up at him. Their gazes locked. Electricity shot to her core, shocked it with desire.

Salvador clutched his length, circled it in her mouth, making the tip brush her teeth and the roof of her mouth. Pre-cum oozed from his slit onto her tongue. "I'm not ready to cum yet." Moaning, he slipped his tool out of her mouth. His hands on her shoulders, he gestured her backwards until she was lying down. Staring at her face, his eyes lowered to her breasts, and then to the slit in her dress. "The slit in your dress is high, exposes your thigh." He fisted the fabric of her dress where the slit was. "Your wedding dress looks sophisticated on you. Turns me on." With his head hovering over her sheathed sex, he kissed her thigh. Edging her panties to the side, he slid his tongue up into her sex and curled.

"Mmmm." Arching her back, Sasha eased her legs up over his shoulders and bucked on his face. Circling her tongue around the outlines of her lips, she closed her eyes. Let her entrance get pleasured with sated desire.

His head motioning up and down between her thighs, he stroked her canal with his long, pink flesh. "Oh, Salvador. I'm about to cum." She'd been waiting on this all day.

"I want us to cum together." Salvador climbed on top of the mattress. Put the tip of his shaft to her center and slowly slid between her creamy walls. When Sasha went to close her eyes, he requested, "Don't close your eyes. Look at me while I make you cum, Sasha." Swallowing, Sasha nodded. Her eyes locked with his, she circled her hips. Inhaled a sharp breath. Her heartbeat thumped erratically beneath her breastbone. "Are you almost there?" he asked, twirling his stem inside her opening.

Her orgasm was brewing up inside her channel like hot liquid. "Yes. I'm almost," quick breaths flew from the small opening in her mouth, "there." Fisting the linen, she heard her sex squishing.

"Me, too. Cum on my dick." He thrust her harder. "Cum, Mrs. Casillas." His eyes linked with hers, he slid his stem to the top of her sex. "Venir!" He slammed his rod into her entrance.

Sasha's sex pulsated. Erupted into a powerful orgasm. "I'm cumming!"

"Ah, yeah. Venir! Keep coming. I feel your pussy exploding on my cock. Feel this." Bam! He slammed into her. His stem jerked wildly inside her channel. "Arrrgh!" Sperm shot from his rod and filled her to the hilt.

Salvador collapsed to the mattress beside Sasha. His breathing slowing, he pulled her in his arms, cradled her to his chest.

Rubbing the tip of his nose on hers, he pecked her lips. "I love you very much. My sweet wife, Mrs. Casillas."

"I love you, too, Mr. Casillas."

The engine of the private aircraft churned. The intercom inside the bedroom came on, and the pilot announced, "Mr. and Mrs. Casillas, congratulations on getting married. Your flight to Dubai is about to depart. Please buckle your seatbelts."

Sasha's mouth dropped open. "We're going to Dubai?! I've always wanted to go there!"

"I'm glad you're pleased with where I'm taking you for our honeymoon."

Sasha cupped Salvador's jaws. "Oh, Salvador. I bet life with you is going to be one wild adventure."

"You have no clue." He slid his tongue into her mouth and kissed her erotically.

The private aircraft sped down the runway, lifted from the ground, and then shot into the dark night sky. After removing all of their clothing, Salvador and Sasha climbed in bed naked next to one another. With her spine spooned to his rock solid chest, she yawned and drifted off to sleep.

A few hours later, as Salvador and Sasha lay in the bed on the aircraft sound asleep, Salvador's cell phone buzzed. Holding a naked Sasha in his arms, Salvador stirred.

Buzz. Buzz. Buzz. Hearing the constant ringing of Salvador's cell phone, Sasha's eyes fluttered open. Her back pressed to his chest, she patted his hand. "Your cell's ringing, Salvador."

Reaching for his cell, Salvador's soft shaft turned hard against her buttocks. "Hello?" A long pause. "What?!" He bolted from the bed. Seemingly severely upset, he paced back and forth.

Terrified that someone had died or something horrible had happened, Sasha eased up in bed and observed her husband's face. Pressing the cell phone to his ear, Salvador's face contorted. His eyes darkened. Silence. Nothing. "Fuck. Fuck. Fuck." Nothing. He stopped pacing. "Thanks for calling me and letting me know."

His jaws clenching, Salvador tossed his cell phone on the bed. He grabbed the sides of his head. "What's wrong?"

Salvador's eyes hardened. He flung his arms up into the air. "Someone burned my house down! Well, not my house, but our house! It's gone! Fucking evil bastard!"

"Ohmygod! Our house was burned?!" Sasha's voice cracked. "How did that happen?" Water came into Sasha's eyes. Naked, she climbed out of bed and stood in front of Salvador. "Did someone start the fire? Did you leave something on inside the house?"

"I don't know how it happened, Sasha. I don't have any of the details yet."

"Well, we have to go back home. Tell the pilot to turn the plane around."

"No! I'm not letting anything stop us from having a welldeserved honeymoon. The house is gone, and there's nothing we can do about it. But what we can do is enjoy our lives together and celebrate the best day of my life—our wedding day." He cursed.

"I want to celebrate, too. But where will we live once we return?"

Salvador shrugged. "I guess we'll have to live at the lake house. Or if you prefer, we can live in the penthouse at the Balfour Hotel."

"The lake house is fine. I'm so sorry about your house burning."

"Not my house...our house. I'll build you another home. One that's nicer and bigger. I'll build you whatever you want."

"For all I care, I could live in the lake house for the rest of our lives.

I don't need a big house. As long as I have you, nothing else matters."

Although Salvador was trying to look strong, he looked devastated. Raw pain pierced his eyes. "I know you could care less about materialistic things. But still, I'm going to make sure you have nothing but the best in life. The best house. The best car." When he wrapped his arms around her waist, she lay her head on his solid chest. "Most importantly, you're going to always have the very best of me."

Salvador put his jeans on, rolled a shirt over his head, and hefted his cell phone from the mattress. "Excuse me. I have a very important phone call to make." He pulled open the door of the aircraft's bedroom and stepped out into the sitting area.

Why do I have the feeling he's not telling me something? Sasha thought, hating her husband had lost everything in a house fire. Sulking, she eased back in bed, pulled the covers up to her chin, and prayed.

NOT WANTING SASHA TO OVERHEAR his telephone conversation, Salvador exited the bedroom, plopped down in the recliner farthest away from the door. Blood pumping fiercely through his veins, he cursed. Laurente set my house on fire. He's out to destroy me and will stop at nothing until I'm dead and until Sasha's dead. I refuse to let that happen. It's time I taught this grown bully a lesson. His thoughts jumbled together, Salvador dialed the one person who could help him put an end to Laurente's craziness—an old friend of his that lived in Puerto Rico—Frank Gotti.

"Salvador! How are you doing, my long lost friend?" Frank answered.

Dread filled Salvador's voice as he stated, "Frank. I need your help."

Frank asked, "Why you sound so frustrated, mi amigo? What can I do for you?"

"Someone is threatening to kill my wife."

Frank chuckled. "Su esposa?! I didn't know you got married?!" "Yeah. Spur of the moment." She's my heart.

"Congratulations, mi amigo. She must be pretty special if she got you to marry her and got you to turn in your player's card." Frank cleared his throat. "I'll take care of the person threatening your wife for you. Okay? When I was down and out, you came to my rescue. Just tell me his name, and I'll kill him for you, okay?"

"The bastard's name is Laurente Lagounov. He lives in Hilton Head. Owns gift shops."

"Laurente Lagounov. I got it. When you want me to kill him?" Frank queried, as if it were no big deal.

"All I need you for is backup. To handle his goons. I'll take care of Laurente myself."

Frank chortled. "You still the little roughneck I trained how to box all those years ago, I see. Just tell me what we gon' do, and consider the bastards dead."

Salvador told Frank, "I haven't quite figured out all the details yet. I'll call you when I do."

Frank cleared his throat. "You sure you want to be involved? I can fly down to Hilton Head tomorrow, toss a got damn grenade in that fucker's house, and blow his ass up."

"No. Don't do that. He has a son that I've grown to care for." Hating the fact that he was going to kill Ivan's father, Salvador's heart grappled. He ended the call with Frank.

Salvador stood. You started this shit, Laurente, but I will finish it. For sure. He stalked back inside the bedroom, slid back into bed next to Sasha. His back to her, she stirred. Moaning, she threw an arm across his waist. Threw her right leg across his thigh.

God, I hate having to break your heart, Sasha. But I must fake my death.

Or leave you behind.

Chapter Thirty-One

Dubai

CUMULOUS CLOUDS FLOATED IN THE powder blue afternoon sky. The helicopte r carrying Salvador and Sasha flew above a curving private bridge. With the sun perched high in the sky, the aqua blue water surrounding the bridge shimmered. In awe of the most beautiful scenery she'd ever seen, Sasha sat in the rear of the helicopter with Salvador. Marveling, her lips pulled into a smile.

Thoroughly enjoying the helicopter ride, The Burj Al Arab Jumeirah luxurious hotel came into closer view. Ecstatic, Sasha looked sideways at Salvador. "Wow. Look at the hotel! It's beautiful! I've never seen anything like it!"

Salvador glanced at Sasha and cupped her hand. "Yes, it is."

Smiling, Sasha began clapping her hands. I can't believe I'm actually in Dubai and will be staying here with my husband. The closer they got to the hotel, the more her heart raced. The more her insides beamed.

The rotor blades on the helicopter chopped the afternoon air. Hovering over the hotel, it began descending downwards. Coming in close proximity to the ground, the helicopter landed on the circular patch of emerald grass encircled in bright yellow.

Salvador climbed out of the helicopter. He turned around, extended his arms to Sasha, and helped pull her out of the helicopter.

Tilting her head back, Sasha' eyes traveled up to the top of the hotel building. Positioned on an artificial island with crystal blue water, the hotel's shape of structure mimicked the sail of a ship. Ohmygoodness. This is incredible.

Holding hands, Salvador and Sasha walked across the grassy land, passed the valet attendants, and walked inside the immaculate hotel.

Sasha's mouth parted.

Salvador looked at Sasha and grinned. "I wish we were inside our room so I could stick something inside your mouth."

Sasha snapped her mouth shut. Giggling, she playfully hit his arm. "Is that all you think about?"

"No. Unlike a lot of men, what I think about most is how I can't live without you." His tone was so serious.

"Well, you won't ever have to live without me. Not unless I die."

Salvador stopped in his tracks. Glaring down at her, he clutched her arms. "Don't ever let 'you may die' come out of your mouth."

"I'm just kidding." Jeez. Salvador seemed uptight, and he had every right to be. His beach house had been burned to the ground. "Just playing," she reiterated.

He released her arms. "Sorry. I overreacted."

Dressed in a white sundress, Sasha's royal blue peep toe heels clicked against the marble flooring. After Salvador checked them in, they stepped onto the elevator. The gold doors glided closed, and they began climbing towards the top. Silence loomed in the air. Moments later, the door of the elevator slid open.

They stepped off, headed down a long hallway, then rounded the corner at the end.

Standing outside their hotel suite, he swiped the card in the door, and it clicked open. He pushed the door open and stepped to the side. "Ladies first."

Sasha walked inside the club one diplomatic suite and just about jumped out of her skin. The inside of the spacious one bedroom suite was just as beautiful as the exterior of the hotel. Simply breathtaking.

Sasha's eyes wandered over the luxurious hotel. "Oh, Salvador. Just look at this suite. It's breathtaking," she said, entering the sitting area. Her eyes traveled up the white marble steps to the second floor. "I had no idea it was two story." A deep purple sofa with gold pillows centered the room. The wide bay window offered a perfect view of the endless Arabian Sea. Leaving the sitting area, she entered the bedroom. A red silk bedspread covered the kingsized mattress, and its posts were draped with red and gold intertwined scarves. "Thank you so much for planning all of this, Salvador. I feel like I need to do something special and nice for you." "Other than your love, I don't need anything from you, Sasha."

"I'm so lucky."

"NO, I'M THE LUCKY ONE," Salvador stated, his heart aching with pain. Contemplating how he was going to leave Sasha in Dubai by herself, he draped his arms around her waist. "Are you hungry?" he asked.

A sensual glow radiated in her cinnamon eyes. "Yes. I'm hungry to make love to my husband." Sasha unbuckled Salvador's belt, yanked his zipper down, and circled her fingers around his shaft. Squeezed him tight. Like magic, his tool lengthened in her tight grip.

"Wouldn't you like to eat first, pussycat?"

She motioned his hard rod up and down in her fist. "Nope. I want to suck my husband's dick first." Clenching him tight, she dropped to her knees. She put his head to her lips, and then sucked him into her slobbery mouth.

Looking down at Sasha, Salvador groaned. "I've already turned my wife into a little freak, I see."

"Mmmm-hmmm." She swirled her tongue over his tip. "You sure have."

Salvador grabbed the sides of Sasha's head. Circling his hips, he rotated his shaft like a windup toy inside her hot mouth. Her head bobbing up and down, Sasha's cheeks contracted and expanded. She hummed and groaned. Scraped her French manicured nails on his testicles.

"Oh, pussycat. Your mouth feels so good sucking my cock." Hot cum bubbled at the surface of his tip. Salvador groaned. He slipped his erection out of her mouth. "I'm about to cum."

"Good. Cum in my mouth." Sasha opened her mouth wide, grabbed his shaft, and sucked him to the back of her throat. Salvador cursed. As he thrust in and out of her mouth, she twisted his shaft in her hand. Rotated it up and down. Flicking her tongue over his head, she sucked him to the back of her mouth.

Fisting her hair, Salvador lolled his head back and shot! Like sweet vanilla milk, Sasha proudly swallowed his spunk. Sasha was his kind of woman. A freak in the sheets, and a lady in the streets, he thought, pulling his semi-hard shaft from between her lips.

ON THE FOLLOWING DAY, SALVADOR and Sasha got up at the break of dawn and went to the Jumeriah Beach Strip. While they were there, they had ridden camels, cruised the sea on a big, luxurious yacht. Sasha herself had drank one too many frozen alcoholic drinks and had ended up drunk and deliriously horny. When they'd gotten back to the hotel later that evening, she and Salvador had had sex five times in one night.

Pressing forward to day three, Salvador rented a four-wheeldrive Safari and drove to the desert. As Salvador drove the Jeep over a large dune in the hot desert like a pro, Sasha squealed out in delight. "Go faster! Faster!" she yelled, clapping her hands.

Dirt kicked up from the tires of the four-wheel-drive Safari. Driving the Jeep across the desert at a fast speed, Salvador chuckled. "You're acting like a wild woman, pussycat."

Smiling, Sasha threw her hands up in the air. "Whoo hoo! Woot! Woot!"

"Hold on!" Coming to another large sand dune, Salvador pressed hard on the gas, and the Safari Jeep hiked upward.

"Weeee!" Sasha giggled, her breasts juggling inside her shirt.

After the fun drive in the desert ended, Salvador and Sasha enjoyed the pleasures of henna paintings, belly dancers, and a hot air balloon ride.

When Thursday evening arrived, Salvador and Sasha found themselves back at their hotel at a restaurant housed deep beneath the sea. Clear glass walls and glass ceilings made up the restaurant's sides and roofs. While enjoying their delicious meals, colorful tropical salt water fish and wild sea life could be seen swimming above their heads through the clear glass ceilings. And at both their sides through the clear glass walls.

Sasha pressed her finger to the see-through clear glass wall to her left. "It looks like the fish are swimming inside the room with us." A grey shark swam past their table on her left. "Oh my, that's a mean looking shark."

As Salvador sat eating the well-seasoned Matchbous dish consisting of spiced lamb, tomato, stew, and rice, his heart ached. Tonight would be the last time he would see Sasha for a while. God, how he hated he had to leave her. He hated he had to betray her trust. Sulking, he inwardly sighed.

If things went as planned, someday he'd return to Dubai and take Sasha back to Hilton Head with him. On the other hand, if he got killed, Sasha would become a widow. A very wealthy widow. But still a lonely widow. She'd also become a single mother and would have to raise their son or daughter by herself. Damn Laurente for putting him in this horrible predicament.

"You're so quiet. Looks like you're lost in thought. What are you thinking about?" Sasha queried, cutting into his thoughts.

Dread filled his heart. "I'm thinking about how much I love you. And how now is the perfect time for me to give you your last wedding present."

Smiling, her eyes stretched wide. "There's more?" She forked a small portion of Tabbouleh into her mouth. The Tabbouleh dish consisted of salad, tomatoes, green onions, cucumber, fresh mint, and lemon juice, and had tasted delightful when he'd sampled it a few moments ago.

"Yes. There's more." Salvador smiled. "You'll get it right after I make love to you."

Bringing her wine glass up to her mouth, Sasha smiled. "I'm getting hot just from thinking about it."

"I'm glad you like the way I make love to you, pussycat."

"Like it? I love it. Do you want a boy or girl?"

"As long as the baby is healthy, it doesn't matter. But something tells me it's going to be a boy."

"Well, I think I'm having a girl. If it's a girl, what do you think about naming her after your mother? Luciana?"

"Maybe Luciana can be our daughter's middle name, but definitely not the first. Perhaps we should name our daughter after your mother—Ava."

Sasha smiled. "Ava Casillas. I like it."

"Me, too. If it's a boy, he's going to be named after me, of course. He's going to carry on the Casillas last name."

"I want him to be named after you, too. As soon as we get home—"

"I'm going to build you another home, Sasha. As soon as we get back to Hilton Head, I'll hire a general contractor, interior designer, and get started on it right away. We can go looking at lots, too."

"That's just it. I like the lot you were already on. The way the house sat up on the rocks, I just loved it, Salvador."

"Okay, well. We'll just clean up the debris and rebuild our new home in the same spot." That bastard Laurente will pay for making

my pussycat upset.

Right as they finished their tasty meals, the waitress lowered a huge piece of

Esh asarya in the center of the table for them to share. Known as "the bread of the harem", the dessert was basically cheesecake with a cream topping, but the texture just melted on your tongue.

Salvador carved a piece of the Esh asarya with his spoon, held it up to Sasha's mouth. Sasha wrapped her mouth around the spoon and ate it. "Mmmm, this is so delicious. Just melts on your tongue."

Salvador ate a huge chunk of the Esh asarya. "It's very light and fluffy. Sort of like how I'm going to make your pussy feel in a moment...light and fluffy."

Sasha's cheeks turned a brownish-red tint. "Oh, Salvador. Having sex with me is all you've talked about for the entire day." "It's all I'll probably talk about for the rest of my life with you. I'll never tire of making love to you, Sasha. Never."

After Salvador and Sasha finished eating their tasty dessert, they went back to their hotel suite. Tugging Sasha's hand, Salvador led her into their immaculate suite. While he stood at the dresser lighting the candles, Sasha held his gaze, and then started stripping off her clothes.

Salvador chuckled. "I see all that talk about sex today has made you horny."

"Yeah. I'm very horny."

Salvador laid the fluid lighter down. His eyes raking up and down Sasha's luscious body, his cock twitched. Not knowing if he'd ever see her again after tonight, he memorized every appealing detail of her sexy figure inside his head.

Her hair pulled back in a low ponytail, the skin on her face glowed. As she swallowed, her neck looked long and slender. Brown breasts perched on her chest. Her nipples were puckered, looked delicious for sucking, and flicking.

His eyes moved down her flat stomach. Grazed over her bald pussy. Down her legs to her red painted toenails, and then hiked back up to her pretty face.

Balls tingling, Salvador swallowed. Eager to slide his shaft between her thighs, he removed his clothing. Walking towards his wife, Salvador's heavy cock swung from side to side.

Their mouths touching, Salvador yanked Sasha off her feet. "I've been wanting to get inside your pussy all day."

Sasha wrapped her legs around his waist, twined her arms behind his neck, and thrashed her tongue inside his mouth. Closing her eyes, she kissed him hard. Like she hadn't had sex in months. Or years.

Flicking his tongue with hers, Salvador released her feasting mouth. He turned back the cover on the bed, and then gently laid her on top of the crimson silk sheets. Aroused, he stalked over to the nightstand, opened the top drawer, and retrieved a blindfold and two scarves.

"I'm going to tie you up tonight," he stated, standing at the foot of the bed.

Sasha's body writhed on the crimson silk sheets like a sexy goddess. "Hurry." When she inhaled, her breasts jiggled. Her tongue gliding over her bottom lip, Sasha spread her legs wide.

Salvador mounted the bed. Hovering over her naked body, his shaft rested between Sasha's juicy, plum looking breasts. "Put your arms above your head."

Her brown pupils shimmering, Sasha brought her arms above her head. Salvador double wrapped the scarf around her right wrist, and then tied it to the bed post. He then did the same with her left wrist. Lowering the blindfold over her eyes, the tip of his erection poked her on the chin.

She writhed. "I can't see a thing."

"You don't need to see. All you need to do is feel and hear, and enjoy." With his knees pressed into the mattress, Salvador was straddled on her chest. Fisting his dick, he traced her lips with the engorged head. Sasha's tongue came protruding from her lips, and she licked his swollen head. "Open your mouth wide, Sasha." When his wife parted her beautiful lips, Salvador slipped his hard tip inside. Enjoying the way his tanned shaft looked gliding back and forth on her brown lips, an electrical current charged up his erection. Made fluid seep from the tip and spill into her delicate, saliva-filled mouth.

Enough of him being selfish, Salvador thought, slipping his tool from her sweet mouth. Ready to satisfy his wife beyond her wildest imagination, he climbed off the bed. He walked over to the dresser, reached inside the ice bucket, and retrieved some ice cubes. Back on the bed, hovering over her, Salvador traced her lips with the ice cube. He then trailed the ice over her chin. Down her slender neck. Between the alcove of her swollen breasts.

HER WRISTS TIED TO THE bed post with scarves and her eyes covered with a satin blindfold, Sasha felt Salvador circle a melting ice cube on her right pointed nipple. Her body writhed against the satin sheets. A sharp hiss spurted from her parted lips. "That's so cold." Cooing, her chest rose and fell. "It feels so good."

Salvador traced her navel with the ice cube. Tracing a line down her bald sex, he dipped his tongue in the hollow of her navel. Now feeling the ice cube between her moist sex, Sasha's labia fluttered. A dull ache formed in her moist center. Her clitoris throbbed. "Lick me. Lick me," she begged, circling her hips. "In due time, pussycat."

Gently circling the melted ice cube over her clitoris, Salvador lifted her right leg, placed it over his shoulders, and sucked her big toe into his mouth. Sasha squeaked out with pleasure. Oh. Oh. Ah. One by one, he suckled a toe into his hot mouth. He then placed her left leg on his shoulder.

Suddenly, the ice cube thing stopped. She heard something click. Then she heard a buzzing sound. "Okaaayyy. What's that noise?"

Salvador stated, "A silver bullet." A silver bullet?! "Have you ever tried one before?"

Anticipating sheer pleasure coming her way, Sasha's sex clenched. "No, but I've heard about it."

"What did you hear about it?" He traced her nipple with the vibrating bullet.

Hearing the bullet churn in her ears as he traced her nipples one at a time with it, Sasha's blood got hotter. Zapped through her veins. "I heard it felt good. And could make your soul jump out of your skin."

Salvador chortled. "I don't know if it'll make your soul jump out of your skin. But I do believe it'll make this drenched cunt of yours jump. Let me see." He circled the silver bullet on her clitoris.

Sparks ignited in Sasha's erected nubbin. While repeatedly circling the bullet on her clit, Salvador inserted his erect shaft inside her entrance. Bolts of electricity coursed through Sasha's veins. Toes curling, her spine arched, slightly lifted from the bed. "Oh God. Oh God."

Keeping the vibrating bullet to her clitoris, Salvador slid his hard tool back and forth inside her. The head of his member knocked against her G-spot with every deep, delicious stroke. Desperately wanting to touch him, she longed for him to untie her.

Bound by the scarves, she wrapped her fingers around the stretched material and pulled. "Untie me, Salvador. Untie me."

"Why?"

She nibbled her bottom lip. "Because I want you to," her sex pulsated. Her breathing caught. Ohmygod. The deep penetration from his shaft and the bullet muted her speech. Made her delirious. Starting with her toes, volts of electricity zapped up her legs. Her head motioning from side to side, Sasha's legs shook violently on the mattress. "Uh. Uh. Oh. Oh God! Oh God! Salvador!" Sasha's sex shattered, her clitoris erupted. Having a clitoral and G-spot orgasm at the same time, she felt cream spurting from her opening, drenching her.

Salvador twirled his stem inside her. Grunted. "I love you, Sasha. I'll always love you." Keeping her tied up and blindfolded, his strokes quickened. The headboard banged against the wall. Knock. Knock. Knock.

"I love you, too, Salvador." The buzzing bullet was still on her clitoris, forcing her towards another over-the-top orgasm. Her head motioned from side to side. "Stop. Stop. I can't take it. I can't take——" She kicked her legs wildly on the mattress. Screaming, her throat burned. Her lungs hurt. Tears slid from the cracks of Sasha's eyes.

Salvador slammed into Sasha. "Yeah. Wiggle your cunt on this cock, pussycat. Aaargh!" Salvador unleashed inside her, forcing her to join him in another mind-blowing, Earth-shattering orgasm.

Sasha lay on the bed breathing raggedly, and exhausted. Sexually fulfilled, her sex was drenched with juices, and sticky.

When Salvador removed the blindfold from Sasha's face, her lips curled into a smile. He untied her wrists. Positioned his back to the headboard.

Staring into his eyes, she thought she saw raw hurt. Trying to read his facial expression, the wet spot beneath her buttocks grew cold. Sexually satisfied beyond measure, she eased up on her elbows, traced a finger down the hard line between his chest muscles. "What's wrong?"

"I have a lot on my mind."

"What?"

"I'll tell you after we shower and I give you your last wedding present." The sullen expression on his handsome face worried her. He climbed out of bed and stalked inside the bathroom.

While in the bathroom, Salvador made Sasha a bubble bath in the garden tub. Turning on the powerful jets, he climbed in the circular garden tub and sat down. She climbed in after him and crawled between his legs.

Resting his back on the curb of the tub, Salvador tenderly held Sasha in his arms. Bubbles floating around their necks, he proclaimed his undying love for her. "I love you very much."

"I love you, too, Salvador."

He sighed. "During our marriage, there may come a time where we may not see eye-to-eye. At some point, I may have to make a decision you don't agree with. But my decision may be in the best interest of you and our child. I need you to say you understand."

Her hand caressed his thigh beneath the water. "I understand. As the leader of our family, I trust you."

"I'm glad to hear you say that."

Sasha scooped some bubbles up in her hands and blew. The bubbles shot into the air.

"Let me bathe you," Salvador decreed.

"Okay." Sasha got to her knees. Soapy bubbles covered her breasts.

Salvador bathed Sasha's breasts with the soapy washcloth in his hand. Lifting her right arm, he washed beneath her armpit, and then did the same to her left arm. Washing between her legs, he pecked her lips, then finished bathing her completely.

Sasha returned the favor by bathing Salvador. Circling the washcloth on his hard chest, she sensed sadness coming from him. Growing concerned, she washed his abdomen. Lifting the tip of his shaft with her index finger and thumb, she scrubbed his length with the soapy washcloth. As she washed his shaft, it began hardening.

Salvador sighed with exasperation. "Jesus Christ. I'm going to miss you, Sasha."

Sasha's hand stilled on his erect rod. "Miss me? What do you mean you're going to miss me? You plan on going somewhere without me?"

"Rinse off, and get out of the tub." His voice sounded so cold. Covered in bubbles, Salvador got out of the tub and began toweling off. Worried, Sasha toweled off beside him. He's going to miss me? What's wrong with him? He sounded like he planned on going somewhere. When she grabbed her red, silk nightgown from the counter, Salvador stated, "Don't put on your nightgown. Put on a pair of presentable jeans and shirt."

Presentable jeans? Sasha sighed. "You keep giving out orders, but you still haven't told me what the hell is going on." Sasha smiled. "Oh, I get it. Does this have something to do with my surprise?"

"Sort of." Salvador stalked inside the bedroom with Sasha on his heels. After getting dressed in a pair of jeans and a cotton black shirt, Salvador grabbed his suitcase from the closet and rolled it to the bedroom's door. He unzipped the side of his suitcase, pulled out a brown envelope.

Okay, I'm getting scared. "Salvador, baby, are you going somewhere? Why did you get your suitcase?"

"Sit down on the bed, Sasha." Confused, Sasha sat on the bed. Standing in front of her, Salvador held a brown envelope in his hands. With a cold look in his eyes, he swallowed. "Remember when I said I had a wedding present to give you?"

She nodded. "Yes."

"This is it." He handed her the brown envelope.

Sasha reached inside the envelope, extracted several sheets of paper, and then sat the envelope beside her on the bed. "What's this?" she asked, searching his face for answers, holding the papers in her hands.

"It's a music contract."

She glanced down at the papers, then back up at his sad face. "A music contract? Huh?"

"After speaking with an A&R at Sony Entertainment, he agreed to listen to your music. I forwarded him the songs you recorded, and he has agreed to give you a publishing contract if you're interested."

In disbelief, gratitude filled Sasha. Her eyes became watery. "Of course I'm interested. Thank you so much, baby," she said in a shaky voice.

Salvador gave her a bland half-smile. "I'll let him know you're interested. I want you to write more music while I'm away."

"While you're away? What? Wait. Salvador, what in the hell is going on?"

Salvador cupped Sasha's face. "There's no easy way to tell you this, Sasha. But I have to leave for a while. Without going into a lot of detail, I'll try my best to briefly fill you in. The person who killed Ben and shot my mother has threatened your life. He has threatened to kill you, me, and our baby."

Sasha became frightened. "I'm confused, Salvador."

A dark cloud seemed to shadow the luxurious room now. Salvador stated, "The same man who killed Ben, who shot my mother, and who threatened to kill you, burned down our house. He's evil and will stop at nothing until he kills my whole family. I'm not going to let that happen."

Sasha trembled. "Oh my God, Salvador. This is serious. Frightening."

"I had everything I own transferred into your name. Just in case I don't come back, I left all my assets to you. My life insurance policy is worth five million dollars. Between the life insurance policy, and the cars, and my houses...if anything happens to me...you'll be a very wealthy woman."

Tears poured from Sasha's eyes. She started shaking. "Why can't you just go to the police and let them handle this evil man?"

"The police won't arrest him. He has ties with the police. The only way to stop a man like him is to—"

Sasha interjected, "Is to what? Kill him? You're going to kill somebody?! I married a murderer?! How could you leave me, Salvador? I'm coming with you."

"No, you're not. It's too risky. You're staying here. In Dubai. Where it's safe."

Sasha jumped off the bed. "Like hell I am!"

"Frank!" Salvador shouted. Four men and a woman burst inside the bedroom, looking like gangsters. Who in the hell are they? Sasha wondered, having never heard them enter the suite. Salvador continued. "Frank, Al, Dennis, Marco, and Carina...this is my wife, Sasha. Sasha, this is Frank, Al, Dennis, Carina, and Marco. We all grew up together. Dennis and Marco will be watching you while I'm gone. Frank and Carina will come with me."

Rolling her neck, Sasha fisted her hips. "Watching me?!"

Dennis walked past Sasha and snatched the telephone cord out of the wall. Marco grabbed Sasha's cell out of her purse.

Salvador's voice was laced with steel as he stated, "Yes. Watching you. You'll be safe with them. However, you won't be able to leave the room until this is over. If you need anything, just let Dennis or Marco know, and they'll go out and get it for you."

Sasha threw her hands up in the air. "This is ridiculous! You're holding me hostage?!"

Salvador's eyes looked like blue ice. "I'm not holding you hostage. I'm protecting you, my wife."

When Salvador went to touch Sasha's face, she slapped his hand away. "Don't touch me! You can take the music contract and shove it up your ass!" She picked up the music contract, ripped it into tiny pieces, and threw it in his face. "I hate you!"

"They say songwriters write their best music when they're troubled. Why don't you try writing something while I'm away? I love you more," Salvador's voice faded, losing its steely edge. Gloom in his eyes, he turned and stalked away.

Watching Salvador walk out the door, Sasha's heart shredded. Shaking, tears streamed down her face. "How could you do this to me?! Jerk! Murderer! If you kill somebody, I'll never look at you the same! Never! I married the wrong man! I married Mr. Wrong!"

Chapter Thirty-Two

SALVADOR STOOD IN THE DRIVEWAY of his beach home, glaring at his burned mansion. Burned to a crisp, only the frame remained, and he could see straight through his house. Debris stacked high on the ground. Scents of smoke polluted the air. The once emerald lawn looked black and torched. Three of the cars inside his garage were completely destroyed.

Salvador's heart twisted with anger. He felt like someone had punched a hole in his chest and had yanked out his heart. Yet as much as this horrific incident pained him, there was something else that could pain him more. Could cause him more grief, the kind he wouldn't survive. And that was losing Sasha and his baby. If something happened to them, he'd roll up in a ball and die.

"You're going to pay for this, Laurente," Salvador mumbled, climbing inside his SUV. He slammed the door shut.

"Are you okay?" Carina asked, sitting inside the passenger's seat.

"Yes. It's time for me to finish the war that Laurente started."

"Let's do it," Carina, his friend since high school, stated.

"I married the wrong man! I married Mr. Wrong!Sasha's last words wrung loud inside Salvador's head as he steered his SUV down the road with Carina posing as Sasha by his side. Sasha's words right before his departure had sliced his heart in half. Had almost brought him to his knees. Disgust for him had been in her eyes, too.

"I had no choice but to leave, Sasha," he uttered, speaking to Carina. If God is willing, I'll be back, my darling little pussycat.
"She's never going to forgive me if I kill Laurente."

Carina patted Salvador's thigh. "Sasha will forgive you in due time. Even if she doesn't, you have to do whatever it takes to protect her and your unborn child. From what Frank and I learned about Laurente, he is a ruthless muthafucka, and he won't hesitate to kill you and yours. He's already killed Ben, shot your mother, and burned your house down. It's high time this damn Laurente learns a valuable lesson."

"And his lesson will come from me," Salvador stated tersely.

Carina nodded. "I got your back, Sal."

"Thanks, Carina." Glancing sideways at Carina, Salvador thought she looked a lot like Sasha in the disguise. "From a distance, you look exactly like Sasha. Same color hair, same skin complexion. Laurente is going to believe you're really my wife."

Carina lowered the sun visor and looked in the mirror. "Yep. I look exactly like Sasha today. We're going to fool that fucker. And when he least expects it, we're going to go in for the kill."

Nervous about his plan to destroy Laurente, Salvador drove his SUV up to Laurente's gift shop and parked. Having rehearsed his plan with Frank and Carina at least a hundred times, Salvador pulled back the lapel on his blazer, spied the gun tucked in his holster. Ready for war, he climbed out of the SUV, stalked up to the gift shop.

Leaving Carina in the car to pose as Sasha, Salvador flung open the door and marched inside the gift shop. With his bowed, Laurente stood behind the counter counting money. The heels of
Salvador's hard dress shoes clacked against the floor. Laurente's head shot up.

A scar running down the side of his face, evil glared in his glass eye, and the other one, too. He put the money inside the cash register and shut it. "Well. Well. Well. If it ain't Salvador. How's the wife?" He looked out the window at Salvador's SUV. "Oh, I see you bought Sasha with you."

Blind bastard. That's not Sasha. I'd never bring my wife around you. Ignoring Laurente, Salvador stalked down an aisle lined with Hilton Head Island souvenirs. Ceramic mugs, key chains, and towels…a little bit of everything was placed throughout the gift shop. Now at the back of the store, Salvador turned and faced Laurente. "You know, Laurente. I'm a little pissed at you."

Laurente laughed. "Me?" He shrugged. "Laurente could care less about why you mad at him. For all Laurente care, you can go suck a dick! And get out of his store."

Salvador hefted a mug in his hand. "Your merchandise is dusty as fuck." Salvador clenched his teeth. "Just like your dusty ass…you sonofabitch. No one interrupts my wedding. Threatens my wife. And burn down my house."

Laurente tossed his head back and laughed. "Ha. Ha. Ha. Yeah, I burned down your house. So what——"

Salvador reached behind his back, pulled out a bat, and swung at the merchandise on the top shelf. Glass ornaments shattered. Pissed off, he swung the bat at the items on the second shelf. Mugs broke. Glass dolphins cracked. Merchandise fractured. Going on a rampage, he broke every got damn thing in his sight.

Right when Laurente whipped his pistol from the back of his pants, Frank and Al walked into the store, pretending to be customers. Never the one to do shit in public, Laurente quickly put his gun under the counter.

Salvador dropped the bat, stalked up to the cash register, and met Laurente's evil stare head on. Leaning into the counter, Salvador clenched his teeth and mumbled, "Go ahead, make a move, I'll blow your fucking brains out right here."

"Excuse me, but do you have any fishing rods?" Frank asked, his eyes roaming around the gift shop.

Laurente pointed to the back of the gift shop. "Yes, they're in the back. Watch out for the glass."

"You bet," Frank said, hefting a fishing rod from a basket.

Still standing at the counter across from Laurente, Salvador narrowed his eyes more. He took a picture out of his pocket and placed it on the counter. "I took this picture of Zena today while she was at the beach tanning. If you ever come near my wife or threaten her again, I'll fuck Zena first, and then I'll snap her neck in half. When I'm done, I'll find you. Put you in a meat grinder and grind your punk ass up like hamburger meat."

Laurente's eyes darkened. "Fuck you."

"By the way, check your surveillance cameras. They're not working. I broke in here last night and destroyed them. You've met your match." Knowing Laurente would undoubtedly seek revenge on him, Salvador stalked out of the store. I'm willing to die and/or
go to prison for murder for my wife.

LAURENTE'S DARK GAZE FOLLOWED SALVADOR as he stalked out of his gift shop. The stupid fuck climbed into his SUV, kissed his wife's Sasha's cheek, and drove off. Fuming, Laurente spied the huge mess Salvador had left in his store. Broken glass covered the floors and shelves. Salvador would pay with his life for coming into his store and destroying his merchandise. No one makes a fool of Laurente. No one fucks up Laurente's merchandise and tries to embarrass him in front of his customers. Salvador is dead meat.

"Whew! It's a mess back here. There's glass everywhere," one of the gentleman that'd walked in earlier exclaimed.

Laurente was so angry, he felt his blood pressure spike. "Sorry about the mess. The customer that just left got mad because I wouldn't let him return an item and get cash back. If the merchandise isn't returned in thirty days, you can only get an exchange," he lied.

The gentleman laid the fishing rod on the counter. "People these days get so mad over the smallest thing."

Laurente rang up the fishing rod, placed it in a bag, and handed it to the gentleman.

The other guy inside the gift shop stalked up to the counter beside him. He placed a blue T-shirt that read 'Hilton Head Island' on the counter. "If someone came in here and messed my store up like this, I'd break his neck. Look at this place. It looks like a hot mess. He must think you're a pussy and gon' let him get away with it."

Salvador made me look like a pussy. I'll get him for this. "Yeah, well if he thinks I'm going to let him destroy my store and do nothing about it, he's dead wrong." Laurente handed the guy his Tshirt inside of a bag, and the two gentlemen left in separate cars.

Now inside the gift shop alone, Laurente dialed his son, Ivan. "Hello?" Ivan answered.

"Hey, son. Your father here has a big assignment for you tonight. I'll be there in an hour to get you. Put on some dark clothing, some jeans, and grab a cap. If you have any leather gloves, bring them with you."

"What kind of assignment?" Ivan asked.

"I'll tell you more about it after I pick you up. Just go get ready. Oh yeah, and wear your hiking boots." They're good for combating. After Laurente ended his call with Ivan, he called up Rob and Troy and told them to get ready for the war of their lives.

Chapter Thirty-Three

INSIDE THE LAKE HOUSE, SALVADOR, Frank, Al, and Carina sat around the kitchen table eating pepperoni pizza and drinking cold beers. Tilting the tip of the beer bottle to his lips, Salvador's heart swelled. It was so good to see his old friends.

Salvador had been born and had grown up in Puerto Rico. Once a member of a ruthless gang, Frank had trained Salvador how to box. The older gentleman also taught him how to become a better person, and how to think before he acted.

Many years ago, Frank had gotten himself into a lifethreatening situation while secretly working the streets. He'd owed   a dope dealer a bunch of money but didn't have it to pay. He'd called up Salvador and had asked him to loan him the money so he could pay the dope dealer. It was the only thing that would spare his life.

By that time, Salvador was a professional boxer and wealthy. Salvador ended up giving Frank a hundred thousand dollars not only to keep the dope dealer from killing him, but for him to have a little extra to spend. He'd assured Frank it was a gift, and not a loan. Ever since then, Frank had felt indebted to Salvador.

Having gone to high school with Al and Carina, Salvador had to get them out of similar situations, too. And that's why all three of them would give their lives for him.

Yet, while sitting here eating pizzas with his friends, who were no longer gang members, Salvador didn't feel right about involving them in his mess. Maybe he should tell them to go home, and just take care of Laurente all by himself. Yeah, that's what he should do. Contemplating his decision, Salvador sighed.

Frank laughed. He hefted his beer to his lips and told Salvador, "You should've seen Laurente's face after you left. He looked like he'd pissed on himself."

"More like shitted," Al confirmed. "While ringing up my shirt, his fingers kept trembling. Salvador, you shot Laurente's blood pressure up, if nothing else."

Carina laughed. "I wish I could've seen how much stuff you broke, Sal."

Frank chuckled. "He broke a whole lot of crap. Glass was everywhere. Looked like a damn tornado had come through the gift shop."

"You think Laurente will show up here tonight?" Carina asked.

Salvador nodded. "I'm positive. Laurente doesn't handle embarrassment well. I'm sure his ego has gotten the best of him by now. If he hasn't already done so, he'll do his research. Find out I own this lake house, and come looking for me."

Frank took a swig of his beer, swallowed, then belched. "And when he shows up here, we'll be waiting."

"I know I've said it before, but thank you guys for your help." Salvador rose from his seat. "The more I think about it, though, I want you to leave. Go back to Puerto Rico."

Frank frowned. "Leave?" he said, standing. "Hell no. We're not leaving you here by yourself to take on that coward, Laurente. I'm in this for the long haul." Frank clutched Salvador's right shoulder. "If it hadn't been for you, I'd be dead. I owe you big time, Salvador.

It's high time I repaid you, too."

Al stood on the other side of Salvador. "Me, too. There's nothing you can do to get me to leave. Nothing," Al said, clutching Salvador's other shoulder.

Tilting her head, Carina smiled. "Don't even think about asking me to leave. I'm staying right here." She hefted a slice of pizza from the box, bit it into it, and threw her legs up on the table.

Guilt rushed Salvador. "Thanks, guys. Just please know…if you change your mind about this…feel free to leave at any time." If anything happened to either of his friends, he'd feel horrible about it for the rest of his life.

Leaving them to enjoy the remainder of the pizza, Salvador pulled open the front door, stepped outside, and called Sasha. The phone pressed to his ear, he looked at the lake behind his home. On the third ring, Dennis answered. "Hello?"

"Dennis. How's everything going?"

Dennis sighed. "Man, this wife of yours is bossy as hell. Quite feisty, too. She's been cussing Marco and I out left and right. She even wrote a song about us called The Kidnapping Thugs."

"Damn right! You can't do this, Salvador!" Salvador heard Sasha's loud shouts.

Salvador shook his head. "Put that wife of mine on the phone."

"Hold on. Hey, Sasha. Your husband wants to speak with you," Dennis said.

"Hello," Sasha said calmly.

Thank God she's calmed down. "Hey, pussycat."

"Don't you 'pussycat' me! You think what you're going through is hell? You haven't seen anything yet! Wait till you get back in Dubai…I'm going to have you arrested for kidnapping!"

Salvador's gut twisted. "Sasha, sweetheart. Can you please stop screaming for a second so I can tell you something?"

Silence. Nothing. "What?!"

"I love you."

"Killer!" Click! Sasha hung up in his face.

A few seconds later, the cell buzzed in Salvador's hands. Spying the Caller ID, he answered. "What's up, Dennis?"

"No! This is not Dennis!" Sasha screamed. "It's me! Your wife! As soon as I get back to the states, I'm going to divorce you!"

Salvador's heart cracked. There was no way he could make his precious wife understand where he was coming from. "Oh, Sasha. Please don't say you're going to divorce me. Can't you see I'm doing this for your own good? For your protection?"

Sasha sighed. "I'll tell you what, husband," she snapped. "If you tell Dennis and Marco to allow me to go get my nails done at the spa, I'll try to understand things from your perspective."

"No. It's out of the question."

"Please, Salvador. Being cooped up in this room all day, locked up like a prisoner, is driving me crazy. Please. I'm going nuts. At least let me go get my nails done and get a massage. Something."

Salvador rolled his eyes. "Okay. But Dennis and Marco will be attending the nail salon and spa with you. You're not going by yourself."

Sasha said, "Thanks. Here. Your boss wants to speak with you." "Hello," Dennis said.

Salvador remarked, "I want you and Marco to take Sasha to get her nails done and get a massage. Stay with her at all times. And don't take your eyes off her, not even for one second."

"I got it, Salvador. I'll tell Marco."

"Thanks, Dennis. As soon as this is over, I'll deposit the other half of the money into your account."

Dennis replied, "Really, Salvador. You don't have to pay me anything. What I'm doing for you and Boss Lady comes—" "Don't call me 'Boss Lady', you thug!" Sasha screamed.

Listening to his wife's rants, Salvador chuckled.

AWAKENING FROM A MILD SLUMBER, Sasha's eyes fluttered open. Yawning, she stretched her legs beneath the soft fabric of the comforter and her arms above her head.

Anxious to go get her massage today, she climbed out of bed. She crossed the bedroom suite to the window and drew back the crimson, thick drapes lined in a bright gold.

The clear blue water surrounding the luxurious hotel shimmered. Gosh, she wished she could go for a swim today. But nooo. Her husband had locked her up inside this suite like a princess desperate to get out of a dungeon inside a castle.

Folding her arms across her chest, Sasha huffed. If Salvador thinks he can keep me trapped against my will, he's wrong. Uugh.

I'm escaping here today. Plotting how she was going to outsmart Marco and Dennis, Sasha opened the bedroom door.

Marco stood outside her door like an FBI agent. "Good morning."

She offered him a fake smile. "Good morning, Marco. I'll be ready to go for my massage in about an hour."

Lying on the couch asleep, Dennis shot up. Sleep in his eyes, he said, "An hour. That's kind of early. I just went to sleep an hour ago."

Too bad. "Thanks for understanding," she replied sarcastically. "I'm going to get ready."

After Sasha tidied up in the bathroom, she grabbed her spa bag and walked back into the sitting area where Marco and Dennis were.

Dennis stated, "Don't try anything stupid, Sasha."

Wearing a pair of yoga pants and a T-shirt, Sasha fisted her hips. Irritated, she rolled her neck. "And if I do, what are you going to do? Tell my husband on me?"

"You sure talk a lot of smack," Dennis stated. Dark circles were beneath his tired eyes.

Speaking of smack, she felt like smacking Dennis and Marco upside their heads. "Whatever." Sasha licked her tongue at Dennis. "Let's go. Kidnappers & thugs. Unh. Hold you against you're will. Keep you hostage. Unh. That's what they do. Who? Who? Kidnappers & thugs."

Dennis spat, "If you keep singing that song, I'm not taking you anywhere."

Marco shook his head. "I'm starting to think this is a bad idea, Dennis."

"Okay. Okay. I'm sorry. I promise I won't sing it anymore. I'm sorry," Sasha apologized.

"Swear on your husband's grave," Marco stated.

"Yeah, swear on Salvador's grave," Dennis mocked.

As mad as she was at Salvador, she didn't wish him any harm. Especially not death. Sasha raised her right hand. "I swear on Salvador's grave that I won't sing the "Kidnappers & Thugs" song anymore. You have my word." Jerks!

Moments later, Dennis, Marco, and Sasha entered the spa. Dennis and Sasha walked up to the receptionist desk. When Dennis draped his arm around Sasha's neck, she cringed. "My wife and I and our friend would like to get a massage."

Wife?! Uugh. Bile rose from the pit of Sasha's stomach. "Thanks so much, baby, for thinking of this." When she winked at Dennis, he pinned her with a strange look.

"You're welcome, babe," Dennis said.

The receptionist stated, "Since you're husband and wife, I'm assuming you'd like to be in the same room." "No," Sasha said.

"Yes, we would," Dennis remarked. He caressed her spine, and she just about puked. Get your hands off me. Dennis stated, "You are too funny, sweetheart. You know you want to be in the room with me. Don't you?"

Hell no. "Yes, babe. You know it," she lied.

The receptionist looked at Marco. "I can put you in the room next to this lovely couple, if you like."

Marco nodded. "That'll be fine."

The receptionist led Sasha, Dennis, and Marco down the narrow hallway. Dim sconces lit the walls along the hallway. Vanilla scents sailed up Sasha's nose. "Thanks for joining me." Dennis yawned. "You're welcome. Whew, I'm tired." Remaining silent, Marco nodded.

The receptionist showed Dennis and Sasha into their massage rooms first, introduced them to their individual massage therapists, and then she left.

"I see you want the deep tissue massage," the therapist told Sasha.

"Yes."

The other therapist looked at Dennis. "And you want the hot rocks and soft massage." Sasha snickered.

"What's so funny?" Dennis asked.

Sasha glared at Dennis' chubby stomach. "You don't look like you'd like a soft massage."

"Well, I do. Okay?"

One of the therapists stated, "After you take off your clothes, you can hang them on the post or put them inside the bags on the chair. We'll leave you two to get undressed and be back shortly." Both therapists left the room, closing the door behind them.

Rolling her eyes, Sasha sighed. "Aren't you going to leave so I can get undressed?"

"No. You might try something."

Sasha threw her hands up in the air, then fisted her hips. She whispered, "Look around. This room doesn't have any windows. I couldn't escape, even if I wanted to."

"True. True. You have one minute to get undressed, and then I'm coming back inside."

Nodding, she gave Dennis a fake smile. "Okay."

Dennis pulled open the door and stepped outside so she could get undressed. Sasha removed her shirt and yoga pants, exposing her bikini, and then climbed underneath the crisp white sheet on the table.

A minute later, Dennis reentered the room. "I'm back. Good. You better not had tried anything." He took off his shirt and jeans and laid them on the chair. Afterwards, he climbed on top of the table. Lying on his stomach, he placed his face on the circular pillow.

Screw you, Dennis. Pressing her face in the circular hole of the soft pillow on the massage table, thoughts of Salvador entered Sasha's mind. "I'm doing this to protect you," Salvador had claimed.

Oh, Salvador. Why didn't you tell me that someone wanted me dead before we got married? I know you're only trying to protect me, but still this is wrong. Just wrong.

The massage therapists reentered the room and started giving Dennis and Sasha their massages as slow music serenaded them.

Standing over the massage table, the therapist squeezed Sasha's shoulders, made the hard knots beneath her skin roll.

"You have a lot of knots in your shoulders. Are you stressed?" the therapist asked.

"No. I just got married. I couldn't be happier," Sasha lied.

"I couldn't be any happier either, babe," Dennis said, enjoying the fact that everyone thought they were married.

Sounds of ocean waves streamed from the speakers to the inside of the room. Finding it impossible to relax, tension built inside Sasha. Oh God. What if Salvador got killed? Her baby would grow up fatherless, and she'd be a widow.

Salvador had left all his assets to her. But so what? She didn't care about being rich. She'd much rather have him than the money. No amount of money could replace her husband, or the love she had for him. I love you, Salvador. Please be safe, my love.

Tension hardened Sasha's neck. Her back. And her spine. Her mind drifted back to Ben and the letters Claira had written him. Ben and Claira had loved each other so much. Like Claira had written Ben letters, she'd written Salvador three love songs since arriving in Dubai. Hopefully, she'd get to share them with him someday. Salvador was her life. Her heart. Her soul. Her everything and—

"Scaaa," Sasha lifted her head from the pillow to find Dennis fast asleep and snoring on the massage table beside her. "Scaaa," Dennis snored.

Ohmygod! He's asleep. I have to escape. Now. Run, Sasha, run! her conscience shouted. Easing up from the massage table, Sasha put her finger to her lips, warning both massage therapists to remain quiet. Smiling, they nodded.

She climbed down off the massage table. Moving quietly, she reached inside Dennis' jeans lying on the chair and retrieved his wallet. She snatched her bag and clothes off the chair, quietly cracked the door open, and left the massage parlor.

Minutes later, Sasha slid the keycard in the door of the hotel suite where they'd kept her hostage. Her heart pounding inside her chest, and still wearing her bikini, her feet scuttled up the ivory marble steps. Now on the second level of the luxurious suite, she burst into Dennis' room, grabbed her purse off the dresser, then hurried back downstairs to the first floor.

She threw back on her shirt and yoga pants. Not caring less about her luggage, Sasha hurried out of the suite. Her purse strapped over her shoulder, she bolted like a flash of lightning from the hotel and never looked back.

Chapter Thirty-Four

NIGHTTIME FELL. DARKNESS SWALLOWED THE dense wooded forest. Right at 3 am, in the wee hours of the morning, two SUVs pulled off the main road and drove into the woods.

Perched in a tree with high -tech binoculars positioned to his eyes, Al spotted the SUVs driving along the dirt path, heading towards Salvador's lake house. "Our guests just arrived," Al stated, speaking into the tiny microphone attached to the inner area of his shirt. Salvador, Frank, and Carina had their FBI high -tech bionic earpieces and wires, too.

"Roger that," Frank said, concealed behind a large oak at the side of the lake house. "We're going to take out everyone. Shoot every last one of them."

"I copy that," Carina stated, crouched down beneath the boat dock in the dirt.

"I'm ready," Salvador stated from inside the lake house.

The two SUVs pulled up to the lake house and parked behind Salvador's SUV. The door on the SUV closest to the lake house flung open. Laurente hopped out and took off running towards the rear of the house. Two men hopped out of the second SUV and scurried up to the front door.

Carina stated, "Laurente is picking the lock on the back door." Pause. "He's headed inside the house now."

His back to the wall, and clenching a gun, Salvador stood in the hallway near the guest bedroom. To throw Laurente off, he'd left the television on a porn station inside the master bedroom. Loud moans and groans streamed from the television and could be heard out in the hallway, and in the den area, too.

Salvador heard the rear door of the lake house squeak open. Inching his head out from behind the wall, Salvador spotted Laurente entering. A second later, he spotted two men entering his house through the front door.

Laurente jerked his head towards the bedroom. All three men tiptoed towards the back of the house, steadily walking closer towards Salvador.

His finger on the trigger, Salvador fired!

"Fuck!" Laurente shouted, firing back.

Pow! Pow! Pow! Pow! Pow! Pow! Gunshots rang out.

"I'm coming in," Frank stated.

"I'm right behind you," Al said.

Pow! Pow! More fire exploded inside the lake house. "Shit, I've been hit!" Frank yelled. Pow! "I shot his ass back. He's dead."

Laurente's other henchman ran from the kitchen and darted out the front door. Al chased after him. "Don't run now, coward!" Al shouted.

Laurente ducked behind the sofa, scurried on his knees to the back door, and ran. "Laurente just ran out the back door," Salvador stated into the wire beneath his shirt.

"I'll get him," Carina remarked.

Salvador stated, "Carina, you see about Frank. I'll take care of Laurente," Salvador shot out the back door, made a sharp left, and ran into the woods beside the house.

Chasing after Laurente, Salvador fired several shots into the woods. Sticks cracked beneath his hiking boots. Breathing harshly, he jumped over a log. Running, he spotted Laurente's shadow and fired.

Laurente's strides slowed. He glanced back over his shoulder and fired back. A bullet grazed Salvador's flesh. Pain shot up Salvador's arm. His flesh burned. Shit! He got me.

Blood dripping down his arm, Salvador ducked his head beneath a tree limb. Running, Salvador's lungs constricted and expanded. He knew these woods like the back of his hand.

Losing sight of Laurente, Salvador halted in his tracks. Catching his breath, his chest rocked. "Don't run now, coward!"

His eyes wandering over the dark forest, Salvador suddenly felt the barrel of a gun press into his spine. His heart dunked. "You're the coward, Coach. Drop the gun, and put your fucking hands up in the air!"

Salvador glanced back over his shoulder to find Ivan standing there, pressing a weapon tight into his back. Ivan. "Ivan. Put down your gun."

Hatred glared in Ivan's dark eyes. "No, Coach. You put down your gun before I shoot you in your back." Ivan's voice sounded cold and heartless.

Shit. Laurente has Ivan involved in this. Salvador dropped the gun to the ground. His hands shot up in the air.

Ivan circled from behind Salvador and now stood in front of him. Aiming his gun at Salvador's chest, Ivan shouted, "Father! Father! I got him! I got Salvador!"

Laurente came from behind a tree and stood out in the open. Gun in his hand, Laurente walked up and stood beside Ivan. He patted Ivan's back. "Great job, son." Hatred for Salvador dulled

Laurente's eyes. "You thought you'd outsmarted me." He cocked his weapon to Salvador's head. "I don't appreciate the way you came into my store and destroyed my merchandise. You stank sonofabitch."

Keeping his eyes on the loaded gun clenched in Ivan's hands, Salvador didn't flinch. I'm so sorry, Sasha. I'm so sorry, my unborn baby. Lord, please take care of my wife and child, Salvador thought, accepting his fate, his life history flashing inside his head. Of all the blessings God had given him, Sasha and their unborn baby were the best. I love you, Sasha.

Laurente lowered his gun to his side. He looked at Ivan. "It's time you become a man, son. I'm going to let you have the honor to kill Salvador."

"Okay." Ivan kept his gun pointed at Salvador's chest and pulled the trigger. Salvador flinched. Nothing happened; the gun was empty. "I'm all out of ammunition. I used them all up."

"Here, use my gun." Laurente handed Ivan his weapon. Ivan cocked the weapon to Salvador's skull. Laurente stated, "Wait. Let me step back. I don't want this bastard's blood to get all over my brand new Gucci shirt." When Laurente took three steps backwards, Ivan turned the gun on his own father, and now the weapon was pointing at Laurente's heart. Laurente's eyes stretched wide. "Ivan, my son...what are you doing?" Laurente asked.

Ivan's eyes were icy and unresponsive. "I'm pointing a gun at you, Father. That's what I'm doing."

Laurente held out his hand for the weapon. "Hand me the gun, Ivan. You don't want to kill me. What about our legacy, my son?"

Tears filled Ivan's eyes. "I'm tired of the beatings, Father. Tired.

I hate you."

Laurente scowled. "You don't mean that, son." With his hand palm up, Laurente wiggled his fingers. "Give me the gun, Ivan. Give it to me."

Frowning, Ivan snorted. "Yes, I do hate you! You treat Mama like crap. Like she's a slave! You treat me like a slave, too!" Snot

slid from Ivan's nose. He continued. "You make me commit crimes. And now you're trying to make me hate Coach Salvador. Well, I don't! Coach Salvador has been nothing but nice to me. I want to be just like him."

Grave disappointment smoldered Laurente's eyes. "You're just as stupid as they come, son. You're nothing but a big crybaby. A big, fat pussy!"

Pow! Ivan fired a bullet straight into Laurente's heart. Laurente's body jerked wildly, his back flew against the bark of the tree. He slumped to the ground on his rear. Eyes stretching wide, he gripped his heart. Blood pouring from his mouth, Laurente's eyes rolled to the white parts, then closed. For good.

Still pointing the gun at his father, Ivan's hands trembled. A loud wail broke from his quivering mouth and echoed throughout the forest. The gun went tumbling to the ground.

Salvador crouched down beside Laurente, put two fingers to his neck, checking for a pulse. There was none. Laurente was dead. Thank God it's finally over.

Salvador stood, wrapped his arms about Ivan's shoulders, and gave him a tight hug.

Ivan's shoulders shook up and down as he sobbed. "Oh God. I killed my father. Who's going to take care of my mother now?"

"I am. I'm going to make sure you and your mother are taken care of for the rest of your lives. I promise."

As Salvador stood in the dark wood waiting for the police to arrive, his cell phone rang. He fished it from his back jean pocket. "Hello?"

"Hey, Salvador. It's me, Dennis. I don't know how to tell you this, but Sasha. Um, well, Sasha escaped."

Salvador's gut whirled. "She escaped?! How'd that happen?!"

"It's a lot to explain, Boss. Anyhow, Marco and I tracked her down at the airport. But by the time we got there, she'd already left on a flight headed back to United States."

Salvador breathed harshly. "Does she have a layover that you know of?"

"Yes. Dallas."

His mind jumbled, Salvador clicked off without saying goodbye. Not only was that wife of his hot and feisty, but she was smart, too. But he already knew that, now didn't he?

Chapter Thirty-Five

PEOPLE CROWED DALLAS FORT WORTH International Airport.
While waiting on her flight to Charleston, South Carolina, to
board, Sasha sat reading a romance novel by Nora Roberts. Holding
the book up to her face, she struggled to comprehend the words
due to the severity of her built up frustration. Sighing, she lowered
the book from her face. Closed it. Put it in her lap.

"Flight five forty -six, heading to Charleston, South Carolina,
will start boarding in fifteen minutes," the female attendant
announced, standing behind the grey stand.

Yawning, Sasha felt like it'd been days since she'd slept.
Worried sick about what was going on with her husband, Sasha held
back her tears. Salvador had held her hostage in a hotel room in
Dubai. Against her will. All to protect her. To keep her safe.

As mad as she'd been at first, she wasn't as mad now. In fact,
she was a little scared now. Scared because she had no idea who was
who. For all she knew, the chubby man sitting across from her
could be following her, and waiting to kill her. Oh God, what had
she done? Maybe she should've stayed in Dubai, as Salvador had
instructed. It's too late for that now.

Growing frightened because she had no idea who wanted her

dead, and because she had no idea what was going on with Salvador, water came into Sasha's eyes. Sniffling, she drew in a deep breath.

Put a hand to her pregnant belly. God, please let Salvador be alive.

I love him so much. The baby and I need him.

Buzz. Sasha's cell phone vibrated inside her purse. She pulled back the flaps of her purse, reached inside, and extracted her phone. Spying the screen, she covered her mouth. Salvador had texted her.

Salvador: It's not good when wives don't listen to their husbands and escape.

Sasha's finger tapped the letters on her phone's screen.

Sasha: You had no right to hold me hostage.

Salvador: As your husband, I had every right to protect you. Your life was at stake. There will be repercussions for your bad behavior, pussycat.

Sasha: Repercussions? What kind of repercussions?

Salvador: When I see you, I'm going to tie you up and spank that round, delicious ass of yours. Hard.

Sasha: Stop texting me. I'm not talking to you!

Salvador: Oh pussycat. Don't act like that.

Sasha: I'm not your pussycat! Goodbye!

Sasha threw her cell phone in her purse. Mixed emotions swarmed inside her. A part of her was mad at Salvador, and then the other part was ecstatic because he was alive. Tired, she put her elbows on her thighs, dropped her face in her hands.

Images of how Salvador may tie her up and spank her behind came into her mind. First, he'd place her in the center of the bed on her stomach. Then he'd wrap scarves around her wrists and tie the material to the bedposts. Hovering over her, he'd slap his bare, thick shaft between the crack of her butt. He'd then raise his hand high in the air, then let it come slamming down on her behind.

Smack. Smack. Smack. He'd spank her something delicious. Sasha's

sex tingled just from thinking about how her husband would spank her, and then make wild, burning love to her.

Holding her face in her hands, Sasha felt someone tap her shoulder. Hating they'd interrupted her thoughts of Salvador, she lifted her face from her hands to stare up at the person. Sasha's mouth fell open. Her heart pounded harsh beneath her breast bone.

With a serious expression on his face, Salvador towered over her. His striking blue eyes bore into her face. Putting a finger to her chin, he gestured for her to close her mouth. She pressed her lips together.

"I love you, Sasha," he said with husky emphasis.

All the anger inside Sasha vanished. Salvador's hands went to her shoulders. Sasha jumped from her seat, threw her hands around Salvador's neck. "Thank God. You're okay. I was so scared."

Salvador caressed her spine. "I know, pussycat. I know." Cupping the balls of her shoulders, he pried her from him. "It's over, Sasha. You're safe now. You and the baby are safe now."

"Did you kill—"

Salvador whispered, "No. I didn't kill anyone."

"Thank God."

He cupped her hand. "I've arranged for us to stay in the penthouse suite at the Balfour Hotel until our home is rebuilt."

"Why not the lake house?"

"Let's just say it's a mess. Now come...the private jet is waiting on us," he said, tugging her hand.

Love swelled Sasha's heart as she and Salvador walked along the terminal at the Dallas Fort Worth International airport. Oh my, how she'd been so wrong to think she'd married the wrong man. If loving Salvador was wrong, then she didn't want to be right.

Epilogue

EIGHT MONTHS LATER, SASHA WOBBLED around the house of her newly rebuilt oceanfront mansion. Pressing the phone to her ear, a dull ache formed in her back. Her belly hard, she put her free hand to her hip and crossed the room to stare out the huge bay window inside her den.

Grey clouds hung over t he huge sea. Ocean waves crashed along the edges of the land. Suddenly, rain drizzled the earth. Pelted the cold sand.

"Say it again, Michael. Say it again!" Sasha stated, speaking to Michael Lang from Sony Entertainment.

"Your song, I've Changed, just h it number two on the music Billboard chart!" Excitement laced Michael's voice. "By the end of the week, I bet it goes to number one!"

Joy filled Sasha. "Oh my God, Michael. I'm so happy. Thank you for everything."

"No, thank you. I knew when I first heard the song, it would be a hit. Now we have to get you set up for tours and concerts."

"Tours and concerts? There's no way I can do tours and concerts and travel the globe with twins."

"Yes, you can. Just hire a nanny or two."

Salvador stalked up behind Sasha, wrapped his arms around her waist. Kissed her cheek. A sharp pain stabbed Sasha's stomach. She gripped her belly. "Thanks for calling....Michael."

"You're welcome. Goodbye." Sasha ended her call with Michael.

Ecstatic about her song, I've Changed, hitting number two on the charts, Sasha turned within Salvador's embrace. "Guess what?"

"What?"

"My song hit number two on the music Billboard chart! Number two! Can you believe that?!" Ecstatic, another sharp pain coursed through Sasha's body.

Salvador's blue eyes radiated with joy. "Yes. From the very first time you sang it to me on our first date, I always knew your song would be a hit."

Sasha cupped Salvador's jaws with both her hands. "Thank you for believing in me, Salvador."

His eyes brimmed with tenderness and passion. "Don't thank me, Sasha. As your husband, it's my job to believe in you. To protect you. To make sure you and the babies are looked after and have the very best. What would you like to do to celebrate your success?"

Sasha already had everything she wanted—a great husband and two babies on the way. "Nothing. Having you and the babies will be plenty of celebration for me."

"You should really celebrate, Sasha. I tell you what...after the babies are born, I'll give you a huge party and invite the executives at Sony, and your friends, and all of our family to attend."

"Okay. Sounds good."

"On another note, I just got off the phone with Detective Carter. He said they finally found Reggie and have him in custody. He's going to finally pay for beating you."

Yeah, that jerk Reggie had been the one to send her an empty box with a zero in it for a bridal shower. "That's wonderful news. I can finally rest—" Sasha's stomach balled. Pain rippled through

her hard belly. Water gushed from her center and splattered the floor. Gripping the sides of her contracting belly, she squealed out in pain. "I'm in labor. Get the bag. It's by the door."

Salvador swept Sasha off her feet, carried her to the SUV, and placed her inside. He sped the SUV out of the driveway and drove like a bat out of hell to the hospital.

Thirty minutes later, Sasha lay on the hospital bed with her legs spread wide open, and pushing. A contraction shot through her body. Squeezing Salvador's hand, she yelped, "Here comes another one! God!"

"I can see the head. Keep pushing," Dr. Constance Chambers ordered.

In gut-wrenching pain, Sasha bit her bottom lip and pushed. Out popped her baby from her center.

"It's a boy," the doctor stated, handing the precious little boy to the nurse by her side. The doctor dropped her gaze back into Sasha's center. "Here comes the other one. Keep pushing, Sasha. Keep pushing."

Salvador caressed Sasha's back. "Push, baby. Push."

Sweat saturated Sasha's forehead. Nodding, she cried. She inhaled a deep breath, blew it out, and then pushed with all her might. As she hollered, pain rippled through her stomach. Out popped her other baby from her center into the doctor's hands.

"It's another boy," the doctor confirmed.

Salvador chuckled. "I have two boys! Yes! Yes! Thank you, Sasha. Thank you."

After wrapping the darling twin boys in blankets and checking their vitals, the nurses handed one of the babies to Salvador, and one to Sasha. With Salvador by her side holding their firstborn son, and her on the bed holding their second born son, Sasha felt like she was in heaven.

the end

ABOUT THE AUTHOR

Sabrina Sims McAfee is your writer of women's fiction, romantic suspense, and contemporary romance. She loves writing about
strong men and sexy strong women, and the adventurous journeys
they travel. In her leisure time, she likes spending time with her family, reading, traveling, and song writing. Her song entitled…This Is Goodbye …is scheduled to be released this summer so stay tuned.

Sabrina loves hearing from her readers, so please feel free to email her at Sabrina@sabrinasimsmcafee.com or visit her online at www.sabrinasimsmcafee.com.

THE BRIDES OF HILTON HEAD ISLAND SERIES

MARRYING THE MARINE
(Braylon & Sandella)

MARRYING THE MILLIONAIRE
(Richmond & Kayla)

MARRYING MR. RIGHT
(Zeke & Taylor)

MARRYING MR. WRONG
(Salvador & Sasha)

COMPLETE SABRINA SIMS MCAFEE AMAZON BOOKLIST
The following titles are also available in electronic format from
Amazon.

SINFUL SEDUCTION
THE PROPOSAL
WANTED
BEDDING THE BOSS

FROM THE DESK OF
SABRINA SIMS MCAFEE

A Writer at Heart
Visit me at my website:
www.sabrinasimsmcafee.com

Dear Readers,
Wow! I can't believe I've completed four books in The
Brides of
Hilton Head Island series. I hope you've enjoyed reading
it as much as I enjoyed writing it. Thanks a million for
reading Marrying Mr. Wrong. I could not be where I
am without my readers. Please know, I truly appreciate
each and every one of you. Reviews, comments, and
likes are greatly appreciated.
Favorable reviews greatly help authors, so thank you.
Fondly,
Sabrina

Also, if you enjoyed the book, please remember you can
share it with a friend via the lending feature. In
addition, you can help
readers find it by recommending it to friends and family,
reading and discussion groups, online forums, etc.

Website: www.sabrinasimsmcafee.com
Email: Sabrina@sabrinasimsmcafee.com

Twitter: www.twitter.com/sabrinamcafee
Facebook: www.facebook.com/sabrina.mcafee.10

Made in United States
Orlando, FL
22 November 2023

39309053R00200